THE REMNANT

THE REMNANT

Christy Kenneally

HODDER
HEADLINE
IRELAND

First published in 2006 by Hodder Headline Ireland

2

A CIP catalogue record for this title is available from
the British Library.

ISBN 0 340 89769 4

Typeset in Plantin Light by Hodder Headline Ireland.
Printed and bound in Great Britain by Clays Ltd, St Ives plc.

Hodder Headline's policy is to use papers that are natural,
renewable and recyclable products and made from wood grown
in sustainable forests. The logging and manufacturing processes
are expected to conform to the environmental regulations of the
country of origin.

Hodder Headline Ireland
8 Castlecourt Centre, Castleknock, Dublin 15, Ireland

A division of Hodder Headline
338 Euston Road, London NW1 3BH

*The Remnant is dedicated
to my wife, Linda, who is the heart of my life,
and to my sons, Stephen and Shane, who are its joy.*

1

Kennedy Airport, New York

'This is as far as we go, sir.'

Michael Flaherty started from his reverie, surprised at the empty seats beside him and the line of gaping lockers overhead.

'You were somewhere else?' the flight attendant added, reluctant to detach: the dark man in the lived-in jeans and rumpled pullover was a possible antidote to the boredom of a three-day stopover in New York. He reached up to rescue his travel bag, and mentally Helen ticked a few more plus signs: six foot something, bare ring finger, firm in all the right places.

The flight director's honeyed tones eased into her ear. 'Helen, would you be a sweetheart and check the bar inventory?' Sarah's smooth black face smiled at her with that infuriating 'girl, I know what you're doing' look.

Helen stomped away to the galley, venting her frustration on tiny bottles until she sensed her colleague hovering at her shoulder.

'Helen, you remember that training course we had on cultural awareness? Always choose a culturally appropriate form of farewell: *le'chaim*, *hasta la vista*, have a nice day. Right?' Sarah lowered her voice and leaned in conspiratorially. 'I guess the Irish version goes, "Are you staying over in New York? Maybe we could meet up for a drink…" Tell me when I'm getting warm, honey.'

Despite herself, Helen laughed. 'Ah, Sarah, you have to admit he had potential.'

'So that's what they call it now, huh? Potential?'

Sarah scanned her clipboard, pink tongue peeking mischievously from the corner of her mouth.

'Doesn't say anything about potential here,' she drawled. 'Flaherty, Michael. Caucasian male, six feet three inches. One hundred and sixty-eight pounds. Distinguishing marks: scar front and rear of left shoulder. Unmarried, travelling on an Irish passport. So far, so good; definite potential. Three little items of interest, though, honey,' she said quietly, and Helen's smile wavered at her tone.

'What?'

'You see his eyes?'

'His eyes?'

'I guess you were looking elsewhere. Well, he had the kind of look my brother had when he came back from Nam. They call it the thousand-yard stare.'

Helen swallowed. 'And the second item?'

'He's a Catholic priest.'

'Shit.'

'Tut and tut. Go wash your mouth with holy water, you good Catholic girl, you.' Sarah slipped her arm around Helen's waist and squeezed comfortingly.

'Three?'

'Say what?'

'You said three items.'

Sarah blew out a long breath before replying.

'Distinguishing marks, scar front and rear of left shoulder, you remember?'

Helen nodded dumbly.

'Bullet wound,' Sarah said bluntly, all humour fled.

★

Passport Control was idling in the backwash from the 747, and the lady flicked cursory eyes from Michael's passport to the screen before pushing it back at him. Instinctively, he checked the arrivals hall for Mal. He felt relieved when he failed to find him. That particular tête-a-tête would come, but not now. His eyes fastened on a small, elderly

Chinese man, made huge in a deer hunter's parka that pulsed with the same dayglo intensity as the baseball cap shading his eyes. The old man's hands, swaddled in heavy mitts, bookended a small card. It had 'Michael Flaherty' printed on it.

'I'm Michael Flaherty.'

'I know.'

'How?'

'Process of elimination,' the little man said, casting a meaningful eye at the empty hall. He swept Michael's bag over his shoulder and led him at a brisk pace to the car park. A half-truck squatted under the diluted warmth of a sodium lamp in the disapproving glare of chrome all around; a solitary shovel lay on a sheet of tarpaulin in the back. It looks like a burial detail, Michael thought wryly. Now we drive to the New Jersey marshes and Fu Manchu whacks me with the shovel. *Arrividerci*, Flaherty.

'What's so funny?'

'Oh, nothing. Just thinking.'

'You look younger when you smile.' The driver reached under the dash and snagged a stiff white envelope. 'Maybe you should read this while you're still happy.'

The envelope, Michael saw, carried the logo of the Archdiocese of New York. The single page of notepaper crackled expensively as he spread it open. The scrawled signature at the bottom was indecipherable. Should've been a doctor, he thought, dropping his eyes to the printed version. 'Monsignor Patrick J. Dalton, BA, BD.' Mal's pal in another life. Mal had once suggested to this particular titled cleric that he do something proctologically impossible with the archdiocese.

Mal. Mal, who had given Michael a home when he had first come to the States after his brother drowned; who had tutted about him joining the Marines and then tutted even more when he swapped their uniform for a clerical one. Mal, who Michael had discovered was his 'minder', who had assured the debriefing brass that Michael Flaherty – the only survivor of a mission gone bloodily wrong in South America – would not divulge what had really happened. At that thought, his left shoulder twinged, and he swept his head in a slow arc. No sign of Mal, the retired cop who wasn't really retired; Mal the friend, who wasn't really... His mind baulked at that and automatically filed it in the Scarlett O'Hara folder: stuff to be thought about tomorrow. Read the goddamn letter, he exhorted himself.

Dear Reverend Father,
His Eminence instructs me to inform you that you will take up residence at the Benedictine Monastery of the Resurrection, Carmel, New York State. This office will notify you in due course as to the time and date of your interview with His Eminence to review your situation.

He folded the letter and stuffed it into his inside pocket. It was, he considered, a typically bloodless letter: no reference to the murder of his brother Gabriel, or to the two people who had died violent deaths on his Island home, or to the man clubbed to death in the sea by the oars of vengeful Islanders.

The protest of the gearbox, the truck squealing on the slick tarmac, brought him back. He noted how the amber sunlight tinged houses and high-rises sepia as they traversed the city to catch the loop that would loft them upstate. The colours flared to ochre as the truck nosed through the wooded suburbs, then umbered to darkness as the sun flared and died.

He was instantly awake and alert when the hand touched his elbow.

'Come.'

Michael stumbled behind the bulky outline, dimly aware of the cloisters that bordered the courtyard. A door winked open before him, spilling a warm oval light on the cobbles. Inside, he stood in a large spacious hallway, letting his eyes caress the rich furnishings and the gleaming staircase that melted up and into the gloom of a gallery.

His companion rustled out of his many layers in a small closet underneath the stairway, and emerged in a sober grey shirt, grey slacks and dayglo-pink bunny slippers. His eyes tracked Michael's gaze. 'You like them?'

'Eh, yes. Very colourful.'

'A young lady made me a present of them. Damn feet always cold.' He offered no explanation for the cotton gloves that masked his hands. 'Hungry?'

Michael's stomach growled in reply.

'Ah, good. Follow me.'

The kitchen was all stainless steel, state of the art. The man motioned him to a small table covered with a gingham cloth, already set for two, and he sat wearily in the cushioned chair, the static of the drive tingling through his feet to the tiled floor. Briskly, his companion magicked food to the table, whisking away plastic covers to reveal a range of healthy options.

'Eat.'

He himself did not eat. Methodically, he positioned various containers within Michael's reach, until Michael sat back, sated.

'Thank you. Quite a place you've got here.'

'Yes, a man with lots of money and no kids found his conscience and left all this to the cardinal. The understanding was, of course, that there would be an annual mass offered for the happy repose of his soul, however much of it still remained. All this' – he gestured vaguely with a gloved hand – 'is just another form of fire insurance.'

He stood and moved to a cupboard, reaching up to take two tumblers and a large bottle of whiskey from the interior.

'Would St Benedict approve?' Michael asked,

smiling, raising his glass to match the other man's salute.

'Benedict is dead,' his host replied simply. 'We're alive. Cheers.'

'You work here?'

The old man laughed silently, placing his glass before him. 'I'm the abbot. Now you're wondering what sort of monastery has someone like me as abbot.'

'No. I'm wondering what sort of monastery is instructed to take someone like me.'

'Not instructed,' the abbot corrected mildly. 'The cardinal said "Please".' He stretched his pink-bunnied feet on the tiled floor, sighing with relief. 'I can call you Michael?'

'Yes, please.'

'My Chinese name would tangle your tongue. My name in religion is Raphael. Michael and Raphael – two archangels.'

There was an Archangel Gabriel, Michael thought suddenly. Gabriel my brother, who couldn't fly.

Silently, the abbot refilled the tumblers.

'Why am I here, Raphael?'

The abbot swirled the liquid in his glass and downed a good third of it before replying.

'There are five men here, including me. I'm the only Benedictine, so names are changed to protect the innocent... well, the residents. You'll meet them around the house or the farm, and they'll ignore you. You'll do likewise. Should your paths ever cross in the outside world, you will give no sign of recognition.'

'You haven't answered my question.' It came out sharper than Michael intended, but the abbot only smiled.

'So impatient, for an archangel. Old men have the right to meander, Michael. Now, where was I? The other four, yes. Father Tobias is a Rwandan priest, a Hutu. The archdiocese had sponsored him to do a course in Columbia University, all arranged, and then the writs arrived from The Hague. It seems Father Tobias may have been involved in certain actions against his Tutsi brethren. While the lawyers discuss extradition, Father Tobias lives here as the guest of the archdiocese. Brother Jonas is a Basque Franciscan friar, who may or may not have carried a suitcase, which he may or may not have packed himself, to Barcelona. He was fortunate enough to travel to New York before anyone caught up with him. His extradition papers are also before the courts. Fathers Anthony and Anselm are priests of the archdiocese with a penchant for certain websites. Alleged penchant. The case is pending.'

He reached for the bottle, relaxing again when Michael waved a warning finger above the rim.

'And you?'

'Ah, yes. I was a Professor of Archaeology at the University of Beijing. Archaeological digs in China are marvellous places, Michael. A person can find anything – a computer, a two-way radio, a fridge, even a wife. All he has to have is money. I found a bishop – Bishop Yuang, an expert in ceramics. I made him a member of my team long before I knew who he really was. To make a long story short, I was converted in China's catacombs. He ordained me – just the two of us and a congregation of terracotta warriors.' Raphael smiled as a memory surfaced. 'During the ceremony, when he asked if the community deemed me worthy of ordination, not a single terracotta warrior voiced any objection.'

Michael watched the light leach from the old man's eyes, and braced himself.

'He was betrayed the next day. I asked permission to interrogate the prisoner, and they gave me five minutes. He ordained me a bishop in three minutes flat. Then the political officer came in, so I spat in Bishop Yuang's face. I was rewarded for my patriotism with a front seat at his trial.'

The abbot moved a gloved hand over his eyes, as if shading them from the light in the room. His body seemed to sag for a moment; then he drew a deep breath and sat erect again.

'They walled him in up in the dig. I stood there, like Paul of Tarsus holding the cloaks of those who stoned Stephen, and I didn't open my mouth. I was terrified that I would be betrayed too. As they put in the last block, I heard him whisper the *De Profundis*. "Out of the depths I cry to you, O Lord."'

He sighed deeply. 'I had one year of freedom

before me at that moment. I was reasonably well known in the worldwide archaeological community, so when I was caught I became something of a cause célèbre. The Vatican leaned on Washington, Washington whispered to Beijing, Beijing bartered one abbot for two phantom fighters.'

'So they let you walk?'

The little abbot smiled bleakly. 'Well, not exactly,' he replied, nodding to his feet. 'Me, they released; my toes are still in China.'

'I'm sorry.'

'I'm not. I'm here and I've got goddamn bunny slippers.'

'And your hands?'

'Fingers without fingernails aren't in fashion this year.' He looked directly at Michael. 'This is a holding house. It's a place where there is no judgement. That will come in its own good time, but, for now, a soul can find some measure of peace here.'

'A soul like mine?'

'Yes, like yours, and maybe mine – who knows? You want some deep Chinese insight? Shit happens, Michael. No choice about that. The choice comes in what we do with it.'

He rose wearily and stretched to gather the glasses. 'Enough. You're at the top of the stairs, first on the left. Good night, Archangel.'

'Good night, Abbot, and thank you.'

'For what?'

'For your story.'

The old man placed the tumblers on the table. He offered his gloved hands, and Michael took them as gently as he was able.

'If you should wish to tell me yours, Michael, I would be honoured to listen.'

Michael nodded and released his hands.

★

He opened his eyes to the sunlight angling through the small window in the roof. When he had showered, shaved and dressed, he draped his weathered windcheater over his arm and raided the kitchen for strong coffee and brown bread. There were tell-tale signs of earlier risers: an inverted mug weeping on the draining board, a scatter of crumbs beneath a chair. He ate and drank, standing, his eyes fixed on a slender tree that flared through the kitchen window.

Raphael was sitting on a rustic bench, surrounded by the corpses of vivid leaves on the close-cut lawn. Michael sat down easily beside him, content to contemplate the morning, listening to the birds vying for the prime spot at the bird feeder that hung from the flame tree, scenting the sweet aroma of a hidden bonfire. His shoulder pulsed. Absently, he crooked his hand back to massage the ache, taking the opportunity to check the stand of trees that bordered the monastery property.

'You ever see our friend Mike these days?' the abbot asked casually.

Surprised, Michael glanced his way and saw him mime a speaking mouth with a gloved hand held close to his chest.

'No, not for a long time.'

'I'll bet good ol' Mike is still out there somewhere,' the abbot continued easily. 'Let's have that cup of coffee, huh?'

Michael followed him into the spacious kitchen, where Raphael placed a finger to his lips and turned the faucet on full. He beckoned Michael closer into the thunder of water drumming on stainless steel.

'You sensed them?' he murmured.

'Yes.'

The abbot nodded and seemed pleased with himself. 'Haven't felt it myself in some time. Not since...' He stopped, and the laughter left his eyes. 'Have I shown you the den in the basement?'

Michael shook his head and followed him obediently down a short flight of stairs, to a low room dwarfed by a full-sized billiard table.

'Parabolic microphones don't work so well through floors,' the abbot smiled.

'Who is it?'

The abbot shook his head, the shadows from the harsh overhead light making him look gaunt and haunted. He picked the black ball from its spot and turned it slowly in his hand.

'Were they here before I came?' Michael asked.

'No.'

'You're sure?'

'Michael, I was a fugitive in a police state. I'm sure.'

'So it's me?'

The abbot replaced the black ball, nodding.

'Look, if it means trouble for you, I could—'

The interruption was swift and vehement. 'No. The chase is what they love.'

Raphael padded to the wall-mounted phone and knuckled in a series of numbers. There followed a rapid-fire conversation in Chinese. Finally, he smiled and replaced the receiver.

'Can I ask what that was all about?'

'Sure. I ordered a Chinese takeaway for some friends,' the abbot replied calmly, but his eyes held a steely glint.

★

Special Agent Dwight Hammond squashed yet another mosquito on his bare neck with a pudgy palm. He cursed quietly, checking the red smear on his palm, and wiped the blood on the camouflaged surface of his leggings. He shifted the headphones fractionally, focusing on what the parabolic dish could trawl from its sweep of the monastery. He was not a man without humour, and he had already chuckled at the thought of bugging monks under a vow of silence. Then he had remembered the lean, humourless faces of his masters and grown sombre again.

His head twitched, like the finger of a fisherman on a taut line, as the dish gathered and magnified two male voices. His expression of intense concentration melted into one of incredulity: they were comparing the merits of two well-known porn sites. He was saved further pain by the blow of the cosh that rendered him unconscious.

Hammond woke slowly to a buzzing sound and automatically reached to his neck before he realised the sound was coming from inside his head. Groaning, he eased himself into a seated position and found himself gazing at a group of nuns wearing identical shocked expressions. 'I'm okay, Sisters,' he called gallantly, to assuage their fright, and then felt cold to the pit of his stomach at the slow, awful realisation that he was stark naked.

2

Rome

Giulio Benedetto was dreaming. It was a pleasant dream, and he smiled as it spooled behind his flickering eyelids. He and his wife Paola were strolling hand in hand between the tumuli of the necropolis in Cerveteri. The evening sunlight sieved through ferns and branches, warming Paola's face, glinting in the sprinkles of silver at her temples. A robin flicked among the stones, angling a bright black eye at the intruders, stopping only to puff up and scold.

'Babies,' Paola whispered, leading him away from the little bird's territory. He smiled at her and wondered, not for the first time, what had opened her heart to the gangly youth whose only other passion was archaeology and who earned a mundane living as a hospital administrator. Every summer, she had organised their vacation to include some ancient site. He remembered pacing around Hadrian's Pool in the Tivoli Gardens, his first-born son sleeping against his chest, finding peace where Hadrian had plotted walls against the nightmare of the barbarians. He remembered jolting his daughter in her pushchair over rutted Roman roads, steering her between the ruts of long-gone chariots. Had he been selfish? Antonio was now Assistant Head of the Department of Archaeology at the University of Rome and Paolina a restorer of ancient manuscripts at the Vatican Museum. The passion of one generation had found expression in the next.

The robin chirped in the distance, reminding him that his fledglings had grown and flown. Now it was just Paola and Giulio, in slanting sunlight and the smell of wild rosemary.

The robin chirped again, sharply, more insistent than before. Wide awake, Giulio groped for the bedside telephone.

'Pronto,' he whispered, swinging his feet to the floor. He padded in total darkness to the bedroom door, with the assurance of one who slept lightly.

Angela Amarone clenched the receiver between her jaw and shoulder and swivelled from the glass frontage of the reception desk for some measure of privacy. 'A thousand apologies for calling you at such an hour, Signor Director. I hope I haven't disturbed the signora. A telephone call, some ten minutes ago… No, no name, Signor, but the caller asked if I would ring you immediately with a message… Yes, Signor, by name. He insisted I write it down and read it back. Twice. Of course I said it was highly irregular, and would he speak to… Oh, yes, Signor, I have it right here. "To the Signor Director Giulio Benedetto, Hospital Santa Sabina… urgent… Code Pietro.'"

For a dizzying moment, lights danced behind Giulio's eyes in the darkness. He was aware of the sweat blossoming above his eyebrows.

'Repeat that please, Angela,' he whispered hoarsely.

With great deliberation, as if speaking to a child, Angela repeated the message.

He took a deep breath and steadied himself with his free hand against the wall. 'Angela, please listen carefully. You must summon Professor Ricci immediately and—'

'But, Signor, the professor is attending a conference in Aquila.'

In a nation of people who could make a casual conversation sound impassioned, Giulio Benedetto was an exception, a man who seldom raised his voice and never lost his temper, but for a moment he longed to scream at his loyal and capable receptionist. He knew the professor's conference was of the extramarital kind, with a willing nurse too young to know any better. Giulio, the man, fervently hoped that the randy professor would die the death of a thousand paparazzi pounding avidly on his hotel-room door. Giulio, the hospital director, said, 'Clear the casualty area now and prepare the private room on the second floor beside the service lift. Have the emergency team on standby, and inform the medical registrar. I'll be there in ten minutes.'

★

At 1.45 a.m., the streetlights on the Via Pio X blinked and died. A sliver of grey appeared, bisecting the dark mass of the wall that stretched along one side of the street. Five shadows eased through the gate, four fanning out to the four points of the compass, the fifth taking the centre spot. Slowly, as if carefully choreographed, each figure pirouetted through three hundred and sixty degrees and stopped. They held their left hands close to their faces; their right arms, crooked at the elbow, held something that sloped close against their bodies under long unbuttoned coats. The figure in the centre inclined his head to his left hand and whispered. The gate swung wide on silent hinges. The ambulance emerged.

An insomniac or inquisitive neighbour, drawn to the window at that moment, might have seen the blur of white moving almost noiselessly on the darkened street. A trained observer would have noted the scuffed appearance of the vehicle, the mute siren, the absence of flashing lights, the tinted windows, and how low the ambulance rode on its wheel rims. But the windows of the overlooking buildings remained dark and shuttered. A few moments after the ambulance had left the Via Pio X, the streetlights blinked awake.

Inside the cab of the armour-plated vehicle, the driver pressed the accelerator until he was just enough above the speed limit not to excite attention in a city where slow and steady was unusual enough to be suspect. His eyes scanned to the limit of the headlamps, his brain racing through the route he had memorised minutes before. He was already deciding on options in the event of obstruction, pursuit or the need for evasive action. Under his right foot, he had enough power to push the heavy vehicle to impressive speeds and ram any impediment with the punching power of a medium-sized tank. He relaxed, moving into the well-practised routine. The man beside him in the cab was in constant motion, swivelling in his seat, holding the Uzi double-handed, its stubby mouth angled to the cab floor.

The patient lay shapeless under a light blanket, his head occluded by soft, white, paper-covered pillows. His face was indistinguishable under a plastic mask. The other three occupants of the back of the ambulance felt rather than heard the regular hum of the engine, almost masked by the sibilant hiss of the oxygen. The woman wore nurse's whites and a short veil over close-cropped hair. She crouched beside the patient, never taking her eyes from him, her concern only evident in the tiny adjustments she made to the mask and blanket. The young man, dressed in sweat-shirt, jeans and sneakers, exhibited all the symptoms of an anxious relative. Too coiled to sit, he rolled on the balls of his splayed feet, his out-stretched arms bending and straightening against the ambulance wall as the vehicle turned. Occasionally, the woman swung her head to smile reassuringly at him.

The man crouched on the seat facing the double doors swayed slightly with the movement of the ambulance, the muzzle of his gun never veering more than an inch from the line where the locked doors met.

★

Giulio Benedetto hesitated before the open wardrobe. Instinctively, he chose his second-best suit. Silently he eased his feet into shapeless black leather brogues, anticipating long hours on marble floors. Looping his tie, he tiptoed to the other side of the bed and bent to kiss his sleeping wife.

'Bye,' she murmured, eyes closed. He tucked the duvet around her back and left.

He was fishing for his car keys in his trouser pocket and almost collided with the policeman.

'*Scusi.*'

'Signor Benedetto?'

'*Si.*'

The door of the police car swung open and he sat inside. The sudden acceleration slammed Giulio against the plastic seat. He fumbled and clicked his seat belt, more in hope than in faith, as the police car slalomed through the quiet streets. Giulio took his battery-powered shaver from his pocket and began to plane his face.

3

Santa Sabina Hospital, Rome

At Giulio's nod, four orderlies moved to the open ambulance and lifted the stretcher. He was pleased to note how efficiently they deployed the telescopic undercarriage without jolting the patient. At their signal, he turned and led the way at a brisk pace to the examination room. He scanned the faces of the emergency team standing gowned and ready.

Dr Eli Weissman, the medical registrar, held his gaze with steady brown eyes. Weissman was Roman-born, from the district of Trastevere, the Jewish Quarter; summa cum laude at the University of Tel Aviv, resident in Bethesda, USA, assistant surgeon at Johns Hopkins, chief surgeon at Haifa University Hospital. Then, after such a meteoric rise, his career star seemed to have blinked out for a year. At the interview for the registrar's position, Giulio had queried the gap. 'Personal reasons,' the young doctor had replied simply. Giulio had employed 'dead air', the oldest trick in the interviewer's repertoire, inviting Weissman to fill the gap with further revelations: nothing.

Hospital directors are no more immune to the conference circuit than their medical colleagues. Calls to Giulio's opposite numbers in Bethesda and Johns Hopkins had elicited enthusiasm, commendations, congratulations, even a request for the name of that 'great grappa' they had supped not wisely but too well at the Trieste conference – but they divulged nothing that Weissman's file didn't already contain and nothing to illuminate the shadowed section in his CV. Intrigued, Giulio had tried his charms on his counterpart in the Haifa University Hospital. But Benjamin, whom he remembered as a powerhouse of fun at various conferences, was strangely awkward when Giulio revealed the nature of his query.

'Weissman? First-class medic; you won't get better, my friend.'

'Yes, yes, thank you, Benjamin, but I am puzzled by this period... Perhaps...?'

Their conversation was an electronic ping-pong game played on some satellite high above the earth, and yet neither the ether nor the time delay could camouflage the wariness in Benjamin's responses. The conversation had petered to an awkward close.

'Well, goodbye, Benjamin. Next year in Jerusalem, yes?'

'Goodbye, Giulio.'

Following his gut instinct, he had hired Eli Weissman and never regretted it. Weissman had presence, the kind of understated self-assurance that calmed patients and colleagues alike. But the archaeologist fretting beneath Giulio's skin still itched to excavate that short, sterile patch of invisibility in the life of Eli Weissman.

The metallic clicking of the approaching trolley brought Giulio back from his reverie. He glanced sideways as it neared the doors of the examination room, registering how the young, casually dressed man and the nurse flanked the stretcher at the patient's head to hide him from the curious. There was a brief flurry of movement on the nurse's side as she broke her stride and bent to lift something that had fallen from under the blanket. At Weissman's nod, the emergency team converged on the table. 'God guide you,' Giulio said softly, and left.

★

At first glance, Fabio was a typical eighteen-year-old boy: a complexity of angles, elbows and acne. Upon closer inspection, it became evident that the synapses in his brain fired a degree less briskly than those of his peers. Even Giulio's vast reservoir of sympathy ran dangerously low when his simplest instructions were digested with irritating incomprehension until the slow, slow dawn of understanding washed over the boy's speckled face. Fabio was a trial even to those who bothered to try.

He was also where he should not have been. Standing in the broom closet, he had been agonising over the choice between brush and mop for his next task as a hospital cleaner, and had missed the evacuation order. At a critical moment, in the shadowed closet, some instinct turned his attention to the section of corridor revealed through the door he had left slightly ajar. He saw the headless bodies cross the space, the patient's head shielded by a nurse's body. As the procession hurried by, an arm slipped from under the blanket and swung briefly from the trolley before the white-clad figure retrieved it and tucked it in again.

They were gone; the swing doors of the examination room sighed closed, and it was quiet. Fabio returned to his task, took a deep breath and chose the mop.

★

Giulio opened his office door and froze. The cleric lounging in his chair behind his desk raised a languid hand, the heavy ring on his third finger glinting in the pool of light from the desk lamp.

'Ah, Signor Director, do come in.'

Giulio turned to close the door behind him, taking the opportunity to mask his dismay and fury.

'Won't you sit down?' The man gestured to a chair set well back from the desk.

'I prefer to stand, Eminence.'

'You know who we are.' The other man turned from his position by the window, and his face was revealed in the wash of the desk lamp. His accent was middle-European, his Italian uninflected so that his words came as a flat statement rather than a question.

'I know who you are, Eminence,' Giulio said to the man at the window. Cardinal Richter, Secretary of State of the Roman Catholic Church, the second most powerful man in the Vatican, looked just like his photographs, Giulio thought, ascetic and disconnected. The adjective popped up from his subconscious, but before he could examine it, the cardinal at the desk spoke again. Giulio was beginning to hate that oily voice, the patronising leer, and the fact that the man was lounging in his chair.

'I am Cardinal Aurelio Alba, the unworthy assistant to his Eminence Cardinal Richter,' the man simpered, plucking his purple skullcap from his balding head and crowning himself reverently again.

Richter cut in peremptorily on his assistant. 'You may wonder why we did not take... the patient to the Gemelli?'

'It would be the norm to take this patient to that hospital,' Giulio replied warily.

'The Gemelli is compromised,' Richter said bluntly. 'The flat roofs of the buildings around it have been rented by television crews from around the world.'

'Like hyenas scenting a kill; vultures drawn to a feast,' Alba interjected angrily. Richter glanced at him, and he fell silent again

'When Professor Ricci has completed his examination,' Richter continued, 'I will speak with him.'

A knock on the door rescued Giulio from explanations.

'Ah, that will be Professor Ricci now,' Cardinal Alba said brightly, depressing the button on Giulio's desk to admit the visitor.

Eli Weissman surveyed the tableau before addressing Giulio. 'I have come to report on the patient, Signor Director.'

'But where is Ricci?' Cardinal Alba demanded.

'Professor Ricci was... uncontactable,' Giulio said. 'Dr Weissman is our registrar.'

'You allow this... registrar to examine...'

'I have complete faith in Dr Weissman.'

'Dr Weissman,' Richter said. 'Do you know who I am?'

'No, Signor,' Weissman responded coolly.

'I am Cardinal Richter, the Secretary of State. Can you inform me of the patient's condition?'

Weissman looked to Giulio, who nodded.

'The patient was admitted exhibiting restricted

breathing and an elevated temperature. We have stabilised the former and reduced the latter. He is now sleeping.'

'And?' prompted Alba imperiously.

'And what?' replied Weissman.

'Doctor.' Cardinal Richter stood directly before him. 'I think my assistant meant to ask for your diagnosis. Please.'

Weissman took a deep breath. 'He is an old man with a progressive, debilitating and terminal illness. I can keep him free from pain, Signor, but I can't keep him alive. The Pope is dying.'

Giulio felt as if all the air had been sucked out of his body. Cardinal Richter showed no emotion.

'So now you are God,' Cardinal Alba spluttered. 'Who are you to say—'

'Enough.' Richter's voice cracked like a whip in the room. 'If you can keep him free of pain,' he said to Weissman, 'it would be a great mercy.'

He strode for the door, leaving it open behind him.

Aurelio Alba found himself marooned behind the desk, struggling for some shreds of dignity.

'You will ensure that no word of this emerges, Signor Director. The Vatican Press Office will call you with detailed instructions.'

'I run a hospital, Eminence, not a prison,' Giulio replied calmly. 'And I do not work for the Vatican Press Office. Now, if you will kindly vacate my chair and my office, I would like to return to my work.'

Giulio's tone stung Alba to his feet. The cardinal's eye caught the framed photograph on Giulio's desk, and a cruel smile stretched his mouth.

'This is your family, Signor Benedetto?'

Giulio walked slowly to the desk and took the photograph from the cardinal's hand. Alba leaned close and dropped his voice to a whisper.

'Your son works for a pontifical institution, your daughter at the art restoration centre in the Vatican. It would be in their interest—'

'Goodbye, Eminence.'

After the cardinal had left, slamming the door en route, Giulio absent-mindedly polished the picture frame on his sleeve and replaced it gently on his desk.

'I don't think they're exactly thrilled to have a Jewish doctor caring for the leader of the Catholic Church,' Weissman offered quietly.

Giulio eased into his chair before replying.

'I'm surprised to hear you say that, Doctor. I understand the Catholic Church owes rather a large debt to a particular Jew.'

Weissman gestured toward the photograph on Giulio's desk.

'May I?'

'But of course.'

The doctor looked carefully at the portrait. 'Your children are very fine, Signor, and lucky.'

'Lucky?'

'The cardinal... he leaned on you, and you didn't bend.'

Giulio stared at him.

'I lip-read, Signor Benedetto. It helps with stroke victims.'

'You're a man full of surprises, Doctor.'

'I'm sorry if my... stubbornness puts you in a difficult position.'

'My children wouldn't appreciate their father bowing to a bully, Doctor, whatever the cost. Anyway, I meant what I said. I have every confidence in you. So what does it feel like to have a pope for a patient?'

Weissman replaced the picture gently on Giulio's desk.

'I tell myself, "Eli, you have a patient who happens to be pope."'

'Does that help?'

'No.'

★

Father Ambrogio Corelli padded away from the locked door of the examination room, his Franciscan sandals squeaking indignantly on the marble floor. The hospital chaplain was known by many names among the staff, a diverse group of professionals united by their aversion to the chaplain. To some, because of his mannerisms and carriage, he was Namby-Pamby. Others preferred the title Ambi Dexteri, because his watery gaze lingered a little too often and longingly on slim male staff. The emergency team, accustomed to communicating in terse acronyms, expanded his initials into A.C.D.C. The chaplain processed the great indignity that had just been visited on his sacred person, and his hand fluttered comfortingly to his chest.

The sudden evacuation of the casualty area and the heightened tension among the staff had drawn him to the exclusion zone. 'I am the hospital chaplain,' he had declared to the man in the short leather jacket who stood before the locked doors.

The man's eyes had frisked the corpulent priest and refocused on a spot a thousand yards beyond Corelli's left shoulder.

'I demand access to the patient,' Corelli had continued petulantly. The man's eyes had stayed elsewhere. His hand had moved slowly to his open jacket, drawing it aside just enough to reveal the holster beneath his armpit.

'The brute,' Corelli mouthed, 'threatening God's anointed.'

As he always did when his fragile self-image was threatened, Corelli thought of food, and he hurried to the dining hall. The long, littered room housed hospital personnel dressed in different-coloured uniforms; like birds of a feather, each colour flocked together around the circular tables. He made his way purposefully between them, oblivious to the way each group expanded to cover any vacant space at their table as he approached, then relaxed gratefully in his wake.

The emergency team always pooled in the top right-hand corner of the dining room, beneath the wall-mounted speaker and close to the emergency doors. 'Incoming,' one of them hissed, and the group huddled closer to create an exclusion zone.

The chaplain swayed for a moment in deliberation and struck. 'Ah, Petronella,' he said, his voice carrying above the general hubbub, 'it's just too sad about your brother. You must be devastated.'

Petronella's brother had featured in all the daily papers as a 'colour' item tacked on to the report of the Roma–Lazio game of the previous evening. Her colleagues had already expounded on the photograph of the exceptionally endowed streaker, and Petronella had fielded their banter with good humour. But the chaplain was an outsider, an intrusion. Abruptly, Petronella surged from her chair and stalked away.

Corelli eased his bulk into her chair. 'Poor dear,' he offered. 'So humiliating.'

The team gave their total attention to what they were eating. 'But I, too, have been humiliated today,' the chaplain continued, injecting pathos into his voice, his eyes dramatically wide and wounded.

An assistant cardiologist, shielded from Corelli's view by two burly colleagues, mimed attaching paddles to his chest, jerked convulsively, then calmly resumed eating. The circle swayed with suppressed laughter. Implacably, the chaplain continued. 'Imagine – I am forbidden to bring the comfort of Holy Mother Church to this... mystery patient in the examination room.'

The group tensed momentarily and then exploded from their chairs, muttering excuses and gulping the dregs of their coffee. Ambrogio Corelli was alone.

'Goodbye, goodbye,' he said softly. 'You too are about the Lord's work.' He waved a vague sign of the cross at their retreating backs before turning to the table, his eyes scanning hungrily for deserted food. The emergency team could always be relied on for rich pickings, if not for information.

'Holy Father.'

Corelli looked up guiltily to see the smiling face of Fabio.

'Ah, Fabio, how good to see you,' he murmured without conviction. Why the administration employed these defectives, he could never fathom. The boy's slack grin and vacant eyes sent a tremor of revulsion through him, so that he hesitated a moment before nibbling delicately at an abandoned bun.

'Holy Father,' the boy said again, nodding happily.

'No, no, Fabio. No one is truly holy but God Himself, but God knows I try.'

'I saw him.'

'What?' How he hated the inanity of it. Conversing

with this loon would reduce him to grimacing and babbling. The bun wasn't worth it, he decided, and prepared to leave.

'In the exa...mi...nation room.'

Corelli folded a paper napkin with inordinate care and pressed it to his lips before speaking.

'What did you see?'

'I was in the broom closet. Mop or brush... which...?'

'Yes, yes, dear child, but you saw...?'

'Busy busy, rush rush, all going by. Hand fall.'

Fabio placed his elbow on the table and let his arm dangle over the edge.

'That's very good, Fabio. Did you say a man's hand?'

Fabio nodded and began to plaster butter on a piece of toast. Sensing his shift of interest, the chaplain leaned forward conspiratorially.

'You see many things, don't you, Fabio?'

'Yes.'

'You saw a man's hand. What else did you see, my son? You can tell me. You know who I am?'

'I know who you are. Father Cor...elli.'

'Yes. Excellent. Father Corelli, your friend.'

'My friend.'

'What else did you see, clever Fabio?'

The boy stretched his hand, palm down, across the table. The chaplain checked his urge to lean back and nodded encouragingly. The boy tapped the third finger of his hand. 'Ring,' he whispered, 'big ring. The Pope – Holy Father,' he added, and smiled.

Ambrogio Corelli sat back, stunned. With a huge effort, he re-engaged his brain. Of course. Evacuation of the area, armed security and tight lips all round. And now this. The boy was not exactly a solid source, but he was too simple to lie convincingly. Corelli patted Fabio's head in hasty benediction and left the dining hall, his sandals squeaking at a higher pitch in his excitement.

He needed a phone. The chaplain should be provided with a mobile phone, he thought, fuming. He had asked, but Angela, that monstrous Amazon, hadn't even looked up from her damned computer screen. 'If we want you, we'll find you, Father.' If? The damned cheek of the woman.

He found himself in the reception area and turned to the public phone booth. An elderly lady in a padded pink dressing gown was perched on the stool behind the glass. She held the phone in her right hand, her left hand weaving beside her head for emphasis. He rapped on the glass. The flying hand hovered, then tightened to a fist with the middle finger extended before resuming its flight pattern. Corelli wanted to kick the glass door. He wanted to grab the receiver from the crone's paw, wind the cord around her scrawny neck and pull.

Breathe, he instructed himself. Breathe. He turned and surveyed the busy reception hall. Something was missing... Angela. Don't rush. Slow and steady.

He detected a faint, sweet smell of perfume on the handset in the office and grimaced.

'*Pronto.*'

The chaplain was immediately soothed by the calm, uninflected voice at the other end and by the music he could hear in the background. '*Sursum corda,*' he whispered. Let us lift up our hearts.

'*Habemus ad Dominum,*' the voice answered. We have raised them up to the Lord.

'I have a report of Peter in chains at the Santa Sabina,' he whispered.

He heard a slight intake of breath and swelled with pride.

'*Fidelis servus et prudens,*' the voice said, and broke the connection.

Corelli felt as if he were floating. He had always regarded himself as a faithful and prudent servant, and now it had been affirmed by no less than—

'Father Corelli.'

He whirled and found himself face to face with the Amazon. Angela out-bulked him, and her fiery eyes invited him to bloody combat.

'You do not use my phone,' she snapped, prodding his chest with a hard finger for emphasis.

'My dear—'

'I am not your dear anything, Father. I am the reception manager, this is my office and you are using my phone.'

Corelli backed away, his hands patting the air between them as if trying to quench a fire.

'Yes, yes, of course,' he spluttered. 'It was… an emergency. A poor soul in need of comfort. It is deplorable that the spiritual director of this institution has not been provided with—'

'Father Corelli.'

She extended her hand, palm up, and he placed the receiver in it, careful not to make any physical contact. Her head slanted toward the door. Cheeks aflame, Corelli backed away and waddled off with as much dignity as he could muster.

Angela's eyes drilled imaginary holes in his departing cassock. Instinctively she crossed herself and made the sign against the evil eye as well, for good measure.

4

Castel Sant'Angelo

Stefan closed the phone. Though his mind wrestled with the information he had just received from Father Corelli, his hand did not tremble. His face was thoughtful, not anguished. In one lithe movement, he left the chair behind the functional desk and paced to the centre of the high-ceilinged room. Giotto cherubs gazed from the plaster above his head as he settled at the music stand. Methodically, he riffled through the sheet music and selected Mahler's Ninth Symphony. To him, music was pure mathematics in liquid form – further evidence, if he had needed it, of divine exactitude.

The light on the stand created a glowing circle

beyond which the room was blurred with shadow. In his right hand, he held the baton across his chest; his left hand operated the remote control. With hardly a whisper, the powerful Bang & Olufsen speakers blinked awake. Raising his hands chest-high, he summoned the music. Mahler swelled and he rode the wave of emotion, his plain brown cassock rippling with the movement, two half-moons of black seeping wider beneath his armpits.

Behind his closed eyelids, the agony began.

He was coming in solemn procession from the rear of his parish church, on a hill outside Srebrenica. Flanked by candle-bearers, and preceded by a young acolyte carrying a gilded crucifix, he had already bowed to the statue of the Virgin that guarded the doors. The congregation rose as one and faced the altar. Stefan knew there were many in the church who admired and even idolised him. For them, he was an iconic figure of strength and single-mindedness in the chaos of their country. There were others who feared him and saw his unwavering belief as parochial and partisan. None of them loved him. He knew he was not a man to be loved, and he did not desire it. That part of himself he had locked away many years before, in his dedication to the priesthood. He regarded it as needy, a weakness, and rooted it from his make-up. If he had a passion, it was for Truth – a concept mapped out in dogma by his Church, encompassing the heavens and the earth. Truth came in primary colours; there was no room in his world view for shade or nuance.

He felt the rumble of heavy vehicles through the floor. The atonal crump of explosions percolated through the walls, and a murmur of unease swelled in the body of the church, but he did not switch his gaze from the altar. He bowed to kiss the altar stone and rose to face his people.

'Let us sing to the Lord,' he proclaimed, his strong voice echoing over the congregation, insulating them from the thin screams that pierced the doors and windows, 'who has done great things for us.'

With a groan, the church doors buckled and fell inwards, quenching all sound. Uniformed men strolled the aisles, swinging their weapons to left and right. Those near the central aisle ebbed away, distancing themselves from the menace that spread through the church like a toxic cloud.

'You dare defile the House of God?' Stefan shouted. A sudden burst of gunfire, magnified by the high walls, startled cries and whimpers from his people. The statue of the Virgin sprayed pieces of plaster, rocking on its plinth. He opened his mouth in horror, but they were upon him, arcing his arms up and outwards behind his back so that he thought his shoulder blades must snap. And yet he kept his head straining upright, glaring his defiance at the militia.

They dragged him from his church and held

him on his knees as flaming torches arced to the timber roof. The angry flames peeled the skin from his face and ate his eyebrows to ash. In his torment he cried out, '*Eli, Eli, lama sabacthani* – my God, my God, why have you forsaken me?' His straining ears heard only the stutter of distant guns. Above the crackling and groaning of his flaming church he heard a pistol being cocked behind his head, and he readied his soul for release.

'No.'

The small man in military uniform had the bland face of a cherub; blond curls twisted innocently from beneath his forage cap. His eyes were deep black pools into which all hope had sunk without leaving a ripple. He brought his face close and gazed into Stefan's eyes for a long moment. 'Save your bullets,' he commanded. 'Let this one live as a warning to others.'

Those who had escaped to the forest straggled back to wail and beat the earth with their foreheads. Two young men peeled away from the knot of smoke-wreathed survivors and dragged Stefan to the shell of someone's house. With infinite patience they stripped him of the vestments welded by fire to his body. The dead are free of feeling, he thought, and made no sound. They dressed him in salvaged clothing redolent of smoke and left him to bury their dead.

Sometime – morning, evening, night, he did not know which – he stood and stumbled outside.

Placing one foot carefully before the other, he skirted the gouges in the earth and the huddled half-human shapes. He walked into the green, waving sea of the fir forest until the sounds of his former life muted and stilled.

They were hunched over a small cooking fire when he stumbled into the clearing. Startled, the young men reached for their weapons. A sharp command stilled them. The woman emerged from behind a tree, a weapon already cocked. She called again, and a young man stepped sheepishly from the forest, buttoning his flies. The sentry, Stefan thought. The woman slapped the careless sentry hard enough to make his head rock. He showed no resistance, only stood there with his head hanging.

The muzzle of her weapon gestured Stefan to the fire, now abandoned by the others, who joined their shamed colleague at the other end of the clearing. She wore a mishmash of uniforms, worn and weathered so that they clung to her like a second skin. Her hair was black and cut close to her scalp, raggedly, as if by a hunting knife. Out of a thin, feral face, dark eyes watched his every movement as he hunkered down. They were the eyes of someone who had seen nightmares in daylight. Those eyes would never again see hope or love. Stefan saw himself mirrored in those eyes.

'What will I do?' he asked the eyes.

'What must be done,' she replied tonelessly. 'Will you eat?' He knew it was not a gesture of kindness but an invitation to a commitment to living. He searched himself for some reason to refuse and found none.

'I'll eat,' he said. 'I'm hungry.'

She crouched by the fire and watched him eat, her weapon always to hand, her head cocked slightly as if listening beyond the crackle of the fire. She noticed with approval how he ate slowly, showing no sign of relishing the food; how he made no effort to engage her in talk, but ate as if alone.

'Your name?' she asked, when he licked the thin gravy from his fingers.

'Stefan.'

'Magda,' she said. 'These others,' she continued quietly, angling her head in the direction of the group who muttered among themselves, 'they were angry. They wanted revenge. But anger and revenge burn like a flash fire: here, then gone. Now they want to go back, to find a new... normal.'

'And you?'

She shook her head. 'I have no normal to go back to.' He watched her closely for signs of emotion and saw none. She raised her head and glanced at the group at the other end of the clearing. 'They have wives and children. Back home, they'll avoid one another's company for a while and never talk about the things they've done. They think that will make it all go away. I stand in the way of that; so, all day, they've been trying to work up the courage to kill me,' she said calmly. 'Can you shoot?'

'I don't know.'

She drew a pistol from her belt and slapped it, butt first, into his palm. The group had fanned into a menacing half-circle, the chastened sentry chivvying his companions with urgent whispers.

'Don't stand close to me, but stay level,' she said calmly. 'The man with the scar – aim for him.'

Stefan felt his heart begin to bang against his ribcage. A kind of madness welled up inside him, so that he had to lock his throat not to laugh. Magda walked directly towards the group, her gun and her eyes marking one man for death. The man she targeted called out hoarsely.

'There are six of us and only two of you, Magda.'

'Yes, Arkady,' she answered, never slackening her steady pace, 'but we don't care.'

Stefan could not contain himself. His laugh was a high, wild sound that sent a tremor through the line.

Magda fired. Arkady's head exploded. The two men on either side of him flinched instinctively from the spray of blood and bone. In that moment she shifted her angle and gut-shot the man to her left; his upper body arched forward and his trigger-finger convulsed, spraying a man on the periphery. Lengthening her stride, Magda took him high in the chest.

Stefan, staring at his target, registered the slaughter in his peripheral vision as a blur. His brain tracked the panic and fear scudding across the scarred face, and he pulled the trigger. The pistol bucked like a live thing in his hand. His target flinched as the round whined over his head. Stefan dropped the muzzle and pulled again, and the man toppled, gargling blood through the hole in his throat.

He sensed Magda gliding to flank the survivors, and watched them raise their hands. In the sudden silence, someone twitched on the ground, and Magda shot him without taking her eyes from their captives. Stefan's head rang with adrenaline and bloodlust. He swept his weapon up again.

'Stefan. Enough,' she snapped.

He came to himself panting and shaking like a wet dog. His fingers were locked, claw-like, on the trigger.

She turned to the two remaining men. 'Go.'

They crabbed away towards the trees, their eyes never leaving hers until they crashed through the undergrowth and the forest swallowed them.

'Why did you let them go?' Stefan asked. 'They would have killed us. They may bring others.'

'No. They lived and others died. How will they tell the story? Will they say it was two against six?' She shook her head dismissively. 'No. They'll say we were more than six...and not human. Shame and fear, Stefan, are weapons also. Remember.'

She shouldered her weapon and began to walk into the trees. Stefan followed.

Later, when they were deep in the forest, their backs to a lichened boulder, she broke the silence.

'You tugged the trigger. Squeeze. Move sideways when there's more than one enemy. An angle makes three men into one; the other two can't shoot for fear of hitting their comrade. Head and gut shots are best at the beginning; brains and bowels spread terror and confusion. Pick one target. Mark him out with your eyes and your voice. Look at him until he knows he is going to die and becomes afraid. Were you afraid?'

'No.'

'Why?'

'Because I didn't care.'

She bobbed her head in a brief, approving nod.

'Thus endeth the lesson,' she said, with the ghost of a smile shimmering under the surface of her bone-white face. Stefan thought she had a cold, unearthly beauty, like the statue of the Virgin at Srebrenica.

In the days and nights ahead they melded into one shadow, flowing through and behind minefields and sentry pickets, never speaking unless out of necessity. But, as the Serb body count grew and the myth expanded, others talked; others tallied.

The sentry outside the village was a boy in uniform. A soldier would never have stood limned in light. A soldier would have found a tree, a rock, a fence, anything to mask his shape. The boy signalled his position by the slow-dash Morse of his cigarette glow. Magda was close enough to touch his puppy-fat, downy face. When she slid the blade across his throat the boy convulsed; his finger tightened on the trigger. Stefan saw the muzzle-flash before he heard the bang. He moved quickly, toppling the boy's body to the side, dragging Magda to the cover of the trees. When he examined her wound he struggled to conceal his horror. There were lights in the distance, bright fingers poking inquisitively between the branches. He heard voices call and then coalesce into a bellow of rage. They had found the boy. He turned to Magda.

'Gut shot,' she gasped, the words bubbling through the blood in her mouth. 'Go.'

A speculative rake of machine-gun fire brought an early autumn to the leaves above his head. Instinctively, he raised his right hand in benediction; then he clasped it over her nose and mouth. She bucked twice reflexively, her fingers scrabbling at the smothering hand, and then her body sagged. He took her hunting knife from her belt and shoved it into his. It was better balanced than his own. Carefully, he backtracked, burrowing deeper into the forest.

He woke, and his senses told him he was not alone. Easing his eyelids open, he saw them. He should have been flattered; at least twenty men and women surrounded him, all heavily armed. A tall bearded man stepped forward from the group and spoke in Stefan's own language.

'You think you're a hero. For every one you killed, they've killed two of ours. If we don't bring you in, the killing won't stop.' He seemed suddenly spent. 'The United Nations soldiers say they will protect you,' he muttered, almost apologetically.

There is always choice, Stefan thought. He could erupt from his prone position and run directly at them. A man to the left had his finger outside the trigger-guard. The woman beside him in the red headscarf held her weapon sloped.

No. Their need for a scapegoat might absolve him of his guilt at surviving. Anyway, without Magda... He allowed them to strip him of his weapons and bind his hands and feet, and 'like a lamb he did not open his mouth'. When they dropped him like garbage in the mud outside the UN compound, he just lay there waiting.

The Dutch UN commander had greying black hair that clung like fish scales to his scalp. Behind the rimless glasses, his eyes were weary.

'Father, there have been many accu— allegations levelled against you. I have sworn affidavits from many witnesses.'

Stefan almost smiled. There were no witnesses.

'Have you anything to say?'

The silence stretched.

'If I put you in the holding camp... I might as well shoot you myself. We have people under guard in the compound from both sides; it was the only way we could stop the killing. They will be processed, and most will be released. But both sides would kill you, Father, for what they allege you have done or for the retaliation that resulted from your actions.'

The commander plucked the glasses from his nose and rested them on the thick pile of documents. Weariness sagged his face into the shape it would have twenty years from now. If he lives that long, Magda's voice whispered calmly in Stefan's head. There is a pencil. It can be driven into his eye. Folded documents can crush his larynx. Look, he's wearing a holstered gun.

Stefan squeezed his eyes shut and listened to the Dutchman.

'These are terrible times, Father. Things have been done... terrible things, by people who were once friends, neighbours... even priests. By people who were once... people. They may become people again if there is some measure of peace.'

He let the word 'peace' hang like a talisman between them as he searched Stefan's face for something, anything. He had noted the slight shake of the head and the hard-shut eyes, but the man who sat before him now was carved from granite.

'I am instructed not to create martyrs or myths. My superiors, in their wisdom, imagine that everything can be forgiven and forgotten, given time. They talk about amnesty and normalisation. Oh, yes, there will be show trials. It is necessary occasionally for one man – or more – to die for the people.' He smiled mirthlessly. 'But not you, Father. It seems the Holy Catholic Church wishes to embrace its prodigal son. It has been decided by the authorities, in the best interests of all concerned, that you should be given sanctuary in Rome.'

At that, the commander stood abruptly, gathered his papers into his arms and left. The door slammed behind him.

Stefan heard and smelled the truck backing to the door of the hut. He displayed no surprise when the two soldiers opened the door and lifted him roughly from the chair. Adjusting his hips, he lessened the impact on his body when they flung him into the truck bed. Before the doors closed he saw a sliver of the holding camp. Lined along the razor wire, standing three deep in total silence, men and women stared at him. He could feel their hatred like a hot wind on his skin. The truck smelled of blood and excrement and he knew the cargo that had been unloaded for him. Empty, empty, Magda's voice crooned. Let it go. Sleep.

The days ahead were a kaleidoscope of sounds and smells. There were trucks of all sizes and levels of discomfort. He heard a ribald exchange, through his covering of burlap sacks, that convinced him he was crossing a frontier. He knew from the way the soldier's voice turned from challenging to conspiratorial that something had changed hands. Time stretched. Boredom is your greatest enemy, Stefan, she counselled. It leads to blindness. Sharpen your senses; whet them regularly on whatever's around you. Remember, the rock you see day after day may hide a marksman today. The path most travelled is where they place the mines.

For days and nights he conjured rooms in his mind and gauged the depths of cellars. He was passed from one person to another and built up pictures in his brain of their ages, nationalities and occupations. Except for the drivers, they were mostly nuns, monks and priests, the underground Church that passed him dutifully from hand to hand. He heard bird calls in forests and, occasionally, a whistle that was not made by a bird. He marked the rise and fall of tension in his minders as a counterpoint on a musical score.

He found sanctuary at the heart of the Church, ring-fenced by the impenetrable power of Rome. And then the Devil came.

His minions preceded him. They bound Stefan to a chair and passed a rope around his neck so that he could not turn his head. The Devil made an offer. It was not an offer of absolution. Stefan had faced that toothless dragon when others along the way had tried to seduce him to repentance. They would have had him beg for forgiveness and become an icon of pardon, to be paraded for the edification of a broken world. Listening to their anxious voices, he had conjured up the taste of blood in his mouth and steeled himself until their pathetic pleadings had faltered.

The Devil was different.

'Father Stefan,' he said calmly, 'you are what you are. Perhaps you are who you were meant to be. That doesn't make you unique, just different. You're a man of action; well, the history of salvation is peppered with them – men and women. As I recall, the children of Israel sang the praises of Saul when he slew his thousands and sang even louder when David slew his tens of thousands. I understand you are unrepentant. Good. Hope is insidious, Father Stefan. When times get tough, the weak are tempted to hope rather than act. The enemy sweeps right over them and they are disillusioned. You have no illusions, and I won't offer you any. My offer is a simple one. I will feed, clothe, house and protect you. I will give you the power of life and death over others. Why? Because I need you. I need a warrior for one final battle. And, when it's over, I give you my solemn oath that you will die.'

It was so novel and unexpected that Stefan was seduced from his shell to consider it. He heard a voice rasping with disuse ask, 'Why should I believe you?' It was his voice, and it seemed to speak of its own volition.

'Because,' the Devil answered, 'I will show myself to you.'

He did not recognise the Devil in his human form, but he knew the significance of his garb and of the ring he wore.

'Are you willing?' the Devil asked.

'*Volo*,' he replied. 'I am willing.'

He listened intently to the difficulty of the task and the enormity of the goal.

'Weapons?' he asked finally.

'Access to information,' the Devil replied.

The boxes delivered to Stefan's living quarters contained a mobile phone and a computer, both state of the art. The password was printed on a thin sheet of paper that he was enjoined to read and destroy. '*Urbi et Orbi*,' it read. 'To the city and to the world.'

There were two other boxes. One contained the Bang & Olufsen music centre and a small collection of compact discs; the other, a statue of the Virgin. Her face was caked with soot. She had bullet holes for eyes.

And now the mobile phone had whispered a critical piece of information. The Rock of Peter had begun to crumble. The universal Catholic Church tilted perilously, and cracks would begin to fissure East and West as powers angled for domination.

He swept the baton across his chest. The music ended.

He sat at the computer console and tapped in the code. It was time to take up arms. The word '*Venite*' – 'Come' – appeared on the flat screen. Like a concert pianist, he raised his right hand and dropped it on the keyboard, index finger extended.

Send.

5

Catacombs of San Domitilla, Rome

Alessandro Cudicini shifted his weight from one buttock to the other and sighed. Beneath the tectonic plates of his ample ass, the shabby taxi rocked in sympathy. It had been six weary hours since the call. Always the same voice, toneless as an answering machine, ordering the pick-up – at a different run-down, shit point in the Eternal City. 'No names, no faces, caro.' Alessandro had never imagined that a term of affection could chill.

Always the same drop: the Catacombs of San Domitilla. Their outer walls glowed a jaundiced yellow in his rear-view mirror. 'Always park backwards. Never look around. Whatever deep philosophical insights your profession has bestowed on you, keep them to yourself. No talk, *capisce?*'

Oh, he understood, all right. Hear no evil, see no evil. 'You break the rules and you learn to sing castrato, caro.'

It took a full half-minute for the trembling to stop. Alessandro fixed his hands on the wheel, knuckles white as death, and waited.

★

'Gabriel?'
  '*Adsum.*'
'Raphael?'
  '*Adsum.*'
'Michael?'
  '*Adsum.*'

The roll call rebounded from the low roof of the burial chamber. Starting with the archangels, it would work its way through the litany of saints and martyrs until the final '*adsum*' – 'I am here.'

The chamber was twenty feet long by thirty feet wide, carved on the orders of some noble Roman family of the first century, long gone to dust in the marble sarcophagus that glowed in the candlelit crypt. Stefan called the names using the sarcophagus as a lectern – or, more correctly, as a podium, since he never used notes. Under his right hand, a primitive fish shape was scratched into the sheen of white marble. In the miles of underground corridors, crypts and grottos were many similar scratchings, the graffiti of the early Christians who had kept the flame of faith alive in the dark under Rome.

'*Fratres, sobri estote et vigilate. Quia adversarius vester diabolus, tamque leo rugiens, circuit quaerens quem devoret. Cui resistite, fortes in fide,*' Stefan intoned in little more than a whisper, his sibilants slipping through the rows of men before him, teasing their attention. It was the admonition Peter the Apostle, the first pontiff, had given to his followers almost two thousand years before. My brothers, be sober and watchful, for your enemy the Devil, like a roaring lion, goes about seeking who he may devour. Resist him, steadfast in the faith.

'Amen,' they chorused. The murmur of a huge truck pounding the street above their heads drummed faintly in the ensuing silence, like a portent of impending thunder.

'You have been tried in the refiner's fire,' Stefan continued in the same whisper, 'and not found wanting. Some of you have known martyrdom: like the blessed Saint Sebastian, you have been pierced by the arrows of the scornful.'

A tall young man with the face of a cherub inclined his head in acknowledgement.

'Like the blessed Paul, others have been persecuted for holding to the true faith.'

To the rear of the group, a squat man with Middle European features stiffened momentarily.

'You have sat like Job on the dunghill of your dreams and seen the rise of lesser men – men who

have traded the truth of the Gospel for the approval
of the godless, who have diluted the blood of Christ
with liberalism, who have sown weeds in the wheat
field of the truth.'

The group seemed to swell as if with suppressed
emotion.

'Lesser men,' he continued, his voice rising
marginally to override the painful images that
flashed in every brain. 'Lesser men who have sold
their birthright for a mess of pottage; men who say,
"Lord, Lord" with their lips and shield the darkness
of their hearts. But, I say unto you, I have come to
cast fire on the earth.'

'Maranatha,' they murmured. 'Come, Lord
Jesus.'

His voice rose another notch, surfing the
emotion in the room. 'The stone rejected by the
builder will become the cornerstone.'

'Amen,' they chorused again.

He allowed the echoes to whisper into silence
before continuing. 'It is time to separate the chaff
from the wheat. Time to pull down those who have
been exalted and raise up the lowly.'

Although his words were largely culled from the
scriptures, no one in the vaulted chamber could be
ignorant of their import. Stefan, the convenor of
these men, knew them intimately and loathed them
for their weakness. They were the disappointed, the
ones whom Mother Church had not favoured; the
loyal sons who had remained dull, dutiful and

therefore invisible, who had watched in envy as their prodigal brothers and sisters were promoted ahead of them. Envy, he knew, was anger in aspic, preserved until it corroded the vessel that contained it. He had courted that anger, holding out the promise of revenge, and they had come to him like hyenas to the promise of a kill. Yes, there would be sacrifices, quarries to be hunted down and dispatched. Some of their enemies must be 'down-sized', 'promoted laterally', to avoid suspicion and make way for the chosen – how he loved the American vocabulary of corporate assassination, so many words crafted to conceal the reality and make it palatable. Others must be terminated. He approved the dark Latin root of that word.

'The hour is at hand,' he declared, scanning the faces before him for incredulity, joy, fear. The fearful he would mark and not forget. 'You remember your oath. You know your duties. Let the gathering begin.'

He closed his eyes, sensing the shock that rippled through them, hearing the sounds of dispersal, the shuffling of feet in the maze of tunnels as they sought the outside world through different exits to avoid arousing interest or suspicion. And still he stood immobile, eyes closed, as if the effigy of the buried Roman in the sarcophagus had slipped from its frieze to stand in contemplation.

'You are troubled,' he said finally, opening his

eyes. They showed no flicker of surprise as they took in the man before him: John Howard, Professor of Dogmatic Theology at St Anselm's Seminary in Sussex, where he read from the same notes he had used for twenty years, as his students pretended to take notes and itched for the challenge of the younger theologians or a few beers at the local.

'I wonder if perhaps we are being somewhat… premature.'

Stefan remained silent, his head angled towards the professor. Howard was not a man who savoured silence. He had long interpreted the silence of his colleagues as ridicule, the silence of his students as apathy. He pressed on, wispy white hair aflutter, heavy spectacles sliding down the ski slope of his nose.

'Of course, you're quite right in everything you say. These are dreadful times for Mother Church: rogue theologians, that liberation-theology nonsense, and so forth.' He wrinkled his nose in distaste and ploughed on. 'But I wonder… I mean, would our cause not be better served by some attempt at balance? What I'm trying to say is, could we perhaps be in the modern Church but not of it – a leaven for change from within, so to speak?'

His voice tailed off into the dark, and the silence returned to unnerve him further. 'I must say that I have occasionally taken up the cudgels against—'

'Caro.'

The word was so laden with inflections that

Howard grew quite still. He seemed to grasp at that one word as if it held all he yearned for: companionship, acceptance, respect.

'You are burdened,' Stefan said softly, and Howard nodded slowly, a tear teetering behind his spectacles.

'Yes,' he breathed.

Stefan moved fluidly to stand beside him, placing his hand gently on the flecked shoulder. He waited until the eyes first squinted and then focused on his own.

'You have toiled in the vineyard of the Lord in the noonday heat, when others, coming late, received the same reward.'

'Yes.' Howard trembled; the tear hung like a diamond on the rim of one large lens before falling silently to the floor. Stefan's strong arm encircled his shoulders, and Howard laid his head against Stefan's chest like a child seeking comfort.

'Come unto me,' Stefan whispered, 'and I shall give you rest.'

He cupped the weak chin tenderly, as if he would tilt up Howard's face. Transferring his other hand to the professor's shoulder, he tugged sharply and heard the neck bone snap. A small sigh escaped the dead man's lips before he sagged to the floor.

'He who would put his hand to the plough and draw back is unworthy of me,' Stefan whispered harshly over the still form.

6

The Irish College, Rome

A bell tolled somewhere in the distance, and Father Hugh O'Neill awoke.

Automatically, he rolled to his knees beside the bed and prayed. Then he showered, dressed in the long black soutane with the flying cape and studied himself in the mirror. The man who looked back at him was of medium height, with mousy blond hair cut Mormon-short. His Irish skin stubbornly refused to tan, compensating with a sprinkle of light freckles on high cheekbones. It was an unremarkable face, and he spent no time considering it, beyond checking the overall image for tidiness. The eyes in the mirror were pale grey, set slightly too far apart under a broad forehead. He would have been surprised to learn that some people found his gaze disconcerting. A friend might have told him this, and might have highlighted other aspects of his appearance and character that set him somewhat apart from his fellows. But Hugh O'Neill had no one in his head or heart filed under 'friend' – except, perhaps, Tom Finn.

He moved to the immaculate desk, opened a file and withdrew an aerogramme. Tom Finn wrote sporadically from various parts of the world, recounting his meteoric rise in the field of surgery at Harvard and Mount Sinai, the tug of home that had landed him back in Derry, and his academic and sexual exploits, for the edification of his clerical friend.

The savage loves his native shore, and the native shore is as savage as ever. Suffice it to say (because I know they read your mail) that I now hold the world speed record for kneecap replacements. In the early days, some of these boys bled out before we could get them on the table. I dropped a wee word at home, drew some pictures for the da – a sort of crash course in trajectories, you might say. From then on, every one was as clean as a whistle: never a nick on an artery. I'll get the Nobel Award for promoting corpses to cripples. Got to dash, Hugh, emergency: a very interesting assembly of anatomical parts of genus femina – Jane by name and pneumatic by nature – just hove into view. You'll have to meet her whenever you opt to forsake the lofty heights and get down and dirty again.

Your friend,

Tom.

P.S. Met Duffy the other day. In for a check-up. Every registrar's nightmare.

'When did you first experience chest pains, Father?'

'1962.'

What can you do? They had to give him an epidural to get the soutane off. I told him how well you were doing. 'As I feared,' he said, gnomic as ever. Write soon. Your letters are so full of the cut and thrust of Vatican intrigue that I'm having them serialised in the Belfast Telegraph.

T.

'You have a fine mind, Hugh.'

Monsignor Francis Brennan, President of the Irish College, peered quizzically at Hugh over his half-moon spectacles. Brennan was Kildare to the bone but all Italian on the surface. Though small and round, he moved from the window to his ornate desk with that languid motion so typical of the Latins. Behind his head, framed photographs hung on the walls, showing him locked in fraternal solidarity with some of the leading Churchmen of the day. On the desk, in a silver frame, he had just managed to nudge himself into focus between the Pope and Nelson Mandela.

'Yes, Monsignor,' Hugh replied.

'You also have the uncanny knack of saying one thing and meaning another.'

'Yes, Monsignor.'

'Definitely diplomatic material,' Monsignor Brennan nodded. He seated himself in the high winged chair behind the desk, carefully adjusting his tiny skullcap. 'Man to man, Hugh, and within these four walls – and all the other clichés I could employ but choose not to – I have something to say to you.'

He paused and searched the face before him for a reaction. But Hugh had long ago learned to wear the mask of inscrutability. Monsignor Brennan nodded almost imperceptibly, as if in approval.

'The Church is in crisis, Hugh.'

He spoke so softly that Hugh leaned forward, unsure if he had heard him properly.

'Great changes all about us, Hugh. As the cynic said, constant change is here to stay.'

Hugh allowed a small smile to penetrate his mask.

'Oh, that line could sum up the Church in any age, I know.' The Monsignor rose wearily from the desk and paced again to the high window, as if anxious for the warmth that pooled there.

'Since the earliest times, people have resisted change. Peter wanted to circumcise the new Christians and continue the Jewish tradition – until, of course, he had a vision. A convenience not afforded many others in times of crisis.' He breathed deeply, and some strength returned to his voice.

'The Church survived the Great Schism, the Reformation, the Enlightenment – how? The Holy Spirit? We'd like to think so.' He turned from the window, his head haloed in sunlight. 'The Holy Spirit breathes where He will, Hugh. You know the quote. But He must have something or someone to breathe through. We call that inspiration. The Church survived because men were inspired to protect her, strong men, the brightest and the best: our own shock troops, dedicated to holding the line until the threat could be overcome or accommodated. And what threatens us today, Hugh?'

He moved from the embrace of the sunlight so that he faced the young man. The unhindered light from the window blinded Hugh and occluded the eyes of the man before him. Deliberately, he shifted his chair out of the light.

'Are you evading the question?'

'No, Monsignor. I'm weighing the question, and…'

'And?'

'And the agenda of the questioner.'

The silence stretched between them. Brennan

turned briskly and closed the heavy drapes. The table lamp, which had been superfluous in the sun-lit room, now cast an amber circle, into which he brought his chair. He nodded his head approvingly, a wry smile teasing the corners of his mouth.

'Very good. Very good. I see you have learned more than theology here. Very well. Let me answer my own question and, in the process, answer yours. In a time when half of the population died at birth and the other half wished they had, the Church was the Porta Coeli, the gate of heaven. If I may mix my metaphors, once you had booked your ticket on the barque of Peter, you were on the only licensed ferry, with a cast-iron guarantee of safe passage to the other side – unless, of course, you threw yourself overboard through mortal sin or walked the plank through excommunication. It was a safe and simple contract for the illiterate, unskilled and unquestioning. Not now, Hugh. Not today.'

Up close, Hugh was surprised to see the brown smudges like old bruises beneath the monsignor's eyes, and the patch of silver stubble the morning razor had overlooked below his left ear. He found them slightly unsettling, as if he had looked closely at a Titian or a Rembrandt and seen the canvas peering through the paint.

Brennan's tone was flatter than before. 'When there was a crisis of heresy, we burned the heretics. When there was a full-frontal attacker, like Luther with his ninety-five theses and his little righteous hammer, we sent in the Marines – the Dominicans to preach and the Jesuits to teach. When there were wars, we blessed the guns – on both sides, of course. We rang the bells, sang the Te Deums and sprinkled the mass graves.' He lifted his head and gazed quizzically at Hugh. 'Do I shock you?'

'No, Monsignor.'

'No. Well, I shall have to try harder. The Church, down through the ages, has survived because she was a whore.'

Hugh stared in amazement at the composed face opposite.

'Ah, now that shocks you, does it? Hugh, Hugh, use that great brain of yours. The Church has always been a whore – but a whore for the sake of Christianity's survival. There are biblical precedents, aren't there?'

'Yes,' Hugh answered softly, after a pause. 'Judith, in the Old Testament, seduced Holofernes, the commander of the conquering army.'

'And to what purpose?'

'To behead him.'

'Indeed,' the Monsignor agreed. 'The Church flirted with Mussolini, danced with Hitler, bedded monarchs, despots and crackpots for centuries. They are gone, Hugh. And we are still here. If I may extend the rather racy analogy, we seduced the Reformation with ecumenism and inclusion. We apologised to the Jews, took out the reference to "perfidious Jews" in the Holy Week liturgy, and –

our master stroke, in your lifetime – we elected a pope who made a pact with the commander-in-chief of the greatest super power in the world. And so the Wall came down and the Iron Curtain, if you'll pardon the pun, rusts in peace. Marx, Engels, Lenin and Stalin – all gone, Hugh; and Castro, their disciple, is beholden to us for handouts.

'So, is Islam the threat? One-fifth of the population of the world falls to its knees five times a day to face Mecca, not Jerusalem, not Rome. They learned quickly from us. "Save Jerusalem" is the sort of soundbite that can inspire a crusade just as "Save Rome" gave us an Inquisition. Their message is so simple: "La illaha illa Allah" – there is no God but God. We have the truth; all others are infidels. We share the same missionary mandate: "Go teach all nations."

'Or is the threat materialism – that great catch-all word that means what, precisely? That people in our Western culture have enough to eat and drink, can have a home, a job, social security, and the wherewithal to educate their children?'

'Surely it means putting material things before spiritual things,' Hugh interjected.

'How many people do you know who consciously make that decision, Hugh? How many do I know? These are things we take for granted. You and I are housed and fed, gratis. We will never have to worry about a mortgage or putting children through college. Supposedly, this allows us the freedom to give more of ourselves. Interesting hypothesis.'

Monsignor Brennan paused, worrying at the little skullcap.

'I believe the greatest crisis is within the Church. There is a fracturing of belief, and where are the defenders? The Jesuits, our Marine Corps, have discovered solidarity with the poor and taken off their uniforms. There are dissident voices questioning the most fundamental tenets of the faith, and they are elevated to media stardom or martyrdom when they are silenced. We have a Trojan horse within the walls of Rome, Hugh, and it is pregnant with the destruction of the Church.'

'But surely we have groups within the Church who champion orthodoxy?'

'Oh, yes. Escriva had quite a cadre, before the move for canonisation and the digging started; Opus Dei influences clerics and laypeople alike, within and outside the Church. But, in times of crisis like ours, many are beginning to think there is a need for an elite. After all, the British have the SAS, the Jews have Mossad, the Americans have Special Forces.'

'Who do we have, Monsignor?' Hugh asked quietly, and Brennan allowed the silence to lengthen before replying.

'I am not avoiding your question, Hugh. I am weighing it.' He smiled, almost sadly. 'And I am weighing the agenda of the questioner.'

'I'm asking out of concern, rather than curiosity,' Hugh answered, with a hint of affront in his voice.

Monsignor Brennan held up a restraining hand.

'Pace, Hugh. We wouldn't be talking like this if I didn't have every confidence in your commitment to the Church.'

He stood creakily and moved around to sit behind the desk again. Hugh sensed the encounter was moving onto some other level.

'We have true believers, at every level of the Church, who have been branded conservative and excluded from positions they should hold. They are no longer willing to stand idly by and see the truth bartered for popularity. Even our enemies have always had a sneaking admiration for the clarity of our teaching. *Roma dixit* – Rome has spoken; that dictum has been enough for generations of believers. Not now. We thought a pope who had resisted communism so vigorously would champion the certainty of the faith.' Brennan sighed and leaned back in the chair. 'Even popes grow old, Hugh, and there are those close to the throne who whisper in his ear about compromise. And so we establish relations with the Eastern Orthodox, the Reformers, the Jews – not to bring them to the one true Church, according to our divine mandate, but to validate them in their error. To put it simply, we need men and women of proven orthodoxy to take positions of influence within the Church and steer it back to its true course.'

'How can you do that?'

'By removing those who have failed to do so.'

'Why are you telling me this?'

The monsignor lifted a heavy folder and placed it before him.

'This is you,' he said, almost absently. 'From your time in school through the seminary to this very day. George Orwell would hardly approve.' He smiled. 'I don't seek to flatter you when I tell you that you're all we hoped you would be. Academically, you have fulfilled your gifts. Tomorrow, you will be granted a First Class Honours degree for your Doctor of Divinity thesis on the Council of Trent. Yes, I know' – he waved a hand to quell Hugh's interruption – 'you haven't submitted the final draft. But your first draft has suitably impressed the examiners. I won't bother your humility with the superlatives.

'And it's not just your mind that has impressed us. We note your character, your single-mindedness in everything you do. In different times, that trait might have caused us concern. It might have suggested a certain narrowness of focus, and there would be annotations in your file about "blinkered vision". But not now. You have come to the attention of certain people within the Church. Excuse the obliquity. For now, it is only necessary that you know this and know you are not alone. There are others who ponder the same questions and read the runes in the same way as I do – and, perhaps, as you do.'

He closed the folder and leaned his elbows on it, giving Hugh the full force of his scrutiny.

'They would like to discuss these things with you, if you wish. There is no obligation on you to do so – but, if you do, then their confidences must remain inviolate. Do you understand?'

'Yes.'

'When you are sure, Hugh, let me know. But you must be sure. This is a plough from which, should you choose to grasp it, you cannot lightly take your hand.'

For a moment, Hugh was chilled, but he replied in a firm voice. 'I will consider everything we've talked about and get back to you, Monsignor.'

'Basta – enough.' The little round man was all Italian again, ushering Hugh to the door. 'We have great hopes for you, Hugh,' he said quietly.

7

The General Hospital, Derry, Northern Ireland

Tom Finn ran a cursory eye over the level in the saline drip and traced the tube to the insertion point in the patient's arm. He let his hand rest coolly on the swollen one beneath it. 'Everything's in order, sweetheart,' he said softly. 'You'll be straining the bedsprings again before too long.'

The young woman in the bed turned weary eyes to him. 'I feel like death,' she murmured.

'God knows, you look like it,' he replied wickedly. 'But not this time, honey, and not for a long, long time to come.'

He segued seamlessly into teacher mode, arms crossed over his chest, head flung back, eyes raking the ranks of medical students circled around the end of the bed. 'Results of preliminary examination?' he barked.

A young man in the front row, lost in a too-large white coat, cleared his throat nervously. 'Preliminary examination suggested a growth in the abdominal area.'

'Good man yourself, Martin,' Tom replied magnanimously, 'but keep the gobbledegook for the exams, will you? She had a wee lump in her belly, boy.'

Martin's prominent Adam's apple bobbed once in acknowledgement.

'And what, pray, did the Flying Finn do?' Tom demanded dramatically. A Malaysian student, demure in veil and floor-length gown, smiled involuntarily, her hand immediately rising to cover her mouth. 'Go for it, Ayesha,' he commanded.

'The surgeon... the Flying Finn,' she corrected herself, 'made an incision, excised the benign tumour and sutured the wound.'

'Bravo, Ayesha, but two additional days on Ramadan for using big words, okay?'

The group laughed dutifully.

'Keep it simple, gang, okay? Remember, if you can't say it simply, you simply don't know it. Thus endeth the lesson,' he concluded with mock solemnity.

Turning to the patient, he lowered his long, lanky frame to eye level. 'I suppose a quickie is out of the question, Mary?'

'Ah, go on with you,' she smiled, 'or I'll burst my stitches.'

Tom hared past reception, dodging trolleys and wheelchairs with all the footballing ease of his schooldays.

'Mr Finn. Call for you.'

'Christ, Kate,' he smiled at the receptionist, 'I can never get past you. You're a better tackler than Maldini.' Better legs, too, he mused as he scooped the phone to his ear.

'Tom Finn.'

The voice in his ear was tight with anger. 'You've been fixing the wrong people, Doctor.'

'Ah, it's yourself again,' Tom replied equably, walking the cord to the limits for confidentiality. 'You know, you should have a wee check-up; all that heavy breathing sounds like heart trouble to me.'

'We warned you already,' the voice snapped, 'not to have truck with them boys. You wouldn't listen then and you're not listening now.'

'Listen,' Tom said patiently, huddling into the phone, 'Paddy or Trevor or whatever, I put my hands inside people every day and I've never found a Prod tumour or a Catholic kneecap. Can you follow that, you thick wee gobshite—'

The phone buzzed angrily in his ear like a trapped fly, and he placed it on the cradle a little more emphatically than he had intended. The receptionist raised an interrogatory eyebrow.

'Fans,' he grinned reassuringly.

He strode across the wet tarmac of the car park, palming the keys from his pocket – a young man with a loping gait, and just the merest frosting of silver in his flying red hair. The BMW – sleek, efficient and instantly responsive to his lightest touch – was his only indulgence.

'Does exactly what it says on the tin,' he muttered happily, and turned the key in the ignition.

*

Hugh plucked the envelope from the table outside the common room and weighed it in his hand, noting the university address and seal. Thoughtfully, he made his way to an armchair flanked by a standard lamp, at the far end of the common room.

The common room was lined with bookshelves, probably the bequest of some long-gone professor from the dim and distant past who had hoped his students might gather wisdom by a process of osmosis. The scattered occasional tables were strewn with magazines; the previous day's *Irish Times* lay spreadeagled immodestly, its sports page exposed. The murmur of talk from the students draped over chairs at the other end of the room vied with the relentless drone of CNN on the television.

Hugh took a deep breath and opened the envelope carefully, his eye translating the Latin text with ease. Monsignor Brennan had been right.

Summa cum laude, et cetera, et cetera. He was now Dr Hugh O'Neill, his doctorate to be conferred at the end of the month in the Gregorian University. For a fleeting moment, he felt a rush of satisfaction. He folded the parchment along its original lines and secreted it in the capacious pocket of his soutane.

'Hugh – hey, Hugh!'

He looked up in surprise.

'On the telly, Hugh – isn't that your neck of the woods?'

He made his way to a position behind the group, in time to see the establishing shot of the General Hospital in Derry. Someone used the remote to up the volume. A reporter stood speaking to the camera, her eyes slightly off centre as she tracked the autocue. The hospital logo was framed over her right shoulder.

'Northern Ireland's ongoing story of murder and mayhem took a new turn today, when a hospital surgeon died in the flaming wreckage of his booby-trapped car.'

The camera shot switched to a close-up of mangled wreckage, still smouldering behind a cordon of fluttering tape. A policeman, squat in his Kevlar jacket, glanced at the camera and turned his back, easing his machine gun into a more comfortable position.

'Dr Tom Finn is just the latest casualty in the tit-for-tat feud that has plagued the province. A Roman Catholic, he was trained…'

But Hugh was deaf to the voice, blind to the picture. Someone stood before him with anxious eyes, mouth moving soundlessly. Someone reached a tentative hand towards him. The room spun and he was running, running for the ordered sanctuary of his room. He sat panting at his desk, breathing deeply in harsh gasps until the drumming in his chest was muted. Carefully he extricated the university letter and filed it away. Then he sat, immobile, staring at the blank space before him.

He didn't hear the monsignor enter. He was unaware of him until Brennan drew up the only other chair in the spartan room and sat beside him.

'I'm sorry, Hugh,' he said gently. Hugh nodded dumbly, grateful that the monsignor hadn't attempted physical contact.

When he met Tom Finn, Hugh had been only a child, a traumatised boy uprooted from his family's farm and transported to Derry in the wake of his father's murder by Loyalist paramilitaries. School had come as a welcome relief. English, Irish, History, Maths were worlds he could enter and close the door behind him. He remembered his first day in the science lab, sunlight slanting through the tall windows, the walls dancing with reflections from a forest of glass and copper vessels. His gaze moved reverently over rows of high desks with fitted sinks, swan-necked taps and stolid Bunsen burners. It was a kingdom of order and harmony, and it smelled of possibility.

He sensed a presence behind him and turned.
Tom Finn had red hair and pale freckles on a pale
face. His shirt was lacking a button near the belt, his
sleeves were frayed hairy at his wrists and his over-
long, shiny trousers tented at his toecaps.

'Welcome to the Demon's Dungeon,' he smiled.

As if conjured by the name, Father Duffy was in
the room, and the boys stilled. Father Duffy was a
creature of myth to the first years, a myth cruelly
expanded by sadistic second years: 'Oh aye, Duffy
will do for you. Collects ears, so he does.' He was
squat and shapeless in a black soutane that might
have been used to mop the lab: it wore a motley of
stains and colours, badges from the elemental world
Father Duffy had ground, diluted, boiled and tested.
Two black eyes strafed the group from under grey-
flecked eyebrows, hairy pelmets over a square face.

Without moving from the door, he spoke in a
voice of rough-ground gravel. 'Some of youse don't
know me, but you will. Some of youse think you
know me, but I'm worse than you'd believe. Out
there' – he nodded dismissively over his shoulder –
'youse can do what you like; it makes no mind to
me. In here, youse do what I tell you, when I tell
you. Or else.'

They discovered what 'or else' meant a half-hour
into the class. 'Twitchy' Moon was living proof of
perpetual motion, his body wired to some inner
charge that powered him to random jerky move-
ments. It was his misfortune to jerk against a tray of

glass beakers, and the row collapsed in gut-squeezing slow motion until the last beaker toppled from the bench. Twenty pairs of eyes followed its flight to the unforgiving floor. Twenty mouths were steeling themselves against the crash when Tom Finn hooked the beaker cleanly between thumb and forefinger.

Hugh's lateral vision registered a black blur, and Father Duffy had Twitchy dangling by his hair. The boy hung limply, his eyes glazed in terror.

'Here you are, Father. No harm done – right as rain.' Tom Finn stood beside the priest, holding the beaker like a votive offering.

Duffy swung his maddened gaze away from Twitchy, and for a heart-stopping moment Hugh thought he might strike the boy before him. Abruptly, he dropped Twitchy to the floor, where all his myriad tics reactivated with relief.

'Name?'

'Tom Finn, Father.'

Something in the priest's expression changed. 'Lar Finn's boy?'

'Aye, Father. I'm his youngest, so I am.'

'Are you planning on being older, Tom Finn?' Father Duffy asked darkly.

'Surely, Father,' Tom Finn said, and smiled. The smile was neither sly, smug, wry nor ingratiating. It was a smile that revealed the open heart that was Tom Finn; a smile that implied all was well with the world, and a big man dangling a small boy was a cloud that had no place in a grand sky.

'I grant you a temporary stay of execution, Tom Finn,' Father Duffy growled, and suddenly there was laughter in the room and the priest himself seemed to struggle not to smile. 'Come on, youse bowsies,' he said grudgingly, ' the world of science awaits.'

Break-time was a mêlée that passed for football. Hugh occasionally glanced up from his book, wondering at the passionate play before him and his own lack of interest. Tom was in the thick of it. Even Hugh, who would have been hard pressed to explain the rules, could see he had an awareness and control that were exceptional. He watched him glide towards the opposing goal, pick up a high cross on his chest, tame the ball with his right foot and send it curling inside the coat goalposts, just beyond the flailing hand of the goalkeeper. He went back to his book.

'So what about ye, Hugh?'

He was startled to see Tom standing before him, ignoring the calls of his team-mates.

'I don't play football,' he said lamely.

'Well, let's be off for a fag, then. Youse lot, keep kickin' each other till I get back,' he threw over his shoulder, and they were away.

Tom smoked as deftly as he played football, jerking the box and trapping the jumping cigarette with his forefinger, tilting it to his lips, dropping and closing the box with a flick of his thumb. He flashed an old-fashioned lighter, stroked it over his knee, then dropped his head to the flame; a quick turn of his wrist and the flame disappeared, the lighter was palmed to his pocket. He dragged the smoke to his toes, the tip of his puckish nose glowing with the effort, then leaned back against the high brick wall of the outside toilet and exhaled.

'I thought Father Duffy was going to kill you,' Hugh said.

'Nah.' Tom's green eyes cracked into lazy slits. 'He knows my da.'

He stood still for a moment, then flicked ash from the cigarette as if he had made a decision. 'You remember internment?'

Hugh nodded.

'My da was lifted, along with my two brothers, and all my uncles, and loads of others.' He smiled at Hugh's expression and then grew serious again. 'Duffy was in my house that night – for a meeting, like. He insisted on goin' in the wagon with the rest of them. Can you imagine?' Tom grinned. 'Duffy sittin' in the Saracen, with the black suit and the dog collar?'

Infuriatingly, he took another long, slow draw on the cigarette. 'Well, one of the squaddies starts a bit of pushin' and shovin' – you know, pokin' with the riot stick and that. Then he waves it at Duffy. "Will you hear my confession, Father?" he says. And Duffy says, "Sonny, I'm goin' to take your wee stick and shove it up your arse if you don't quit." They beat the livin' shit out of him in the cells, but not before he'd stretched two of them. He got a month in the Kesh.'

'Jesus,' Hugh breathed.

'D'you know somethin', Hugh?'

'What?'

'You've a terrible dirty tongue, so you have.'

Hugh's memory skipped. He saw two young men sitting on a bench, under a tree top-heavy with August leaves. Both were engrossed, poring over the single A4 sheets that were a measure of six academic years. Neither was willing to ask the other the only question.

'How did you do, then?'

Father Duffy, brusque as ever, simmering in his black soutane, his hand extended. He held Tom's exam results at arm's length, like a volatile substance.

'Good,' he grunted, and they both knew he had checked his own subject first. 'What'll you be doing, then?'

'Thought I might have a go at medicine in Queen's, Father.'

'Not far enough away,' the priest muttered. 'I'll have a word. You'll be away home to tell your ma and da, then.'

It was a flat statement, and Tom didn't need subtitles. 'See you, Hugh.'

Father Duffy eased into the vacated space and read Hugh's exam results. Hugh was inordinately pleased to see what passed for pleasure on the craggy face.

'Good,' he grunted. 'You worked for it.'

It was the ultimate accolade, and Hugh's heart soared into his throat so that he had to cough for relief before he could answer the next question.

'What'll you do?'

'I was thinking I'd be a priest, Father.'

Father Duffy rose abruptly and stamped away under the tree, his frame mottled with sieved sunlight, hands clasped behind his back, rocking on his heels. He wheeled and returned. He loomed over the boy, blocking out the light.

'You've a good brain, Hugh.' It was the first time he had used the boy's name. 'If you go to the seminary from here, it'll be just more of the same.'

He rubbed his jaw furiously and looked away. 'The priesthood... well, we priests give up a lot, like having a wife and family. They're the very things that keep a man earthed, you know; without them, a man can easily be twisted out of true. As time goes by, it becomes easier to move on than to move out, because it's what you know... it's all you know. Ah, you've been with us long enough; you know what we're like.'

Though Hugh was young, he understood the revelation that was being made and the cost to the revealer. 'I...I know it's not the easiest, Father,' he stammered. He calmed himself; when he spoke again, he met the priest's eyes. 'But people – some people – do it well, and they make a difference.'

It was the longest sentence he had ever spoken

to an adult, and his jaw seemed to ache with the effort. Father Duffy reddened at the compliment, and now it was he who seemed hesitant.

'It's just… it's just that you have it in you, lad. I wouldn't like it to be… well, wasted. There's more to life than the job. You follow me?'

'Aye, Father. But I think it would suit me.'

Father Duffy looked at him keenly for a moment before dropping his eyes. 'And that's what bothers me, Hugh,' he said wearily. 'All right, then. Your mother will want to be seeing you, so away home.'

'Aye,' Hugh replied quietly. 'Thank you, Father Duffy.' He extended his hand. The man's grip was surprisingly gentle, and then he was striding away, kicking the hem of his soutane ahead of him…

Hugh remembered Tom's one and only visit to Rome, the tall figure weaving through a scrum of embracing Italian families in Fiumicino to stand before the black-garbed figure in Arrivals.

'Welcome, Tom,' Hugh had said, extending his hand.

'Ah, feck it, Hugh,' Tom had countered, 'when in Rome,' and he had smothered Hugh in a huge embrace, leaving him red-faced, scrabbling for the small flight bag.

Tom had stayed three days, bunking down in a spare room at the college. His exuberance had spun them through the sights at breakneck speed. 'A bit full of themselves, these Roman boys, eh, Hugh? Any time they farted they put up a statue to themselves… Three coins in the bloody fountain? Christ, that's some scam. Some wee Italian hoor with a net must be laughin' all the way to the Vatican bank... More wine, Francesco. Bring her here, boy. My friend here, the Black Knight, has a hollow leg for the stuff.' Barmen, touts, street girls and vendors melted before his boundless bonhomie.

On the third day, Hugh took him to mass in St Peter's. Even there Tom was irrepressible, commenting in a loud stage whisper despite the forbidding looks of the faithful: 'Wow, imagine what it's like on bingo night.' He was a huge redheaded stork, striding through the Sistine Chapel, gaping at the pictures on the walls and ceiling. 'All them nudes, Hugh. My faith can't stand it.'

The flight home to Dublin was delayed.

'Come on – last chance of a real cappuccino before I go home to hospital sludge. Cheers.'

And, suddenly, he was serious – as serious as someone like Tom could ever be.

'How's about ye, Hugh?'

'What? Oh, I'm fine.'

'"Fine", in my vocabulary, means the patient is in excruciating pain but doesn't want to displease the doctor.'

'I'm not in excruciating pain, Tom.'

'I grant you that, but are you happy?'

'Happy?'

'Ah, Jesus, Hugh, if a man needs an etymology of the word or a list of symptoms to describe the condition...'

He saw the stricken look on Hugh's face and was instantly contrite. 'Sorry, Hugh.'

'No, it's all right—'

'No, it isn't. I'm way out of line here. It's just...'

'What?'

'Hugh, I want to tell you, I loved Rome. I really did. I mean, Jesus, who wouldn't? Except maybe Jesus.'

'Jesus?'

'Don't swear, Hugh.'

'I'm—'

'Hugh. It's...' Tom raked his hands through his mad red hair, tufting it in new directions. 'It's just the Church that gets up my nose. It's so solid and staid.'

'Not such bad qualities, in a shifting world.'

'Yeah, right, I know, but it...it takes itself so seriously. D'you follow me?'

'You mean *I* do, Tom.'

'No – well, yes, dammit to hell. When I came off that plane, you were looking so stiff in your black bib that I thought, if he sneezes, he'll shatter.'

'Tom—'

'Hush up, Hugh. The Flyin' Finn has the floor.'

Hugh smiled and spread his hands in mock surrender.

Tom leaned over the dregs of his cappuccino and locked eyes with him. 'You were a quiet, serious lad in school. No harm in that: Mother Nature's balance for noisy bastards like me. And maybe that's why we clicked – who knows? But, these last few days, I've seen you drink more than your usual sensible single glass of wine, and you were laughin', Hugh, and talkin' to strangers. You were so alive, man. But I see you with the other clergy and you're… different. And now I'm afraid you're going to backslide without me.' He tried a grin, but it didn't make it. 'I'm afraid this place will drag you back into being who they want you to be.'

His voice trailed off and he dropped his eyes. 'Jesus, Hugh,' he whispered in mock horror, 'tell me quick, which one of us is the priest?'

He had such a comical look on his face that Hugh laughed.

'God, it's good to hear you laugh, lad.' Tom smiled, that old glorious Tom Finn smile from years before, and suddenly Hugh's eyes began to haze.

'Hugh?'

'It's okay, Tom – it's okay.' Hugh blew his nose in a huge, perfectly white handkerchief and smiled wanly.

'What are you thinkin', boy?'

Tom watched him struggle with something deep inside.

'I was thinking things…things might have been different for me.'

'Attention, please. British Airways Flight 173 is now boarding immediately at Gate 24.'

'You'd better go,' Hugh said.

'Ah, bollocks. Listen, will you come over for a

weekend? Just pack a wee bag, puff out the sanctuary lamp and skip.'

'Sure I will, Tom.'

But they both knew he wouldn't. Already, Hugh was working at making a distance. It was in his eyes as he stood and extended his hand.

'You don't expect me to shake that bloody thing, do you?'

Tom opened his arms wide, and Hugh stepped into his embrace.

'See you, lad,' Tom whispered fiercely in his ear, as he thumped him on the back. 'See you.' But Hugh could only nod against his shoulder.

Hugh opened his mouth to howl, but no sound came. With a conscious effort, he ground his teeth tightly closed.

'Would you like me to stay a while, Hugh?' The monsignor's voice reeled him back to the present. Receiving no reply, Brennan rose quietly and went to the door.

When Hugh spoke, there was a chilling bleakness in his voice. 'Monsignor?'

'Yes?'

'I'd like to speak to those people you told me about. I would like to be of service to the Church.'

Monsignor Brennan hesitated, weighing the offer against the agony in the young voice. At last, he sighed.

'I will arrange it, Father,' he said formally, and left.

8

The Church of San Luigi Di Franchesi, Rome

They were an unlikely pair, the ascetic young priest and the roly-poly monsignor; but clergy are as ubiquitous in Rome as yellow cabs in New York, ubiquitous and invisible. The strains of a Palestrina motet wafted out the door of the church as they entered the vestibule. They sat quietly in the rearmost pew, letting the glorious polyphony wash over them, two shadows immersed in their own thoughts. Hugh remembered bringing Tom there to see the three Caravaggio paintings of Matthew the Evangelist; he had been mildly surprised at Tom's enthusiasm, particularly for the depiction of Matthew as an old man.

'An old man with dirty feet. I'd say that's as real as it gets.'

'A lot of Church people at the time didn't like it for that very reason. Couldn't stomach the idea of an apostle with dirty feet.'

'Why am I not surprised, Hugh?'

His face quirked into a small smile at the memory.

The conductor left the podium and the choir resolved from angels into real people, storing their robes in plastic shopping bags, leaving in twos and threes by a side door, their sotto voce conversations turning to vivace on the pavement outside. Hugh heard someone turn a key in a lock and glanced at the monsignor.

'What now?'

'Now you go to confession,' Brennan whispered, inclining his head to the confessional at the top of the side aisle, close to the Caravaggios.

'Confession?'

'Yes. Usually, only the confessor is bound by the seal of secrecy – but, if you step inside, you'll be committing yourself to that seal also. Do you understand?'

'Yes.'

Hugh knew the seal of confession could not be broken, ever. He swallowed and rose, genuflecting in the aisle before making his way through the dim church to the little light that beckoned over the confessional door. Carefully, he lowered himself onto the cushioned kneeler. As his eyes adjusted, he could see the wire-mesh grille between himself and the confessor. It was already retracted, and the faint outline of a man's profile was visible on the other side.

'My name is Hugh O'Neill,' he began in Italian. 'Sacerdos sum – I am a priest.'

'I know who you are,' the shadow replied in English. 'Perhaps it would be better if we spoke in the native – I beg your pardon, the adopted – language of your country?'

It was a mellifluous voice, as layered with nuance as the motet. Hugh resolved to listen carefully.

'You would be of service to the Church?'

Was there an inflection of scepticism or sarcasm? Hugh couldn't tell. He could feel the heat rise in his face, and he consciously tempered his own voice before replying.

'Yes.'

'Why?' the shadow asked flatly.

'Because it has always been my purpose and remains my purpose.'

'A noble sentiment, young Father. And what would you be willing to do in the service of the Church?'

'Whatever is asked of me.'

'Indeed. So spoke Peter the first pope, who lapsed into Simon the fisherman when accused by a servant girl. So spoke Judas, who kissed his master and pocketed the silver.'

'I am neither pope nor traitor,' Hugh replied evenly.

The other man remained silent. Hugh was comfortable with silence; he waited him out.

'You don't protest your loyalty; that is good. Some, as the English say, "protest too much"; and then, when a cold wind blows...'

He allowed the sentence to hang, and Hugh made no reply.

The figure hunched forward slightly. 'I think it is time to speak plainly.'

'I would appreciate that.'

'As you already know, there are some within the Church who are loyal to the Gospel, who suffer at the attacks on orthodoxy from within. They – we – are called the Remnant. You understand the name?'

'I do. The Remnant are the ones who stand firm when all others depart.'

'Quite so. Yes. The Remnant are dedicated to a Church that claims primacy over all others. The foundation of the Church by Christ fulfils the promise of the Old Testament and renders the Jewish faith obsolete. Islam, Hinduism, Buddhism and all the other so-called religions bud from the political or cultural humus of their civilisations. They will find their way to Christ and to his Church in time. In the meantime, the Remnant must ready the Church for their arrival, by removing those liberal offshoots that sap its strength and stunt its growth. We will do this with the steel of the Crusaders and the fire of the Inquisition, until the Church is purified. Only those who share this great purpose, and who give it total obedience and dedication, are entrusted with that mission. Are you such a one?'

'I would hope to be such a one, with God's help.'

Again, the silence lengthened.

'Very well,' the man said curtly. 'Monsignor Brennan will speak on our behalf. Go in peace.'

The shutter closed.

★

Monsignor Brennan hung his soutane in the heavy, camphor-scented wardrobe and eased out of his shiny black brogues, aligning them toe to heel on the wire rack. His living quarters were bare and functional, his bedroom no more than the word suggested – a room with a bed. The bed was neatly made, and he sat carefully on its side and sighed, plucking the spectacles from his nose, rubbing the weal they left behind. Without the black carapace of his soutane, he was a small man with a paunch ballooning his shirtfront.

Resting his elbows on his knees, he lowered his forehead to his palms and thought of his father. Perhaps it's what we do when death looms clearer on the horizon, he thought. We get this compulsion to check the journal of the voyage. Where have we come from? Where are we going?

Their home in County Kildare had been the classic Irish village: one street, one church, four pubs and a draught of wind. Young Francis Brennan's world was bounded by the flat green land that stretched out like a verdant sea on all sides of the island village; horse country, where his father was someone. He remembered the gleam of the big cars, winking between the curtains of their cottage as the 'gentlemen' called on Jeremiah Brennan, the horse whisperer. The big men, cowled in hats and crombies and smelling of cigars, swamped the humble kitchen chairs as they consulted his father. 'Mr Brennan, could you talk that bastard stallion out of the box for us tomorrow? Savin' your presence, ma'am,' they added as an afterthought, impatiently swatting his mother's offer of tea aside, eyes fixed hungrily on the whisperer.

He remembered the exhilaration of riding in the same gleaming cars with his father, seated behind a driver, as they motored to any of a dozen arenas of pounding hoofs and hearts, flying hats and flung race cards. His father, a slight man in a soft hat and drab brown trench coat, would amble through the knot of anxious owners to the horsebox.

'Leave down the door,' he'd say quietly.

'Jaysus, Mr Brennan, he'll kick the livin' life out of you.'

'Leave it down anyway, and we'll see.'

Francis would stand alone, peering between the shoulders of the grooms, as his father spoke gently to the huge animal with the flaring nostrils and rolling eyes. He would incline reverently towards the horse's head, whispering. From his vantage point at the rear, Francis would watch the horse's mood reflected in the way the men let out pent breaths or laughed with relief. His father would palm-stroke the horse's neck, almost absent-mindedly, and leave the calmed animal.

'He'll be fine now, lad,' he'd say to the jockey, shivering in silks. 'Take him gently for the first few furlongs.'

Francis would watch him pass the huddle of owners, already lost in their race cards, as if embarrassed at their own raw emotions and the non-chalance of the whisperer. Francis expected them to clap him on the back, shake his hand, lighten the wads of notes in their sheepskin-lined pockets.

'They didn't say thanks, Da.'

They were on the bus going home. There was never a gleaming car and a driver on the return journey.

'They're not thanks kind of people, boy.' Jeremiah plucked the pipe from his mouth and tamped the bowl with a calloused finger. 'And I don't do it for the thanks, or the money.'

Francis knew the money would come via a yardman or a stableboy when the race was well over. The crombies wouldn't call again until the next crisis. 'All the same, it wouldn't have killed them.'

Jeremiah was touched by his son's vehemence. 'A man who works for thanks is always beholden to the man who has the givin' of them,' he said. 'D'you follow me, son?'

'Yeah,' Francis answered, dropping his head so his da would not see the reservation in his eyes.

His father leaned closer. 'Francis, lad, look at me now.'

Reluctantly, he raised his eyes to engage the mild blue gaze.

'Whatever job you do in life, do it for yourself. Do it because it's your gift and it's the man you are. Otherwise, you'll always be someone else's.'

Francis nodded slowly.

'Would you fancy the horse game yourself, lad?'

'Ah, no, Da.'

The whisperer was nothing if not patient.

'I was thinkin' I might be a priest,' Francis blurted.

His father nodded slowly, savouring the confidence. Francis stole a look at his face and something was revealed to him. It's not the whispering at all, he realised; it's the listening. Everybody shouts at the bloody horse, pulling and shoving at him. My da just listens, and the horse quietens to the quiet of the man. He was enthused and terrified in equal measure at the idea.

'Da?'

'Yes, Francis.'

'It isn't the whisperin' at all, is it, Da?'

The shrewd blue eyes twinkled sideways through the curl of smoke.

'You're the bright one, Francis,' he smiled. Then he placed a finger on the boy's lips and leaned in to whisper.

'We'll keep that wee bit of wisdom between the pair of us.'

As the bus ground tiredly into the village, his father leaned close again.

'Between ourselves, son, a priest can be owned like any other man – more likely than another, maybe, because he has no natural anchor in a wife or child. D'you follow me?'

'Yes, Da,' Francis replied automatically, but the steady eyes continued to hold him, parsing his answer.

'We'll do our best by you,' his father said finally. Francis followed him from the bus and sensed a sadness in the man before him.

Monsignor Francis Brennan found himself sitting on the side of his perfectly made bed, his finger placed against his lips and tears slipping down his stubbled cheeks. Slowly, he planed them away with his palms and sighed.

'You were right, Da,' he whispered to the empty room. 'A man who seeks regard from others is never his own.' He was chilled by his own words.

The telephone rang. He rose and padded into the small living room, unsteady on his stockinged feet, reaching before him against the imperious ringing. He tried to steady his breathing before putting the receiver to his ear, but his voice was hoarse.

'*Pronto*?'

'Our young friend,' the voice said, as if taking up a conversation from a moment before. 'I find him peculiarly strong-minded.'

'Hardly a fault,' Brennan responded, before his natural caution could stay him.

There was a long pause. The monsignor felt the prickle of sweat on his forehead and grimaced in self-disgust.

'Quite,' the voice said finally. 'A keen brain, also, and a sharp Irish tongue to serve it.'

Rebuked, the monsignor remained silent.

'He can be of use to us.'

Brennan's mind baulked at the word 'use', but he chose to salve his conscience with the thought that the convenor was not speaking in his native tongue.

'Something perturbs you?'

'No, no. My mind had moved on to consider where he might be of service.' He didn't mean to correct the convenor, but the linguist in him overrode his caution.

'He will be assigned as a theological consultant to his Eminence Cardinal Thomas.'

'The American? But he isn't sympathetic to our cause, and I understand he chooses his own consultants.'

'What is it the Chinese sage said, Monsignor? Know your enemy. Our young friend will be close to Thomas, and Thomas is close to the pontiff. Too close. Our information is that he champions détente with the Muslims and whispers that poison in the pontiff's ear. As to Thomas' own consultants,' the convenor continued, 'unhappily, one of these will be indisposed. Your protégé will be chosen to replace him.'

The sweat on the monsignor's forehead grew cold, and he looked at the closed door in search of the chill.

'I pray he will be worthy of the task.'

'I know you do, Monsignor.'

The call ended.

9

The Monastery of the Resurrection,
New York State

The routine of the days gradually took hold, kneading the knots out of Michael's mind and body. There were even nights when he slept through to dawn without thrashing nightmares, without seeing the drowning faces dissolve and re-form into all four men lost to the sea during his time on the Island. His body tautened and hardened as he worked, alone or side by side with the other silent men, gleaning the last the land had to offer before it died for the winter. His relationship with Raphael grew in long, amiable silences, founded on the sure knowledge that theirs was a brief time out of time and that the clock ticked inexorably towards a moment when they would part, perhaps never to meet again.

Raphael was a master of silence; sometimes, when Michael sat with him, he imagined he might never speak again and be content. Contentment was a state he longed for, and he approached it in the unthinking ritual round of work.

'It's in the action, Michael,' Raphael told him as he swept the cloister of leaves, 'not the result.'

More bloody fortune-cookie aphorisms, he thought, wiping the sweat from his eyes. As if reading his thoughts, the abbot continued lightly, 'Yes, I know, New Age bullshit.'

He smiled, patting the bench beside him. Michael sat gratefully, allowing the broom to rest against his shoulder.

'A mother buries her baby and feeds her neighbours. Is she thinking, have we enough rice to go round? Can we afford to burn paper money at the shrine? No; she's using the serving of rice, the care of the guests, as rituals to keep her body busy, so that her heart can begin to carry her baby as a blessing, not a burden. You can't leave the dead unmourned, Michael. Unmourned is unburied.'

'God, my back is killing me,' Michael said, stretching.

'No. Your back hurts, yes, but you're killing yourself.'

Then, one night, there was a tap on his door. It came from the heel of a hand, and Michael was unsurprised to see the abbot enter. Something in his bearing made Michael rise. He had been reading a book by Thomas Merton, and he closed it without marking the page.

He gestured to the other chair, and the abbot sat. Slowly, the old man held out a white envelope. Michael weighed it in his hand, never taking his eyes from the abbot, whose expression was unreadable.

The letter was, as he had expected, typically terse and impersonal, giving the date and time and emphasising punctuality.

'Tomorrow,' he said finally.

'Too soon,' Raphael said softly. 'A spirit needs time to wither a season before it can hope to bud again.' He smiled slowly. 'Fortune-cookie proverb, my friend. I wish I could offer you more.'

Michael attempted to return the smile, but he couldn't quite shape it.

'If you wish,' the abbot said softly, 'you can take the time remaining to tell your story.'

Michael felt a surge of emotion rise from deep within him. He clenched his teeth, burrowing his chin to his chest, until the moment passed.

'I'm sorry, Raphael,' he said huskily.

The abbot bent forward and placed one gloved hand on his. 'I know what it's like to carry secrets, Michael. Should you ever wish to share yours, I am here.'

★

Michael waved once at the retreating truck and
imagined he saw a raised glove reciprocate, then he
turned his face to St Patrick's Cathedral. For a long
moment he stood on the sidewalk, letting the
passers-by eddy round him, watching the grey
façade flicker in their colourful stream. From his
vantage point, the building appeared enormous,
soaring up like the mediaeval cathedrals of Chartres
or Rheims, spires pointing imperiously to the sky –
a sky bracketed with the tall glass towers of
Mammon, bulking in on every side. He took a deep
breath and climbed the steps.

Cardinal Wall's waiting room was decorated like
some Vatican version of a Sears Roebuck catalogue.
It was heavy on mahogany furniture and purple
velvet drapes. A tentative sunlight tiptoed
apologetically across a vast rug emblazoned with
the cardinal's coat of arms. Ranged around the
perimeter, high straight-backed chairs, built for
attention rather than comfort, formed a guard of
honour along the walls.

There were two other penitents – supplicants,
sacrifices, he couldn't quite settle on the
appropriate word – in the room. Angling his head,
Michael stole a glance at the priest five chairs to his
left. He was a stockily built man somewhere in his
fifties, clothed in a rumpled black clerical suit, a few
inches tighter than snug, a few dry cleanings

beyond its best-before date. The man within seemed to pulse with a nervous energy that thrummed through his fidgeting fingers. His face was puffed and patchy; purple deltas radiated from his nose to web his cheekbones, and even in the cool of the high-ceilinged room he was working on a sheen of sweat. The other occupant was limned by sunlight from a window behind her, shifting in and out of silhouette as the light waxed and waned. She had a flat leather briefcase on her lap, and her hand occasionally flashed white as she turned pages on her makeshift desk. As Michael watched, she shuffled the papers into a neat file and zipped them out of sight. She stood and walked purposefully across the coat of arms to stand before him, her hand extended.

'Hi, I'm Kathleen O'Reilly. We who are about to die salute you.'

Nonplussed, he reciprocated her firm handshake. 'Hi, I'm Michael Flaherty,' he said, and followed with the first thought that came to his tongue. 'I didn't know gladiators wore trousers.'

'Actually,' she replied with a smile, 'in the Church arena, it's definitely pants for the gladiatrix. Anyway, it really pisses off the emperor. May I join you?'

'Oh, sure – sorry.' He pulled a chair closer to his own and she sat, crossing one trousered leg comfortably over the other. Michael was to fashion what Attila was to art, but even he knew the tailored navy suit and the luminous white blouse meant big bucks. The oval face, free of makeup, would have been unremarkable but for the intelligent green eyes under shoulder-length auburn hair. Her under-stated perfume was a welcome antidote to the aroma of beeswax polish and body odour that permeated the room. He realised he was staring and dropped his gaze.

'Are you new here?' Kathleen asked, leaning in a little closer.

'You come here often?'

She laughed throatily, tilting her head back. 'How very Irish of you to answer a question with another. Okay, me first. I'm Professor of New Testament Studies at Columbia University and a Sister of Mercy, so I'm indicted regularly on both counts.'

He threw an enquiring glance in the direction of their fidgeting neighbour. Kathleen's face softened as she followed his eyes.

'Oh, Larry Breen is a lifer here. I'm afraid he has a tendency to solicit alms for Armalites. Second-generation Irish, second-hand patriotism… it's a heavy cross to carry. Therapy is a weekly ball-busting session with his Eminence.'

Michael was still digesting this when she added lightly, 'So who did you kill?'

Her green eyes registered the shock on his face, and she was instantly contrite.

'I'm sorry, Michael. Did I mention I'm a motor-mouth?'

The door to the inner office creaked.

'Uh oh, here comes Cerberus,' she whispered.

Monsignor Patrick J. Dalton stood with his back to the door of the inner sanctum as if afraid of contamination. Or he likes to play games with space, Michael thought, beginning to recover from the body blow. The monsignor was four foot eleven, stretching for the magic five with elevated black brogues and ramrod posture. The black soutane was stippled with pearly black buttons and slashed midway by an angry red sash. His small, rounded face had melted with the years and reset into a permanent scowl of suspicion. Steel-framed spectacles worked hard to provide some gravitas to watery blue eyes, but they were punching way above their weight.

'Sister Kathleen.' The voice was carefully modulated, pitched below his normal register – a newsreader's voice, Michael thought.

'Why, Monsignor Dalton, how fetching you look in skirts.'

She swept by him into the cardinal's office, seemingly unaware of the baleful expression on his face. As the door clicked behind her, Dalton turned his gaze on Michael. Michael returned his stare until the monsignor dropped his eyes and hurried from the room.

Michael glanced sideways at his remaining companion, who was smiling broadly.

'That Kathleen,' he wheezed, 'boy, is she a pistol?'

Unfortunate simile, Michael thought, but right on the money.

*

Cardinal Wall's office was an extension of the waiting-room motifs: heavy drapes, shiny brass, a mahogany desk that dominated the space, a spindly chair for the visitor placed beyond the power zone of the crested carpet.

'Sit.'

Michael sat, letting his eyes roam the room, as the man in the high-winged chair angled himself to the light from the window, his fingers peeling through a dossier. The wall to Michael's left was obviously the glory gallery. It was decorated with photographs of his Eminence locking grins with Reagan, grim-faced beside a clearly nervous Clinton, smiling wolfishly down on a slightly puzzled-looking Bush. A short illustrated history of Church–State relations, Michael thought. He felt suddenly tired, tired of snatching at distraction, exercising the surface of his senses to keep reality at bay. The monastery might have been his chance to excavate the charnel house where his heart had once been.

He realised the cardinal was staring at him.

John Henry Wall was easily two inches taller than Michael, and broader to boot. Rumour had it that the Pope had chosen him for the red hat from a group photograph because he couldn't see the others behind him and thought he was the only candidate. Bronx-born and Bronx-bred, Old

Stonewall, as he was none too affectionately known, was the classic rags-to-red-robes story the Irish Diaspora loved. He had a cigar-roughened voice and tended to tilt the ends of his sentences, turning the most innocent observations into accusations.

'Hell of a story, boy,' he growled, tossing the dossier on the desk. 'Is it true?'

'I haven't read it.'

The grey eyes regarded Michael. 'Sorry about your brother.'

'Thank you.'

'I wanted to leave you a while longer with Raphael. He chewed my ass good and proper for calling you back here.' Wall shook his head admiringly. 'Hell of a guy. Well…' He pulled on his spectacles. 'Looks like you may have won the lottery, young Flaherty.'

Michael looked at him uncomprehendingly. The cardinal plucked a piece of paper from his desk, holding it gingerly between thumb and forefinger.

'The Sacred Congregation for the Propagation of the Faith requests an assistant to his Eminence Cardinal Thomas. In fact, they want you. Why?'

Michael shook his head. 'I have no idea.'

'Curiouser and curiouser,' Wall muttered, staring at the letter as if he could glower some further revelation from it. He laughed suddenly, a sharp bark that flushed his face a littler redder. 'I should send them Kathleen I-wear-the-trousers O'Reilly. Jeez, that would set the cat among the *paisanos*.' He regarded Michael. 'You want the job?'

Michael searched himself for any feeling, one way or the other, and came up dry.

'The maxim of the law is that silence gives consent,' the cardinal growled. 'I take that as a yes.'

He scribbled something in the margin of the letter and tossed it aside. 'Look, Michael, listen to me. All this stuff…' He gestured at the dossier. 'Shit happens, okay?'

'That's what Raphael says.'

'I'll bet he does. Dirtiest mouth I ever heard in an abbot. Let me add my own ten cents. Shit also travels, get my drift? So, if you don't want Rome, say so now. I can wangle something, get someone to break your legs, I don't know. I can send you back to that half-assed Abbot Raphael.'

The faces of the dead surfaced from Michael's subconscious. He saw his brothers, Liam and Gabriel, and his old mentor Father Mack; they seemed to look at him reproachfully… He shook his head until they faded. Not now, he thought. He was not too emotionally wasted to recognise kindness in the cardinal's rough humour. 'That's good of you, Eminence, but maybe it's time to move on.'

'Okay,' the cardinal said slowly, 'it's your call.' He leaned back in the chair. 'Ever been to Rome?'

'No.'

'I go every now and then, for committees and such like.' He plucked the purple cap from his head and massaged the vacant space before crowning it again. 'Rome is…' He paused, as if weighing his words. 'You know what they say in Ireland: the nearer the Church, the further from God. Does that shock you?'

Michael recognised a rhetorical question and let it go. Cardinal Wall was on a roll.

'Hell, some of the guys over there are so ambitious they'd stab you in the front.' He barked again, pleased at his own joke. 'Now I'll have to go to confession and accuse myself of calumny – or is it detraction?'

'Maybe exaggeration,' Michael suggested wryly.

'I wish,' the cardinal muttered ruefully, more as an aside than as an answer. He was all business again, slamming his spectacles to the bridge of his nose. 'You'll fly out in a few days – I'll get Dalton to sort out the arrangements. My car will pick you up from the monastery.'

He got to his feet, hand extended. 'If the Pope asks after me, say I'm busy, okay? And, Michael, remember, I'm still your bishop – though you might not have noticed, up to now.' He plucked a card from the desk and tucked it into Michael's top pocket. 'You want to talk any time, call this number. Don't come through the switchboard.'

Michael searched the cardinal's eyes for explanations, but they were unreadable.

★

Cardinal Wall sat for a few minutes after Michael's departure, drumming his fingers on the dossier.

'Poor lad,' he muttered finally, 'poor lad.' He pressed a button on his desk and heaved himself from the chair to the drinks cabinet.

Mal O'Donnell entered and sat in Michael's chair.

'You heard?' Wall asked.

'I heard.'

'What'll it be?'

'What is it ever?'

'God,' the cardinal said resignedly, 'the savage loves his native shore.' He replaced the single malt Scotch and reached to the back of the cabinet for the Jameson. 'Are you driving?'

'Nah, Hanny's picking me up.'

'Same danger,' the cardinal chuckled, pouring a generous measure into each glass. He handed one to Mal and pushed his chair back from the desk, so that he was beyond the light of the lamp. The daylight had fled the window behind, and the yellow haze that passed for the night sky pulsed biliously over New York. Wall sipped thoughtfully at his glass.

'The dossier, Mal – is it true?

'Yeah. Understated, if anything. In the heel of the hunt, we had a Seal on the ground and a sub listening offshore. So, yeah, it's true.'

'So what's troubling you?'

Mal took a long pull at his glass before replying.

'There's stuff you don't have in your file, Eminence,' he said slowly. 'Before Michael studied for the priesthood, he was in Special Forces.'

The cardinal placed his glass carefully on an occasional table and settled himself in the chair. 'Let's hear it,' he said.

'We had a general running his own private drugs war in South America. He figured, if he could set the cartels at each other's throat, he could take over the powder pipeline to the States. So he hired this guy Major Devane and sent him south of the border with a group of soldiers. They were effective and invisible, the general saw to that. But word got out, and Washington had to sort them out before they caused an international incident. They sent a squad of Special Forces.'

The cardinal raised a quizzical eyebrow.

'Yeah, Michael was one of them. The only one who came back alive. He was badly wounded and strung out. I saw him in the secret medical facility in Virginia, between debriefing sessions.'

Mal shook his head with distaste and drew hard on the glass. 'Now he was a problem for the brass. What if he talked after he was discharged? There was talk of a witness relocation programme. So I cut a deal. At the time, I was working on tracing Major Devane and his sidekick. The deal was, if they released Michael to me, I'd be his shadow. There was always the chance that Devane would get wind of the survivor and make a move on him, and...'

'And Michael became the tethered goat – the lure to draw them out?'

'Yes.'

'Does he know about this?'

'Yeah, I think he does.' Mal sighed. 'I thought they'd never find him. When he went to seminary, I figured it would keep him out of circulation. Later, he lived with me and Hanny while he was chaplain in the prison. I figured I had covered all the bases – and then his brother Gabriel went missing, and Michael went home to the Island.'

'The file says that's where your Major Devane was running his drug factory,' the cardinal prompted.

'What are the odds against that? When it was all over, I thought Michael would come back to Hanny and me and go back to work in the prison, and everything would be the same old, same old. I even went to a meeting in Virginia to tie up any loose ends. I laid it on the line: the bad guys are no more, the drugs line is shut, the dirty one in Washington has fallen on his sword, case closed. Michael Flaherty has gone above and beyond the call of duty for his country; it's time to give him back his life.'

'Hell of a speech,' the cardinal said quietly.

Mal leaned forward so that the light shifted shadows on his face. Wall thought he looked haunted. 'And now they say they've had a request from this Cardinal Thomas in Rome for an assistant and they're sending Michael, just like that. And I'm thinking, how come this request ends up on a desk in the State Department before it lands on yours, Eminence?'

'I didn't know that until now,' the cardinal said thoughtfully. 'But Michael could have refused.'

'He might have, if he had spent more time with Raphael and got his head sorted. These people play mind games, Eminence. I know how they operate. Putting that agent in the monastery grounds was just part of their game to keep Michael off balance. Michael is working at staying one step ahead of his pain, and this is their way of pushing him. I guess if he didn't go to Rome, he'd just go somewhere else.'

Mal's voice trailed away and his shoulders sagged.

The two old men contemplated their glasses in silence for a time. Theirs was an unlikely friendship, the powerful, acerbic prince of the Church and the blue-eyed ex-cop from the Bronx. Mal was one of the few people who talked to Wall as if he was a fellow human being, and when Wall lost the plot and acted the cardinal, Mal just waited him out until he returned to himself. The cardinal saw his friend's sadness. 'You care about him, don't you, Mal?'

'That I do,' Mal confessed, after a long pause. 'You know Hanny and me never had kids of our own.'

The cardinal nodded and waved his glass to indicate that he should proceed.

'Well, I guess I took Michael in for his sake, but I kept him for mine. He kind of grew on me.'

The doorbell buzzed peremptorily and the cardinal leaned over casually and pressed the locking mechanism on his desk. It buzzed again, longer and angrier than before. Mal raised an enquiring eyebrow.

'Nah,' the cardinal said. 'That's just Dalton. Who definitely has no need to know,' he said meaningfully, and Mal returned his nod.

'What's the story on this Cardinal Thomas?' Mal asked quietly.

'Thomas is a hotshot, what they call a papabile – you know, throne material. What he asks for, he usually gets. Maybe you're just being a wee bit over-protective, Mal.'

'You mean possessive, don't you?'

'I mean I envy you your son, Mal,' the cardinal said gently. He tilted the last few drops from his glass and set it firmly on the desk. His eyes were steely again.

'Let's say you and I keep a watching brief on our boy, okay?'

10

The Janiculum Hill, Rome

The Janiculum was not one of the seven fabled hills of Rome, and the tourists, taking a tip from history, seemed to pass it by. That appealed to Hugh O'Neill. Whenever he needed time alone, outside the fortress of his room, this was where he came. Today, at 5.00 a.m., it was as silent as any place in Rome could be. He stood leaning on the parapet at the top, savouring the cool air and the sleeping city. Occasional sounds just seemed to emphasise the quiet, as a dog barking from a neighbouring farm had provided punctuation for the night-time hush of his childhood. In the distance, a police car blared its siren once, almost apologetically. He heard a metallic drum roll – probably the metal grille of a shop or bakery ratcheting up, he thought, and instinctively sniffed the air for the smell of new-risen bread. It had been one of the dominant smells of his childhood, that, and the moist, comforting smell of the steam iron. In his mind's eye, he saw his mother plane his father's collarless shirts smooth with long strokes, before pegging them above the kitchen range to dance gently in the rising thermals. He dropped his head tiredly as the image faded.

The boast of Paul of Tarsus – 'I am a man of no mean city' – filtered into his mind. 'I am not of this city or any other,' Hugh whispered to himself. Abruptly, he started walking again, taking a path through the trees, breathing their evergreen smell, moist and energising now, before the Roman sun rose to fry it dry and acrid.

At the statue dedicated to the wife of Garibaldi, he paused. The last time he had come here was with Tom. He had savoured his friend's pleasure as the early light washed colour over the night-smudged city, bringing a gentle blush to the terracotta roofs, a luminescence to the green cupolae. They had stood together in companionable silence as the light edged down into the dark canyons between the tall buildings, sculpting them into sharp relief. Hugh smiled, remembering how they had walked to this very spot to look at the statue of the wild woman on horseback, her hair streaming behind her, one hand clutching a baby to her bare breast, the other brandishing a pistol. And Tom had laughed, a clear, effortless laugh that had surprised some pigeons into brief applause.

'What's so funny?' Hugh had asked.

'I was just thinking of the difference between Italian statues and the ones at home.'

Hugh gazed fixedly at the statue until the ache in his chest eased. He turned to go, and gasped as a young woman collided with him.

'Scusi, Signorina.'

'Prego,' she muttered, and hurried on.

Slightly winded, Hugh found a park bench and sat there listening to the birds greet the new day, wondering where the woman had come from and where she was going in such a hurry. The man who sat down beside him was bulked out in a long overcoat against the morning chill, a brown fedora shading his face from view.

'You will be needing this, Father,' he said softly in English, sliding Hugh's wallet across the bench between them. Before Hugh could catch his breath, the man was striding into the burgeoning light so that only his silhouette was visible, then the trees bisected and swallowed him.

Gingerly, Hugh picked up the wallet and scanned the contents. He riffled the banknotes and stopped. Slowly, he withdrew the folded piece of paper and thumbed it open.

'Fontana Del Moro, noon,' it read.

★

The Piazza Navona was thronged with tourists, street artists, pigeons and pickpockets, and Hugh touched his jacket to check the bulge in the inside pocket. There were three fountains in the oval piazza. The dominant one was Bernini's Fontana dei Quattro Fiumi, depicting the four great rivers of the world, but Hugh hardly spared it a glance; he homed in on the southern end of the piazza. The Fontana del Moro – the Fountain of the Moor, also from the Bernini school – showed the fantastically playful figure of a moor surrounded by frisking dolphins with remarkably sharp tccth. Hugh sat on a dry section of the parapet, a black asterisk in a sea of colour, and waited. It was 11.55 a.m.

'*Caro.*'

The voice was inflected with a tone that stilled his urge to turn.

'Listen carefully and do not speak,' the voice continued. 'You are to assist the prince who would debase himself before the moor. Your letter of appointment is already on your desk, beside your Biblical Commentary. See this letter as an extension of the Book of Revelations.'

Hugh steeled himself against the mocking voice.

'Work diligently in the prince's vineyard, caro, and bring me the fruits. I want names, dates and places, particularly anything pertaining to the moor. Then I will set my axe to the root.'

The figure in his peripheral vision turned and disappeared into the crowd. A mime artist turned to catch Hugh's eye. His silvered face cracked into a grotesque smile.

★

Carefully, Hugh turned over the envelope and checked the wax seal. It was intact. The letter within, couched in careful Latin, confirmed what the speaker had told him.

His collar felt suddenly hot and constricting. He plucked it two-fingered from his throat, feeling the stipple of sweat on the smooth surface. He bit down on the anger that welled up inside him, and a tiny muscle spasmed in his forehead and grew still.

'Hugh?'

Monsignor Brennan seemed somehow shrunken and uncertain. Hugh beckoned him to a chair, and he sat carefully. Hugh noticed that the morning razor had spared even more of the old man's stubble and thought he caught a faint scent of alcohol.

'Are you troubled, lad?' The rheumy eyes settled on a spot below Hugh's eyeline.

Dispassionately, Hugh recounted the events of the day.

'And now?' Brennan prompted in the ensuing silence.

'Now,' Hugh replied, 'I'm not sure what I feel. At some level I feel violated.' He picked up the letter from the table and tossed it back again. 'I didn't earn this position,' he blurted angrily.

'And?'

'And I don't relish being an informer.'

'Ah, I see,' the monsignor said, shaking his head,

a smile already twitching his lips. '"Informer" is the great Irish swear word, isn't it, and the deadliest insult? They were the ones to be drowned like pups in the rain barrel and buried in the bog; pariahs, to be hunted to the far corners of the earth and dispatched as a warning to others. Stop me if I'm getting too melodramatic, won't you?'

When Hugh failed to yield a smile, the monsignor leaned forward.

'History is a funny old thing. One man's terrorist is another man's freedom fighter, and both men write the history with the benefit of hindsight. You know, of course, Moses sent Caleb and a companion to spy out the Promised Land – which probably goes to show the patriarch had no great problem with the concept... But I digress. Tell me this: what does the Vatican run on? And please' – he raised a cautionary hand – 'spare me the Holy Spirit. We've both been here too long for that.'

'The Vatican is where decisions are made that guide and govern the Universal Church,' Hugh said without enthusiasm.

'Very good, young Father,' the monsignor said gently, his eyes softening the patronisation. 'And what are these decisions based on?'

Hugh answered in the same lifeless voice. 'On the revelations in the Scriptures, the teachings of the Church and, I suppose, the needs of the faithful.'

'Absolutely. The first two the Vatican can handle

in house, so to speak, but how does it determine the needs of the faithful?'

'I suppose...'

'Suppositions be damned, lad. Sorry, I spoke harshly, but it doesn't do to beat about a burning bush. I'll answer my own question. Information, Hugh.' He savoured the word, elongating the syllables as if explaining to a slow student. 'Think of it. We have nunciatures and Apostolic Missions all over the world. Why? To represent our views to various governments? Yes. To maintain and monitor the local Church? Yes again. But also to gather information and feed it to here, where decisions are made. Who should succeed an ageing bishop, which government minister should be cultivated, should the cardinal oppose state policy, how should the Vatican assist the local Church to bring about change? This information shapes the minds and decisions of those who plot the Church's course. Now ask yourself: what happens if we have the wrong man in the right place? What happens when there are even some close to the Throne of Peter who pursue and promote their own agendas? Even those called to the highest council are not immune to championing causes that serve their own. *Quis custodiet ipsos custodes?*'

'Who minds the minders?'

'Who indeed, boy?' The monsignor leaned back in the chair. 'We are called to be the servants of the servants of God, bound by the three vows of poverty, chastity and obedience. What happens to obedience when poverty and chastity move a man to consider that he has nothing and no one to lose? He may well search for something to give him the illusion of being someone – something like power, perhaps. Lucifer fell like lightning to the earth because he wanted to be more than the light-bearer. If the angels can fall, what about mortal men? We stumble seventy times seven times, and that's on a good day. Young priests believe the oil of ordination grants them some kind of immunity from their humanity. When it doesn't, they become disillusioned. They believed in the illusion of perpetual purity. Some can't live with the reality – especially if their purity has become their pride.'

Hugh felt the colour rise in his face.

11

St Patrick's Cathedral, New York

Sister Martha sat stiffly on the edge of the pew, clutching a large manila envelope. Every few seconds, she swung her head towards the confessional, checking the little red light over the door, waiting for it to blink and release the penitent inside. More haste, less speed, girl, Momma's voice whispered in her head. Resolutely, she fixed her gaze on the altar, ignoring the tension in her neck and the impulse to turn and check again. She felt the slick of sweat on her forehead and took a hand from the envelope to dab it with tissue, poking stray strands of greying hair under her veil.

You're no oil painting, dear, said the whiny voice in her head.

'Yes, I know, Momma,' she agreed wearily, and anchored her hand to the envelope. This was her second visit to her confessor in two days.

Martha had drifted into rather than opted for the religious life, and her career had been a series of appointments of ever-decreasing importance. She worked in kitchens, usually below ground, behind barred windows. She had become, as one of her more caustic Sisters said, 'the only nun in the history of the congregation who had started at the bottom and gone down'.

And then the Second Vatican Council had happened. By the time that tornado had whirled off into the history books, those Sisters who remained in religious life either couldn't or wouldn't reconstruct the paradigm originally created by men. While most of her Sisters were careering determinedly down the Yellow Brick Road of liberalisation, Martha was left behind, yearning for Kansas. She shied away from the narcissism of discarded veils, modern hairdos and hints of make-up, and the total abomination of sweat pants in the Community Room.

The veil, the habit and the weekly confession were the flotsam she clung to. Every Saturday, she made the pilgrimage to St Patrick's, freighted with the details of her many transgressions – only to emerge burdened and dissatisfied. The young confessors had blithely dismissed her lists as 'scrupulosity' and offered the catch-all panacea of general absolution.

So she had watched the traffic flow to and from the various confessionals, instinctively suspicious of the popular ones with a fast turnover. Near the sanctuary, there was one little light that rarely gleamed to signify occupancy. Only the aged and the unwary ventured there. The former emerged after lengthy periods, looking relieved; the latter tottered out faster than they had gone in, dropping to their buckling knees in the pews, perhaps to make fervent vows never to return.

He had listened carefully to the details of her every real and imagined infringement, giving equal weight to both. He seemed to possess a bottomless well of sympathy, and he had clucked at appropriate intervals when she ventured into paeans of dismay at the changes in the Church, the liberalism of her Sisters in religion, her own envy of young, gifted Sister Kathleen...

The light blinked.

When the slide eased back, Sister Martha began to speak hurriedly, in a strangled whisper. 'I have the document you asked me to—'

'No need to rush, Sister,' the confessor's voice soothed. 'I never doubted you for a moment.'

Sister Martha released her pent-up breath in a huge sigh.

'In this time of great turmoil and trial within the Church, there are few who make a stand for our values and traditions as you do, Sister,' her confessor continued gently, and Sister Martha felt her heart swell at his words. 'Does anyone know you have the document?'

'Oh, no – I photocopied it in the Women's Centre in the convent basement, where I work. I was able to put it back in Sister Kathleen's room while the community was at prayer. Sometimes I miss prayer because I have to tidy the kitchen and—'

'Sister.' She closed her mouth with a snap. 'You feel isolated in your religious community?'

'Oh, yes,' she breathed. 'They think I'm old-fashioned. One of the Sisters said I was the last nun standing. I didn't know what she meant, but the others laughed.'

'Remember the scriptures, Sister,' he whispered. 'Be cautious when they speak well of you. The true believer will always be scorned. When you first came to this confessional, you were worried for the well-being of the Church; so many have discarded our precious heritage, so many are questioning her unchangeable truths and teachings.'

'Yes, I was, and—'

'But you, Sister, have had the courage to resist. This Sister Kathleen you told me of… her voice is listened to. She could be a champion of the Church in these times, but she chooses to be critical. To counter her errors, we must have knowledge of them. This is why I asked you to bring me a copy of her speech. You understand, don't you?'

'Yes…yes, I·do. It's just that…'

'What, Sister?'

'I don't like taking it without her knowing.'

'Of course, Sister, and that is to your credit. But, for the sake of the truth…'

'Yes, yes, of course,' she whispered.

'Please leave the envelope beneath the kneeler before you go,' he said. 'And remember, what you have done today is to the glory of God and in defence of his Church.'

The slide closed and she was in the dark. Quickly, she eased the envelope beneath the kneeler and hurried from the confessional to drop on her knees in a pew.

Sister Martha felt elated. In her confessor, she had rediscovered Kansas.

Momma's voice came needling into her head. Tell-tale tattler, buy a penny rattler. Shaking her head, Sister Martha hurried from the church, but the voice would not be still.

Convent of Mercy, 42nd Street, New York

Kathleen O'Reilly had finally conceded defeat at 4.00 a.m. Sleep just would not happen, she had concluded. Lying wide awake, she had found herself thinking about her father.

It was Father Joe, of course – Father Joe, who throughout her childhood had listened tirelessly to Momma's alcoholic ramblings, golfed with Dad, acted as conciliator between him and his tearaway sons and suffered with equanimity the slings and arrows Kathleen regularly threw his way – who had precipitated the showdown. He and John O'Reilly had been on the ninth hole on Pelham Parkway municipal golf course – Dad's nod at egalitarianism. John O'Reilly was driving like a demon, whacking his ball out of sight, only to find it nestling behind a tree or half-submerged in scrub or sand. 'Isn't that a pity,' Father Joe remarked in consolation, dropping his own ball in the cup from yet another safe lie. 'Another lucky stroke – sure, I was way offline.' O'Reilly was already on the point of frustrated implosion when the priest applied the touch-paper.

'I hear Kathleen gave as good as she got last Wednesday.'

'How's that?' O'Reilly asked, pausing mid-swing.

'Ah, you know – the carry-on with Stonewall.'

'I do not.'

The expression on O'Reilly's face would have semaphored disaster to a more sophisticated and less innocent soul.

'Sure, he has her on the carpet for a roasting every Wednesday, regular as clockwork. I hear he's demanding editorial rights over anything she wants to publish. Hasn't he a lot to bother him? John? John?'

But O'Reilly was already pounding for the clubhouse, leaving his golf bag lying on the green and Father Joe wondering if perhaps he should have dropped a few shots, out of charity.

Monsignor Dalton had been adamant. 'It is customary – and, indeed, common courtesy – to make an appointment to see his Eminence, Mr O'Reilly.'

'Monsignor Dalton, I was brought up never to raise my hand against a man of the cloth. In your case, I could make an exception.'

The office door banged against the wall and rebounded closed behind the furious O'Reilly.

'This is a pleasant surprise,' Cardinal Wall said.

'Maybe for you.'

'To what do I owe—'

'You can spare me the bullshit, Cardinal. I have something to say, and I want you to listen.'

'Ah, I gather you've been talking to your daughter.'

John O'Reilly placed two meaty hands on the desk and leaned into the cardinal's face. 'She's not mine, Eminence. I fathered her, but I don't own her – and neither do you, nor the Pope, nor the Holy Catholic and Apostolic fucking Church. Are you with me? Kathleen O'Reilly is her own person, has been from a child – sometimes a total pain in the ass, but always, always her own person.'

'I understand,' Wall said mildly.

'The hell you do. Maybe from the neck up. You have no goddamn gut idea of what I mean, and don't pretend you do.'

'You're right,' the cardinal said.

'What?'

'I said you're right, goddammit. Sit down. Sit the hell down. The last man who talked down to me was my father; I didn't hit him, but, by Christ, I wanted to. Now, turn about is fair play.' He surged to his feet. 'You listen to me, John O'Reilly. You know where I come from and all the humble beginnings horseshit. My dad was a nightwatchman who didn't manage to drag himself up by his bootlaces to the American dream. They didn't want me in the seminary, but I studied myself blind, aced every exam they put before me, and gave them no good excuse to fire me. This is the only life I know, and I'm damn good at it. So, before you shit on it, understand it.'

Cardinal Wall left the desk and stood before the window. 'Kathleen O'Reilly is the finest brain this archdiocese has produced for years. She's also a theological pain in the butt, pushing women's issues at every possible opportunity. Now, for better or for worse, I happen to be the ward boss here – and there are politicos above me, all the way to the Vatican, who would like nothing better than to drop-kick Kathleen's butt into some kind of Catholic gulag. So I call her in every Wednesday, like clockwork, and dump on her. That's the story on the bush telegraph. That's the story that keeps Rome off my back and hers. But then we do something they don't know about. We drink whiskey, Mr O'Reilly, and we talk. We have knock-down, drag-out fights on every issue under the sun, and then I shout a bit more and

Kathleen leaves. And I'll tell you this, for whatever it's worth to you. If I ever longed for a child of my own – and believe it or not, Mr O'Reilly, even cardinals do have some feelings below the neckline – I would want Kathleen for a daughter.'

'I'm sorry.'

'So am I. It's a damn stupid world we both inhabit, so we learn to play the game.'

'I won't bother you again.' John O'Reilly struggled to his feet.

Cardinal Wall held out his hand. 'That's what they all say,' he said gruffly. 'Here, shake hands now. What'll you have?'

Kathleen had wrung, cajoled and demanded the story from good old loose-lipped Father Joe, and her eyes misted at the thought. Invigorated, she swung her legs from the bed and strode into the bathroom.

Today, she would stand at the podium in Columbia University and deliver a paper on 'Women and Ordination to the Priesthood', subtitled 'If You Won't Take the Daughters, You Can't Have the Sons'. Instinctively, she grabbed a clump of the auburn hair at the nape of her neck and tugged. Ever since she had been a child, she had coped with stress this way. She knew they would all be there: faculty members, the cardinal, the papal nuncio – a conservative Italian who could oil his way through locked doors – the Mother General of her Order, friends from the UN... Jesus, she thought, and tugged harder. She let the water in the shower run cold, to centre her, and towelled herself vigorously.

In a pale-blue dressing gown, her dripping hair turbaned in a towel, she sat at her desk. Immediately, she was in the zone of concentration she had perfected in childhood. Nothing, neither her mother's drunken ramblings nor her father's entreaties nor the rough and tumble of her raucous brothers, had ever penetrated that shell. She laid her paper before her, and for the next two hours she was totally absorbed.

★

'Sister, Sister!'

The insistent knocking drew Kathleen out of her fugue state. It had to be Martha; only Martha still clung grimly to titles, despite repeated pleas to do otherwise. Kathleen padded to the door on bare feet.

Martha was suitably apologetic and awkward, already in reverse mode when Kathleen opened the door. 'Sorry to disturb you, Sister, but the congressman called an hour ago. I didn't want to disturb you.'

'Come in, come in.'

Martha had long ago developed the gift of invisibility, of melting into the background, always putting others' needs before her own. It wasn't healthy, Kathleen knew, and she felt a pang of guilt. She was aware she took Martha for granted, and she longed to warm her with inclusion.

'John Fox called?'

'Yes.' Martha brightened in her role as the bearer of good tidings. 'He said he'd be there and you were to knock their socks off.'

Kathleen stripped the towel from her head and kneaded her hair. 'I'm thinking of wearing the cerise trousers and the Madonna halter top.'

Martha's lower jaw detached from the rest of her face.

'Joke, Martha, okay?' And they were both giggling like schoolgirls.

'Can you come?' Kathleen asked.

'Well… I'd really love to, Sister, but it's a busy day at the centre.'

'Come later. There'll be wine and stuff. You can corner the cardinal about funds.'

Martha's expression warred between joy at the invitation and horror at the implications. 'Well, I suppose I could come by for a while.'

'I'd really like that.'

'But I'm no theologian, Sister. Maybe it would all be over my head?'

'Rubbish. Theologians just make up fancy words for what people like you put into practice every day. Anyway, I'd appreciate your support.'

'Really?'

'Really. Now get the hell out of here. I have to

get glammed up and pick up a few things from the university.'

'Okay,' Martha said, backing for the door. 'I'm sorry if I've delayed you, Sister.'

'You just be there, okay?'

When Martha left, Kathleen reflected for a moment on what kind of Church encouraged the Marthas within it to feel second-rate. Harness your anger, she told herself sternly. Sharpen your lance, girl; the windmills await. With that quixotic thought in the forefront of her mind, she dressed, packed her briefcase and left the Convent of Mercy.

As a matter of principle, Kathleen didn't take cabs – not because she felt threatened by the omniscience of the drivers, she liked to say, but because she believed that solidarity with the people of God demanded she use the subway. Unconsciously, she was mimicking the egalitarianism she had always mocked in her father.

The subway station smelled of fried air and hurry. She passed a beggar on the stairs; her attention was snagged by his yellow leggings and parka, the cowl pulled up over his head, leaving his face in shadow. A Buddhist beggar, she thought whimsically, but he wrung her heart for five dollars. Conscience money, she chided herself; a good luck charm, just one step above touching the back of a hunchback.

She stood on the platform, waiting for the whoosh of warm air that would signal the arrival of her train. So the congressman had called. Fox was a

Republican, but somebody had to be. He was heir to his father's seat, and she knew he had little enough wiggle room, politically; but he was the only one who had braved the Women's Group when they had invaded Congress the year before, baying for male chauvinist blood. Kathleen had been annoyed and then disarmed by his infuriating good humour and by the fact that he had substituted a paper clip for a missing cufflink. The acuity of his brain hadn't hurt, either. She knew there had been chemistry between them, sparked by her acerbic comments and his unassailable calm. He was also a widower. Steady, girl, she admonished herself; friends will do just fine.

She felt a warm breeze lift her hair and moved forward on the platform. Automatically, she checked her watch. Good: plenty of time to...

She sensed a presence behind her and began to turn, a bulky figure blurring in her peripheral vision. The Buddhist beggarman, her brain recorded, just before he slammed into her. She felt the air rush from her body and her head whiplash back, and instinctively tightened her grip on the briefcase. The impact carried her stumbling forward to the lip of the platform, and she had a brief sensation of flight. When she opened her eyes, her vision filled with the details of her death: the driver's rictus of fear, the startled eyes of the headlamps, the arcing sparks from the futile brakes, and the screaming, that awful mounting wail.

'Daddy,' she whispered.

★

The Buddhist beggar struck the toilet door with his shoulder and stumbled inside. He steadied himself and turned to latch the door, leaning his face against the graffiti, splaying his hands against the sticky surface as if to ward off pursuers. For one gut-wrenching moment he thought he heard someone pounding, until he realised it was his own heart trip-hammering in his chest. Slowly he peeled away from the door, frantically struggling out of the yellow top and leggings, kicking them behind the bowl. Spinning the toilet roll, he blotted sweat from his face and neck, and tossed the wad into the bowl. Finally, he flushed the toilet and stepped calmly to the washbasins. He considered sluicing water on his flushed face, but didn't want to attract attention.

As he approached the exit, the door opened and a railway security officer filled the space. His breath hitched in his throat; but the officer politely stood aside.

'Thank you,' he stammered.

'You're welcome, Father,' the officer replied.

Outside, on the pavement, he scanned the traffic, the wail of approaching sirens driving his fear up several notches. A white Taurus eased to the kerb. Leaning back into the seat, he exhaled, a long, ragged sigh.

He pulled a mobile phone from his jacket pocket

and punched numbers with an unsteady finger. 'She is cast down,' he whispered, and broke the connection.

★

Samuel Elroy Jones wished to sweet Jesus his goddamn hands would stop shaking. The white powder slipped in and out of focus on the paper he held waveringly under his hungry nose. 'Shit,' he gasped as the door to the stall beside him slammed, rattling the partition. He gazed in a mixture of rage and longing at the precious snow-cloud drifting to the sticky floor.

Goddamn horse's ass, he fumed, now he's doing the Watusi or something. Samuel's remaining brain cells beamed a ray of pure hatred through the cubicle wall, his body twitching to the rustling and grunting. Should get down on my knees and yank the sucker's ankles, drown him in the can, yeah. He heard the flush – felt it run right through his raw nerve endings – then the scratch of the door as the guy exited the stall. Samuel slumped down on the toilet lid, letting his head fall forward. His eyes brightened momentarily as he contemplated his sneakers. So cool. Like regular Adidas. He had liberated them from a street vendor in 42nd Street just one hour before. White, so white – like snow... His grin disappeared. He jerked upright and fought with the door, stumbling outside to the washroom.

Slowly, he focused on the only other occupant. Hell, maybe it's Johnny Cash. He giggled. Maybe he'll gimme a few bucks. He followed the man on rubbery legs towards the exit and saw the door open before him.

A subway cop filled the frame. Shifting his eyes sideways, Samuel saw the priest stiffen, his hands convulsively clench to fists at his sides. Then the cop stepped aside and Samuel's salvation, his bright white hope, was walking away. He stumbled forward. 'Hey, buddy,' he called, and felt the flat palm of the cop against his chest.

'Just ease up there, bro,' the cop said quietly. 'Don't go bothering folk.' Over the cop's shoulder, Samuel watched the priest mount the steps to the street, his body gradually disappearing from the head down. Finally, only his feet remained in view; and then they were gone.

'I'll be damned.'

'More than likely, my friend,' the cop said gently, 'especially if you go bothering a reverend.'

'He's no reverend,' Samuel said with confidence, achingly lucid for the first time that day. 'You ever seen a reverend all dressed up in a black suit and wearing top-dollar running shoes?'

12

St Patrick's Cathedral, New York

Cardinal Wall hunched at his desk, working through yet another directive from the Vatican. He riffled through a thick Latin–English dictionary, index finger stabbing the word he needed to translate. Pain in the ass, he thought. Why these Curia nerds couldn't just write in plain English… He shook his head and grunted at his own naïveté. Latin was the language of the Universal Church; it was safe because it was dead and couldn't be fiddled with. How he'd love to spend a few hours with an English thesaurus and fax back some optional versions of the directive.

In the background, Sinatra sang from the CD player, begging Joe to lay yet another round on the bar. The glass case beside the CD player was jammed tight with Wall's favourite artists. He had Fats, Ella,

Bennett and a few other golden oldies; all the rest were Sinatra.

He picked up the phone on the second ring. 'Yes?'

'Eminence, this is Congressman Fox. I hope I haven't disturbed you?'

'Not yet.'

'Ah, okay. I'd like to meet with you.'

'When?'

'Now.'

The cardinal twisted his wrist to check his watch. 'Son, have you any idea what time it is?'

'Yes, and you can ignore Sinatra, Eminence: it's nowhere near quarter to three.'

Wall thumbed the remote and the room was silent. 'Okay, let's start again. You want to see me now?'

'Yes.'

'Why?' He pushed back from the desk and stood to relieve his cramping muscles. 'As I read it, George has a ways to go yet, and Condi's the hot ticket to take over. Anyway, I don't deliver the Catholic vote; never have, never will.'

'Eminence, in the event that I ever run for the primaries, I'll do it on my merits and without your blessing.'

'Anyone ever tell you, Congressman, that you have a sassy mouth?'

'That queue is longer than a bread queue in Moscow.'

'Okay, okay.' Wall relented. 'So you want to meet? Where?'

'I'm in my car, across the avenue from St Patrick's. It's a black BMW, registration—'

'Congressman, listen up. We're talking Fifth Avenue here. The word "private" doesn't spring to mind.'

'Well, how about—'

'You got a pen? Write this down. Be there in one hour, and press the buzzer.'

'Your Eminence.'

'What?'

'I happen to have a disc of Sinatra singing that song a whole lot later in his career. On your disc, he sings like he means it; on mine, like he knows it.'

'You a Frankophile?'

'Yes.'

'Maybe there's still hope for the state of the Union,' the cardinal said grudgingly.

He took his time replacing the receiver, long enough to hear a click before it reached the cradle. 'Damn,' he muttered.

Digging his mobile phone out of his pocket, he jabbed a series of numbers.

'Mal? I got a favour to ask... No, you needn't throw the golf game Saturday; you'll lose on merit, my son. Listen, I have to meet someone sub secreto... Look it up, peasant. Okay if we come to your place? ... About one hour.'

He was shrugging into his overcoat when

Monsignor Dalton appeared – right on cue, the cardinal thought.

'Oh, your Eminence is going out?'

'Right in one, Monsignor.'

'May I ask where your Eminence will be contactable?'

'No, Monsignor, you may not. Should some cataclysm occur in my absence and the president calls for my advice, tell him I said he was to finish reading his kiddie book and I'll get back to him. You got that?'

'Ye…yes, your Eminence. Shall I summon the car?'

'No.'

'Your Eminence is walking?'

'It's allowed. Go check canon law. And Monsignor…'

'Yes, your Eminence?'

'Don't wait up.'

★

Cardinal Wall pulled his hat brim a little lower and tucked his chin inside the raised collar of the long black coat. Quickly, he checked the other occupants of the subway carriage. A group of kids chattered noisily; near the door, an old man with a white cane sat alone. Wall slanted his face to the window. The platform gathered speed and blurred as they hurtled into the catacombs under the city.

The old man hawked and said, 'You tell me when this damn train gets to the Bronx, fella?'

'Yeah, sure,' Wall said.

'Missed the damn stop once before and ended up in some jungle. Mary gave me merry hell for that.'

'Mary your wife?'

'Nah, my daughter. My wife's gone these ten years now. Cancer, you know. Quick, though; I'll give the doctors that. Quick and easy – more than some.'

He fell silent again, nodding at some memory.

'Started bumpin' into things,' he resumed. '"You been at the sherry bottle, Sadie?" I says. "You know I prefer Johnny Walker," she says. "Well, he's walkin' you into the goddamn furniture," I says. I got a good ear, you know, ever since my eyes… Well, anyways, she couldn't fool me, not after all them years. A man gets to read a woman's voice. Isn't that right? You married?'

'No.'

'Yeah, and I can tell from that one little word that you never was. Am I right?'

'Right.'

'Well, Mary – that's the daughter – says, don't be a stranger. Kids need to see their grandpa, even if he can't see them. I says, what's a blind old man gonna do for them kids? Well, heck if they ain't like two little guide dogs draggin' me all over the shop. I go up Tuesdays to give her a break – you know, let her get to the store and stuff. Only Tuesdays, mind; don't want to wear out my welcome.'

'You sound Irish?' the cardinal asked.

'Damn right. Patrick Joseph O'Malley. Come over – oh, long time back. Nothing at home, see. I figured it's no good pining for what was, like a sick pup; gotta get up and get on. You're Irish too, huh? I can hear it in your voice.'

'This is Pelham Parkway coming up.' The cardinal linked the old man's arm, helping him to rise.

'You're a priest, ain't you, son?'

'Yes. How did you know?'

'Priest or doctor, I figured. Same kinda listener, but a doctor would've asked more questions, about my eyes and such. You're a good 'un, son.'

'I...'

'Hell, it ain't nothin' to be ashamed of.'

The old man was gone, tapping his stick before him. Wall saw a woman hurry to meet him. She kissed him and hugged his arm, her head already bobbing with talk the cardinal couldn't hear.

The old man's parting shot lodged in his gut as he pounded the sidewalk, the shabby Bronx Park attempting some kind of dignity in the twilight. It ain't nothin' to be ashamed of.

It was that time of evening when the daytime city stopped yelling and took a breather before the night-time city started. High cirrus clouds, tinged with pink, furrowed the deepening blue sky. 'A

mackerel sky,' his father would have said. Ah, that
man, Wall thought. A bum job and not a pot to piss
in, rich in unsubstantiated opinions and generous
with useless advice, but he was... What? Happy?
Sappy damn word; didn't fit in with arthritis and a
pittance for a pension. What had he had to be
happy about?

Me, he thought, and his heart ballooned in his
chest so that he stopped walking and stood there
staring at the sky. Me, the tow-headed kid who ate
the books and blew away the Ivy Leaguers. Me,
who ducked away when he went to ruffle my hair.

He was Cardinal Archbishop of New York, local
boy made good, back-slapper and ball-breaker in
equal measure. It was all downhill from here, he
knew. Soon the letter would arrive from HQ: well
done, thou good and faithful servant; time to step
aside for the next man, maybe become a 'pastor
emeritus' in some nice suburban parish where the
faithful would be affluent enough to welcome a pet
cardinal. And when he popped his clogs, they'd give
him one hell of a send-off, all the great and good
'making devout' in the front pews. He knew the
script by heart; hell, he'd read it over his
predecessor.

And, after that, the judgement. Different
measures there. 'Safe pair of hands, effective
administrator, builder of churches and schools' cuts
no ice here, fella. Where's the kid we showered with
brains and balls? Who's the soft, flabby guy in the

fancy dress? Seems you lost your soul in transit, old man…

The voice brought him back from his reverie.

'Jesus isn't coming, your Eminence,' Mal said softly. 'It would've been on the news.'

Wall kept his back turned a moment, wiping his sleeve across his face. When he turned, Mal looked him up and down appraisingly.

'I checked "sub secreto" in the dictionary while I was waiting, and you ain't it.'

The cardinal spread his arms in apology. 'It was this or the golf gear.'

'The lesser of two evils, then. Come in.'

★

'Hanny!'

'I'm not deaf, old man,' Hanny shouted from the kitchen, 'and I have only one pair of hands. So, if you want hot scones for your mystery guest, better let me be.'

'Hanny, we got a visitor.'

'If it's Richard Gere, tell him I'm married… just.' She appeared at the kitchen door. 'Well, Lord God Almighty.'

'Close, Hanny, but no cigar,' the cardinal said gravely.

'Here,' she said, 'get that coat off you; you'll have the benefit of it when you leave.'

She peeled the coat from his shoulders, folding

it over her arm. 'I'll put this in the closet and make myself scarce.' The cardinal made as if to protest, but she cut him off. 'Your Eminence, I been a cop's wife for over thirty years. I know when it's time to visit a neighbour who doesn't need visiting.'

She turned to Mal. 'I'll be down the hall with Raymond. He'll have seen you coming up. It'll make his day when I tell him we have a cardinal in the kitchen signing the annulment papers.'

Mal kissed her on the forehead. 'Thanks, Hanny.'

'You're a lucky man, Mal,' the cardinal said as the door closed behind Hanny.

'Yeah. Hanny is… Hanny.'

'Who's Raymond?'

'Oh, he's the gay guy in 3C; unofficial security officer for the building, you might say. A rumour couldn't get by Raymond's door. Hanny likes to keep an eye on him, which probably means we're down two scones.'

★

They sat at the kitchen table, sipping whiskey in companionable silence, Hanny's scones cooling between them. The door buzzer sounded, and Mal pressed the button. 'Use the stairs,' he said, 'the elevator is iffy.'

When the introductions had been made and the glasses refilled, the cardinal nodded. 'The chair recognises the Congressman for New York State.'

Congressman Fox wore a blue suit that hung on his spare frame and a tie that belonged to some other ensemble. A razor nick below his left ear had leaked into his shirt collar. He had the blue tinge beneath his eyes that suggested a man whose nights were not particularly restful, and as he spoke his long hands planed the sides of his face, making him appear haggard.

'I want to thank you, Mr O'Donnell—'

'Mal.'

'Mal. Thank you for having me in your home.'

'You're welcome, Congressman.'

Fox turned to the cardinal. 'You probably know that Sister Kathleen O'Reilly and I were friends.'

'Yeah, I know that, and I know she thought highly of you.'

Fox digested that kindness, his throat tightening for a moment, before he resumed.

'I think she was murdered.'

The two older men exchanged glances.

'I'm a cop,' Mal said, after a pause. 'Do you have any kind of hard evidence to back up that theory?'

'No – well, nothing that would stand up in a court of law, but…'

'Spit it out, son,' the cardinal said, setting his glass on the table, shaking his head at the bottle Mal inclined.

'After… the funeral, I talked to some people – a detective at the precinct, the Sisters at the convent. According to the report, a news-stand guy says he saw some fella in a yellow slicker run away from the scene. They had a garbled account from a junkie who said he saw someone acting weird in the men's room. The detective said the witness seemed to be flying high on some substance or other at the time.'

'Not a very dependable witness,' Mal offered gently.

'No, I know, Mal.' Fox picked up his glass and took a long swallow.

'I have a question,' the cardinal said quietly. 'Why am I here?'

Fox took a deep breath before replying. 'The junkie claims the guy he saw acting weird in the men's room was dressed like a priest.'

'So far, so nothing,' the cardinal said evenly. 'Even priests take a tinkle.'

'Yes, your Eminence, I know that, but... Kathleen was a hellraiser. She went to bat on some seriously controversial issues, Church matters. Maybe I'm way out of line here, but I wonder if there's a connection. And there's something else. I called some friends in the State Department, to see if Kathleen was under any kind of surveillance or if they knew of any right-wing groups who might take more than a healthy interest in what she was doing. Okay, it was a long shot, but I got a call back from a guy asking lots of questions about my interest in this particular case. He read me the riot act about my duty as a congressman to respect the integrity of the local police force, the whole nine yards. And

I'm thinking, what gives here? Kathleen is dead, and no one seems too eager to tidy up some loose connections – and someone is really concerned that I keep my nose out of it.'

The cardinal raised an eyebrow at Mal.

Mal turned his glass for a few moments, looking at the swirl of the amber liquid as if it held some mystery. 'I could check around some, I guess. Wouldn't do any harm. I know the guys at the precinct.'

'I'd be really grateful, Mal.'

'I'm a cop; it's what I do, Congressman,' Mal said, holding the young man's gaze. His look said that what he was doing was neither a favour nor an act of subservience.

He saw the red-rimmed eyes and the haggard face and relented. 'Maybe you could do something for me,' he said softly.

'Sure.'

'Eat one of Hanny's scones, will you? She went to a whole heap of trouble baking them for his Eminence.'

'Better check them for ground glass first,' the cardinal said gravely.

13

NYPD Station House, 42nd Street

'Quiet day, Harry?'

'Yeah.' The detective bumped his door open with a practised hip, ushering Mal away from the mayhem of the station house to the littered oasis he called an office. 'All human life, and then some,' he grunted. 'Coffee?'

'That what they still call it? Okay.'

Harry filled two mugs from a battered thermos, adding two sugars and a slurp of milk to Mal's without asking. He sat down, angling his chair so he could keep a weather-eye on the comings and goings outside. Mal turned his mug, warming his hands.

'Sister Kathleen O'Reilly, Harry.'

Harry's eyes flicked up. 'Personal?'

'No.'

'Don't tell me you've gone private, Mal?'

'Nah. Could be some connection with other stuff, you know how it is.'

'Okay…' Harry plonked his mug on the blotter. A little brown tsunami crested the rim and slopped over. He yanked the filing cabinet open so hard it squealed. 'All of it?' he asked tightly.

'Yeah, why not.'

The file landed about an inch from the edge of the desk. Harry walked away to lean on the partition, looking sightlessly at the notices hanging there.

'Something you want to say, Harry?'

'No – yes, goddammit, Mal. The damn cabinet is full of files; cases we can't close because we don't have the manpower to knock on doors, or because the labs are all tied up – or because most of the victims are just John and Jane Does and don't have the connections to call in someone like you, and nobody gives a flying fuck one way or the other.'

'Sit down, Harry.'

Reluctantly, Harry hooked the swivel chair with his foot and angled himself into it.

'Harry, listen up. I been a cop for thirty-five years. That adds up to a hell of a lot of John and Jane Does towed to Potter's Field, and no perp brought to book because we didn't have the foot soldiers or the D.A. wouldn't run with the evidence – or, yes, because the victims didn't have professional parents or a rabbi at City Hall; because they weren't connected enough to matter. But they mattered to me. Still do. So if a cop came sashaying into my precinct one day and said he'd like to see a file, sure, I'd think what you're thinking, and I'd be pissed as hell. Is she someone special? Heck, she's a nun – bright and feisty, they tell me – with connections all the way up to City Hall and St Pat's. But she's also a man's daughter, and it seems some bastard may have pushed his girl under a train. Now, if I can do anything to help you put that guy away, I'll do it. If you have a problem with that, just say it, and we'll shake hands and I'll be out of here.'

Harry shifted in his chair and rubbed a meaty hand through his hair. 'You play real dirty, Mal, you know that?'

Mal sipped his coffee and grimaced.

'Suppose I say no. What do you say to your people?'

'They're not my people, Harry, and I'm not their man. If I say I'm out, that's it; no reasons, no names.' Mal pushed the mug away and placed his hand on the file. 'Look, Harry, I know you can't give me the file or let me make a copy of it without putting your ass in a sling. So is there someplace here I could nose through it?'

Harry thought for a moment, and a small smile softened his face. 'One of the cells is free.'

'Thanks a bunch, Harry.'

★

The desk sergeant was one of those fussy cops who always ended up promoted sideways to administration. To Sergeant Ben Crouch, Mal was an interlude between a bevy of streetwalkers, all answering to Marilyn Monroe, and a junkie who had slipped a baggie inside his cell mattress and was screaming entrapment.

'Maybe I should take your belt and shoelaces, Mal? You get to make one call, big guy.'

'Lock the door, Ben.'

'Jeez, Mal, you gonna be in some movie or something? You know, I read about these, like, methodical actors—'

'Method.'

'Yeah, right. Anyways, they gotta climb inside their roles, you know, so—'

'Ben.'

'What?'

'Lock the door.'

'Okay, okay. Artistic friggin' temperament. Next thing, you'll be complaining the guy next door's got a bigger cell than you.'

Mal placed the file on the scarred table Ben had requisitioned from somewhere, took off his jacket and slung it on the pallet. Opening a murder file was something he had never done casually. Something in his gut revolted against parsing through the intimate details or pinning up the glossies of a man or a woman defiled by violent death. 'Sorry, kid,' he whispered, and opened the file.

★

Some time later, he closed the file and scribbled a final note on the yellow pad beside it. Carefully, he tore out the written pages – including the blank, indented page underneath – and folded them into his jacket pocket.

'Sergeant,' he called, 'I want out.'

'So do we all, sugar,' replied a languorous female voice from another cell, and the block echoed with wild laughter.

It was Harry who opened the door. 'You want more coffee, Mal?'

'I know the routine, Harry. You're the good cop; who's the bad cop?'

'Coming right up, Mal,' Harry said wickedly, holding the door a little wider.

The woman who eased past him into the cell was all of five two, despite vertiginous heels. Mal's eyes travelled up over the fishnet tights, miniscule skirt and flimsy top to the radioactive-red wig. She flung the wig on the table and sank to the pallet scratching at her lichen of black hair.

'Jesus, these damn things itch like crazy,' she muttered.

Mal raised a quizzical eyebrow.

'Meet Detective Torres, Mal. She's been doing a little undercover work for the Vice Squad,' Harry added helpfully. 'She's your new assistant.'

Mal and Detective Torres stared at each other in mutual disbelief.

'Harry,' Mal said evenly, 'could I have a word outside, please?'

In deference to the racket all around, he and Harry bowed towards each other like confessor and penitent.

'Run it by me slowly,' Mal said.

'It's not my doing, Mal, I swear. After our little chat I got a call from…' Harry raised his eyebrows and pointed a finger towards the ceiling.

'God?'

'Next best thing: the DA Quote, full co-operation, all the assistance the precinct can provide, unquote. How'd he know you'd be coming here?'

Mal held Harry's gaze for a beat, and Harry leaned even closer. 'Some heavy hitters involved in this case, Mal,' he whispered. 'You're in deep water, old friend.'

'I walk on it, Harry.'

'Better learn to dance. This water's hot and gonna get hotter.'

'And Dolorosa Torres is the fullest co-operation and all the assistance the precinct can provide?'

'She's a good kid, Mal. And hey, she's got you – the detective's detective. Like Domingo, right? The tenor's tenor.'

'You're a man of many parts, Harry.'

'Yeah, and I'd like to keep them together. Don't tell them I put you in a cell. Okay?'

'Who's "them"?'

But Harry was already bustling back to his office.

★

'Hanny?'

'Who's calling, please?'

'Hanny, look…'

'This is a recorded message. The lady formerly known as Mrs Mal O'Donnell has cashed his pension and run off with the Avon lady, citing mental cruelty 'cause he forgot to put out the garbage… again.'

'Sorry, Hanny, okay? Look, I got a favour to ask…'

'The last request of a condemned man. So ask.'

14

En Route to Kennedy Airport, New York

Eddie, the cardinal's driver, had obviously not been chosen for his fluency, Michael concluded as his third attempt at conversation died a death by monosyllables. Eddie was a Robert Mitchum lookalike, even to the same slightly amazed eyes under arching eyebrows; Michael remembered reading somewhere that Mitchum had been an interviewer's nightmare, with a reservoir of answers that went all the way from 'yep' to 'nope'. He contented himself with wondering who lived in the tiny, two-storey wooden houses that peeped timidly at their auto-shop neighbours and the growling Parkway. Something in his Island upbringing resonated with the claustrophobia of these relics of times past, their only surrender to the modern age the square nostrils of air-conditioning units that flared under the sad eyes of shuttered windows.

Eddie spoke. 'Company, Father.'

Michael resisted the urge to turn his head, leaning instead on the armrest in the middle of the back seat. Obligingly, Eddie tilted the rear-view mirror and Michael scanned the traffic behind. A camper van with Oregon plates bulked innocently in the mirror. He waited. Then a black Cadillac, with tinted windows, nosed out of its lane and back again. 'Peekaboo,' said the taciturn Eddie, fishing a mobile phone from the dash.

'Are you sure he's tailing us?'

'Do bears...? Excuse me, Father.'

Eddie muttered for a half-minute, then stashed the phone as the tollbooth loomed ahead. Michael watched him drop his coins – and then the seat back hit him solidly between the shoulders as Eddie went to Mach 1.

After a terrifying two minutes of slaloming around everything before them, to a chorus of plaintive horns, they slowed again to cruising speed. Michael flexed his shoulders and remembered to breathe.

'So?' he said, opting to play Eddie at his own one-word game.

'Yeah?' Eddie was not so easily budged into conversation. Michael remembered a journalist remarking that Kipling's five Ws were the only sure-fire tool against the hesitant interviewee.

'What was that all about?'

Eddie easily aced that question with a shrug. Four to go, Michael thought, the adrenaline rush making him whimsical.

'Who are those guys?'

'Spooks.'

'Where'd you get that idea?'

Eddie never took his eyes from the road. He raised his right hand from the wheel and tapped his head with a forefinger.

It occurred to Michael that Mal had pulled a similar stunt once before, on the way to the airport. It felt like a lifetime ago, but he had to ask.

'Two more questions, Eddie,' he said casually. 'Who did you call?"

'Tollbooth cops.'

'So the spooks are back there answering a thousand trivial questions?'

'That's three,' Eddie said calmly.

'Let me go for broke here, Eddie, okay? You know a guy, an ex-cop, called Mal O'Donnell?'

'Mal O'Donnell? Nah. I know a Pete O'Donnell – could be some relation. Lived out Queens direction, as I remember. Small guy with a toupee, retired about two years ago, July. I seen him a couple of—'

'So you don't know Mal?'

'Nah. Like I said, there was—'

'Eddie?'

'Yeah.'

'You're full of shit.'

Eddie watched the priest make his way through the automatic doors of the terminal building. He checked his rear and wing mirrors for a black Cadillac with tinted windows: nada. His eyes still scanning, he punched numbers on his phone.

'Cadillac, smoked windows,' he grunted. 'Before the tollbooth… Yeah, I lost them… He knows… I'm sure, Mal,' Eddie said.

★

Michael paused and turned before entering the departures area. While apparently inspecting the departure times, he scanned the busy concourse, all the time tensing his left shoulder in anticipation. Nothing. No spooks, no Mal. Same difference, he thought angrily. But he stayed a few minutes longer, just in case.

★

Hugh knew St Peter's Basilica was a collection of architectural afterthoughts. Ever since Julius the warrior pope had goaded Michelangelo into drawing the plans, and then changed the shape from a Greek to a Latin cross, successive popes had hired and fired some of the greatest names of their eras. Bernini, Bramante, Modena, Raphael and a whole galaxy of architects and artists had blazed through, leaving their marks. It had been built to dominate the Roman skyline: pilgrims would glimpse the distinctive shape as they entered the city, drawing them into the embrace of the encircling colonnade. At this early hour, the massive church and dome loomed over Hugh, and there was something desolate about the empty square that matched his mood.

He checked his watch again and walked quickly between the pillars to an open doorway. A long corridor stretched before him, rising through a series of stairways like locks on a canal. Presently he arrived at a closed door flanked by two Swiss Guards. Tom's voice whispered in his memory: 'Will you look at them boys in pyjamas, Hugh? Living proof that the Swiss have a sense of humour but take it very seriously.' He might have smiled, but for the figure seated at the desk before the door.

The black-clad figure inclined his head. 'Prego.'

Black eyes scanned Hugh's letter of appointment, the pale, pared features registering nothing. Languidly, the long fingers of one hand stretched from their black sheath to initial the margin, while the other raised a metal stamp and pressed the papal coat of arms onto the page. The functionary slid the document to the lip of the desk, and the pale hands retreated. No eye contact, no small talk: the bureaucracy of a theocracy, Hugh thought.

'Grazie,' Hugh said. The black eyes fixed on some point to the left of Hugh's shoulder. Welcome to the Vatican, he thought. The Swiss Guards straightened their halberds perfunctorily as he passed, the deepening gloom of the vaulted hallway dimming the vivid colours of their uniforms.

He was lost in a maze of corridors bracketed with identical doors. He spent a frustrating ten minutes searching for the right one, and he could feel the beads of sweat at his hairline. Pausing just to dab his forehead, he took a deep breath and entered.

Cardinal Thomas studied the chunky Rolex on his wrist. 'Do I bawl your ass out or send this back to Switzerland?'

'I apologise for being late. I'm afraid I went astray—'

'Apology accepted. Sit down.'

Hugh sat on the straight-backed chair set just inside the ambit of the desk lamp. On the other side of the desk, Cardinal Thomas flipped a folder open, ran his finger down a page and closed it abruptly.

'This is some piece of work,' he grunted. He leaned forward to give Hugh the full benefit of his stare.

Some of the cardinals Hugh had encountered looked incongruous in their prelate's garb. Bartoli, who had chaired the viva voce for Hugh's defence of his doctorate, was a scrawny man with a pointed head that emerged from his collar when he asked a question and retreated again during the answer – he was known affectionately as 'the Turtle'. Cardinal

Richter seemed totally unaware of his regalia, as though he would have been equally at ease in a banker's pinstripes. Alba, Richter's assistant, was a diva, using his cassock, sash, cape and skullcap for operatic effect. Hugh's own criteria, when it came to sartorial selection, stretched from 'clean' to 'dry'. But Thomas wore his robes like a second skin. A coiled energy radiated from him. Hugh had never known precisely what 'presence' meant, until now. There seemed to be a concentrated stillness at Thomas' core, and when he moved a hand to the file on his desk, there was a fluency and grace in the gesture.

'Civil service gobbledegook,' Thomas snapped. 'Age, rank and serial number – all the stuff you don't need to know about a man. Sure, there are observations.' He drew out the word, tasting it and finding it wanting. 'Observations by those who claimed to know you: deans, professors, et cetera, et cetera… But, hey, these guys are company men – lifers, every one. They know the score: shaft not and you shall not be shafted, right? I have a damn degree in semiotics, and even I can't read this stuff.'

He closed the file and pushed it away.

'Here's how we proceed. When I served in the US army, we had rank and file. Rank said "soldier", file said "sir". Command and obey. Works damn well in wartime, hell of a waste of time in the Church. Leads to stagnation – lots of guys sticking to the straight and narrow and no one thinking outside the box. Now, we had a tradition in the

Marine Corps known as "no rank in the locker room". Get my drift?'

Hugh nodded warily.

'Good. I give you five minutes in the locker room, Hugh O'Neill. You talk straight or you take off. Did you research me before you came here?'

'No.'

'Why not?'

'The same reason you find my file inadequate. The same people who wrote about me would talk about you. They didn't know me; why would they know you?'

'What are they not telling me about you?'

'What's private to me and none of their business.'

'And none of mine?'

'Yes.'

'Family?'

'None.'

'Close friends?'

Hugh paused. 'None.'

Thomas was on it like a terrier. 'Come on, Hugh, why the hesitation? Are we talking former lovers who could surface in the popular press someday and bite your ass, or what?'

'No, no one like that.'

'Okay, let me fill in some of the blanks. You already know the various departments in the Vatican. I – we – don't exist officially. The others range from bean-counters to firefighters, like

Richter's mob. Their mandate is to hold the fort; ours is to keep an eye on the future of the Church. Our immediate brief is Islam.'

'I know very little about Islam, apart—'

'Look, Hugh, I got Islamicists on tap here, guys who've got doctorates in how many hairs there were in the Prophet's beard – all past tense. We're talking the future here, like who's the coming man in Mali. We've got someone on that already, but we need to know other stuff: who are the movers and shakers in Egypt? Is US foreign policy a help or a hindrance in the East? We need to gather the *sensus populorum*, the mood of the people. If we get it right, the Pope can alter the course of the Church accordingly. If we don't, we crash and burn – and there are plenty of folk hereabouts who pray devoutly for that eventuality.'

'Eminence, I'm an academic. I have some competence in canon law. How can I be part of your project?'

'Son, I'm an American. I don't sleep nights unless I have access to a lawyer. You keep the local wolves from my door. Also, with respects, you're low enough in rank to pass beneath the radar. People won't adjust their answers to your title. It's just possible that you may hear and see things as they actually are. I want you in. Are you on side?'

'Yes.'

'Good.' Thomas glanced at the gleaming Rolex. 'Gimme a minute; I have to make a call.'

After a few moments, Hugh heard the bass voice rumble from the other room and rose to scan the documents strewn on the desk. A memo caught his eye, and he angled it under the desk lamp. 'To Archbishop Leclerc, re: Mali meeting…' Before he could read further, he became aware of the silence from the other room. Quickly he picked up a marble letter opener and began to examine it.

'A parting gift from the clergy of my diocese in the States,' the cardinal said breezily. 'Not very subtle, are they?' He grinned, reseated himself behind the desk and shuffled some papers. 'Good. I think we've covered all the bases. Oh, one more thing: there's another Irish guy flying into Leonardo Da Vinci today. Pick him up and bring him to the Villa Farnese for eight. We're invited to a party. Mingle and listen. Have him here at seven sharp tomorrow morning. That's Swiss time.'

Cardinal Thomas opened a folder on his desk. Hugh was dismissed.

*

Hugh sat on a bollard in St Peter's Square and waited for his heart to stop racing. He took a handkerchief from his pocket and blotted away the perspiration that stung his eyes. He started at the voice but didn't turn.

'Our mutual friend asks if you have information to convey, Dr O'Neill.'

It was a woman's voice, and in the blur of his peripheral vision he caught a glimpse of her black religious garb.

'There was a memo,' he whispered. 'I…I didn't have time to read all of it, but it was to an Archbishop Leclerc, concerning a meeting in Mali.'

'It is sufficient,' the voice said.

15

Leonardo Da Vinci Airport, Rome

Why name an airport for an artist? Hugh wondered idly, waiting for the transatlantic flight to release its passengers. 'Come on, Hugh, smell the pigment, boy,' Tom laughed in his head. 'We're not talking any old dauber here. Da Vinci was da man, the daddy of all Renaissance painters. Bastard son of a Tuscan lawyer, sweet-talks the old man into shelling out the shekels for his apprenticeship – and then what? Out-paints his friggin' master.' They had been standing before the 'Baptism of Christ' by Verucchio, and Hugh had been aware of the whispering tourists ebbing away from his tall, noisy companion. 'Da Vinci was firing on all pistons, Hugh. Old Veruca just couldn't keep up with him.'

'Verucchio.'

'That's what I said. Now, according to this here brochure, Verucchio painted this picture – but listen to this, Hughie, and learn. "It is generally believed that Da Vinci painted the angel on the left." Look at the angel painted by Ver-what's-his-face. Cripes, he's like an altar boy in the Falls Road – all snubby-nosed and bored out of his skull with the baptism, and getting an eyeful of the wee lassie angel. She's the Da Vinci. Look at that face, and the hair, and the way she's holding the cloak…' And when Hugh had countered that Da Vinci rarely finished a painting, Tom had been at his explosive and irrational best. 'Plenty of apprentices only dying to do the fiddly bits. The master doesn't mix the paint or frame the friggin' picture. Leonardo had vision, Hugh; other men had to settle for sight…' God, how Hugh had loved those wild conversations, Tom gesticulating wildly over cheap wine in some shabby café. Tom had been the visionary and Hugh the canon lawyer, an anchor dragging against the mad race of the gale, trying to keep the ship steady and on course.

He felt the absence of his friend as a dull ache in the pit of his stomach. It lay in a part of him that he regarded as *terra incognita*, an unknown land of mythical and fantastical beasts that tempted and terrified him so that he took refuge in the known world of his head, mapped out in the bold black and white of canon law. 'Come out and play, Hughie,'

Tom had teased. 'Leave your wee intellectual toys for once and dance on the friggin' table, ye boy ye.' But Hugh had been afraid; afraid to let go, in case he never got back.

Hugh became aware of the tightness in his throat. He swallowed with difficulty and turned his attention to the concourse.

That has to be him. The man was alone – not just unaccompanied, but solitary. It was something he wore like a coat. He was tall and sallow, with raven-black hair, and his head swung slowly from left to right as he walked. Hugh was certain the man had seen him, but still his head moved, left and right, left and right. He felt the sweat cool on his body.

That has to be him. Michael Flaherty took stock of the slightly built cleric, unremarkable in his plain black coat and dog collar. He thought of Raphael waiting at Arrivals, all iridescent in his parka and mittens. He thought of Mal – in another time, another life – feigning indifference in the throng at the departure gates, and steeled himself.

Automatically, he scanned left and right for signs of undue attention; old instincts die hard. He let his eyes trawl over the sweepers, pushing their brooms with Buddhist detachment; the kiosk vendors, reanimated by the fresh influx of passengers from his flight. The phalanx of taxi drivers eyed the stream of passengers speculatively, occasionally calling 'Taxi' without enthusiasm. The nun – cased conservatively in severe black, only her facial features visible in a starched white frame – would have been incongruous anywhere but in Rome; she stood alone, eyes cast down, waiting. Michael was distracted by the delighted screams of a family rushing in the direction of a boy who walked hand in hand with a female flight attendant. He looked about twelve years old and apprehensive as the wave of affectionate humanity surged to claim him. The laughing, weeping, welcoming party broke over him, and he was gone.

Something squirmed in Michael's subconscious, clamouring to surface. Old-fashioned nuns travel in pairs. When he looked back, she was nowhere to be seen.

The man in the plain black coat had a Northern European pallor and grey eyes.

'Hi, I'm Michael Flaherty.'

The grey eyes took in Michael's black roll-neck sweater, the creased jacket and trousers, before they rose to meet his. 'Welcome to Rome, Father Flaherty.' The accent was homogenised Northern Irish, impossible to place within the province. The handshake was dry and perfunctory. 'I'm Father Hugh O'Neill. Cardinal Thomas instructed me to meet you.'

'Instructed' is an interesting choice of word, Michael thought. It puts both of us in our places.

'Your bags?'

'You're looking at them.'

'Very well; we can go directly, then.'

The car reflected the man, Michael thought as he got into the small Fiat. The interior was bare and functional. There were no magnetised Virgins or crucifixes, no discarded newspaper or fag ends or any of the normal debris. A pool car, he concluded, a vehicle for going from A to B. Used by everyone, it belonged to no one.

Hugh O'Neill drove sedately, keeping the speedometer needle rock steady, about ten kilometres shy of the speed limit. He seemed oblivious to the affront this occasioned other motorists, who flashed the Morse Code of their frustration in his rear-view mirror or accelerated dramatically by, wagging single-digit salutes. Only when they were safely in the slow lane of the highway did Hugh speak again.

'The cardinal also instructed me to tell you that we are to attend a party in the Villa Farnesina this evening, at eight o'clock sharp. Do you have something more... eh... formal to wear?'

'Did he instruct you to ask that?'

'No, it's just that—'

'Listen. Officially, I sign on tomorrow, so the cardinal's writ doesn't run tonight. Unofficially, I've been in the air for over six hours. I would like to wash, eat and sleep, in that order. Can you organise that, Father O'Neill, or do you have to check with the cardinal for further instructions?'

Hugh studied the road in silence for a few

moments before replying. 'I've arranged a room for you at the Irish College. We can go there now, if you'd like to shower and change. I'm sure his Eminence will understand if you decline the... invitation to the party. To be perfectly honest, I find these affairs a bit contrived.'

Michael let his anger sluice away in a long sigh.

'Look, I'm sorry, Hugh. As they say, I had only one nerve left and you were getting on it. How about I get cleaned up, and we borrow some glad rags and go to the ball?'

'I think we could manage that... without further instructions from the cardinal.'

Be careful, Hugh O'Neill, Michael thought. I think you nearly smiled.

★

Michael leafed through the *Eyewitness Guide to Rome* as Hugh's driving created its own private tailback. The Villa Farnesina merited a two-page spread, together with pictures of its treasures and a floor plan. It was like essential reading for a search-and-rescue mission, he thought. He imagined Lieutenant Bryson's drawl: 'Listen up, you guys. Force A lobs the smoke in the loggia. Force B strafes anything at head-height, except the god-damn statuary; someone already beat us to that. No shooting, I repeat, no shooting inside the villa, what with all them priceless works of art and all. You do not wish to go down in history as the guy who took out a Ray-fay-el.'

He might have smiled if the picture hadn't come, unbidden, of a jungle clearing where Lieutenant Bryson's torso lay at some distance from his legs. Michael shook his head to dislodge the memory. 'Let the memories come up from the dark, Michael,' Raphael whispered in his mind. 'Nightmares are memories we don't look at in daylight.'

'We're here,' Hugh said.

The garden of the Villa Farnesina was hung with coloured lanterns, illuminating the boles of the trees so that their crowns melted into darkness. On a raised dais, a group of musicians bowed their heads to Monteverdi, seemingly oblivious of the tinkling glasses and raised voices competing with their music. The two priests gravitated to the comparative quiet of the vestibule, standing beneath an up-lit fresco.

'Hugh,' Michael whispered.

'What?'

'Maybe we should stand somewhere else.'

He inclined his head to the three naked ladies on the wall behind them.

'Oh,' Hugh said, and blushed to the rim of his collar at the expanse of naked flesh.

'Guidebook says the lady on the left was the owner's mistress. Wouldn't want to damage your ecclesiastical career by association.'

Taking Hugh by the elbow, Michael steered him

to stand near a more sedate Madonna and Child, plucking two glasses from a passing tray en route. 'Here; you don't have to drink it. Just hold it. It'll help us look less like two clerical sore thumbs. So where's the instructor?'

'Who?... Oh. That's him there, talking with the Contessa Farnese.'

Michael looked at the couple standing close together in an area of shadow between the illuminated pools of the lanterns. He saw Cardinal Thomas lean closer to whisper something in the contessa's ear. Her head inclined to him so that their faces almost touched.

'I should introduce you,' Hugh said.

Michael shook his head. 'He looks pretty occupied to me. I'm reporting for duty tomorrow morning; that's soon enough.'

Suddenly, Cardinal Thomas straightened as if aware of being observed; he took the contessa's elbow, leading her in the direction of a knot of guests who were conversing noisily. The contessa, Michael thought, seemed reluctant to end the moment of intimacy. The cardinal eased away from her, giving his undivided attention to a young lady who seemed suddenly animated by his presence. The contessa offered her hand to a distinguished-looking man, who sucked in his cummerbund before bowing carefully to kiss her fingers.

'Who's the guy in the bellyband?' Michael asked.

'Beck. He's the US ambassador to the Vatican.

Second-generation Polish; an unsubtle appointment, considering who sits on the Throne of Peter.'

'I think I'll stroll around for a bit. It might keep me awake.'

'Whenever you want to leave, just say so.'

Michael made his way across the garden, depositing his glass on yet another passing tray. Various guests gazed and glazed as he passed. He had the impression they were scanning him for signs of rank, and his plain black coat put him way below the pecking order. 'Black is the absence of colour, Michael,' his old mentor, Father Mack, had said. For a shuddering moment, he saw Mack's face, and the blood in his mouth, and his own hand opening to drop him into the sea below the cliff.

'You.'

The imperious voice snagged at Michael's ear, but his pace didn't falter.

'You. I'm speaking to you.'

A heavy hand clamped on his shoulder. He turned slowly and faced the source of the voice.

The man before him wore the red sash of a monsignor. He was about Michael's height, but his belly overflowed the band around his waist. He had a face that might once have modelled for a Botticelli cherub but was now melting into his collar, rendering him more satyr than angel. The young clerics in his entourage wore plain black cassocks and identical expressions of simpering anticipation.

'Didn't you hear me call you?' The monsignor

thrust his face close enough that Michael could smell the alcohol on his breath. 'I want another gin and tonic.' He used the hand on Michael's shoulder to pull himself upright again. 'Those damn waiters are all hiding as usual. Probably in the kitchen, drinking my mother's wine.'

His attendants laughed dutifully, never taking their eyes from the monsignor. His eyes turned to Michael again, as if surprised to find him still there. 'Gin. Tonic,' he said, as if speaking to someone hard of hearing. 'Now.'

'Do I look like your mother?'

The colour erupted in the man's fleshy face, and his hand clenched to a claw on Michael's shoulder.

'You dare to speak to me like that?' he muttered incredulously.

Michael was aware of the silence that had rippled out among the other guests.

With his right hand, he gripped the hand digging into his shoulder and removed it. Stepping closer to the other man, he raised their locked hands between them, shielding them from the others. 'Monsignor,' he said softly, 'you have choices.' Slowly he squeezed, bending the trapped fingers backward. 'You can continue in this vein, in which case, I will snap your fingers.' He bent the hand another degree to illustrate the point, and the colour drained from the monsignor's face. 'You may, however, choose to smile and apologise, and this matter will be ended.'

Drunk as he was, the monsignor knew that the man before him would be as good as his word. Beads of sweat collected on his forehead; he drew a shuddering breath, and his jowls quivered as he twisted them into a rictus of a smile. 'I'm sorry,' he croaked. 'I mistook you... for someone else.'

Michael matched his attempt at a smile with a mirthless one of his own.

'It seems you did, Monsignor,' he said lightly, and released his hand. He walked quickly away, aware of the resumption of chatter in his wake. Hugh stood with his mouth open as Michael walked past him into the Villa.

He opened a door at random, and stood transfixed at what was before him. He was looking through pillars at a Roman skyline that couldn't have existed for a few hundred years. As his eyes grew accustomed to the shadows around him, he realised that he was looking at a mural.

'Extraordinary, isn't it?' a voice said from the shadows to his left. He saw the glow of a cigarette briefly illumine a man's face. 'Come and sit, Padre. The illusion is best appreciated from here.'

Michael eased himself down beside the man on the stone bench.

'You are looking at the Perspettive, Padre. Tell me what you see.'

'I see a view of the city through marble pillars.'

'Yes, remarkable, isn't it? Chigi, the Siennese banker, had it painted in the sixteenth century. And then Cardinal Farnese bought the Villa. This is the Farnese who became Paul the Third.'

'The counter-reformation pope?'

'Yes, indeed. The pope who thought he would reform the Catholic Church and bring Luther's children back to Rome. A dream, Padre. An illusion, just like the Rome painted on the wall before you. There are always people who long to preserve what has been. This villa' – the man waved his hand so that the cigarette tip made a glowing parabola above them – 'it was once a great salon for the bankers and nobility of Rome. Cardinals, even popes, all came here. Their spirits still whisper here, still plotting to bring about an illusion – a time and place painted on wet plaster... But excuse my manners. I am Vittorio Spenza, the husband of the Contessa Farnese and the father of the man who offended you.'

'It's okay, Signor. It was nothing.'

'My son has yet to learn that those who would hunt tigers must be prepared to meet one,' the old man said regretfully. There was no counter to that, and Michael remained silent.

'You are new to Rome, Padre?'

'Yes, I arrived today. My name is Michael Flaherty.'

'Ah, you are Irish. You know your ancestors battered at our gates and gave our children nightmares?'

'And your ancestors didn't bother to invade our country.'

The old man cackled happily and began to cough. It bent him double; it seemed he would never breathe regularly again.

'Can I get you some water?'

'Very kind of you, Michael Flaherty,' he wheezed, 'but Roman water is a cure worse than any disease. In the not-too-distant past, all this was malarial swamp. No, no water, thank you.'

No sooner had his breathing steadied than he drew on his cigarette as if dragging the smoke down to his toes.

'Our history tells us that a Roman was not considered a proper man until he had... what's the English word? Outdone! Yes, outdone his father. I look at my son and I wonder: why this ambition... this hunger that eats up the heart? I love my son Sebastiano. How is it possible, do you think, that a father could love his child so passionately and yet find him... incomprehensible?'

'Father and son is never the easiest relationship, Signor.'

'You speak from wisdom.'

'No, I speak from failure.'

The old man laid his hand gently on Michael's arm. 'I never believed that a Roman could envy a Celt,' he said quietly, 'but I envy your father, Michael Flaherty.'

'Papa, Papa! I know you're in here.'

Signor Spenza offered the cigarette to Michael. 'If you would save me from an Amazon?' he pleaded. Michael took it and tried to appear nonchalant.

The young woman surveyed them with suspicion.

'You were smoking,' she accused her father. The old man raised his arms in a gesture of wounded innocence.

'Excuse me,' Michael interposed, 'I'm the one with the cigarette.' She glowered at him.

'Michael Flaherty,' Spenza said, 'this is Emilia. She is my daughter and my doctor. Like Janus, the Roman god, she wears two faces. One moment she's breaking her father's heart, the next she's listening to it with her damned stethoscope.'

'Papa...'

'I know, I know, I have been a poor host. I must go back to the party.'

He turned to Michael and dropped his voice.

'Be careful in Rome,' he whispered. 'Come and see me again.'

'Thank you, Signor. I'd like that.'

'You must make our guest welcome, Emilia,' Spenza said, and ambled off reluctantly. Michael and Emilia looked at each other for a moment.

'You don't really have to stay, Signorina,' he said.

'And you don't really have to hold that damned cigarette as if you knew what to do with it, Signor.'

'Sorry,' he said sheepishly.

'No, no need to be sorry. Of course I... what's the English word for when you say something again and again?'

'Nag.'

'Nag? A nag is a horse, no?'

'Yes – I mean, it also means a horse.'

'Okay, okay, sometimes I nag him.' She turned and looked away from Michael, towards the fresco. 'I hate that stupid picture,' she muttered fiercely. 'I hate all this… pretence.'

He suspected she was crying, and dug in his jacket pocket for a large white handkerchief.

'I'm afraid I came in borrowed garments, Signorina. I can't guarantee the provenance of this handkerchief.'

She turned and smiled. 'Thank you.' She dabbed at her eyes and handed him the handkerchief.

'You're a doctor?' he asked, trying to lighten the mood. 'Do you work in a hospital?'

'No, I work in a night shelter for women in Trastevere.'

'Trastevere?'

'Oh, sorry. Trastevere means "across the Tiber". Hundreds of years ago, it was a place for Jews and the poorest people. My mother doesn't approve. She thinks a descendant of the Farnese shouldn't work in a place like that.'

'The Farnese have long memories, don't they?'

'Yes – like the Irish, I think,' she said, smiling. She glanced at her watch. 'I'm afraid I must go. I'm working tonight.'

She offered her hand. Her grip was firm, and she prolonged it as she spoke. 'My brother Sebastiano is a Farnese, Michael. He won't forget or forgive. He'll try to hurt your career in the Vatican.'

'I don't have a career in the Vatican.'

'Then they have no reason to protect you,' she said enigmatically. 'Go carefully.'

Leaving the villa, Michael saw Hugh hunched over a mobile phone and waited. He noticed the tension in the other man's body and how he stared at the phone after the call had ended.

'Shouldn't you turn that thing off?' Michael asked.

'Wha...? Oh, yes – of course. Eh, I'm afraid I don't know how. I'm not used to...'

'Here, I'll do it.' Michael had the phone in two quick strides and turned away to press End. 'You just press that button with the red telephone,' he said lightly, slipping the phone into Hugh's pocket.

After you've memorised the number, he could have added. Why did I do that? hc asked himself. Had Emilia's warning put him on edge, or was that simply the place he had come to inhabit, ever since... When? Since Lieutenant Bryson had got the unit killed because he stopped checking? The whole unit, except Michael.

It's over, man, he chided himself. Let it go.

★

But he couldn't shake it – neither the vague feeling that something wasn't quite right nor the very real ache in his shoulder. He remembered picking up a book, in an airport somewhere, entitled *Your Body Speaks Its Mind*. For a mad moment he imagined his shoulder whining, 'It's like in the movies, everyone gets shot in the goddamn shoulder...'

He must have made some sound, because Hugh looked at him quickly from the driver's seat. 'What?'

'Nothing. I was just thinking how kind up-lighting can be to old buildings. They look almost better at night.'

They were driving along the Tiber and Michael was scanning, his head swinging slowly left and right. He stretched his legs for comfort, and then tensed.

The car he saw in the wing mirror was being driven by a Hugh-clone, who was maintaining a sedate speed and a respectful distance. The motor-cyclist, dead ahead, seemed tethered to their front fender by a twenty-foot rope. Michael saw the bike's indicator blink as it peeled away to the right. Hugh turned to follow in its wake, and the car behind shadowed them into the turn.

Two pilot fish, Michael thought. So where's the shark?

'I thought you might like to see the Pantheon,' Hugh said. 'It's usually crawling with tourists during the day. We'll have the piazza to ourselves at this hour.'

Michael's brain raced as he began to slot the

pieces of the jigsaw together. Hugh O'Neill acts furtive on the phone, and suddenly we have an escort of outriders. 'A little midnight sightseeing, Father?'

'Why not, Father? We'll have the piazza to ourselves.'

The hell we will, Father, he thought grimly, and considered his options.

He fingered the *Eyewitness Guide* in his lap and bent forward to open the glove compartment, as if he were stowing the book there. He saw two or three flimsy brochures and a torch. He slammed it shut and sat back, slipping the torch into one pocket and the book in the other. He deepened his breathing and worked at relaxing his muscles. An old memory tape began to spool in his head, flickering images on his inner eye.

The man who had walked into the Instruction Room had no identifiable insignia. He stood just a shade under five feet, and he had an economy of movement and an aura of self-effacement that made him instantly forgettable. A chameleon, Michael had concluded, and he had wondered at the respect in the sergeant's body language. The session had been flagged on the bulletin board as 'Weapons Training', but there wasn't a single weapon in the room that Michael could see, and the lecturer was not introduced.

'Who's the midget?' someone asked softly at the back. 'Kowalski's lunch,' someone answered, and the room trembled with swallowed laughter.

The unit groaned when Sarge wheeled in Herbert, the rubber mannequin used for hand-to-hand demonstrations. The little man's voice was paper-dry, little more than a hoarse whisper. 'You fellas may be wondering where the weapons got to,' he said. 'Well, this room is a pretty good arsenal.'

For the next thirty minutes he proceeded to inflict appalling injuries on the uncomplaining Herbert, using a pencil, a paper clip, a rolled document and any number of other readily available objects. 'The thing is, fellas,' he whispered, 'the enemy will disarm you and then relax. That's when he's most vulnerable. Any questions?'

There were no questions. Michael sneaked a look at his companions and registered the shock in their faces. He also realised that he was the only one taking notes. For whatever reason, he concluded, the little man had become a killing machine, the ultimate soldier. That he had been a twenty-four-carat looper as well, Michael couldn't deny – but he had kept the notes.

That evening, he had walked into the dormitory with a toothbrush in his hand, and the entire unit had covered their heads in perfectly synchronised mock horror. 'Not the toothbrush,' Kowalski had wailed. Boy, how they'd cracked up at that one. They were all dead, even Big Kowalski, who had coughed his lungs up in Michael's arms before the killing bullet passed right through him and Michael's shoulder.

The ache in his shoulder brought him back. The piazza was deserted, the cafés shrouded with shutters for the night, their large umbrellas folded like daisies in the dark. The Pantheon hulked huge and shadowed along one side. Hugh turned off the engine and they sat in silence for a while.

'Okay?' Hugh asked.

'Whatever you say,' Michael said easily. He walked around to Hugh's door, letting his eyes adjust to the light.

'Better put the alarm on,' he said.

'At this hour? No need, really.'

'Better safe than sorry,' Michael said, standing at his shoulder. Hugh pressed the keyring, and the car blinked twice before hunkering down to sleep.

Michael heard the faint sound of car doors closing, in an alley somewhere to the side of the Pantheon, and picked up the percussion of feet on cobbles coming from the same direction. On the other side of the fountain, metal grated on concrete. Bike-stand, he thought. Two coming from the left of the Pantheon and one from our rear. He considered dragging Hugh into the shadow of the colonnade and dismissed that option: it was a confined space without exits. The Marine instructor barked in his head: 'When all else fails, get mad. Do the un-expected. Remember, the badasses also read the manual.'

'Sorry, Hugh,' he muttered, and hit him. He caught him as he slumped and hauled him up the steps, laying him at the base of the fountain. One down and three to go, he thought.

He heard the slide of leather on leather and swung upright, jabbing the torch to life. The beam dazzled the man momentarily, long enough for Michael to smack the torch across the bridge of his nose. The man screamed and dropped to his knees. Nose is good, the instructor inside his head said approvingly: lots of blood, and waters the eyes.

Yeah, and makes shit of the torch, Michael thought wryly, hurling the mangled shaft in the direction of the two burly figures running at him.

The best form of defence, Flaherty?

Attack.

Attack what, grunt?

Attack, sir. As the men reached the second step he launched himself at them, arms outstretched, and they clattered back together on the cobbles. He rolled over the one on his left, short-jabbing his throat with his fist.

He was back on his feet when the third man came at him, arms widespread. Too big to wrestle, he thought. He clutched the book in both hands at chest height and waited. The man wrapped him in a bear hug. Wait. He felt the vice-grip squeeze the breath from his body, lifting his feet from the ground. He saw the big head rear back to butt him. Now.

With all his strength, he jerked the folded book up under the man's jaw. He heard the click as the teeth smashed together. Involuntarily, his opponent loosened his grip as his mouth filled with blood. As Michael's feet touched the cobbles, he kicked sideways and heard a satisfying snap. The man groaned and sagged away, his left knee twisted out of true. Too much time, too much time, the instructor roared. Tag team coming back, and, boy, are they pissed.

Buy time, Michael thought frantically. Maybe the cavalry are coming. He ran for the car, footsteps pounding behind him. He hit the driver's door with his shoulder; the car rocked on its springs, and the siren echoed around the piazza.

In the intermittent glare, Michael saw the men loom like fantastical creatures, then they were on him, grappling him to the ground. He covered his head, trying to roll with the kicks to his sides. They redirected their blows to his thighs and torso, and pain lanced through his body. Fuck this, he thought savagely. He rolled and swung his right elbow up and out, catching Motorbike Man off balance. The other man swung his leg and Michael grabbed it, giving it just enough lift to put the man on his ass. He was on him, hammering his head into the cobbles.

An arm closed over his throat, a hand gripped his hair and he was dragged up and back. You want to dance, let's dance, he thought wildly, accelerating backwards so that the man lost his balance and fell. He spread his arms to save himself, and Michael snapped back his head, catching him on the chin.

He was sitting astride the man's chest, flailing him with punches, when he was dragged off. Someone pressed something hard across his throat in a choke hold, and his vision began to blur.

'Michael, Michael!' Someone was shouting in his ear. Hugh's face swam into soft focus.

'It's the police, Michael.'

16

Rome

Michael was spent. It was always like this after combat. The frenzy over, the mind tripped a switch to prevent overload. He remembered soldiers who couldn't find the switch, didn't want it to be over; they craved the buzz that blunted pain and blasted them beyond the ordinary they inhabited. As the adrenaline ran slower in his veins, the pain came. His shins and kneecaps burned. He tried to breathe deeply, but it stung his ribs. In his peripheral vision he could see the curve of his right cheekbone where he had never seen it before. He leaned forward to inspect his hands, and his neck muscles spasmed.

Presently he became aware of Hugh sitting beside him, careful not to make contact when the police car swerved, the siren bouncing against alley walls. The car jerked to a stop and he was thrown forward against the hazy plastic partition. Uniforms hauled him out of the car, one pressing down on his head so that he wouldn't bump it. He had a sudden urge to laugh and bit down on his lip, tasting blood.

Inside the police station, they were frog-marched to adjoining cells, and the doors slammed behind them. Michael sat on the bare pallet, taking slow deep breaths and flexing his fingers. He heard the faint murmur of voices from Hugh's cell.

A key groaned in the lock, his cell door swung open and Emilia Spenza walked into the room, accompanied by a policeman. She spoke rapidly to the policeman, who withdrew. For a long time she stood there staring at Michael.

'Oh, Michael,' she whispered, 'who did—?

'Good evening, Doctor,' he said politely, and shot a meaningful glance towards the other cell. She nodded and moved beside him, looking at his injuries, her face pinched and white with shock.

'Smoking damages your health,' he said lamely.

'And that of others,' she added, and tried to smile.

She ran her fingers lightly over his face and shone a small torch in his eyes. Carefully, she unbuttoned his shirt and peeled it from his body. Her fingers prodded his ribcage, and he winced. She touched the round, puckered scar on his shoulder and walked around him to see its evil twin on the other side. 'Entrance and exit wounds,' she noted.

His torso was mottled with angry weals that would graduate through black to yellow, but he had no broken bones, as far as she could tell without an x-ray. Swiftly, she upended her bag on the bed and began to apply a cream to his bruises.

'What's that?' Michael asked.

'Arnica,' Emilia replied. 'You know you should go to hospital for x-rays?'

'No, no hospital,' he said flatly.

When she had finished, she helped him into his shirt and fastened the buttons.

'The women's clinic where I work is just round the corner,' she whispered. 'The police often call for whoever is on duty, if there's something they want to keep secret. Is there anyone you would like me to call?'

'No – no, thank you.'

'Michael…'

A policeman ducked inside the door and beckoned to him.

★

Hugh was already sitting on a hard plastic chair when Michael was brought into the interview room. He glanced up sheepishly, but Michael ignored him. He counted four police officers in the room, all armed, and dressed like extras in a Gilbert and Sullivan opera.

A man entered, and the officers stiffened to

something like attention. The man looked as if he had been called from his bed and had dressed in the dark. His shirt collar angled out on one side like the broken wing of a small bird; he wore a lived-in, shapeless cardigan and had missed a button on the way down, so that the little bulge revealed the end of his tie every time he moved. Somewhere in transit, the long sparse hairs he normally combed over his bald crown had given up the unequal contest, and they hung down limply over one ear. His eyes were those of a disappointed basset hound. Slowly, he took wire-framed spectacles from his cardigan pocket and shook them open. He rested them on the tip of his nose with a heavy sigh.

Hugh rattled a long stream of Italian at him, but the man waved him to silence with a graceful gesture, as if he were moving a butterfly to a window.

'I speak English,' he said in a tired voice. 'I am Detective Fermi.'

He lifted his head and inclined it fractionally. Reluctantly, the police officers shuffled from the room; the last to leave glared at Michael from a puffed eye socket before slamming the door.

'Detective,' Hugh began, 'we are priests employed by a Vatican department. We are therefore under the protection of the Holy See—'

Again, the beautiful wave. 'Reverend Father,' the soft voice said. 'Whatever you do within the Vatican is the Pope's business. What you do in the Republic of Italy is mine. Now that we have clarified your position, perhaps I may ask you some questions.' He glanced at a single sheet of paper on his desk. 'Father O'Neill, my officers tell me they found you unconscious at the base of the fountain near the Pantheon. Can you tell me how you came to be there?'

Hugh glanced quickly in Michael's direction. Michael stared forward impassively.

'I believe I was showing my colleague the Pantheon and slipped on the steps of the fountain, hitting my head.'

Fermi nodded sagely. 'Do you usually show visitors the glories of the Pantheon after dark, Father?'

'No.'

'I see.'

The detective leaned forward and pressed a button on his desk. Immediately, the door opened and a police officer stepped inside.

'Father,' Fermi said sympathetically, 'I fear you may have suffered a mild concussion. Carlo here will take you to the infirmary, so that you may rest. I have no further questions for you at this time. Thank you.'

'But I—'

'Thank you, Father.'

When the door had closed behind Hugh and his escort, Fermi pulled off his spectacles and set them carefully on the table.

'You, Father, I suspect, will give me no more than your name, rank and serial number.'

There was a hint of a smile softening the corners of his eyes, but Michael showed no reaction. Sighing again, the detective pulled a sheet of paper to him and began to read. 'I will translate,' he said. 'Please pardon me if I get something wrong.'

His forefinger slid along the report as he read. 'Police alerted by a passer-by who witnessed a disturbance near the Pantheon. Officers were dispatched and apprehended five males. Four were unconscious and one was... let us say, making an unconscious man even more unconscious. While restraining the conscious male, Officer Borza received an injury to his right eye and Officer Rovere a blow to his testicles.' Fermi winced slightly. 'The other three males have been taken to the Emergency Department at the hospital of Santo Stefano. Ah yes, the medical bulletin: two broken noses, a bruised larynx, six stitches inserted in a head wound, a partially severed ear, a detached patella, et cetera, et cetera. All have regained consciousness and share a profound and collective amnesia concerning what happened in the piazza. Have you anything to say, Father?' he enquired mildly.

'No.'

'May I ask how long you have been in Rome?'

'About twelve hours.'

'And how long do you plan to stay, Father? I ask this so that a state of emergency may be declared.'

When Michael remained silent, Fermi leaned back in his chair. 'Let me be frank with you, Father. Very soon, I think, a very senior police officer will appear and ask me to vacate this chair. Within maybe ten minutes you will be driven, along with your companion, to the Vatican. Once you step inside St Peter's Square, none of this will have happened. No record will be kept of our conversation. The police officers know this, and they are angry. Would you indulge an old man, please, while he... conjectures?'

He leaned back in his chair and fixed his eyes on the ceiling. 'I believe you are, as your friend has claimed, a Catholic priest attached to a Vatican department. If my ear does not deceive me, you are Irish, though I think you have lived in the United States. I would surmise, from the injuries inflicted on the other men, that you have been in the army – maybe Special Forces. There are two things I find puzzling.' He raised a finger. 'The three men you disabled are known to us; they have a history of violent crime. Why would they give attention to two Catholic priests, and why in such an organised way? Two in a car and one on a motorcycle is not their usual modus operandi. They are known for their muscle rather than for their brains, Father. So who is the brain?'

'That's three questions.'

'Choose any two you prefer.'

'Off the record?'

'Yes.'

'On your honour?'

Detective Fermi sat upright. 'There is no answer to the question that need not be asked, Father,' he said firmly.

Michael nodded. 'We were followed from the Villa Farnesina by a car,' he began. 'The motor-cyclist stayed in front. When he signalled, all three vehicles went to the Pantheon. I was attacked there.'

'So Father O'Neill followed the signal?'

'I can't say that. We were going there anyway.'

Detective Fermi gave him a long, hard look. 'And the flashlight and book found at the scene?'

'I found them in the car.'

'So you knew this would happen?'

'I suspected.'

'And your companion?'

'I knocked him out, to keep him out of the way.'

'That wasn't what I was asking.'

'I know.'

The sound of raised voices swelled outside the door. Detective Fermi looked resignedly at his watch. 'Twelve minutes,' he murmured. 'I am, as you say, losing my touch.'

Quickly, he plucked a card from the desk and offered it to Michael. 'You have only delayed them, Father,' he said urgently. 'When you discover this for yourself, you will call me.'

Michael took the card and tucked it out of sight as the door opened and a police officer, wearing more gold braid than a four-star general, pushed past a protesting policeman.

'Thank you, Detective Fermi,' he said briskly, inclining his head to the door. 'If you please.'

The detective stood slowly. 'Good evening, Commissioner,' he said politely. He turned to Michael. 'Goodbye, Father Flaherty.'

As Fermi left the room, the commissioner peeled off his cap, set it under his arm and saluted stiffly. 'I am Commissioner Falcone. I must apologise, Father Flaherty, if you have been shown any disrespect. Father O'Neill is already in the car. I will transport you myself to the Vatican.'

'I've been treated with the utmost courtesy, Commissioner,' Michael said evenly.

'Good, good,' the commissioner replied. 'Did you perhaps speak of your ordeal with Detective Fermi?'

'Detective Fermi was most concerned about my injuries,' Michael replied tightly.

'Oh, but of course – how thoughtless of me. Please, we shall leave now.'

The commissioner did not speak again until he had parked the car at the end of the Via della Conciliazione, near the mouth of St Peter's Square.

'Cardinal Thomas wishes me to say that you, Father O'Neill, will convey Father Flaherty to the cardinal's office. He will be accommodated there. I will wait and bring you to the Irish College.'

The cleric at the desk in the Vatican corridor

narrowed his eyes as they approached, but remained seated. His hand was unsheathed from his sleeve and gestured them through. Only when they had passed the Swiss Guards did his hand reappear and reach for the telephone.

'*Sursum corda*,' he whispered into the receiver.

★

Michael knocked and entered. A golf ball slid across the carpet and bounced against his foot.

'Being in the wrong place seems to be a talent you've perfected, Father Flaherty.' Cardinal Thomas gestured with the putter. 'Sit down before you fall down.'

He wore an open-necked white shirt with the sleeves rolled up; apart from the ring, he wore no symbol of his office. 'You play golf?'

'I was born and brought up on an island, Eminence. It played hell with my long game.'

The cardinal smiled. 'I partner Archbishop Fortunata sometimes. He introduces me as his handicap.'

He leaned the putter against the desk and poured from a decanter into two heavy crystal tumblers. 'What do you say in your country?' he asked, raising his glass in a toast.

'We say "sláinte". It means "health".'

Cardinal Thomas looked critically at the marks on Michael's face. 'Under the circumstances, maybe "cheers" is more appropriate.'

Michael sipped, and felt the warm liquid infuse his body.

'Why are you smiling?'

'I was remembering a friend of mine on the Island. Whenever he broached a bottle, he'd throw the cap in the fire. It was his way of showing you were welcome.'

'Past tense?'

'Yes.'

'Why am I not surprised?' Cardinal Thomas sank into an armchair facing Michael. 'I hope you won't take this amiss,' he said, 'but you look like shit.'

'You should see the other guys,' Michael said grimly.

'I have – well, I've read the reports. Fortunately we have friends in high places within the police and the media; otherwise, your little escapade at the Pantheon would be manna from heaven to the more hysterical newspapers hereabouts. God, can't you just see the headlines: "Celtic Assault on Ancient Rome".'

'Why am I here, Eminence?' Michael spoke softly, but his tone signalled that the casual conversation had moved to a different plane.

'Long or short answer?'

Michael waved a hand, palm upwards.

'Why,' the cardinal said lightly, 'how very Roman of you.'

He settled his tumbler on the ornate occasional table beside him.

'Okay. Why are you here, as in here in my office tonight? Because Rome is and always has been a village, and the Vatican is a village within it. In this village, information is a marketable commodity; in its absence, rumour is a thriving black market. Add to the mix a hierarchical Church, a multi-tiered civil service of ambitious celibate men, all playing the information market for personal advantage or, God help us, for the glory of God... This is a theatre of war where I've learned to keep my friends close and my enemies even closer.'

'Which category do I fall into?'

'Time will tell. I'm hoping you'll feature among the former.'

'So why am I here?'

'You asked that already.'

'You told me why I'm here in your office. I'm asking why I'm here in Rome.'

'I asked for a soldier, and they sent you. I didn't expect you to go to war quite so soon.'

'Let's be clear on something, Eminence,' Michael said evenly. 'I went to war, as you put it, on my own terms. I didn't do it for you or for Mother Church, or even for the glory of God.'

'Okay, then let me try you with the long answer. You want to fortify yourself with a filler?'

'Will I need it?'

The cardinal filled both glasses before continuing.

'I already said that I asked for a soldier. That

may sound a tad dramatic to you, but I wanted someone like Agricola, the Roman general who left his farm to fight for his country and then went back to the plough after his triumph. I needed someone who has no ambition for advancement within the Church, who wasn't going to see me as a stepping stone. Your file says you're that kind of man. I need you because I'm at war – it's as simple as that.'

He heaved himself out of the armchair and went to a globe that stood beside his desk. 'The West fears a Third World War with Islam, China, maybe North Korea... That's all someday stuff, Michael, sometime down the line. What we have right now is a civil war within the Catholic Church. There are those who want to go back to the old certainties; those who've bought into the system. Their hope was that a pope from a ghetto church in a totalitarian state would take all the defensive skills he needed to survive there and bring them to the Universal Church. They under-estimated him, just as they underestimated John XXIII; the company man who broke ranks and called a Vatican Council.

'I... we believe those reactionaries are selling tickets for the Titanic. We believe the future is in the decentralisation of Church power, respect for cultural and religious difference, and a unity based on like-mindedness rather than sameness. I need someone to help me fight for these principles. That someone could be you, Michael Flaherty. Heck, I'm talking you to death. You want to go to bed?'

'In a while. Tell me about Monsignor Sebastiano Farnese.'

'Farnese is the Deputy Head of Vatican Radio, and he's longing to drop the adjective. The head honcho in Vatican Radio is old school – Curia to his marrow, safe and steady. The station is about as predictable and controlled as Tass or Pravda used to be. After just three months in the job, Sebastiano found the money to expand the service: new, powerful equipment, more correspondents on the ground. Now it has the capacity of a world service, but it has a gap where South America used to be, and the coverage of the US has expanded to fill the space. Lots of interviews with the president on abortion and the Secretary of State on the security of the Western world – and, of course, the Catholic ethos gets plenty of airtime.'

'Could he have got the money in America?' Michael asked.

'Yeah, it's possible. No shortage of philan-thropists when it comes to spreading the Gospel. Wealthy Southern Baptists wouldn't balk at piggy-backing on Vatican Radio, even if they figure its call-sign should be six-six-six.'

'What if it's not private?'

'Ah, now that opens up a much more sinister can of worms. "In the national interest" is such an interesting concept. Under that banner, you can set up Noriega, the Sandinistas and Saddam, and then send in the gunboats when they bite the hand that feeds them. Naïve or stupid – who knows? What we do know is that Reagan and the Pope were cosy. Reagan needed a lever to crack the Berlin Wall, and along came a Polish pope. How's that for timing? The cowboy's cowboy finds his partner Sundance, in the Vatican of all places, and suddenly Solidarity, the Polish trade union, is swimming in dollars. No guns, tanks and missiles this time, thank you very much; that's an Armageddon scenario. The guy with the birthmark in the Kremlin would have had to press the button on that one, or have it pressed for him. So it was photocopiers for inflammatory pamphlets, and the Pope went off to pray to the Madonna in Czechostowa. How's the movie so far?'

'I read the book. I know the ending.'

'Yeah, roll the credits as Reagan and Rome ride off into the sunset, the guys who won the West. Might is right because right is might, curtain and applause, sweep up the popcorn and Oscars all round.'

'But…?'

'Ah, yes, the inevitable but.' The cardinal spun the globe. 'Despite all the best efforts of mediaeval mapmakers and theologians, retired cowboys and Polish popes, the world is round. And round here' – his index finger stabbed the spinning globe, bringing it to a halt – 'round here, the natives are restless. Islam, Michael, has more believers than any other faith on earth. It has no Church, no priesthood, no dogma worth a damn, just a simple message for a largely illiterate population. La illaha illa Allah. There is no God but God. They look west and see Mammon ruled by infidels. If – when – they start to move, the fort ain't gonna hold them out. It's time for a different kind of treaty.'

'How do I feature in this movie, Eminence?'

'I need time. I have connections on both sides of the line, but my biggest problem is right here.'

'The Pope?'

'The Pope is dying, Michael,' Cardinal Thomas said flatly. 'The vultures are gathering, and I'm mighty high in their pecking order, if you'll pardon a bad pun. It doesn't bother me; I've been around long enough to play them at their own game. But there are rumours about another group – and if they're true, these new guys on the block make Opus Dei look like the Sistine Choir. We're talking people, at every level of the Church, who are thinking Crusade and who believe the end justifies the means.'

Slowly, he walked around the desk and sagged into the chair. 'There's something else you should know. I didn't tell you because... maybe I didn't want to scare you off. Before you and O'Neill showed up, I had two assistants, one from Rwanda and the other from Munich. The Rwandan got a call from home, some family matter he had to go back and sort out. He was a Hutu.'

'Past tense?'

'Yeah. They identified him by his dental records.'

'And the German?'

'Walked into a lake in Bavaria. Left a note tucked in his shoe. He confessed to having a predilection for... well, it doesn't matter. So now you know. It's your call whether to stay or go.'

'I'll sleep on it.'

'Okay. Get up when you're able. Good night, Michael. Pleasant dreams.'

17

The O'Donnell Apartment

'Over my dead body, Mal.'

'Unfortunate turn of phrase, under the circumstances.'

'Quit playing it for laughs, old man,' Hanny snapped. 'You're not using that room to play Sherlock Holmes with Rosa Luxemburg.'

Mal sighed. 'Torres, Hanny; Detective Torres. Can you keep the volume down, please?'

Hanny leaned across the kitchen table. 'I don't care if she's Frances Fu Manchu, there's no way—'

'Hanny, will you listen to me, *cailín*…'

'And you can shove the tooraloora where the sun don't—'

'Hanny, listen. You and me been walking on

eggshells ever since… well, since Michael left. No, hear me out now. You miss him, bad; I know that. For what it's worth, so do I.'

'Well, you did precious little to stop him going, Mal.'

'He's a grown man, Hanny. He had things to do and he did them.'

'That's not what I'm talking about, and you know it.'

'Okay. He's pissed with me. The army wanted him where they could keep an eye on him, in case he ever took it into his head to spill what he knew about that cock-up in South America. I argued different.'

'You let him go home to the Island because you needed bait for bigger fish.'

'I did. I risked him. There, it's said. And I did it because it was his only chance at anything like a normal life. He doesn't see it that way. He thinks I used him, and that hurts me… deeper than even you know, Hanny.'

They paused for breath. Hanny walked tiredly to the kitchen window and jerked it up a few inches. Mal wasn't sure if she wanted to let air in or let something more toxic out, but he was grateful for the waft of what passed for air in New York, and for the ordinary sounds of the city. She reseated herself and stretched her hand to his across the table. He took it and gently kneaded the back of her hand with his thumb.

'Look, Mal,' she began, and the anger had evaporated from her voice, 'I've been a cop's wife for thirty-odd years, so I know all about need-to-bloody-know, which means "don't ask" – and I don't. But… well, here goes nothing. I thought you had retired, and you hadn't. I thought you'd retired again, and suddenly I'm baking scones for a cardinal and a congressman who are doing some hugger-mugger with you in my kitchen. And now you want to set up a cop-shop in Michael's bedroom?'

'Who told you about the congressman?'

'Oh, for God's sake. Raymond told me – Raymond the all-seeing eye. And then you sashay home with—'

'Hanny!'

'"No scones this time, Hanny. We just want Michael's room."' She stopped talking and looked away. 'It's all I have left of him, Mal.'

'Oh, Hanny, I'm sorry… Look, let's forget the whole damn thing. I can scrounge someplace downtown.'

'I haven't asked my question.'

'Okay, so ask.'

'What are you investigating, Mal? Tell me now and shoot me later.'

'A nun fell under a train, Hanny.'

'Oh, Jesus.'

'Yeah. Except she was a savvy kid, a New Yorker, not the kind of girl who stands too close to the edge.

From what the congressman says, and the cardinal doesn't say, she had enemies inside the Church. His Eminence also says so far, so nothing, except that maybe a witness saw a priest acting strange in the subway station. And there's something else you should know. The guys in Virginia, the ones who wanted to keep tabs on Michael, say they got a request from a cardinal in Rome for an assistant. They sent Michael.'

'I don't understand.'

'Neither do I, and neither does Cardinal Wall; he's right out of the loop on this one. He says he'll keep an eye on things, but it just doesn't sit right.'

Hanny squeezed his hand. 'You wanna shoot me now?'

'Maybe after coffee.'

'So go fetch Dr Watson while I put on the kettle.'

'Detective Torres, Hanny.'

'Yeah, yeah.'

Torres was leafing through a pile of *National Geographic* magazines in the sitting room, sprawled in Mal's recliner, one leg tucked under her for comfort. For a brief moment, he wondered what it would be like to have a daughter.

'Like some coffee?' he asked.

'Hey, I don't know. They got a big article on coffee, right here in the *National Geographic*. Some people are saying the stuff is poison, you know.'

'If it makes you feel any better, we can switch cups when Hanny's not looking.'

★

They pulled the desk into the centre of the room and pushed back the bed. Mal tried not to look at all the things associated with Michael.

'This your son's room?' Detective Torres asked.

Diplomacy wasn't her strong suit, Mal thought. 'We had a friend staying for a while. Hanny and I don't have kids.'

'Oh. Okay. So, Detective O'Donnell, where do we start?'

'We start with you calling me Mal, if that's okay.'

'It's okay, if you call me Dolorosa Esmeralda Conchita.' She saw the expression on his face and laughed. 'Rosa is fine.'

'Dolorosa. Why did your mama give you such a sad name?'

'You should've known my papa,' she answered simply, all humour flown.

Time to move along, Mal chided himself. 'Maybe you could talk to the junkie and the news vendor, and I'll tackle the subway cop.'

'Whoa there. Do I detect a little stereotyping? The white cop speaks to the white cop, and Señorita Dolores Esmeralda Conchita Torres gets the two Hispanics.'

'You talk the language, Rosa,' Mal protested. 'I could miss something.'

'You, miss something? Never.'

She delved in her shoulder bag and pulled out a

huge pistol. In one fluid movement she checked the magazine and safety, before sliding it back into the bag. 'Let's go.'

'That's one hell of a piece, Rosa.'

'Yeah, I've had it since I graduated from cop college. The knife, I have since I was twelve years old.'

She looked at him, but he didn't ask.

★

When they got back from their interviews, Mal brought two mugs of coffee and a plate of buttered scones balanced on a tray into their make-shift incident room.

'Clear a space,' he grunted. 'An army marches on its stomach. What's so funny all of a sudden?'

'A Hispanic man in a kitchen is a tourist. Believe me, I know; I got six brothers.'

'Okay,' Mal said. 'To work.' He toasted her with his raised mug. 'Dug up any pearls of information?'

'Pearls come from oysters,' Rosa said dryly. 'You know, like seashells. No digging needed.'

She flipped her pad. 'Samuel Jones, Hispanic male, five ten. Distinguishing marks: five-inch scar on left cheek. Says he cut himself shaving. So he shaves with a chainsaw. We already know from the files about his love life with the powder, so let's move on. Says he heard banging in the next stall. When he came out, he saw a priest standing by the basins, except he wasn't.'

'Wasn't what?' Mal grunted around a mouthful of scone.

'Wasn't a priest. Says he had the black suit and the shirt and the…?' She pointed at her throat.

'Dog collar.'

'Really? That's what they call it? Boy, I never knew that.'

'Rosa.'

'Yeah, well, Samuel says this wasn't no priest, 'cause priests don't wear all that fancy stuff and walk around in hundred-dollar track shoes.'

'How'd he know what the shoes cost?'

'He moonlights selling track shoes on Madison, right outside the Nike store. He says they can't stand the competition, always calling the cops.'

'What did the priest look like?'

'I was getting to that. About six one, six two – bigger than our friend, anyways. Had a pale face.' Rosa threw her eyes up. 'So what's new? Black hair, combed in on both sides at the back.' She put her hands behind her head to demonstrate. 'Like John Travolta in that dance movie,' she added helpfully.

'It's called a duck-ass.'

'Really? That's what it's called? I never—'

'Rosa.'

'Okay, okay. That's it from Samuel.'

Mal wrote 'track shoes' on his pad and circled it. 'And the news vendor?'

Rosa swallowed a mouthful of coffee to fortify herself. 'Oh, boy. Roderigo Arroyo. Can this guy talk. Tell me you don't need to know about his sick wife, his six kids and his mother in the Dominican Republic.'

'No.'

'Neither did I, believe me. Says he knew the Hermana Kathleen. Sometimes she buys a paper to read on the train. Always asks…asked about his kids. Must have missed a lot of trains.'

She saw the expression on his face. 'Sorry, Mal.'

He waved her on.

'Roderigo says he saw a beggar in a yellow slicker near the stairs, when he was using the bathroom earlier. Noticed him 'cause he had the hood up. It wasn't raining that day, and it sure wasn't raining in the station. And yes, before you ask, Roderigo saw the track shoes. They looked too good; he wondered where the guy had stolen them. At the time of the accident, he says he saw Slicker Man running away. I checked him on the "away".' Mal nodded approvingly. 'He says everybody's running to the edge of the platform, and this one guy's running away from it. That's all she wrote.'

Mal underlined 'track shoes' within the circle. 'Okay, my turn. Subway cop saw a priest exiting the bathroom. He got distracted by the junkie – thought he was hitting on the padre – so very few details. White guy, black hair. A whole lot of nada.'

'Hey, you speak Spanish. Bueno.'

'I've just used up my entire Spanish vocabulary, Rosa.' Mal got up and began to pace. 'We got a priest, or a guy dressed as a priest, wearing new track shoes.'

'As you say: *nada*.'

'Maybe, maybe not. Let's just assume for a moment we're talking a genuine priest here. He's young, tall and has black hair.' He realised he was holding a framed photograph of Michael, taken in the seminary some years back, and replaced it quickly on a shelf.

'What about an identikit?' Rosa asked.

'Too little to go on. You got a street map of Manhattan?'

'Never leave home without it.'

He cleared the tray, and she laid it on the desk between them.

'Okay,' Mal said. 'See how many Catholic churches we can find in a ten-block radius of the subway.'

Rosa counted. 'I make it five. Think we should knock on doors?'

'No, not yet. Priests are like everyone else: they talk. Start rattling the bushes, and the bird will fly. I think we should pay a visit to St Patrick's Cathedral.'

'But it's outside our circle,' Rosa said, finding it with her finger on the map.

'We're going to see Cardinal Wall.'

'He's a suspect?'

'No,' Mal laughed, 'not yet.' He passed her coat across the table. 'You ever been to St Patrick's?'

'Nah. They give you a blood test at the door. No green, no beer, no entry.'

'Not funny, Rosa.'

18

Cardinal Wall's Office,
St Patrick's Cathedral, New York

'You want what?'

'I want the files on all the priests currently serving in these churches.' Mal handed the list to the cardinal.

'You got a warrant?'

'No, but I got someone willing to co-operate fully in the discovery of any and all material pertaining to the current investigation.'

'Who?'

'You.'

'And if I refuse?'

'I'll write to my congressman.'

The cardinal glowered at Mal and switched his glare to Rosa, who smiled.

'Monsignor,' Cardinal Wall said, 'I need the key to the archives.'

'Archives?'

'Yes, that's what I said.'

Monsignor Dalton looked suspiciously at Mal and Rosa before ushering the cardinal a little way down the corridor.

'Eminence,' he whispered, 'it is most irregular to grant access to the archives to… outsiders.'

'They're cops, Monsignor, and this isn't the Vatican State. The laws of the US apply to us, same as anyone else.'

'I presume they have a warrant?'

'You may indeed presume that, Monsignor, and you may further presume that I have seen and accepted it. The key, please.'

Under Monsignor Dalton's baleful eye, the cardinal unlocked a heavy oak door and the detectives passed through. The door was closed in Dalton's face, and he flinched as the lock turned from the inside.

He hurried to his desk and picked up the telephone. 'Sursum corda,' he whispered when the connection was made. He spoke rapidly into the receiver and listened intently to the response. Then he depressed the cradle and dialled again.

★

Mal laid the ten files on a long table in the aisle between towering shelves. 'I think we can manage from here, your Eminence,' he said evenly.

'Mal, a word. Excuse me, Miss.'

Cardinal Wall led the way into a narrow passage between the shelves. A mere six inches separated the two men when he turned to confront Mal.

'Let's be clear on something, Mal. There may be stuff in these files that's no one's goddamn business. So how do we proceed from here?'

Mal held his gaze. 'Well, your Eminence, this is how I see it. With regard to it being my goddamn business, let me remind you that I'm a cop. There is no file in the United States, from yours to the president's, to which I may not have access while pursuing an investigation.'

'What guarantees do I have that anything that isn't relevant to your investigation won't be divulged or acted upon outside this room?'

'I didn't have a warrant, Eminence. The DA couldn't run with it. Anyway, priests don't divulge what they discover in confidence. Why would you presume a cop would be any less ethical?'

'You should have been a Jesuit, Mal,' the cardinal said gruffly, but Mal's face remained impassive. 'Look, I'm sorry. It's just… I'm going way out on a limb here.'

'You know what they say, Eminence: you take the job, you take the bullet. It goes with the territory. Happens in our line of work all the time.' Mal's voice softened. 'We'll be out of here as soon as we can.'

For a moment Cardinal Wall looked as if he might say something; then he turned and left abruptly.

'Lock the door, please, Rosa,' Mal said. 'Okay, step one: we just look at the mug shots. Anyone who looks even vaguely like our man goes here.' He pointed to a clear space on the table. 'The others go straight back on the shelves.'

When they had finished scanning and sorting, the space on the table held three files.

'What are we looking for now?' Rosa asked.

Mal took a deep breath and exhaled. 'Rosa, I have to say this, okay? These files hold all sorts of stuff about these three priests, personal stuff that's got nothing to do with us. At least, that's true of two of them. You got any ideas on how we should handle this?'

She looked at him steadily for a moment. 'Need-to-know, huh? Seems to me there's no point in both of us reading the same stuff. So why don't you wait outside?' She laughed at his expression. 'Kidding! No, you read them, okay? Then you can tell me what I need to know.'

'Thank you, Rosa.'

'De nada, Mal.'

★

The Church of the Holy Spirit stood back from the street behind a cracked concrete car park. Compared to its high-rise neighbours, it looked hunched and self-conscious, shabby as a bag lady reflected in the shiny windows of the stores on Madison Avenue.

Some of the roof shingles lay askew, Mal noticed, and green damp deltas spread on the walls around the copper drainpipes.

'We're looking for a Father Bernard Roberts,' he said quietly, never taking his eyes from the church. 'This is his parish.'

'Three guys in the files had black hair and sallow skin, Mal. Why did you pick this guy?'

'You're right,' Mal conceded. 'All three fit the description you got from Samuel and Roderigo, but…'

'But what? Come on, Mal, don't tell me we're working on a hunch here.'

'Yes and no.'

Rosa rolled her eyes.

'No, hear me out. Let me ask you this. What do cops do when a partner goes bad?'

'We don't talk about it – well, not to outsiders, anyway.'

'Right. Now, what do the brass do?'

'I guess they unload the guy on another precinct, or call Internal Affairs to investigate.'

'So mostly it gets handled in house, right?'

'Right.'

'Why?'

Rosa shifted uncomfortably in her seat. 'Because… hell, I don't know. Maybe it's loyalty, or because we don't want civilians to know a cop can go bad.'

'The Catholic Church is the same, Rosa. They shift priests from one parish to another, maybe hoping the new place will straighten them out, or trying to keep them one step ahead of getting nailed and having the whole damn mess go public. Roberts' file had lines like "in the interests of discretion", "at the request of his pastor" and "to avoid scandal". That, and the fact that this guy has been moved four times in three years, add up to what?'

'Trouble,' she muttered.

'Yeah. And just how much trouble is what we have to discover.'

Glass fragments crunched beneath their feet as they passed the wire-meshed windows. The parish house stood a little apart from the side of the church, but seemed joined to it in shabby solidarity. A car parked outside crouched like an old hound, the bonnet snuffling down between the front tyres. Mal pressed the bell, and a single toll sounded deep in the unlit house. A square of light appeared through the frosted-glass panel of the front door, and a man's shape was silhouetted from behind.

'Who is it?' The voice sounded old and hesitant.

'Father, I'm Detective Mal O'Donnell and my partner is Detective Rosa Torres. I'm putting my ID through the mailbox, okay? We'd really appreciate a few minutes of your time.'

They saw the shape bend and straighten again. A bolt slid back, and then another. A key turned, and the door opened a crack.

'What is it this time, Officers?'

The breathy voice seemed to carry a freight of

fatalism. Mal saw a stooped, grey-haired man, about seventy years old. His face, in the yellow wash of the sodium lamps on the street, had the colour and texture of old parchment. Cracks radiated from the corners of his eyes and fissures from the sides of his nose. He wore a once-fawn cardigan, and one of his hands clutched the place near the top that was shy a button.

'Father John Lane?'

'Yes, that's me.'

'We'd like to chat for a few minutes, Father.'

'All right.'

'Inside, Father, if that's okay. More private.'

'Oh, yes – yes, of course. Please come in.'

Father Lane padded before them, down a long hallway that smelled of mould, and led them into a kitchen at the rear of the house. Mal thought Hanny would have described it as 'man-clean'. The plain wooden table was wiped bare, the washbasin was free of crockery and all the cupboards were shut.

'Will you sit down and I'll put on the kettle?'

'Please don't make anything for us, Father,' Mal said gently, easing himself into a kitchen chair. Rosa picked the one at the other end of the table, so that the old priest was left in between them.

'You see, Father, we're working on an investigation, and we're asking the clergy hereabouts for help,' Mal said. 'Are you alone here?'

'Eh… yes. Father Roberts is away.'

'Father Bernard Roberts? Where would he be?'

'Oh, he comes and goes. Hard to say.'

'It's just that we'd like a word.'

'Well, if… when he comes back, I'll get him to give you a call.'

Rosa's eyebrows semaphored: 'if', not 'when', and 'back' instead of 'in'.

Mal nodded. 'I know this is an unusual request, Father Lane, but I wonder if we could see Father Roberts' quarters. It's just a routine thing.'

'Well… I don't know, him being away and all. Is he in some kind of trouble?'

He nearly said 'again', Mal thought. 'Well, it's more that we want to eliminate him from our enquiries,' he said. He stood up, and Rosa followed. 'Upstairs, is it, Father? No' – as the old man made to rise – 'no point in putting the bother of the stairs on you.'

'It's right at the top,' Father Lane said.

The door at the top of the creaking stairs was locked. Rosa took something from her bag and jiggled it in the lock.

'They teach you that at cop college?' Mal whispered.

'Nah, my brother Pepito could open Fort Knox with a hairpin.'

'Bright boy, your brother.'

'Yeah, he graduates from Riker's Island Prison next fall.' She turned the handle, and the door swung open.

The small sitting room was spartan, the few

pieces of furniture edged perfectly around a square of thin carpet. A bookshelf, packed tight with solid hardbacks, flanked one wall. A small occasional table held pamphlets and magazines, their edges perfectly aligned.

'Mal,' Rosa whispered, 'this guy is so anally retentive he straightens cushions every time he stands up.'

'You start in the bedroom,' Mal murmured. 'I'll mosey around here.'

When she had stepped inside the bedroom door, he went to the bookcase and began to scan the spines. They were dogmatic and moral theology texts – of another era, he judged, from the plain hard covers and the solid script. The lower, more accessible shelves were crammed with devotional works: *The Heresies of the Second Vatican Council*; *The Church in Chains*; *Lefevre, the Last Catholic Bishop*… Mal was no theologian, but he had provoked Michael regularly and good-naturedly on Church topics, and had listened carefully as Michael talked of the various opinions within the Church. From what he remembered, the choice of books before him betokened a priest firmly fixed in the past and to the far right.

He switched his attention to the pamphlets and magazines on the low table. The right-wing motif continued as he checked the titles and contents pages: 'The Angelic Call to Arms', 'Why the Mass in English is Heresy'… Near the bottom of the pile, he found a magazine entitled *Armageddon: A Guide to the Final Conflict.* There was a dedication written in furious black: 'To Father Roberts, God's chosen and anointed servant.' Good for God, Mal thought, shaking his head.

He was copying the signature into his notebook when Rosa called.

He carefully aligned the pamphlets as he had found them and went into the bedroom. Apart from a large wardrobe,there was only a bed. Rosa was standing just inside the door, her back to the wall. She had her arms crossed, her hands tucked into her armpits as if she was cold.

'You okay?'

'Bad vibes here, Mal.'

'What've we got?'

'Okay,' she said. 'Bed's made up like maybe the guy was in the army sometime. In the wardrobe, he's got black shirts, socks and stuff, and vests – who wears vests, for God's sake?' She sounded angry. 'Black shoes, two black suits and a white collar.'

'Dog collar,' Mal said.

'Yes, dog collar,' Rosa said, and shivered.

'No track shoes?'

'No. Mal... look under the bed.'

He reached in and pulled out a small black suitcase. 'Was this locked?'

'It was,' Rosa said, keeping her eyes averted.

He reached inside and took out the magazines, giving them a cursory glance before he dropped them back and closed the lid. He stood and wiped his hand on his coat. 'Bad,' he said distantly.

'Sick bad, Mal,' Rosa said fiercely. 'He's got pictures of little boys and—'

'Rosa. Lower your voice. I'm sorry you had to see that stuff.'

He felt anger well up in him as he watched her pinched face. No goddamn track shoes, he thought. He took a deep breath and let it go.

'Let's get the hell out of here and have some coffee. My treat.'

'And a muffin?' she asked shakily.

'Hell, yeah,' he said, looking away as she struggled with tears. 'Let's blow the budget and have two… each. You go on out; I'll talk to the padre.'

Mal went back to the kitchen. 'Sorry for taking so long, Father. I think we're all done here.'

'Are you sure you won't have a cup of tea before you go? It's no trouble, no trouble at all.'

He detected a note of pleading in the old priest's voice and thought of Rosa waiting.

'No, thanks, Father. Maybe another time. You make sure to put the locks on when we're gone, okay?'

★

They sat on uncomfortable steel stools, picking at the muffins, their senses assaulted by rap music and the heady aroma of coffee flavours beyond counting. Mal looked at the frothy concoction in his mug and pushed it aside.

'Mal.'

'Yeah.'

'I'm sorry… about inside.'

'*De nada*, Rosa,' he said softly.

Rosa's eyes brimmed and tears slipped down her face, dropping into the ruins of her muffin.

'It's just my brother,' she said brokenly. 'The one I told you about.'

'Pepito?'

'Yeah. My father wasn't a good man – not a proper father, you know.'

She took the handkerchief he offered. 'Thanks.' She dabbed her eyes as if afraid to wet the hand-kerchief.

'So Pepito… he never told anyone, not even me, his sister. We only heard about it when he went to prison, the first time, and cut himself. The social worker there, he told her everything. He didn't tell me, Mal, all that time – his big tough sister.' She covered her eyes with the bunched handkerchief.

Out of the corner of his eye, Mal saw a beaming waitress bearing down on their table. He gave her the full benefit of a fierce blue-eyed stare, and she rocked on her heels before scurrying back to the counter. 'Give it a good blow, Rosa,' he said. 'Never mind the damn handkerchief.'

He looked away while she did running repairs to

her face. 'Why don't I drop you home? We can go dragon-hunting in the morning.'

'Thank you, no,' Rosa said huskily, and he welcomed the light in her eyes. 'I'm a cop,' she added simply. 'Anyway, an old guy like you, what you gonna do if you meet some badass – hit him with your walking stick?'

He feigned indignation, and she laughed, until she saw his expression and stopped.

'What is it?'

'Father Lane had the door bolted. He wasn't expecting Roberts back, and he's scared. I could feel it coming off him. Look, I'm going back, but you don't have to come. I can drive—'

'The hell I don't,' she drawled.

'That's the worst John Wayne imitation I've ever heard.'

'Hey, gringo, what'd you expect? We were the ones outside the Alamo, remember?'

*

On the way back, Mal asked Rosa to stop at a liquor store. As he stashed the bagged bottle at his feet, she said slyly, 'In cop college they call that entrapment, Detective.'

'Where I come from they call it *uisce beatha*, the water of life, Detective,' he said easily.

Father Lane went through the same door bolt ritual with agonising slowness. 'Did you forget something?'

'Nothing important,' Mal said, steering him into the kitchen. 'We thought we'd have a nightcap, and then Detective Torres figured you might join us in a drop.'

'That's very kind of you, young lady,' the old priest whispered, and Rosa blushed. Mal poured three generous measures into tumblers he had snagged from the kitchen cabinet.

'Great changes in the world today, Father,' he said when they were on their second glass.

'Oh, Lord, yes. All of them newfangled things nowadays, computers and the like – I can't make head nor tail—'

'Even in the Church?' Mal cut in.

'Even in the Church.' Father Lane sighed. 'You know, in my day it was a lot simpler. But, sure, that's change, and we have to move with—'

'A priest I know – Cardinal Wall, as a matter of fact – was telling me the younger priests are a different breed altogether.'

'Well, that's the truth. I don't know, they're more... closed, very serious. Isn't it extraordinary for them to be hanging on to the old ways?'

'Here,' Mal said, 'a bird never flew on one wing.' He splashed more whiskey into the priest's glass.

'Did I tell you I was in Cardinal Wall's class in seminary?' Father Lane said shyly.

'You did not. Aren't you the dark horse?'

The priest smiled self-deprecatingly. 'Ah, now, we weren't really close or anything. He was a great brain altogether. I knew he'd go far, and he did. I'd see him now and then, but after he got the big job he was busy. You know how it is. There wouldn't be much reason for his Eminence to come here. Neighbourhoods change when the young people marry out; there's only a handful of the old crowd left. It's all offices, you see; commuters rushing in and out to the city. I try to keep the church nice – well, inside, anyway – but... anyway, that's the way.'

'Did Father Roberts have any close friends?' Mal asked.

'No. Well, nobody called to the parish house, anyway.'

'What about phone calls, Father?' Rosa asked.

Father Lane seemed about to speak, but then he pressed his lips together.

'Maybe he got some calls from other priests,' Mal urged.

'Well, it's the oddest thing, but sometimes the phone rang twice and then stopped. He'd be down the stairs straight away. I'd tell him it was probably a wrong number, but he'd stand there in the hallway and then it would ring again. This morning, I was just in from mass, hanging up my coat, and it rang right beside me. At first I thought there was nobody on the line, but then the caller asked for him. No "hello" or anything, just "Father Roberts, please".'

'A man's voice?'

'Yes.' Again, Father Lane's lips stretched and tightened.

'I think maybe you knew the voice, Father Lane?'

'I couldn't…I couldn't be sure.'

He paused and seemed to carry on an internal dialogue, nodding to himself. Mal shook his head in Rosa's direction, and they waited.

'I think it was that fella in Saint Patrick's.'

Mal cocked a quizzical eyebrow.

'Ah, you know – Dalton.'

'The monsignor.'

Father Lane nodded.

'No love lost there, I think, Father?' Mal said quietly.

'No. I find him a bit… abrupt.' He leaned closer to Mal. 'I know the Good Book says we should prize charity above all else… but…'

'He can be difficult,' Mal offered.

'Difficult? Yes. I heard a priest say one time that we had only two total shits in this diocese, and Dalton was both of them. I hope I haven't scandalised you?'

'No, not at all. And was Father Roberts here this morning, to take the call?'

'Yes. Afterwards he was away out the door, without a goodbye or anything.'

'He's not coming back, is he, Father?'

'Is he in trouble?'

'I'm not sure.'

'I wouldn't wish trouble on him, but I'm glad he's gone.'

'There's one last thing, Father Lane,' Mal said

apologetically. 'We searched his room for a pair of track shoes. Couldn't find any trace of them.'

Father Lane bent down and began to untie his laces.

'They were a bit too big for me anyway,' he said quietly.

★

Carefully, Mal sealed the shoes in a plastic evidence bag. They drove in silence for a while.

'You know, Rosa, I'm not proud of my performance tonight. I poured whiskey into a lonely man and then pumped him dry.'

'It's the job, Mal.'

'I couldn't figure any other way.'

'What happens now?'

Mal was already on the phone. 'Harry. I need a favour.'

★

'I ain't done nothin',' Samuel Elroy Jones said, with more hope than defiance. He wished he could control his twitching fingers and tried to anchor them to his knees. Mal sat across the table from him and Rosa leaned against the side wall, so that Samuel's head swung from one to the other.

'You said the guy you saw in the subway station was dressed like a priest?' Mal said.

'Yeah, but he wasn't.'

'Wasn't what?'

'Wasn't a priest.'

Rosa grunted with impatience, but Mal fixed Samuel with a steady gaze. 'Why not?'

'I seen his track shoes. He's got all this priest stuff on, and he's wearing these track shoes.'

'You saw them clearly?'

'Yeah. The subway cop didn't want me botherin' him, but I seen him go up the stairs. That's when I seen his shoes.'

Mal bent and dipped into the bag at his feet. He placed the track shoes on the table, toes facing Samuel. After a moment, Samuel reached out and turned them the other way. 'Like this,' he said. Hunching over the table, he lifted the heels and held them close to his eyes. For what seemed to the two detectives like a long time, Samuel turned the shoes every which way, examining them carefully. Then he placed them back on the table and sat back. 'Yep,' he said.

'You saw a guy walk upstairs. You saw the backs of his shoes. So how come you're so certain?'

'I plead the Fifth Amendment.'

'Oh, for crying out loud.' Rosa wheeled from the wall and got in his face. 'Listen, Samuel. You give us grief—'

'Detective Torres!'

The steel in Mal's voice brought her up short.

'Detective Torres,' he continued mildly, 'I think Mr Jones would appreciate a coffee.'

Samuel smiled. 'Make it strong and black, honey, with four sugars.'

Rosa opened her mouth to protest. 'Thank you, Detective,' Mal said firmly. She threw him a withering glance as she left.

Mal slouched more comfortably in the chair and stretched his legs. 'Mr Jones,' he said easily, 'I figure I'm in the presence of a man who knows shoes.'

'You got that right, Detective.'

Samuel mirrored Mal's relaxed pose and cocked back his head. 'My first steady job was in Feinstein's. Jeez, we did the whole range, Bally and everything – handmade stuff, not like this crap.' He flicked the track shoes with a dismissive finger. 'Now, it's all mass produced, no hand lastin', no hand stitchin'.' He sat up abruptly and lifted the shoes. 'This is what you get when you pay ten cents an item to some poor bozo in North Korea. Heck, it's a livin' for the guy, but shoes they ain't.' He placed them before Mal. 'They got no stayin' power, Detective, you know what I'm tellin' you?' There was something in his tone that touched Mal.

'Kind of like me,' Samuel continued quietly, as if talking to himself. 'Most guys workin' in shoe stores just fit the feet. Me, I always fit the person, try to find out what they really want.' Mal saw a new energy creep into his gestures and heard it in his voice.

'Say a young guy comes in and he's lookin' for flash. Okay, we can do that, and in a nice box and a fancy bag with the logo big on the outside, and thank you, sir, have a nice day. Older guy comes by, big belly, ain't seen his damn feet like forever; we talkin' comfort. This is the shoe for you, sir, slip-on, soft upper and a real leather sole that's gonna let your feet breathe.'

He let out a long sigh and lapsed into silence.

'It's a rare thing to meet a guy nowadays who takes such a pride in his work,' Mal prompted.

'Took, Detective,' Samuel said. 'That's all long gone. Blew it all up my damn nose, you know how it is.'

'Yeah, I know,' Mal agreed softly. 'Fact is, Mr Jones, I would appreciate the benefit of your expertise. I could take these shoes to Forensics and hear a lotta stuff that won't help, but…'

He let the sentence hang and watched Samuel sit upright and flex his fingers like a concert pianist.

'So what we got here, Detective?' Samuel said, and Mal found himself cast in the role of apprentice to the master.

'A pair of track shoes?'

'No, sir,' Samuel declared with a shake of his head. 'Not a pair. What we got here is two track shoes. This one here' – he tapped the right shoe – 'is top-of-the-range. With its brother, it can set you back more than a hundred dollars.' He nudged the left shoe with his knuckle. 'This one is the poor relation. It's a fake, Detective.'

'They look identical to me,' Mal said.

'Yeah, to you, maybe. Look here. The stitchin' is shot to hell and the laces are topped with cheap plastic, already comin' loose.' He spun the shoes so the heels faced Mal. 'Okay, right shoe got dark blue at the back, and the left shoe? Yeah, he's shadin' to sky-blue. See this? The left heel worn way down; so either this guy hops on one leg a lot, or we got two different shoes.'

'Hell of a thing,' Mal breathed. 'Tell me more, maestro.'

'Listen and learn,' Samuel said and laughed at Mal's expression. He looks different when he laughs, Mal thought. He looks younger.

'These shoes come from a street vendor, most likely someone like me. We talkin' off the record here, Detective?'

'Just you and me, Mr Jones.'

'Okay, here's the scam. You know how shoe stores keep just one shoe on the shelf. Who's gonna steal one shoe? Me, that's who. One shoe here, one shoe there, pretty soon I got a dozen shoes. So then I go downmarket, like way down. I'm talkin' street guys with boxes of shoes or guys at Sunday markets. I'm lookin' for copies. Same colour, and they got the logo, but now it's spelled Nika, you with me?' Samuel brought his two hands together. 'Now, I got my pairs.'

He got to his feet and began to mime to his own narrative. 'I'm on the street. I hand the good shoe to the mark, put it right in his damn hand. I lean in close and start to snow the guy. Look at the colour, stitchin', logo, the whole nine yards. Fit it right on. Feel the cushioned toes and spring heels, yeah, flex your toes, sir. Ain't that good? How many guys you think ever look at the other shoe? The price is half the shoe-store price and the guy thinks the stuff is hot, but hey, who knows and who cares, and the cops don't ask to see your goddam shoes. Pop it in the bag, your change, sir, and you too, sir.' Suddenly exhausted, Samuel flopped back in the chair.

Mal lifted the shoes from the table. 'Are these the shoes you saw in the subway, Mr Jones?' he asked formally.

'Well, if they ain't, they're as close as never mind,' Samuel said firmly.

Mal shoved the shoes under his arm. 'It's been an education and a privilege, Mr Jones,' he said, and held out his hand.

'My pleasure, sir,' Samuel Leroy Jones said, and shook it.

★

Rosa kept her eyes fixed on the battered kettle in the dirty kitchen.

'A watched kettle never boils, Rosa,' Mal said helpfully. 'It helps to plug it in,' he added.

'What happened in there, Mal?' she asked.

He heard the tightness in her voice and closed the door, putting his back to it. 'Well,' he began, 'two detectives were questioning a guy who had information they needed, and one detective got in his face, so her partner gave her an out.'

'Like be a good little girl and fetch the coffee?'

'If she chooses to see it that way.'

Rosa leaned forward and stabbed the power button on the kettle. With her back to him, she exhaled. 'I blew it, didn't I?'

'No, as a matter of fact, you didn't. You might have, if you'd climbed on a high horse. Thanks for not doing that. Rosa, you gotta trust that I won't score points on you. We're partners, remember?'

She turned and smiled wanly. 'Did he sing?'

'Like a canary.'

19

Kennedy Airport, New York

Father Bernard Roberts had bought a soft holdall and packed it with underwear and socks before checking in. He sat in the departures area, behind the shield of *The New York Times*, tensing for the sound of a police siren or a tap on the shoulder. As the flight boarded, he saw he drew more deference than suspicion from the cabin crew; but the tension still knotted his stomach until the wheels lifted from the tarmac. At that moment, he exhaled and rubbed his palms on his knees.

'Really gets to you, huh?' the large man in the seat beside him grunted companionably. 'Getting it up and putting it down are the tricky bits. Old lady asks the pilot, "Son, are you sure you can get us down?" "Ma'am," the pilot says, "I ain't never left no one up here yet.'" He laughed at his own joke, his big frame heaving silently. Father Roberts smiled politely and became engrossed in the in-flight magazine.

Passport Control was a nod and an inclination of the head from a bored officer, and he was in Rome. 'Sursum corda', the sign read. It almost eclipsed the elderly nun who held it up defiantly amid the other placards. She looked like a tiny black asterisk in the multicoloured moving tapestry of Arrivals.

'Habemus ad dominum,' Father Roberts said. 'We have raised them up to the Lord.'

The hostel was perched on the slopes of the Janiculum Hill, set back from the road behind high walls and an ancient gate. He followed the Sister through a side door in the building and, by way of three flights of echoing stairs, to his room. Having tutted over the bunch of keys until she discovered the right one, she finally unlocked the door. He stepped inside, placing his bag on the tiled floor. When he turned to thank her, she had gone.

The room pleased him. It had a bed, a table, a chair, a small wardrobe and a kneeler. He stepped into the small, spotless bathroom and cupped cold water to his face.

As he unpacked the holdall, an envelope on the bedside locker caught his eye.

Caro —
Your service to Mother Church has been
exemplary. When you have refreshed yourself,
take a taxi to the bus station marked on the
enclosed map. You will come to Hadrian's Villa,
in Tivoli outside Rome, so that I may
congratulate you in person. Follow the signs to
the Maritime Theatre and remain there after the
official visiting hours end. I will make contact
with you.

It wasn't signed. Father Roberts tore it into small
pieces and placed them carefully in the wastepaper
basket beneath the table.

★

The sun was low in the sky, slanting long shadows
from the ruins across the lawns. The Maritime
Theatre consisted of a round pool with an island in
the middle, surrounded by stone columns. A group
of Japanese tourists trotted after their tour guide,
pausing to raise their long-lensed cameras. The
shadows between the columns flickered in the tiny
lightning burst and seemed to grow darker. Father
Roberts averted his face as they passed. When they
had gone, he walked across the causeway to the
island and stood gazing into the green, still water.

'This is where Hadrian found peace, Father
Roberts.'

The voice startled him, and he turned awkwardly on the smooth stones. The figure on the causeway had the garb and stillness of a Benedictine. A long cowl shadowed his face, and his hands were invisible in the voluminous sleeves.

'Imagine,' the man continued, 'a man who ruled over sixty million subjects came here for solitude.'

He had a preacher's voice, a voice that carried perfectly in the still air. Father Roberts felt a chill tickle his spine as the figure advanced.

'Like all the Romans,' the man said, 'Hadrian was a magpie. He gathered the shiny pieces of other civilisations and brought them here, or had his artists copy them. And what could possibly disturb such a man and keep him from his sleep?'

He paused between two shoulder-high columns.

'The barbarians might wish to recover their gods. And so Hadrian built a great wall and set garrisons along the fringes of the Empire. It was not enough. Perhaps the gods wanted more... a sacrifice. Hadrian loved art and architecture, but he loved Antinus – a boy, Father Roberts – even more.'

'I have been faithful,' Father Roberts whispered, and trembled at the strange, strangled voice that spoke from his own mouth. 'I killed the woman, the enemy of Mother Church.'

'Yes, you did, Father Roberts, but the barbarians are already in pursuit and will soon be battering on the gates of Rome. They must not find you.'

'Hide me.'

The figure stepped forward and unsheathed his hands from the long sleeves. Whatever faint hope still survived in Father Roberts died at that gesture. He inflated his chest to scream, but a hand locked on his throat. The air trapped in his lungs strained against the grip that closed his windpipe. He heard the blood pound in his ears as the figure pressed him back and over the edge of the pond. The water was only waist-high, and he thrashed to find his footing on the slimy bottom, but the other man had stepped into the pond with him, never easing the stranglehold.

'Hadrian took his boy lover Antinus to this very place, Father Roberts,' he said in that calm, chilling voice, 'and made of him a god.'

He bore down heavily until Father Roberts was on his knees, his upper body arching back. Tepid green water closed over his head, and his fingers scrabbled madly at the death-grip until they slowed and slipped away. Stefan gazed for some time into the sightless eyes, as if he might divine some mystery there.

★

Ippolito D'Este hated his job at Hadrian's Villa. He was a man who had turned disappointment into an art form. He had first worked at the villa as a gardener, but in his first week he had lost control of a mowing machine and reduced a priceless

Egyptian statue to fragments. In his brief career as a guide, he had led a party of Germans to a near-death experience on a monumental staircase that ended abruptly when, to his way of thinking, it should have continued. Now reduced to the rank of security officer, Ippolito was allowed to strut the grounds and glare at tourists to his heart's content; all he had to do was ensure they were all outside the gates at closing time. Apart from the courting couple, the twenty-six schoolchildren and the irate nun, this evening hadn't gone too badly.

He set his torch on the lip of stone that bordered the pond, so that the beam made a path across the still water. Carefully, he plucked two terrapins from his pockets and placed them on the bright racecourse. As they paddled forward, he imagined a million-euro bet riding on the fragile shell of the one to the left.

Typically, it bumped into an obstruction and stopped swimming. Ippolito's first reaction was to be disappointed. His second was to wrestle his walkie-talkie to his ear and call for help.

20

St Patrick's Cathedral, New York

'Is it past your bedtime?' Mal's voice asked, over the phone.

'Where are you?' Cardinal Wall said.

'Outside.'

'Come on up; you know the way.'

The cardinal replaced the phone and smiled. He recognised both his own lack of tact during their earlier conversation, and the olive branch Mal was offering now.

'I'll have a small one,' Mal said tiredly. 'Fill up your own.' He stretched his legs on the rug, and his knees cracked.

'Your days on the beat are behind you,' the cardinal remarked dryly.

'You can set that to music,' Mal replied, taking a sip from his tumbler.

He knew the cardinal would never ask, so he began to speak. 'I think Father Roberts may be our man.'

The cardinal halted the tumbler on its way to his lips. 'Roberts?'

Mal didn't help him.

'Heck, I can't put a face on the guy.' Wall sat up stiffly in the chair. 'Roll it out, Mal.'

'Roberts, Bernard, thirty-five years old, black hair, pale complexion, immaculate quarters except for the locked suitcase full of little-boy magazines under his perfectly made bed.'

Cardinal Wall's hand reached instinctively for the glass. With an effort of will, he withdrew it.

'Jesus,' he whispered.

'He has a whole raft of books,' Mal continued. 'You're the expert, but I'd say they start at the Council of Trent and go back. Pamphlets and magazines, too – Armageddon, the Rapture, take your pick. Is this a sickness or what?'

'If it is, it's an epidemic in the Church. A lot of the young guys… well, so I read, anyway…' The cardinal's voice trailed away. 'I don't know them, Mal; simple as that. I sit up here most days reading reports from the brass and writing orders for the grunts. I'm a damn desk sergeant.'

'I need you to find Roberts for me, Eminence. And when you do, I want him.'

'I'll do what I can. Anything else?'

'Yes, there is. The archives – who has access?'

'Me, and Dalton.'

Mal waited him out.

'Until today, I hadn't been inside the door for years. I give stuff to Dalton, and when I need information he gets it.'

'I can't talk about what I read in there today,' Mal said slowly, 'but it wouldn't be such a bad idea if there was just one key and you had it. That kind of information, in the wrong hands…'

There's a fine line between delegation and desertion, the cardinal thought. I gave Dalton access because it suited me not to be involved in the day-to-day. And, because I detest the bastard, I thought of it as a kind of punishment.

In Mal's eyes, he seemed to have aged since the conversation began. The energy that inflated him seemed to have run out, and he sagged in the big chair. But there was more, and he needed to hear it.

'I spent a bit of time with Father John Lane,' Mal said, 'the pastor at Holy Spirit.'

'Ah, yes, John Lane. We were at seminary together.'

'Have you been down that way recently?' Mal asked.

'No. I have the assistant bishops, young guys; they do the legwork.'

'Yes, of course. Lots of changes there. You know what a neighbourhood starts to look like when the kids go to the 'burbs?'

I don't know, Cardinal Wall thought, and you know I don't. Oh, Mal.

But Mal wasn't finished. 'Father Lane, your classmate…' He sighed. 'You know what Hanny did once? We weren't long married at the time. She had this old uncle, real black sheep of the family. Came out here because he was too odd even for Ireland. Worked in construction for years. Big money, big thirst… you know the story. He ended up on welfare in a basement room in Queens. Well, Hanny started asking the relations about him – and when Hanny asks, people better answer. One day I get home from the precinct and she's sitting at the kitchen table, still in her coat. So I sit down. We were maybe two years married, long enough for me to know when to say nothing. "Mal," she says, "what kind of human beings would let one of their own live like that?"'

He got up and stretched. 'We had him stay… oh, maybe eighteen months. He called me "cop" to the day he died. Is that the time? I'll be away home. Good night, Eminence.'

The cardinal didn't think it was, but he said, 'Good night, Mal,' anyway.

*

Cardinal Wall was learning. He was learning that, when it came to talking about its clergy, the Church had a code of *omertà* that made the Mafia appear garrulous. Five telephone calls later, he was also wondering if amnesia was a prerequisite for priesthood, and learning that silence was much more effective than shouting. Silence created a vacuum that sucked people into revelation.

On the sixth call, he struck pay-dirt. When the call was completed, he picked up the receiver and dialled again.

'Are you alone?'

'Just me and Rosa,' Mal said.

'Same difference,' the cardinal said generously. 'Write this down.'

After he replaced the receiver, he went to the window. The illuminated spire of St Patrick's filled the frame.

Never did see a damned thing from here, he thought.

The O'Donnell Apartment

Mal grinned. 'Rosa, gimme five.'

'You been drinking again?'

'The "again" hurts, Rosa. I got news for you. Our man is in Rome, staying in some hostel run by real nuns.'

'Real nuns?'

'You know, nuns like in the old days.'

Rosa gave him a look.

'Well, maybe my old days. Okay, here's the scene. I'll take the first flight I can get. You collect all the bits and pieces and drop them with Harry – only Harry, okay? Tell him nothing: need-to-know. Then follow me. I'll call and let you know where I am.'

'Rome,' Rosa said. 'What will I wear?'

'Doesn't matter,' Mal said absently, rummaging in a drawer for his passport.

'Gee, thanks, Detective,' she said sweetly.

'What? Oh, no – I didn't mean it like that.'

'Maybe I should wear armour – you know, like in the old days, when you were young. We'll be hunting dragons, right?'

Right in the dragon's lair, Mal thought, with Michael the archangel.

Church of St Rose of Lima, New York

Father Xavier raised his hands to give the blessing. It was, as usual, a lengthy one, and the server stifled a yawn.

'The mass is ended, go in peace,' the priest bellowed.

'Thanks be to God,' the server answered, with relief.

In the sacristy, Father Xavier folded his vestments with great precision and bedded them in the long drawer. He went to kneel before the icon of the Madonna and Child. It was a copy of Raphael's *Alba Madonna*; she held a book in her left hand, her index finger inserted like a bookmark to hold the page. 'Let the words of thy Holy Scriptures find an echo in my heart,' he prayed fervently. His eyes followed the Madonna's gaze to the focus of her attention, the Child in her lap. The Child gazed at a cross held by the child John the Baptist. 'Let my eyes be upon your cross, and let me accept martyrdom in your service,' Father Xavier pleaded. 'If this be thy holy will,' he added.

He couldn't resist looking down at his clasped hands for signs of stigmata. They were strong hands, roped with thick veins but, as yet, unpunctured by celestial nails. He sighed. How he longed for a sign that he was of the elect… Perhaps, he thought, the task he was about to accomplish today would elevate him out of the ordinary. The voice on the telephone had assured him it would.

Father Stefan had spoken of a policeman who stalked a faithful servant of the Church. Even now, he was on his way to Rome and would not turn from his task. 'He must be turned,' Father Stefan had whispered. 'He is a threat to our work. If we cannot strike his evil heart, let us strike what his heart holds dear and draw him back from the chase.'

Father Xavier had listened to his instructions. '*Volo*,' he had said firmly. 'I am willing.'

The O'Donnell Apartment

The elevator wheezed upward. It did nothing to improve Hanny's humour when it paused, a foot shy of her floor, before juddering level. Damn elevator is as old as I am, she thought.

She was three paces beyond apartment 3C when she heard the creak of the door. There were still things in this world she could bank on: death, taxes and Raymond.

'Oh, hi, Hanny.'

She loved the surprise in his voice, as if he didn't have her timed and hadn't acted out the same scene every goddamn day for… She had forgotten how many years. Today, it felt like forever.

Raymond was about half her age and twice her girth. His voice was muted, and his face was always immobile, lest any expression – interest, joy, sadness, any emotion at all – might be construed as unseemly by an onlooker. 'That's the thing with Raymond,' Hanny had once said to Mal. 'He acts like he's being watched all the time.'

'You been in his apartment?'

'Yeah, plenty of times.'

'Has he got a picture of his mother on the wall?'

'Mal!'

'You know, like the ones with the scary eyes that follow you around the room?'

Mal was impossible, she thought fondly; and he was on his way to Rome. She was in the Bronx with tired feet and Raymond.

'How was your day, Raymond?'

'Oh, pretty good. You know.'

Raymond was wearing tan deck shoes, lemon socks and off-white hopsack pants that tied with a cord. His sweater extended the lemon motif. It had a whitish pall, as if he had pressed the material with a very hot iron, and there was a drag mark puckering on one shoulder.

'Mal was in a hurry,' Raymond whispered.

'Isn't he always?' Hanny countered easily, and went on the offensive. 'You made that doctor's appointment?'

Raymond drew a sharp, shallow breath. 'Yes,' he said.

Lie, Hanny's antennae told her. She had noticed that scabby place on his left ear about a month before; as more and more of the ear reddened and turned raw, she had intensified her campaign to get Raymond to see the doctor.

'I'm putting on the kettle,' she said, 'if you'd like some tea.'

'Thank you, Hanny, but I have some chores.'

She hung her coat in the closet and kicked her shoes in for good measure. Coming home to an empty apartment wasn't unusual, but usually she knew Mal would be home, sooner or later. Snap out of it, she chided herself. Get the kettle boiling and switch on the idiot box. That's what old people do: they create artificial sound and light to fill the emptiness. She slammed the closet door shut.

St Rose of Lima Church

Father Xavier had never quite recovered from a stint as an army chaplain. Celebrating mass on parade grounds, without the benefit of amplification, had permanently upped his decibel and blood pressure levels. Even in repose, tension sparked from him like static electricity; sitting still was a form of exquisite torture for him. His deafening sermons were apocalyptic and uncompromising. The Kingdom of God could not come fast enough for Father Xavier, and, in his infrequent reflective moments, he liked to fantasise about the torments that would afflict those who whispered behind their hands as he passed. He felt their snide comments as barbs in his flesh. 'Xavier could preach in Los Angeles without ever going there... Xavier wanted to take 'Attila' as his name in religion... Xavier got a telegram from the Pope saying, "Cool it"...'

God, how he hated those dullards who spouted pseudo-liberal opinions and diluted the Gospel to meaningless platitudes. They were content to fiddle while Rome burned. They were content to tap their feet to the beat of the heretical band as the iceberg loomed. He alone shouted a warning from the mast. 'Repent, for the day of reckoning is at hand. Repent.'

He opened his eyes and looked down with surprise at the scratch marks on the prie-dieu. His fingernails were rimmed with brown varnish.

Someone coughed.

'What?'

'Would you like a glass of water?' the sacristan enquired tentatively.

The mocking voices rose once more to chorus in his head. 'There goes Xavier, one thumbscrew short of an Inquisition... There goes Xavier, two faggots short of a burning...'

And behold, he thought, in his torment they offered him hyssop on a sponge, to slake his thirst, and he would not drink of it. 'No,' he bellowed.

Would no one watch in his Gethsemane? Had he not called out in the night, begging for deliverance from the agony of his tortured mind, for some small ease for his soul? And that creeping Jesus, his Father Superior, had suggested that he might have been unwise not to continue seeing the psychologist... He remembered his last appointment – the panic rising in him, a surge of black, bitter bile; only by the grace of the all-powerful God had he resisted the urge to... His frame shuddered as he released the breath that burned in his chest. They sought to leech him of his fire, bleed away his passion so that he would be like them, ordinary. They were devils in his desert trial, and he would vanquish them.

He rose from the kneeler. 'Thank you, Mr Brown,' he said to the sacristan in calm, formal tones. As he closed the door gently behind him, the sacristan wiped a shaking hand across his eyes and wondered why Father Xavier was even more frightening when he was calm.

NYPD Station House, 42nd Street

Rosa spent fifteen minutes fielding Harry's questions and telling him absolutely nothing. Mal would be pleased, she thought. Harry was not.

'The deal was, what Mal knows, I know.'

'Sounds fair to me,' Rosa said.

'C'mon, Rosa, where the hell is he?'

'He said he'd be in touch. Bye, Harry.'

She spent forty-five minutes explaining the Rome trip to her mother in rapid Spanish.

'But, *querida*, Rome is in Europe, no? And who is this man you're going to?'

'Mama, listen to me. Europe is maybe six hours from New York. I couldn't drive to Canada in six hours.'

'You want to go to Canada? Why? It's always winter in Canada.'

Someday, Rosa vowed, she would write to the *National Geographic* Channel and threaten to sue if they didn't feature at least one programme on Canada that didn't include snow. 'Mama, I am not going to Canada. I'm going to Rome, in Italy.'

'With some *gringo*.'

'Detective O'Donnell is my partner, Mama. *Dios*, he's an old man, old enough to be my father.' She grimaced. Too late to bite her tongue: she had mentioned the F-word.

'Say God's name with no respect. This is what you learn in the cops?'

'Please tell Pepito I'll see him when I get back, okay?'

'Your brothers, Antonio and Pedro, they don't go away.'

Rosa glanced into the sitting room, at the two figures sprawled before the television, and wished they would go away. Preferably to Canada, in winter, and freeze their *cojones*. If they had any.

Bus 44, Manhattan to White Plains, New York

Father Xavier was being borne aloft on angels' wings, above the denizens of the sidewalks and the halls of Mammon on Fifth Avenue. 'Amen,' he breathed.

'Amen,' echoed the elderly black lady sunk in the seat beside him, her knitting needles never missing a beat.

My hour is almost nigh, he thought, and resolved to be silent. And, like a lamb, he opened not his mouth.

Click, click, click. The needles darted and plucked at the wool, like wolves harrying a flock.

New York

Rosa was packing. Passport, bag, money... Shit. Hanny. Rosa hadn't had a chance to thank her and say goodbye, and she felt guilty. Damn, she'd been practically living in the O'Donnells' apartment since all of this started, eating the scones and sandwiches Hanny dealt up with all the disinterested cool of a Vegas croupier. She and Hanny hadn't become close, and Rosa had found herself instinctively reserved with the older woman. Hanny seemed to like it that way. But, occasionally, they would lock eyes over Mal's head when he was being particularly stubborn, and there was a complicity in that look that warmed Rosa. Just go, she thought.

The O'Donnell Apartment

Hanny almost smiled when she heard the doorbell. Doesn't matter a damn who it is, she thought happily, Raymond or Mormons or the Avon lady; they're coming in. Out of habit, she flipped the spy-hole open before unlocking the door. Some of her euphoria evaporated, but beggars can't be choosers, as her mother had remarked when Hanny brought Mal home for the first time.

'Evening, Father,' she said, before she toppled backwards into the dark.

Father Xavier pocketed the cosh, stepped inside and shouldered the door shut. Hanny lay spreadeagled in the small hallway. He got his hands under her shoulders and dragged her into the sitting room. Her heels made a sighing sound on the carpet. Feverishly, he propped her in Mal's rocker and pulled a roll of industrial adhesive tape from his pocket. He wound it round her mouth and head, then tore strips for her wrists and ankles.

He sat on the sofa, breathing heavily. He would wait until she regained consciousness. Then he would recite the Act of Contrition, get her to nod her compliance and cut her throat.

★

Rosa loved the flowers. They had long, graceful stems and shy heads of yellow, red and purple, folded in on themselves as if embarrassed by their own beauty. Their scent seemed to envelop her, and she took a last satisfying sniff before she got out of the elevator.

★

Someone was speaking in Hanny's sleep.

'Do you have headache, nausea?' the voice asked.

'Yes,' Hanny whispered in her dream, 'and then some.'

'Take Dypsol,' the voice continued. 'Guaranteed to ease those aches away.'

'You pour it and I'll drink it,' Hanny murmured.

She opened her eyes and saw a bright-green sachet. She read the word 'Dypsol', and then someone moved and blocked the television screen.

'Don't be afraid, Mrs O'Donnell,' the priest said gently. 'No one is outside the mercy of God.'

★

'Jesus!' Rosa was already reaching for her gun when her brain kicked in. Why did Raymond always just appear like that? 'Oh, hi, Raymond,' she said shakily.

'Lovely flowers.'

'Hanny likes them. Sorry, Raymond, I have to run. Talk to you soon.'

'I hope nothing's amiss.'

'No, no, just a flight to catch.' Her finger was already stretching for the bell-push.

'I meant with the clergyman and all.'

'What clergyman?'

'He's just arrived. I hope he isn't the bearer of bad tidings?'

His eyes widened as Rosa's hand darted to her bag and swung up her gun.

'Raymond, call the cops, now.'

He backed into his apartment as she turned to Hanny's door. If it's bolted, I'm in deep shit, she thought. No way to pick this one. She took a swift pace back and ran at the door.

*

'And I firmly resolve, with the help of Thy grace, never more to offend Thee and to amend my life,' Father Xavier intoned. 'Say "Amen" in your heart, Mrs O'Donnell, and nod your head so I know you understand.'

He was a dead ringer for the pious young priest she had hated as a girl, Hanny thought. Except for the hunting knife.

*

The door flew open, and Rosa catapulted into the hallway. The polished wooden floor emptied her lungs on impact and she slid on her back, watching in a kind of slow motion horror as her gun slid out of reach. He was on her before she could rise, straddling her chest so that his knees pressed her arms to the floor.

As he raised the knife, Father Xavier heard a voice.

'May I be of some assistance?'

Instinctively, he half rose and turned. Rosa kicked. The priest screamed and dropped away on his knees. Damn, Rosa thought, he's between me and my gun. She was aware of Raymond framed in the doorway, and then the priest was coming at her, his face contorted, his knife extended. She knew Hanny was behind her in the living room. There was nowhere to go.

Her hand dropped to her ankle and brought the knife from its sheath. It was the one she had confiscated from Pepito all those years ago. 'Give it to me, *hermano*; I'll keep it safe for you.' At the time, it had looked huge and hungry, lying across his little-boy's palm. Now, face to face with the dragon, it was a toothpick. The dragon grinned and took a step forward.

Rosa thought the hallway bulged outward with the blast. The top of the dragon's head erupted, and she was blinded by a spray of blood. 'Hanny!' she screamed, but she was dumb; her throat ached, her mouth formed the word, but she heard nothing.

Faintly, behind the terrible ringing sound, she heard a voice. 'Rosa – Rosa!' Someone was wiping her eyes. Her vision smeared and cleared, and she was looking at Raymond's round face, at the bloody towel bunched between his hands. His lips moved, and she thought his flat whisper was the most beautiful sound in the universe.

'Rosa, I shot a priest,' he said, and his bottom lip trembled.

She reached forward, and he gave his face to her hands. 'You killed a dragon, Raymond,' she said. 'You're an archangel.'

*

Hanny clutched Rosa's hand. 'Call Mal and tell him I'm okay, please, Rosa?'

'Sure, Hanny,' Rosa said, and kissed her gently. She didn't look okay. Her left temple had risen to an angry bubble, the skin stretched taut and shiny. Her left eye was a slit, like the cleft in a plum.

But there was nothing wrong with the other eye, which held Rosa's gaze. 'You did real well, sweetheart,' Hanny whispered. 'He'll be so proud.'

The medics cranked the gurney and wheeled her away. A flashbulb popped and Rosa flinched. She saw Raymond sitting in the kitchen, a cassette recorder on the table winding in his story for the file. White-garbed figures moved like wraiths in the hallway, gathering the details, all the pieces of the picture that had juddered so violently through the shutters of her consciousness.

'You okay to make a statement, Detective?'

The man was young and black, and he gave

Rosa his full attention rather than looking at what lay behind her.

'Who are you?' she asked.

'Detective John Staines, Bronx Precinct.'

'How do I look, Detective?'

His perfect teeth snagged his lower lip for a second; then he leaned forward and whispered, 'Girl, you look like you rolled around in an abattoir.'

'I'd like a favour. Make that two.'

'Genie always grants three wishes,' he said seriously.

'I'd like to shower and change. I keep a bag here.'

He nodded.

'I'd like you to drop me to JFK; I have a flight to catch to Rome.'

'And the third?'

'I have to walk... through there.' She inclined her head to where the corpse lay behind her. 'Could you walk with me, please?'

John Staines smiled the most beautiful smile she had ever seen. Why is everyone and everything so beautiful? she wondered. Because I'm alive. 'Ma'am, it would be my pleasure.'

He walked beside her, shielding her from the corpse already squared off in yellow tape. She held his arm, and a silence fell over the Forensics team as they passed.

She was surprised to see Harry standing at the door. 'Picked it up on the wire,' he said. 'Sorry I'm late.'

He hugged her awkwardly. 'Way to go, Detective,' he whispered huskily. She could feel his body trembling.

En route to JFK Airport, New York

Detective Staines pressed the 'record' button and passed the cassette player. 'In your own time, Detective,' he said, switching on the revolving roof light and flooring the accclcrator.

Rosa kept her sanity by concentrating on her statement, and kept her own counsel about what she and Mal were investigating. Finally, she pressed 'stop' and stashed the recorder in the dash. Staines never took his eyes from the road.

'That's it?'

'That's it.'

'I get the impression you just told the complete story of *War and Peace* in six minutes.'

'It all happened very quickly.'

He seemed to chew on that for the rest of the journey. When the blur passing the window finally resolved itself into Arrivals at JFK, he turned in his seat and looked at her.

'Can I ask, Detective, what brought you to the O'Donnells' apartment in the first place?'

'I brought flowers for Mrs O'Donnell. Freesias.'

'Freesias. And when Raymond informed you that a Catholic clergyman was visiting Mrs O'Donnell, what brought you through the door like Annie Oakley?'

'Who's she?'

'C'mon, Detective Torres, your average Catholic priest does not constitute clear and present danger.'

His tone irked her. 'You know something, Detective Staines? In my experience, limited though that is, perps don't advertise. This "average Catholic priest" happened to have the mother of all hunting knives, and he was going to carve his way through me to get to Mrs O'Donnell until Raymond shot the top of his head off. Sorry.'

'No need to be, but it still doesn't answer my question. You know all that stuff now; you didn't then. So why did you think Mrs O'Donnell was in danger?'

'I can't answer that,' Rosa said tiredly.

'Can't or won't?'

'Both. It would jeopardise an investigation I'm working on. It's need-to-know, Detective; you got to take that on faith.'

'That's one hell of a leap of faith.'

'I drove to the airport with you, didn't I? What kind of leap of faith was that?'

'Detective Torres,' Staines said, 'I think you'd better give me your gun.'

'And the badge?'

'Only the gun. Unless you want to vacation in Guantanamo Bay.'

21

Santa Sabina Hospital, Rome

The guard's eyes were frisking Eli Weissman as soon as he turned into the corridor, checking the flapping white coat, especially under the arms. He's good, Eli thought. He flashed his ID and the guard nodded, his eyes sweeping back to the corridor.

The Pope was raised on a mound of pillows. His right hand sprouted an intravenous line that climbed to a suspended bottle. A clear plastic tube snaked from his nose. For a moment, Eli paused to look at the most photographed face in the world. The cheeks, he noticed approvingly, were less hectic. The corner of the Pope's mouth sagged a little, but the eyes, despite the drooping eyelids, were open and alert.

Eli stood at the foot of the bed. 'Good morning. I'm Dr Eli Weissman, the houseman in this hospital. I'd like to examine you, please.'

He would have said exactly the same to any other patient. 'Courtesy costs nothing,' he always told his team. 'Always introduce yourself. This is the patient's room and you are a guest. Always ask permission before you examine the patient or perform a procedure; it's bad enough to lose your health without losing your rights as a human being as well.' He knew they rolled their eyes in private, but he continued to press the point, and he always put his principles into practice.

The Pope nodded.

Eli moved to the side of the bed and adjusted his stethoscope. 'I'll listen to your heart first,' he said quietly. Vigorously, he rubbed the metal disc on his sleeve to warm it before applying it to the patient's chest. 'Your heartbeat is regular,' he said. He continued his examination and commentary through lungs, glands, ears and eyes.

When he had finished, he brought a chair to the bedside and made sure he was in the patient's eyeline. 'Have you any questions?' he asked.

The patient's lips moved soundlessly for a moment.

'You said, "I can't speak."'

The Pope stared at him for a moment in surprise, then he nodded.

'I lip-read,' Weissman said.

'Where I live, that would be an advantage,' the Pope mouthed. 'I have a question, Dr Weissman. Why don't you call me "Your Holiness" or "Holy Father"? Everyone else does. I'm not complaining, just curious.'

'I'm Jewish. In Trastevere, we don't get to talk to popes very often.'

The old man gazed at him intently, and then his shoulders began to shake. Eli realised, with relief, that the Pope was laughing. With trembling fingers, his patient tried to take a handkerchief from his sleeve, but it eluded him. 'May I?' Weissman asked; when his patient nodded assent, he took the handkerchief and dabbed it gently around the Pope's eyes, then folded it away again in his sleeve.

'I would like to be called something,' the Pope mouthed. 'My name is Karol.'

'Why don't I call you Pope?'

'Pope?'

'Yes. It's a job description, like "Doctor"; it's not too fancy or familiar. What do you say, Pope?'

'I think Pope will do fine, Doctor.'

'I must go do my rounds now. I'll call again later.'

'Give your other patients my blessing.'

'I don't think so, Pope,' Eli said, smiling. The Pope's shoulders were shaking again as he left the room.

★

Eli Weissman walked to and from the hospital in all weathers. He liked to change his route regularly and be surprised by a statue in a piazza, a weather-beaten wayside shrine tucked in a corner, or just the wind in his face and the strip of sky over his head. Home was Trastevere, across the Tiber, and his footsteps quickened as he turned by the synagogue into the warren of narrow streets.

Signora Fulvi waylaid him on the first landing. 'Signor Dottore, it's Filippo; he's coughing again.' Eli spent ten minutes diagnosing bronchitis and writing a prescription on the kitchen table, and then another ten minutes refusing a fee. There would be fresh bread in a basket outside his apartment door in the morning.

'You were ambushed,' his mother called cheerily from the kitchen. Sarah Weissman was a small, sprightly woman. She was standing on a low stool as she washed vegetables at the sink. Eli wrapped his arms around her from behind and swung her full circle until her feet dropped on to the stool again. She smelled of herbs. 'Dinner in twenty minutes,' she said, 'time enough for you to go to war with your uncle.'

'I'm starving,' he said.

'No, love,' she said calmly, 'you're just hungry.'

'I think I must have been good in a former life for God to give me a mother who's Jewish and Italian.'

She laughed, and then turned on the stool to face him. 'I worry about you, Eli.'

'Mama. Please.'

'I worry about what will become of you when
I—'

He put his finger to her lips.

'Careful, Mama: from your mouth to God's
ears.'

She took his hand and held it in both her own.
'Hearts mend, son, and life goes on. Believe me, I
know.'

'Eli,' a man's hoarse voice called from the sitting
room.

'You have been summoned to the war cabinet,'
Sarah said.

What would it be today, Eli wondered: the Stern
Gang, the Six Day War, or maybe Masada and Bar
Kochba? Uncle Ari had a tribal memory reaching
back, with great clarity and attention to detail,
almost to the Great Flood. Eli smiled as he
remembered his small-boy questions.

'And did our ancestors fight with King David,
Uncle Ari?'

'Fight with him?' the old man had said, for he
was an old man to Eli even then. 'Fight with him?
Your ancestors stood behind him and slung a
second stone at Goliath. King David couldn't hit a
barn door from inside the barn.'

Eli had been amazed at how much history he
had to unlearn when he went to school.

Uncle Ari sat where he always sat, in the chair
beside the window. Eli kissed his uncle, enjoying the

old man's feigned reluctance, and sat before him. He thought Uncle Ari looked a little more fragile than usual and resolved to invent some excuse so he could examine him later. Ari was his mother's big brother, lanky where she was petite, measured and method-ical where she was energetic and spontaneous. Today, he seemed more sombre and still than usual.

'Today, we talk about a pope,' he said abruptly.

Eli tried to mask his shock. 'Which one?'

'How many they got?'

'Just the one.'

'No, not that one. Any pope who gets himself shot by a Turk can't be all that bad. No, today we'll talk about Paul the Fourth. He's the one who put us here in Campo Di Fiori. We Jews came to Rome in the second century before the Christian era – so called; it has yet to kick in. Remember what Gandhi said when they asked him about Christianity?'

'Yes, he said, "I think it would be a good idea."'

'You're a bright lad, Eli,' his uncle said. Eli sensed he was none too pleased at having his punchline stolen, and resolved to give him free rein.

'So what happened after the second century?' he prompted.

'A Golden Age, boy. Jews were famous in Rome as moneymen and doctors. You see, nephew, you're in the right profession in the wrong century.'

'And Paul the Fourth?'

'In the sixteenth century, the Church had taken on all the vices of the world and raised them to the level of high art. But the pendulum always swings back, and Paul the Fourth almost swung it right out of the clock-case. Rome was the Augean Stables, boy, and could this pope shift shit.'

'Sounds like one of the good guys.'

'Yeah, you got that right,' Uncle Ari sneered. 'The problem with the Crusaders, boy, was that there was no handbrake on a horse. They started out charging the Moors in Jerusalem, and they carried on through the Jews, and even other Christians, before they could halt their gallop.'

'So Paul did the big clean-up of the Church. What then?'

'Paul was no Alexander. He wasn't going to weep because he had no more worlds to conquer. So he turned his beady eye to a new target. Guess who?'

'The Jews.'

'Did I tell you this before?'

'No, Uncle.'

'Then you must be getting smart or something. Where was I? Oh, yeah: July twenty-fifth in the year 1550, Paul serves an eviction order on Rome's Jews.'

'Where did they go?'

'Here, boy. It was a place of high walls, narrow streets and malaria. You're living in the original ghetto. Every Sunday, our people were marched to the Church of Sant'Angelo in Persoleria to hear a Christian sermon.'

'Well, those days are over,' Eli said soothingly.

Ari swung his eyes from the window and looked at his nephew. All the mad, gleeful rhetoric was gone from his voice when he spoke. 'I'll bet you a million euro that a professional man of your age said exactly that after Jerusalem, Masada, Paul the Fourth, Torquemada, Mussolini and Mengele. Bastards are boomerangs, Eli, they always come back. Tell me there isn't someone right now, in Iran or in the Vatican, who's hatching a jihad or a crusade – and tell me that, when they've purified their own in the refiner's fire, they won't come for the Jews again.'

Leonardo Da Vinci Airport, Rome

Someone, maybe John Staines, had put the cabin crew wise to what had happened. Rosa was upgraded and fêted all the way.

'Champagne, Madam?'

'Why not?' Hell, she thought, one glass of champagne is allowed in international airspace. As she raised the glass, she saw a single speck of dried blood on her thumb. She barely made it to the toilet before throwing up.

The Delta representative in Rome was straight out of *Vogue*, lean, tanned and courteous beyond the call of duty. He insisted on carrying Rosa's bag, and she regretted not having borrowed her friend Ligia's fancy suitcase. *Vogue*-man charmed her through Passport Control and Customs to the

arrivals hall, where, to her embarrassment, he kissed
her on both cheeks before gliding away.

In that moment of confusion, she looked up and
saw Mal. He was standing just outside the railing, up
to his broad hips in gesticulating Italians. 'Hanny's
fine, Mal,' she said.

'Yeah, I know. It would take more than that...'
And then his throat closed and he gulped.

Rosa wanted to put her arms around him, but she
hesitated and the moment passed. 'Thanks, partner,'
Mal said gruffly, and he was back to himself.

'You got your international driver's licence?' he
asked as they walked to the car park.

She patted her shoulder bag. 'Yes, sir. And my
passport, various items of clothing, footwear,
toiletries, complimentary eye-mask and inflatable
pillow – courtesy of Delta – and a St Christopher
medal from my mother, sir.'

'At ease, Detective. The St Christopher medal
should come in handy: you're driving.'

He talked her though the snarl of the highway and
under the Renaissance gateway of Porta Settimiana
to the Via Della Lungara, rubbernecking all the way
like a tourist, while Rosa hunched over the steering
wheel, hanging on with bloodless fingers.

'Left here... Okay, this is the Janiculum Hill,'
Mal said as the road curved upward. 'The hostel
should be somewhere over the top to our right.'

'Tell me I'm not hallucinating, Mal. Did I just
see a lighthouse over there?'

He laughed. 'Yeah, that's the Manfredi, a gift from the Italians in Argentina to the city of Rome. Heck, Rome is maybe sixteen miles from the sea, so who was pulling whose chain? Slow down here.'

Mal rolled out of the car and bustled to the gate. He stuck his finger on the buzzer and kept it there.

After a full minute, a small shutter snapped back. '*Prego*?' an irate voice called from the other side.

'*Polizia*,' Mal grunted, waving his ID swiftly across the aperture. He heard the bolts begin to move and got back in the car.

'Like a bat out of hell, Rosa,' he murmured.

Even before the gates opened wide enough to admit them, she was revving against the handbrake. They sped through, spitting gravel at the gate-keeper, who jumped smartly off the driveway. Mal repeated his finger-to-buzzer ritual at the heavy, iron-flanged front door, until it swung open to reveal an elderly Sister. '*Polizia*,' he barked again. 'Father Roberts, *per favore*.'

The Sister hurried back down a long, dim hallway, gesturing for them to follow. Mal and Rosa dogged her heels, pounding the marble floor. She stopped abruptly and opened a door with a flourish. '*La polizia*,' she announced, and hurried away.

Mal and Rosa stepped into the room, and the door was closed behind them by a uniformed police-man, who put his back to it. The man sitting at the desk looked at them with an expression of wry amusement.

'If you are the *polizia*,' Detective Fermi said, 'then who are we?'

★

Detective Fermi, or so his admirers claimed, could spot a policeman at a hundred yards on a nudist beach. Even his detractors were prepared to admit that he was a cultured and intelligent man, for a detective; only his friends knew of his two private passions, his wife Cybele and Westerns. He looked keenly at the unlikely pair. The man was a policeman, he concluded: John Wayne without the pigeon-toed strut. He didn't doubt the man could play the aw-shucks charmer when need be, but he had a gunslinger's steel in his eyes. The woman was Hispanic, with more than a hint of Maya around her nose and eyes; where the man was calm, she was coiled, her eyes ranging the room for escape or advantage.

'Please be seated,' Fermi said, and nodded to the uniform. The door opened and closed.

Fermi raised a finger. 'Option one: we talk police talk – no bullshit, as you Americans say. Maybe we arrive at common ground. Option two' – another finger flicked free of his fist before it closed again – 'you play… hardball? Yes, hardball. You want to talk to your embassy, et cetera, et cetera. Then I play "impersonating police officers" and many other silly bureaucratic games, which keep you wrapped in red tape until Uncle Sam sends the US cavalry riding over the hill.' He sat back with a contented smile.

'Option three,' Mal said calmly. 'We lobby American movie distributors to place an immediate embargo on the export of all Westerns to Italy, and most of your vocabulary goes down the toilet.'

Fermi smiled. 'Okay,' he said slowly, 'you show me yours and I show you mine.'

'Jesus,' Rosa grunted, and rolled her eyes.

'Detective Mal O'Donnell and Detective Rosa Torres, New York Police Department,' Mal said.

'Detective Giuseppe Fermi, Police Department of Rome.'

'We're looking for a Father Roberts, a priest of the Archdiocese of New York. He's a suspect in the possible homicide of Sister Kathleen O'Reilly.'

'I beat you to the draw,' Fermi said without humour, plucking a photograph from a folder and sliding it across the desk.

Mal and Rosa leaned forward to examine it. It was a standard mortuary portrait, functional rather than artistic, but horror was stamped indelibly on the dead face.

'Cause of death?' Mal asked.

'He was drowned.'

'Accidentally or deliberately?' Mal said.

'He was held beneath the water. There are marks on his throat.'

'Scene of the crime?'

'The Maritime Theatre in Hadrian's Villa. It is near Tivoli, outside Rome.'

'So,' Mal said slowly, 'this Father Roberts flees New York and finds sanctuary here. Anything in his room?'

'No, but his personal effects back up your flight theory. Everything was bought at the airport in New York, even the bag.'

Mal nodded. 'Shortly after his arrival, he leaves Rome for this villa and is murdered by person or persons unknown. Why?'

'Let's consider the first "why",' Fermi said briskly. 'Why would he leave the hostel? It is, as you say, his sanctuary. Why risk travelling to the city, and then to a popular tourist site like Hadrian's Villa? Now to the second "why": why was he murdered?'

'There's a third "why", Detective Fermi.'

The two men turned to Rosa.

'Why aren't you surprised by any of this?'

Fermi tried to look surprised. 'You know, Detective Torres,' he said, 'the artist Titian painted a portrait of a lady just like you in the sixteenth century. It is a delight.'

'You know, Detective Fermi, I painted my mama's kitchen sky-blue last spring. She hated it.'

Fermi drummed his fingers on the desk for a moment, an abstracted expression on his face. He sighed and looked directly at Rosa.

'I will answer your question, Detective, but not here.'

He had resolved to show them something that had never been seen outside the sanctuary of his home.

The Fermi Apartment, Rome

Cybele Fermi pecked her husband on both cheeks and ushered her guests into a drawing room. It was obviously Fermi's den, lined with books and strewn with papers. An almond-eyed Ethiopian saint gazed impassively from a gilded frame on the wall, and three armchairs squatted around a square of Persian carpet. Signora Fermi looked at the mess and sighed. She turned to Rosa and made a face that said, in any language, Men!

'You see this Persian carpet?' Fermi pointed. 'Twenty-five years we have had this, and I still can't find the mistake.'

Mal and Rosa looked puzzled.

'The Muslim weaver will always make a deliberate mistake. It is a mark of respect for Allah, who alone creates perfection.'

Mal and Rosa sat in the armchairs, careful to keep their feet from the carpet. Signora Fermi ghosted back into the room with a tray of coffee and pastries, edging the pastry plate a little closer to Rosa before she left.

'Now that you are guests in my home, perhaps we can dispense with formality,' Fermi said as he poured viscous liquid into tiny china cups. 'I am Giuseppe.'

'Rosa.'

'Mal.'

'Short for what name?' Fermi enquired, taking a heaped spoonful of sugar.

'Malachy,' Mal said reluctantly. 'He was an Irish saint.'

'You are the second Irishman I have met recently,' Fermi said conversationally. 'The other was named for an archangel – Michael, Michael Flaherty.'

'Michael,' Mal breathed.

'Yes. A warrior-priest.' Fermi smiled. 'You know him?'

'I might. You were going to explain…'

'Ah, yes, forgive me. I have the mind of a magpie, distracted all the time.'

He stood and opened a filing cabinet. Rosa caught Mal's eye and raised an eyebrow; he immediately found his coffee extremely interesting. Later, partner, she thought.

The file Fermi placed on the low coffee table between them was bulky with documents and photographs. He took a last fortifying sip of what Rosa was beginning to believe was napalm, and began.

'For some time, we… I have been interested in crimes involving Catholic religious persons.'

'As perpetrators or victims?' Mal asked.

Fermi shrugged eloquently. 'Possibly both,' he said distantly, flipping the file open. 'This is a priest, an English theologian. He was found floating in the Cloaca Maxima.'

'The what?' Rosa interjected.

'Ah, pardon – the Cloaca Maxima. It is the remains of the great sewer of ancient Rome. These days, it is a place for tourists. I believe a Japanese tourist discovered the body and twenty-five others recorded it on film.'

They both smiled before they realised he was serious.

'Was he drowned, too?' Rosa asked, reaching for a pastry.

'No, his neck was broken elsewhere. Also, it was difficult to establish identification. The rats, you see.'

Carefully, she put the pastry back on the plate.

'There are, perhaps, seven others: four priests, two Brothers and a Sister. Of the eight, one was in Florence, one in Naples and the rest in Rome.'

'What kind of time frame are we talking here?' Mal asked.

'A six-month period,' Fermi replied woodenly, and closed the file.

'All murders?'

'Yes.'

'I don't know how to put this diplomatically,' Mal said, and Fermi waved him on. 'It sounds to me like some sort of vendetta, or...'

Fermi completed the sentence. 'Or a jihad – no, that is not the correct word when speaking of Christians. Perhaps "crusade" is more correct?'

'Was there any link between the victims, apart from the fact that they were all religious?' Rosa asked.

'I suspect there was a link.'

'You suspect?'

Fermi sighed. 'There is something I must explain to you, if it does not try your patience.' This time it was Mal who waved permission to proceed.

'Italy is a republic,' Fermi began, 'but the Vatican is a state within a state. In my experience, any crime involving clergy is… influenced. By the Vatican. There are people within the police department who have connections with the Vatican. High people,' he added, pointing helpfully at the ceiling. 'These people are invited to the Vatican for visits, with their wives and families. They have an audience with the Pope, get a photograph, you know. Sometimes they receive honours, like a knighthood.'

'But not you,' Mal said quietly.

'No, not me. I am *persona non grata*, you understand?'

They understood only too well. Substitute New York for the Vatican, and the story still played the same way.

'So things happen. Someone there speaks to someone here, and files go missing, evidence is lost. And I… a detective is moved from this case to that case.'

'Sounds just like the Mafia,' Mal said.

'The Mafia are innocents compared to the

Borgias, and the Borgias produced popes and poisoners.'

'So you collect this stuff and investigate it in your own time?' Rosa asked.

'Yes. You asked about links. Five of the seven victims held important positions in the Church: a First Secretary in the Vatican Diplomatic Corps; an editor of an influential magazine; the head of a commission to investigate the sexual abuse of African nuns – that was the Sister.'

'Who abused them?' Rosa prodded.

'Allegedly, Catholic clergy,' Fermi answered. 'Another was a television presenter, very popular among the young, I believe.'

'And the fifth?' Mal asked.

'The fifth was my younger brother,' Fermi said quietly.

In the sudden quiet, Rosa heard a clock ticking. Her eyes found it on a highly polished side table studded with photographs in heavy silver frames. The one nearest the clock showed a young man in clerical cassock and collar. He was smiling, as someone does who has an aversion to being photo-graphed but would never risk offending by refusing. Fermi's hand hovered over the file as if he was working up the courage to open it.

'Just a minute.' Rosa went to the table and lifted the photograph. With both hands, she offered it to the ashen-faced Fermi. 'Is this your brother, Giuseppe?'

Tenderly, he took it from her. 'This is Francesco,' he said, as if to himself, rubbing the photograph softly with his thumb.

'He was very handsome,' Rosa murmured.

'Thank you,' he said with difficulty. 'He was my younger brother. As you can see, he took after the handsome side of the family.' He placed the picture on the table between them. 'Francesco got all the brains as well, but he wanted only to be a priest. Even Mama tried to change his mind, but no. After he was made a priest, he became a theologian and taught other priests. Many students, many lectures, many books and articles,' he said proudly. 'He didn't come home very often, always busy, busy. I asked him to visit here, but always he had a deadline, or he had to meet a visiting theologian from South America... Then he came, one day, and what did I say? I said, "Francesco, you are a wonderful priest but a lousy brother."' For a moment, Fermi's face was stricken. He swallowed and continued.

'He was pale and his hands trembled, like an old man's. I said, "Are you sick?" He said nothing. He showed me a letter. It said, "If thy right hand sin against thee, cut it off and throw it away. Is it not better that one part of the body should perish than that the whole body perish in everlasting fire?"'

Some deep instinct tightened Rosa's stomach. She knew what was coming and wished she didn't.

'I begged him, "Don't go back,"' Fermi said, his

voice no more than a murmur, his eyes unfocused. "'Stay with us, your family, and we will protect you. I will protect you." He said to me, "They are everywhere, brother. I must trust the Church to protect me.""

He snorted a terrible travesty of a laugh.

'And then, he was not at his lectures in the university. His room was empty, as if he had just left a moment before and would return. His friends had not seen him or heard from him, his superiors had no idea where he could be. I am a policeman for almost thirty years, I didn't need a lie detector, and no one has invented a fear detector; but they smelled of fear, and I am certain some of them lied.

'They found him in the Campo Di Fiori market, hanging from the statue of Giordano Bruno – who was a Dominican, like my brother, and was executed for heresy. The verdict was suicide. Everything was *in camera* – closed court, you know. To avoid scandal, they said. Suicide by hanging is something I have seen too many times, my friends, but never by someone who has first cut off his right hand.'

They sat in silence for a long time, listening to the rhythmic tick of the clock. Then Fermi seemed to shake himself. 'You must be tired,' he said to Rosa, 'and you also, Mal. Maybe tomorrow I can come to your hotel and we can, as you Americans say, shoot the breeze.'

This is how he deals with horror, Rosa thought: taking refuge in one kind of jive-talk or another, making bad jokes to keep the party going, until the lights go out. And then?

They stood, and Rosa surprised Fermi and herself by kissing him on both cheeks.

22

Alitalia Flight 190,
Rome to Bamaka, Mali, West Africa

Archbishop Jean-Baptiste Leclerc touched his shirt pocket for comfort as the jet bucked in the thermals over Mali. His new passport bulked reassuringly inside the fabric. He swung his head to the window, watching the brown landscape gather speed below.

'Please fasten your safety belts and put your seats in the upright position. We will shortly be landing at Bamako Airport.'

Instinctively, he made to cross himself and thought better of it, lowering his hand to touch the talisman in his pocket one more time. He knew every page of it by heart: the entry stamps from the countries he'd never visited, the perfect copy of his visa, the line that listed his occupation as 'ornithologist'. Only the photograph was genuine; the usual expressionless photograph from an airport booth – except, of course, that it hadn't been taken in a booth but by a very professional young Franciscan Brother in the Vatican, who had worked hard at making it appear authentic.

'And what do you know of birds, your Grace?' the little Italian ornithologist assigned to prepare him had asked.

'I could write my entire knowledge of birds on a postage stamp, Signor Agnelli, and still have space for footnotes.'

Agnelli's hands had fluttered like agitated sparrows before coming to roost again on his pinstriped knees. 'I think we can dispense with my "birds of the world" lecture and concentrate on the birds of Mali,' he had sighed.

Whatever his admitted ignorance of Avis Avis, Archbishop Leclerc was blessed with a photographic memory, and he had duly amazed his diminutive tutor by riffling through the presented text and reciting it back, almost verbatim.

'Perhaps his Grace is similarly blessed in the subject of racehorses?' Agnelli had enquired slyly.

Leclerc had spread his hands in apology.

'Ah, such a waste of a gift,' the little man had grumbled.

The same eidetic memory had been a boon in other ways. Leclerc spoke seven languages fluently, including Arabic.

Once more, his hand went to his pocket as the wheels kissed and then gripped the tarmac. He joined the conga line of sweating tourists standing vainly under a single fan that turned with infinite slowness through the treacly air. His shirt was already moulded to his body by the time he emerged into a maelstrom of beggars. '*Mange, mange? Porteur, monsieur?*' 'Bic, Bic!' the little ones chirped, hoping for a biro. His briefing had been thorough, and he distributed the rank of pens in his top pocket to their delight.

A tall black man in a starched brown safari suit waded towards him. 'Monsieur Bergerac?'

'Yes.'

'Come this way, please.'

The driver had left the engine running, and the cold air inside the Land Rover prickled Leclerc's skin.

'Djenne,' his driver announced.

'Yes, Djenne,' he answered, settling himself for the four-hour journey.

Eight hours later, they arrived at the ferry crossing outside Djenne. Leclerc had not been briefed on the intermittent roadblocks along the way, where police and army personnel palmed the money and barely glanced at his papers. Mali was perhaps the poorest country in Africa, he reminded himself. Once the crossroads for traders going between the Sahara to the north and the tropical forests to the south, it had been a rich centre of

Islamic learning; but then the Caravelle had replaced the caravan, and Mali had nothing to sell which the world wanted. Leclerc looked out at the unrelieved drabness of the landscape, at the children and hawkers and beggars who clustered and clamoured like flies at every halt on the road, and prayed that the pilgrimage he had undertaken might bring some relief to the sufferings of these people.

It was a short, bumpy ride from the ferry dock to the city of Djenne itself, and it was the smells that first heralded the town. No book can prepare you for this, Leclerc thought, breathing shallowly through his mouth. The smell was almost as tangible as the mud-brick houses that flitted by, but as varied and textured as the houses were similar and bland. The light was fading fast, in this country without twilight, when they bumped into the square and Leclerc saw the silhouette of the largest man-made mud-brick building in the world. It bulked before him in the half-dark, but his prodigious memory supplied the details.

The entire structure was made of mud bricks, mud mixed with rice husks for binding; the Hebrews had performed the same miracle in Egypt, using straw in the mix, and then rebelled when the pharaoh demanded more bricks for less straw. There were minarets jutting up from the flat roof; each one was topped with an incongruous ostrich egg, a symbol of fertility common to mosques, churches and temples all over West Africa. Leclerc knew there were palm poles jutting out at intervals from the plastered exterior; these served as scaffolding for the annual replastering, and allowed for the expansion and contraction that occurred throughout the torrid days and cooler nights. He knew there were little vents in the roof that released warm air and cooled the interior; these had decorated ceramic lids and were operated by women.

'Follow me, please.'

They had parked close to the wall of the mosque, so their entry would be occluded by the Land Rover. Leclerc followed his driver to the steps, passing a sign that he knew prohibited the entry of anyone not 'Mussulman'. Outside the door, he shuffled out of his shoes, aware that his driver was doing likewise, aware also that the driver would gather both pairs to avoid suspicion. As his eyes adjusted to the gloom of the interior, he saw the outline of a man seated on a square of carpet that was colourless in the interior darkness.

'*La illaha illa Allah,*' Leclerc whispered in greeting. 'There is no God but God.'

'And Mohammed is his Prophet,' the man echoed, gesturing to the carpet before him. Leclerc sat down gratefully, folding his long legs beneath him. The man before him was Ibrahim Sharif, an imam, the religious leader of the liberal Muslim faction in Mali. He was also chief of a progressive and successful tribe, which some reports suggested would soon replace the present government and reform the country.

'Good friend,' the man began softly, in French, 'we will excuse each other the usual courtesies. What we must say has to be said quickly and simply.'

'Very well.'

'Our world is awash with blood,' the imam continued. 'We wonder if perhaps civilisation is but a *djinn*, a desert spirit that seduces in the night and is no more than a mirage in the light of day. Some of us consider the popular text, "An eye for and eye and a tooth for a tooth," and conclude that it will result in a world that is unable to see or eat. We are weary of never-ending jihads that sacrifice the gullible in the name of Allah.' He touched his breast briefly in blessing. 'These bring bloodshed and heartbreak among those who share with us the one God. We would have change; we will have change. But our people listen to louder voices – voices that proclaim Christians as infidels and enemies of Islam, agents of the nations of the West that have bled our country dry. When there is little to live for, a glorious death as a strike against such nations grows ever more attractive. If the people are to be persuaded from this path, they will need a sign.' He sat back.

Leclerc left a few moments' silence as an acknowledgment of the imam's contribution.

'You speak honestly and generously,' he began. 'We too have our warmongers in government and in Rome. They claim a long lineage stretching back to the Crusades. I am instructed to say that there are those in Rome who share your fears and your hopes. I am further instructed to say that there will be a sign, a gesture from Rome, to your people.'

The imam raised his hand in the gloom. 'My friend will not take offence if I suggest that such generous gestures in the past have come at a price. While the gift was to allay the sufferings of the body, the intention was often the acquisition of the soul.'

'I am further instructed to say this,' Leclerc said firmly. 'A father has two sons. If they are true sons, they will not vie with each other for the father's love. It is immense, beyond imagining. There can never be the possibility that either son has less or more of it.'

The imam nodded approvingly. 'This is a tree well planted,' he said. 'It will bear much fruit.'

'*Insh'Allah.*'

'Yes, God willing,' the imam whispered fervently.

Leclerc sensed his driver materialise behind him and began to rise. He heard a coughing sound and watched in horror as the imam toppled slowly sideways, a black stain spreading on his chest. At the same moment, powerful arms encircled his head and shoulders. He felt a sting in the side of his neck, and then the scene pulsed in and out of focus and faded.

*

At dawn, a crowd swarmed and murmured like disturbed bees around the mosque. Young men linked arms, jumping up and down; little ones flickered in and out among the crowd; the elders clustered together, a little apart. Their heads tilted to the ostrich eggs high above the building.

Someone had climbed up and stuck a human head on the tower. The white face gleamed in the first light of dawn.

23

Santa Sabina Hospital, Rome

Eli Weissman bumped through the double doors of the Emergency Department, his scuffed leather bag in one hand, the Polish loaf from Signora Fulvi nestling warmly under the other arm. He was oblivious to the stares of his colleagues as he passed.

The first sign of anything amiss was the absence of the guard. Eli bent awkwardly and pushed open the door. The empty bed stopped him in his tracks. The room had been swept clean of any evidence of its previous occupant.

He didn't bother to close the director's door behind him.

'Where is my patient?' he demanded.

Giulio Benedetto looked up. 'You came in the back way?'

'Yes.'

'I'm sorry, I told Angela to have you come directly to my office.'

'My patient?'

'We don't own them, Doctor,' Giulio snapped, with an uncharacteristic flush of anger. 'Please close the door and sit.'

Giulio sat tiredly in his chair and waited for Eli to be seated.

'The Pope has returned to the Vatican,' he said.

'You mean he's been returned,' Weissman corrected coldly.

'Yes, been returned, at three this morning.'

'On whose instructions?'

'Cardinal Alba was acting on the instruction of Cardinal Richter. Alba was accompanied by the Pope's secretary and the nursing Sister. Both had the good grace to look embarrassed.'

Giulio lifted a heavily embossed page from his desk and read. 'The Vatican wishes to express its deep appreciation to all the hospital staff. May God bless and reward, et cetera, et cetera. Signed, Cardinal Richter, Vatican Secretary of State.' He let it fall from his hand.

'This is Italy, Signor Benedetto. There are laws. A patient may not be removed from the care of a hospital physician without the physician's signed consent. I signed nothing.'

'And to which papal knight should I complain, Doctor – the Chief of Police or the Minister of Health? Anyway, they thought of that. The papers were already signed by Ricci.'

'But—'

'Dr Weissman, it is a fait accompli, and Italy has no extradition treaty with the Vatican.'

'But why? The man is dying. We could have helped him die in peace.'

'Dr Weissman,' Giulio said tiredly, 'the Pope is not a man. No, let me finish, please. Karol Wojtyla stopped being a man when his name was read from the balcony in St Peter's Square. He became the Supreme Pontiff of the Holy Roman Catholic Church, the religious leader of millions and Christ's vicar on earth.'

'And he forfeited his right to die in peace like any other human being?'

'Eli, please listen to me. I'm a Roman Catholic, sometimes. I know how the system works. When a man accepts the throne of St Peter, he accepts a life sentence. From the day they place the Fisherman's Ring on his finger, he must stop thinking of himself as a person like you and me. He must think of the Church, first, foremost and always. Did you know that some of his predecessors never again used the word 'I' after their coronations? They said 'we'. To be pope is to live in a small apartment in a very large palace. It is to sign papers and meet other heads of state and select groups who are vetted by *apparatchiks*, faceless men who decide if it is appropriate and in the interests of the Church. It is to see, hear and know only what this Praetorian Guard filters to your senses. Do you think someone can drop in casually for a gossip? Is there a café in the world where he can meet a friend? There are convicts in Roman prisons who are freer than the Pope.'

He sat back and sighed. 'Did you know he did some acting when he was a young man? Oh, yes. Now he has the biggest role on the largest stage in the world, but he must follow the script.'

'Even in his dying?'

'Yes, even in his dying. Even that will be stage-managed. Communiqués – light on medical information, heavy on edification – will be issued by the Vatican Press Office. We will hear that the Pope prayed, received the sacraments of Holy Mother Church and kissed the crucifix. We will never be told if he was afraid, or wept, or if any other human being held his hand to comfort him.'

'And this is the Christian concept of love?'

'No, this is the Church, Eli, dedicated to its own continuity. Everything and everybody, even the Pope, is subordinate to that. So, if his predecessor was murdered or died alone and in agony, they would say he was reading a spiritual book and died at peace. If Pius the Twelfth asked for the nun who was his friend and housekeeper for many years to be with him, they would have denied her access to his bedside and sent her somewhere else before his body was cold.'

'Is this true?'

'I have a friend who worked in the Vatican at that time. Retirement has loosened his tongue. He said the Vatican officials were jealous of her influence; they called her "La Papessa". After Pius died, my friend saw her leave the Vatican forever carrying a bag and a birdcage.'

Eli rose slowly to his feet.

'I'm truly sorry, Eli,' Giulio said. 'For the Pope, for you, for all of us.'

When the door closed, Guiulio lifted the telephone. 'I was thinking of taking the afternoon off and I was hoping my wife might indulge an old man and go with him to the Caravaggio exhibition… What old man? Me, of course.' He laughed. 'I love you, Paola … No, nothing's wrong… About one o'clock. *Ciao.*'

Eli did his rounds in a dutiful daze and delegated the rest of his duties to an assistant. 'I'm going home,' he told the bemused medic.

Angela Amarone saw him as he approached the reception area, and left her desk to meet him. 'I'm very sorry, Dr Weissman,' she said gently.

'Thank you, Angela.' Eli smiled. 'Oh, I have something for you.' He plucked the loaf from under his arm and handed it to her. 'I got this for… bronchitis,' he said absently, and walked away.

Angela stared after the disconsolate figure. She switched her gaze to the loaf in her hand and sniffed it suspiciously. Strange man, she thought. Why does he think I have bronchitis?

Trastevere, Rome

Eli saw the black car with the distinctive Vatican number plates parked outside his apartment building, and his steps quickened. As he reached the landing, Signora Fulvi put her head around the door and raised her eyes to the floor above; then she went inside again, and he heard the bolts shoot home.

When he opened his apartment door, he thought for a moment that he was looking at a posed photograph. His mother sat, small and upright, in the over-stuffed armchair. Uncle Ari stood behind her, his hand resting protectively on her shoulder. The two priests sat awkwardly together on the low sofa. 'Eli, my son,' his mother said, 'they have come for you.'

The two clerics rose with difficulty, and Eli recognised the younger one as the Pope's secretary.

'The Holy Father asks that you come to see him,' he said formally.

'When?' Eli asked.

'Now.'

*

As they drove into St Peter's Square, Eli looked up at the obelisk, an exclamation mark against the sky. I've crossed the line, he thought.

The Pope was dressed in a white cassock and skullcap and seated in a straight-backed chair. He was flanked by two cardinals whom Eli recognised as Richter and Alba.

The Pope raised his head with effort. 'Thank you for coming, Doctor,' he mouthed.

Eli nodded. 'You wished to see me, Pope.'

The cardinals flinched on either side, but the Pope smiled. 'Please tell them that I wish to speak with you in private.'

Eli relayed the message. Immediately, Cardinal Alba began to protest. 'It is unthinkable that the Holy Father should be alone with this—'

The Pope raised his hand, and the cardinal's mouth snapped shut. The Pope's lips moved again, and Weissman watched them intently.

'The Pope wishes me to say that he doesn't appreciate being spoken of in his presence. He says it's normal practice to avoid doing so until the Pope has died.'

Eli saw Alba stiffen and withdraw into himself. He thought he saw the suggestion of a smile on Richter's face.

'If you will excuse us, Holy Father, we will wait outside.' With a short bow, Richter left the room. Alba followed hurriedly.

'I sense you are angry, Doctor,' the Pope said.

'I don't like it when my patient is kidnapped.'

'So you have come to pay the ransom?'

'I wish it were that easy.'

'Thank you anyway. I must apologise. You

should have been consulted. Now that you are here, I have some questions.'

'Certainly. What can I tell you?'

'The truth.' The Pope registered the surprise in Eli's eyes and continued. 'People tell me very little; perhaps the Pope overawes them. I would like you to tell me about yourself, please.'

'Me?'

'Yes, Dr Weissman. It would be a privilege to know you better. Please, can you sit here, on this low chair? Not out of deference, but because I find it difficult to lift my head.'

It was said so simply that Eli could feel his reservations loosen. He sat on the low chair and thought of Uncle Ari as he looked at the old man.

He began to speak about his life – at first hesitantly, but the attention in the Pope's eyes encouraged his flow. When his narration took him to Israel, he faltered and stopped.

'Stories are like that,' the Pope said gently. 'We begin to tell a story to another, and the story begins to speak to ourselves, to a deep part of ourselves; and then... we stop. But often, the story longs to be told – to be recognised and acknowledged.'

Eli began again.

'I volunteered to work in a kibbutz, in the attack zone. I was young and I thought of myself as brave. I... we were taken in a raid, a... friend and me. They kept me for a hundred and sixty-two days in a gas tank, underground. Did you know, the earth makes sounds?'

'And your friend?'

Eli shook his head. 'Then there was an exchange of prisoners, and I came home to Rome.'

'And now?'

'And now I like to work. I like to walk and feel the air on my face and look at the sky.'

They sat in easy silence for a while, and then the Pope spoke.

'I saw Jews in Poland, after the war. Many people could not look at them – not because they were so gaunt, but because they looked at ordinary things with such wonder. Some survivors never left the camps, you know. The horrors they had suffered were like a barbed-wire fence, standing forever between them and the ordinary things: laughter, tears, love. It takes a special kind of bravery to live, Dr Weissman. Are your parents living?'

'My mother and my Uncle Ari.'

'Tell me, what is it like being a Jew in Rome?'

Eli told him of Uncle Ari's stories. 'My mother says he's tired of watching for the next Holocaust, but there's no one who can tell him he can stop.'

The Pope considered that for a long time as they sat in silence. 'I have a further question, Doctor,' he said finally. 'Am I dying?'

'Yes. The condition you have is irreversible. When we take into account other factors, such as your age and the injury you suffered, we're talking sooner rather than later. But you are alive today, Pope.'

'Thank you for treating me as a human being, Doctor. I would like you to be my physician, if you are willing?'

'I am. I'd like to continue with my hospital work for now, but if – when – you need me more often, I'll delegate it.'

'Thank you. There is one last thing. It is not a question, it is a request. Will you tell me when it is time to stop watching for the future of the Church?'

24

Cardinal Thomas' Apartments, The Vatican

Michael was clinging to the keel of a capsized currach, the thin canvas membrane of the Island boat bucking beneath him. His brother Liam was hanging on to the other side.

'Michael!' Liam's cry was torn from his mouth and blown ragged by the screaming wind. 'Michael!'

'I hear you, Liam. Just hang on, they'll come for us.'

'Oh, Jesus, Michael, I'm so cold, so cold.'

His heart chilled at the desolation in the thin voice. 'Liam? Liam?'

He woke with a gasp, the taste of bitter salt on his tongue. Cardinal Thomas was looking at him impassively.

'You okay?'

'Yeah. Bad dream.'

'You need to see this.'

Michael padded in his shorts to the other room, where the cardinal was fiddling with a video recorder.

'This was broadcast just a few minutes ago,' he said tonelessly.

The earnest face of a CNN reporter appeared on screen. A strange building loomed behind him in the frame.

'What brought Archbishop Leclerc to the Djenne Mosque, the biggest mud-brick building in the world, remains a mystery,' the reporter intoned. 'It was to be his final pilgrimage.'

The camera tilted up, to the tall spires of the building behind him. Michael saw what looked like large eggs impaled on a number of them. The camera zoomed in for a close-up and revealed a human head.

Cardinal Thomas leaned forward and stabbed the 'stop' button. 'He was mine,' he said simply. 'He was my emissary to a powerful Islamic leader.'

'Who knew that, Eminence?'

'Hell, no one. It was top secret.'

'A secret is something that's known by only one person. So come on – who knew?'

'A Franciscan ran up the passport, and an ornithologist, a layman, helped with the cover story.' Cardinal Thomas shook his head dismissively.

'They're both pros; I've worked with them before.'

'Which leaves you.'

'What the—'

'Who did you talk to?'

'I… oh, Christ.' The cardinal rubbed his hands down his cheeks. 'When O'Neill came for interview, I had a memo on my desk dealing with Leclerc's trip to Mali.'

'Did he see it?'

'He can't have. I was right there… No. I left the room once to make a call. But you don't think he—'

'I don't know.'

'Why did you hit O'Neill, Michael?'

'I had to take him out of the equation. They would have killed him.'

'And that's the only reason?'

Michael remained silent.

'Listen, Michael, I want you to do two things. One: find the connections. Maybe O'Neill is mixed up with this Remnant mob, I don't know. O'Neill is the original canon lawyer: imagination will never be his strong suit, and he's too inconsequential to be anything more than a foot soldier. Find the links, Michael, and follow them to the top. You find the head and I'll cut it off.'

'And the second thing?'

Cardinal Thomas smiled wryly. 'Keep me alive, soldier.'

Hotel Bernini, Rome

Mal picked up the phone and dialled. 'Terence,' he said, 'I need a favour.'

Terence was thirty-five and single. Mal had arrested him for hacking, used all his finagling skills to prise Terence's tapping fingers from a sentence of six to ten, and pulled in some heavy-duty favours to set him up as a computer consultant to a large Manhattan bank – with some pro bono work for the police department on the side.

'I feel my sphincter muscle tighten, Mal.'

'That explains you being such a pain in the butt.'

'Oh, now it's with the cruel jokes. Okay, speak, Master; your servant is listening.'

'Is this line secure?' Mal asked.

'Tighter than a duck's ass.'

'I want the phone records of the offices of the Archdiocese of New York, for the last six months. You're looking for calls to Rome, and maybe one call to the Church of the Holy Spirit in Manhattan made in the last few days. I need times and numbers. Add faxes and… what do you call the damn things you can send by computer?'

'Emails, Detective.' Terence sighed theatrically and hung up.

One hour later, the mobile phone chirped Mal awake.

'Who is it?'

'I am who I am.'

'Shoot, Terence.'

'Hopefully, there's a silent comma between "shoot" and "Terence". Okay, you got a sharp stick and a piece of bare ground so you can scratch down the following information?'

Mal printed the numbers on a small pad. 'And faxes? ... Okay, text it to me, will you? Any joy on the Holy Spirit number?' He scribbled again.

'Hang that Judas until his bowels burst open, Detective.'

'G'night, Terence.'

The Spenza Villa, Rome

Sebastiano swung his feet to the bedroom floor. He had been dreaming of the walls of Rome and of a great host, with banners massed, outside the walls. In his dream, a figure stepped forward from the ranks and raised a fiery cross. 'Rome or death,' he shouted, and the force of his voice boomed against the walls so that they rippled as in a heat haze and began to crumble. With a terrible cry, the multitude began to charge...

He glowered at his wristwatch. It showed 3.00 a.m., and he knew he would not sleep again. Might as well go to Vatican Radio now, he thought; it would impress the director. Quickly, he showered and shaved and slipped down the broad staircase, making his way to the front door.

As he reached for the latch, he heard a voice call his name.

'Sebastiano.'

He swung around wildly and saw no one. 'Sebastiano,' his father's voice called again. It came from the study off the hallway; the door was ajar, and he pushed it open reluctantly.

The old man sat at the head of the long table, a book spread in the wash of light from a lamp that placed his face in shadow. 'Come in, my son. I want to talk to you.'

'I'm going to Vatican Radio. It's urgent.'

'At three o'clock? What can be so critical in the Holy Roman Empire at such an hour? Come, sit.'

Sebastiano ignored the chair indicated by his father and sat grudgingly at the other end of the table, beyond the reach of the light. Two can play that game, he thought spitefully.

'Sebastiano, there are things we should talk about, as father and—'

'What things?' The question came sharply from his mouth. The old bastard hides in his books for thirty years, he thought, and suddenly, there are things we should talk about.

Signor Spenza allowed a measure of silence to absorb the interruption. Then he continued to speak, as softly as he had before. 'We had a guest, Sebastiano, a young priest. I think you forgot your duties as a—'

'So this is what you wanted to talk about?' Sebastiano exploded, rising from the chair. 'The professor finally bothers to talk to his son – and about what? My career in the Church? My friends? Anything to do with me? No, he's just worried about the feelings of a barbarian who got above his station.'

Signor Spenza rose with difficulty. 'I don't consider the priesthood a career,' he said grimly. 'There are good men who offer their lives to priesthood – to serve the people of the Church, not for their own advancement. And, as for your friends... I've seen them, Sebastiano, and I'm not too bookish or divorced from the world to know what they are.'

'What's all this shouting?' The contessa swept into the room in robe and slippers and placed herself between the two men. 'What is the meaning of this?' she demanded.

'The professor is trying to lecture me about that... priest, at the Farnesina,' Sebastiano snapped.

'That is a matter of no importance,' the contessa whispered fiercely, rounding on her husband.

'It's a matter of honour when a guest is—'

'Honour?' she spat. 'How dare you mention honour to me? What honour have you brought to our name? What kind of example have you been to our son? You've lived on dusty books and so-called scholarship, and for what? To be a professor at a second-rate university where your staff laugh at you behind their hands. All this fantasy is only possible because I've paid for it.'

'Your money means nothing to me.'

'You've been a kept man all your life, Vittorio

Spenza, and now you're angry with my son because he wants to make something of himself.'

'I've seen what our son has made of himself, Ottavia, and it is not a man.'

Sebastiano pointed a shaking finger at his father. 'You listen to me, old man. You've spent your life studying history; I'm going to make history. You read about the heroes of the past; I walk with the men who will shape the future. We are the Remnant, and our convenor is the Wrath of Righteousness. And the day is coming when we will sweep away the—'

The slap sounded like a dropped book in the room. Sebastiano held his stinging cheek, his tearing eyes fixed in surprise on his mother.

'You forget yourself,' she said harshly. She pulled his hand from his cheek and cupped it in her own. 'Make me proud,' she crooned as she thumbed the tears from his eyes. 'But now, go to your room and wash your face, my darling.'

Sebastiano hurried from the room. Spenza heard the door slam and sank into his chair. His wife gazed at him with contempt.

'You're a failure, Vittorio,' she hissed. 'You're a failure as a husband and as a father. You've ruined your daughter with foolish talk of service and dedication, and lost the respect of your son. You might have been someone, but you had no hunger.'

When she had gone, Spenza sat in the bitter silence, gazing sightlessly at the open book.

*

The contessa switched off all the lights in her room and went to the wall-to-wall window that framed a spectacular view of the city. She allowed her eyes to sweep over the skyline, the familiarity of every spire and dome, until she was calm. It's said, at last, she thought; no more masks. We haven't been husband and wife for years. It was never more than an infatuation. I thought he had the potential for greatness, but he's what he always was: the diffident man with no interest in meeting influential people, always more interested in the past than in the future, the dead rather than the living. He'll be dead soon enough; he can while away eternity with Plutarch and Herodotus. I am alive, and my son will be someone of influence.

She let her thoughts stray to the man who had cuckolded her husband, and felt a flush of delicious warmth course through her body. Now, there was a real man – a man who listened with respect to her dreams for Sebastiano, and who would do anything in his considerable power to aid his rise.

She picked up her mobile phone and punched the numbers with practised ease.

'You were sleeping? Poor dear. Alone, I hope?' She laughed. 'Soon,' she promised, 'very soon. There's been such a scene...'

He was a wonderful listener, never interrupting her flow, prompting her gently to tell him everything, down to the very last detail. 'You'll see that my Sebastiano has his reward?' she asked. 'Thank you, darling; I knew I could count on you.'

The man at the other end of the line hung up and dialled another number.

25

Castel Sant'Angelo, Rome

Stefan paged through the score, hearing the music in his head, but something niggled in his subconscious; some discordant note repeated and repeated. He dropped the score and put the telephone to his ear.

'It is time,' the Devil said. 'It is time to loose the wolf among the flock and strike the shepherd. There is another matter, of no great consequence – but I do not wish it to become of consequence.'

Stefan listened intently to his instructions. When the Devil had concluded, he asked one question.

'And when these things come to pass, will you remember your promise?'

He listened to the reply, and smiled.

He strode to the computer and tapped in a single word: '*Venite.*' 'Come.' Another tap and his message soared out into the ether, calling the Remnant for the last time.

★

Vittorio Spenza heard Sebastiano's heavy tread in the hallway, and for a moment he thought of inviting him to some kind of reconciliation, but then Sebastiano's phone chirped.

'*Pronto*,' Sebastiano murmured.

'*Caro*,' Stefan said, 'you must go to the Colosseum, to the ruins beneath the walkway. I will find you.'

'Why the Colosseum?' Sebastiano blurted.

'It is a place made holy by the blood of the martyrs. We will draw inspiration from their sacrifice.'

Spenza heard the front door close.

'To promote evil,' he whispered, 'it is enough for good men to do nothing.'

He stood stiffly and walked to the hallway, swaying slightly and steadying himself with a hand to the wall. Resolutely, he plucked the telephone from its cradle.

The Catacombs of San Domitilla

Stefan stood on the Ponte Umbetto, flanked by two suitcases. The taxi driver popped the trunk from inside the cab, his eyes fixed on the road. Carefully, Stefan stowed the suitcases and sat in the rear.

There was no need to give any instructions; Alessandro Cudicini had delivered this passenger to his destination before.

Stefan knew the winding labyrinth of the catacombs as well as he knew his own quarters, and he moved swiftly through the dark passageways. The central chamber of the catacombs was a hub from which four passageways ran to the four points of the compass; he left the suitcases in alcoves at the ends of the north and south passageways. Then he rested in an alcove pocked with loculi, the small niches in which the bones of the early Christians awaited the Resurrection. Behind his left shoulder, a first-century Christian graffitist had scraped a crude cross on a marble slab. Two words were carved unevenly underneath: *IN PACE* – In Peace.

At the appointed hour, Magda's whisper nudged him awake. It is time, Stefan.

They were already gathered when he entered the central chamber and took his accustomed place. A frisson of anticipation rippled through the group as he prepared to speak.

'Already, the ungodly have felt our wrath,' he declared. 'In America, in Europe and in Africa, the Angel of Justice has spread his wings and snuffed out the light from their eyes, as he once did to the Assyrians when they threatened the elect. You have been tried and found worthy. Make your souls ready to receive the Kingdom prepared for you from the foundation of the world.'

He could hear ecstatic murmurings from the ranks before him.

'Abide in this place, among the bones of the blessed, until I come again to proclaim your deliverance.'

'Amen,' they shouted, and he left them.

He made his way quickly through one of the passageways closed to the public and climbed a stairway of ancient stones to a door at street level. The taxi slumbered in the darkness between two street lamps. When the door closed, the driver pressed the accelerator.

After they had travelled a short distance, Stefan said, 'Here.' Taken by surprise, Alessandro slewed the taxi to the kerb. Stefan got out and walked off into the dark.

Alessandro watched him in the rear-view mirror until his outline had faded. He gulped air, like someone who had been holding his breath for a very long time. Still shaking, he fumbled with the handbrake and drove away.

Stefan sat on a stone bench in a little park, a shadow among shadows. He checked his watch and drew a thin metal box from the deep pocket of his robes. Holding it before him, he pressed a button and watched a silver wand rise before his face. A small red eye winked on the face of the box, pulsing like a tiny heart. '*Requiescant in pace* – may they rest in peace,' he whispered, and pressed the button once more. The red eye faded to black.

*

The simultaneous blasts followed the line of least resistance, roaring down the narrow corridors so that those gathered in the chamber were caught between them. Forced head to head in the chamber, the fireballs swelled upward, punching a hole in the floors above. The seismic shock sent a wave of hot air racing through the honeycomb of tunnels, first expanding and then collapsing them as it passed.

Alessandro felt the jerk in the steering wheel and thought, Earthquake. He slammed the brake pedal and spun the taxi in a perfect circle. He saw a fireball flower into the sky and estimated where the source of the blast was. He was still sitting, dazed, at the wheel when the policeman screamed at him to pull over and allow the emergency vehicles through.

*

Sebastiano locked his car and walked to the Colosseum, buoyed up by the memory of his mother, a she-wolf defending her Romulus. The nightwatchman didn't appreciate being woken up, but the sight of money improved his humour. In a few hours, the traders would be fleecing the tourists, the pseudo-centurions would be holding plastic swords to the throats of giggling ladies for photographs; everybody would be coining it, except him, he thought sourly. Night visitors were rare and sometimes dangerous – crack-heads, bum-boys and drunks – but now he had had two safe ones in the one night, both anxious to pray in the place of martyrs and both willing to pay for the privilege. May the holy martyrs rest in peace, the watchman thought happily as he turned the key.

Like most Romans, Sebastiano visited the monuments only out of duty. When the Catholic Broadcasters Convention came to Rome for their annual meeting, the director of Vatican Radio was quick to delegate the guide work to Sebastiano. He remembered the red-faced American bishop, a tiny rooster suffused with self-importance. 'Say, Sebastiano, what were these little bitty stones for?'

'Oh, the bollards, your Lordship? How perceptive of you. They held the *velarium*, the awning that spread over the top as a kind of giant sun umbrella.'

'Sure could do with that today.'

'Here, let me take your bag, your Lordship.'

It never hurt to be seen as obliging. Sebastiano's view was that the American Catholic Church, like the country itself, was populated with ignorant peasants who wouldn't know their apse from their elbow; but they were rich, and, as one famous archbishop had put it so pithily, 'The Church is not run on Hail Marys.'

He was in one of the internal corridors, making his way carefully in the dark to the opening that would give him access to the arena. He never told the honoured guests that most of the marble cladding had been filched for palaces and villas, even for the construction of St Peter's. And he most certainly did not tell them that, in the not-too-distant past, the Colosseum had been the haunt of pretty boys and a magnet for the men who enjoyed their favours.

He was on the walkway that lofted over the ruins of rooms and passages where the animals had been kept in ancient times.

'Sebastiano.'

The voice whispered from below, and he shivered. He had a visceral dislike for this gaunt monument that stretched up out of Rome like a broken tooth. It still had the whiff of decay and corruption. That whisper from the darkness below tickled the follicles on his neck, and they rose to attention.

Stepping warily, he began to climb down into the brick ruins beneath the walkway, into the shadowed bowels of the Colosseum.

'Sebastiano.'

The acoustics were throwing the whisper round and round, and it was darker down there. A section of the dark seemed to solidify and move forward to meet him. 'Sursum corda,' it whispered.

The blow set lights spinning in Sebastiano's head. The dark embraced him before he hit the ground.

Cardinal Thomas' Apartments, The Vatican

The ringing telephone rescued Michael from a watery nightmare, and he shook his head like a surfacing swimmer, ridding it of ghosts. The telephone drilled insistently until he stumbled into the other room and lifted the receiver.

'Father Michael Flaherty, please.'

'Speaking.'

'Father, this is Emilia Spenza. We met at the reception in the Villa Farnesina, and again... later.'

'I remember.'

'My father wants to see you.'

'When?'

'Now. I'm sorry. It's early, but...'

'Where are you?'

'I'm parked on the Via Della Conciliazione. From St Peter's Square, it is the street directly in front of you. On the left, there is a café. I will watch for you.'

The morning air was crisp, and Michael sucked it into his lungs to clear his head. A black Audi blinked its lights as he approached the shuttered café.

He checked the mirrors as they pulled away. Nothing.

'Do you always do that?' Emilia asked.

'Yes. It's a habit from another life.'

'That must be the life you almost lost when they shot you in the shoulder?'

He remembered her fingers probing his back in the cell, and said nothing.

The Spenza Villa was perched on the side of the Esquiline Hill, behind a screen of cypresses. The sky was beginning to lighten a little and the big evergreens were feathery with cobwebs. The occasional sound of a car in the distance merely emphasised the stillness of the garden. Michael detected the smell of the resinous trees combining with that of turned earth.

Emilia locked her car and turned to watch him. He stood, slightly hunched in that lived-in jacket, his head cocked as if he was listening.

'What is it?'

'Nothing; just the morning.'

For a moment he looked weary and vulnerable. Who are you? she wondered. She realised that she would happily have stood there with him, simply enjoying the morning, and then shook herself free of that fancy.

'Shall we go inside?' she said.

Vittorio Spenza sat at a long table, the middle finger of his right hand drumming the polished surface. His face, in repose, seemed to hang in folds from his broad forehead.

'Papa.'

There was a suspicion of cigarette smoke in the air, and Emilia chided herself for noting it. What did it matter, in her father's case?

'Papa, Father Flaherty is here.'

Spenza made an effort to rise, but Michael took his outstretched hand and pressed him gently back into the chair.

'Thank you for coming. Please sit – and you also, Emilia.' The old man took a deep breath and straightened in the chair. 'My daughter Emilia told me what happened to you by the Pantheon, Father. My son—'

'Signor,' Michael interrupted, 'I don't make that connection.'

Spenza nodded in silence for a moment.

'You are kind – for a Celt,' he added, with just a trace of humour in his voice. 'But I am afraid there may be a connection. When Emilia told me of the attack, I confronted my son about his behaviour at the Villa. I am ashamed to say he was unrepentant. My son is a Farnese like his mother. The Farnese have always had an inflated sense of their own importance, and a taste for revenge when they consider themselves slighted. Emilia has the Farnese beauty, but she has a different kind of heart.'

His daughter stretched to squeeze his hand, as much to strengthen him as to acknowledge the compliment.

'My son said more; I think he was so angry that he said more than he intended. My wife overheard us and took his side, as she always has. I won't burden you with family difficulties, but Sebastiano began to rave about the vengeance of the Remnant and their leader, the Wrath of Righteousness… My wife slapped him and ordered him to be quiet. I fear for my son, Father Flaherty, and I fear for you.'

'Have you any idea where your son is now, Signor?'

'Before he left, I heard him speaking on the telephone. He said, "Why the Colosseum?"'

26

The Colosseum

The pain in Sebastiano's wrists and ankles nagged him awake. When the fog cleared from his eyes, he tried to scream, but the tape across his mouth pushed the sound explosively through his sinuses, and he snorted mucus. Raw fear sharpened his senses. He could feel the rough timber beam he was tied to and knew from the caress of cold air on his body that he was naked. Raising his head, he could see along a straight passage that stretched between the ruins; in his peripheral vision, the empty amphitheatre loomed silent and menacing on either side.

About twenty paces in front of him stood a figure in the white robe and black scapular of a Benedictine, his head hooded in a long-tailed cowl.

'Sebastiano,' the dry voice whispered, and he imagined the sound rasped over his bare skin, so that he shuddered and writhed against his bonds.

'Sebastiano, the Christian, ladies and gentlemen,' the voice continued in a grotesque parody of a tour guide. 'A member of the Emperor's Praetorian Guard – from Praetor, the Roman consul responsible for the games.'

With a dramatic flourish, he dipped into the bag at his feet and swung something upright over his shoulder. Like a shotgun, Sebastiano thought, but not a shotgun. Oh, Jesus – Jesus.

'Sebastiano was a member of this elite corps dedicated to the protection of the divine Emperor.'

The sky was beginning to lighten, making the shadows recede and harden. Sebastiano's bulging eyes deciphered the lines of the object: a crossbow. He began to sob, huge tears spilling down his puffy cheeks, but he could not tear his eyes away.

The figure stooped again, and in his other hand he held a stubby bolt, one end obscenely feathered for flight. 'But Sebastiano the Praetorian sold his soul to another god and sealed his fate.'

Sebastiano heard the stutter of sound as the bowstring ratcheted back. He saw the bolt slide smoothly into place, smelled his own pungent waste as it slid down his bare legs.

'And, by order of the Emperor Diocletian…'

There was a blur of movement, and Sebastiano grunted as something struck him. He craned his

head forward and saw an inch of feathered bolt pro-
truding from his thigh. He stared at it for a moment
in disbelief, then the pain surged up and exploded in
his brain. In agony, he smashed his head against the
beam, craving unconsciousness; but he was lucid, all
too lucid, when the second bolt sang its brief song
through the air and split his right knee like a dry stick.

The third bolt passed cleanly through the muscle
of his right arm, and the pain became a roaring in his
ears. They are applauding me, he thought, his
maddened eyes swinging to the empty tiers of the
amphitheatre. I have fought the good fight. I have
borne the pain, and the emperor will raise his right
thumb and…

Abruptly, the roaring ceased, as the last breath
was punched from his body. He strained to draw
another, but it would not come. The bolt in his chest
pinned him to the beam. 'Mama,' he mouthed, as a
wave of darkness lapped over his eyes.

*

A combination of Emilia's driving and the early hour
brought them to the Colosseum in twenty minutes.
'Please wait with the car,' Michael said. 'If you don't
hear from me in fifteen minutes, call this number.'
He gave her Fermi's card and hurried away.

The nightwatchman, stamping up and down outside his hut, looked up in surprise at the approaching
figure.

'Do you speak English?' Michael asked.

'A little.'

'Did you see a man go inside? A big man, black hair, maybe thirty years old?'

'A man? Maybe; not sure.'

Michael dug in his pocket and stuffed some notes into the eager hand.

'*Grazie*, Signor. Yes, I see a big man. A very kind man.' The watchman played thoughtfully with the notes in his hand. 'Also, I think I see something else…'

Michael took a step closer and caught his wrist in a vice-grip. '*Per favore*, Signor,' he said coldly.

'Okay, okay, I remember. Another man come in – before the big man.'

The Colosseum had the eerie quiet of all empty buildings. Michael contemplated taking off his shoes and decided against it: the corridor was strewn with litter, and his shoes were valuable weapons.

★

Stefan checked the impaled figure for signs of life, but Sebastiano's eyes were locked on some other world. He returned to the bag to stow his equipment.

This kind of killing is different, Stefan, Magda whispered.

He paused. 'These are different times,' he explained gently. 'This is a different kind of war.'

★

Michael made his way stealthily to the walkway. He distrusted wood; even old wood could flex beneath a foot and make a sound, and sound was the hunter's enemy. He decided to bypass the walkway and wormed his way deeper, dropping down into the ruins below, moving swiftly in dark shadow.

The beer bottle was what his old mentor Father Mack would have described as a temporal anomaly. Discarded by a modern tourist, it stood on a single brick, probably fired in the thirteenth century, when the Frangipani family had turned the Colosseum into a fortress. All this ran in fast-forward through Michael's brain as his foot struck the brick and the bottle toppled.

We have company, Stefan. Fight or flight?

'Fight, then flight,' Stefan answered grimly, ratcheting the crossbow.

Michael heard a faint creaking and cocked his head. It seemed to come from the end of a long central passage, but the acoustics of the amphitheatre could bounce sound into places distant from its origin. Now there's an idea, he thought. He threw the brick to his left; as it clattered away, he darted to his right, keeping low and scanning the ground for safe and silent purchase.

A question, Stefan, Magda said, as the sound subsided.

'Yes,' he said absently, his finger fitting the bolt to the drawstring.

Civilian or soldier?

He sniffed the air as his mind worried the question. 'Soldier,' he smiled. 'He will go in the direction of the sound he has made.' He was already moving, flitting between the ruined brick walls, crossbow at the ready. He stopped. Nothing.

Not just any soldier, Stefan.

'No, Magda. This is one who is worthy of us.'

★

Michael eased his head around the corner of a wall. There was something in the passage ahead, silhouetted against the gathering light. He leaned back and considered his options.

Assume the other guy is armed, the Marine instructor's voice boomed in his head. Distance is his friend. He can take you out any number of times as you approach. Get close, soldier; get right in there and dance with the devil.

But first Michael needed to check out that thing in the passage. He was on the move again, grateful for any patch of shadow and for the black jacket and trousers that cloaked his body. He kept his face averted from where he thought the target might be; a moving white blob was way too tempting for a marksman. Crouching low, he peered into the passage.

Michael Flaherty the priest was appalled at the ruin that had once been Sebastiano. Michael Flaherty the soldier, prompted by a more primitive instinct, was already rolling on his shoulder when the bolt slammed into the brick wall behind him.

Crossbow, his brain screamed. Run.

He ran directly at the spot from which the bolt had come. Crossbows take time to load – but how much time? His stomach tightened in anticipation of the death blow.

He's coming, Stefan.

Stefan was already discarding the crossbow when the running figure levitated and kicked him in the chest. He rolled to lessen the impact and was back on his feet, a knife appearing in his hand from a wrist sheath.

He was facing east, and the red ball of the sun burned through an aperture in the great wall; Stefan blinked. His opponent was on him, rolling him over and under, crushing his knife wrist in a drowning man's grip. Stefan spread his arms suddenly, drawing the other man closer, and butted him with his forehead. The grip on his wrist relaxed and he was on his feet again, knife held low and forward.

The man feinted toward the knife, and Stefan slashed upwards. He felt the resistance of ripping cloth; then his right leg buckled backward from the force of a kick to his knee. His feet scrabbled for purchase on crumbling brick. He felt himself falling and spread his arms.

Michael had blood in his eyes. He dashed his sleeve across his face, and his vision cleared. The other man was gone. He raced forward to where he had last seen his target and stopped. The level patch on which they had fought dropped away suddenly to another level about ten feet below. He saw no sign of his opponent.

He sat in a shadowed alcove, waiting for his breathing to become less ragged. Time to check for damage, he thought tiredly. Father Mack's windcheater would cheat no more, he discovered, as his finger traced the rip from belly to collar. He followed the trajectory along a stinging line in his jaw to his split earlobe. His hand came away sticky with blood.

He checked his watch. It had been thirty minutes since he had entered the Colosseum; Emilia would have made the call. Michael leaned back and waited for Fermi.

27

Hotel Bernini, Rome

Rosa was already into her second coffee when Mal appeared and sank into the other chair.

'Hey,' she said. 'You look the way I feel.'

'A lotta miles on the clock.'

'Boy, this hotel is really something. The rooms are all one-way: you walk in, you back out.'

'Sorry, Rosa, it was all I could get at short notice.'

'Nah, it's okay. It's got... character. You know, Mal, I could never figure out what that word meant, until now. That's him over there – the character himself. Don't stare. He's the concierge, night porter, waiter, and all-round pain in the butt. "Orange juice, Signorina?" "Yes, please." "It is buffet." A real charmer.'

The character approached with a coffee pot and poured a half-cup for Mal before shuffling off.

'I see what you mean,' Mal said.

'Mal?'

'Yeah.'

'Who's Michael?'

'An archangel,' Mal muttered, never missing a beat.

'You know, Hanny's a saint to put up with you.'

'So she says.'

Rosa wasn't about to let it go, but she caught sight of Fermi striding through the foyer. 'Better sit up straight, Deputy,' she growled. 'Sheriff's here.'

'Good morning,' Fermi said briskly. 'Ready to roll?'

Café Janus, Via Labicana, Rome

Detective Fermi stopped the car and got out.

'I think we're parked,' Mal whispered to Rosa.

'Good. I can open my eyes now.' She blinked in amazement. 'Parked? He calls this parked?' The front of the car leaned into the street; one back wheel was hitched rakishly up on the pavement. 'It's like a dog having a—'

'Rosa!'

Outside the café, three barrel-chested men were already going through the greeting ritual with Fermi. They wore identical black pants, white shirts and inscrutable expressions. Fermi introduced them to Mal and Rosa as the Orsini brothers, 'friends of mine'. Assets, Mal interpreted mentally; every cop had them.

The room they were ushered into was stacked around the walls with bags of coffee. With a flourish, the Orsini brothers produced a metal table and three chairs. When they were seated, Mal leaned forward.

'Giuseppe, we have a little problem. Rosa and I had to leave our... equipment in New York.'

A slow smile crinkled Fermi's eyes. 'Of course. Don Quixote and Sancho Panza can't fight the dragon without the lance.'

'It was a windmill,' Mal corrected.

'And that would be Doña Quixote,' Rosa added tartly.

Fermi was already out the door. He returned carrying two boxes, both whiskery with dust.

'I'll organise some coffee,' he said casually. 'When I return, I will be surprised to discover that the boxes of plastic spoons I left on the table have disappeared.'

When he had gone, Rosa looked at Mal. 'Did you follow all that?'

'Yeah, I think so,' Mal said slowly. 'Ladies first.'

She lifted the cover from the top box and revealed a Walther handgun, cocooned in clear plastic. Underneath, six clips of bullets rested on a springy mattress of bubble-wrap.

'So what did Santa bring you?'

Mal lifted the lid of the second box with a tentative finger. 'The same, but in blue.'

When Fermi came back with the tray of coffee, the table was bare.

'Okay,' Mal said, 'some person or persons unknown are involved in taking out liberal Catholic clergy who have influential positions in the Church. I made a few calls last night to some people I know.'

Quantico, Rosa thought, spooks and covert-operations hardasses in Langley, Virginia.

'It seems we got the same pattern in the US and Europe,' Mal continued. 'The rest of the world, they don't know about – except maybe South America, and the information from there is scrappy.'

'The US likes to keep their *amigos* in South America real close,' Rosa said bitterly, 'so close that they don't see the disappeared. You know, under some of the juntas down there, a liberal priest is a threatened species.'

'Two things,' Mal said. 'I had a call from a friend. I asked him to check out communications from Saint Pat's. He says Dalton faxed Sister Kathleen's speech to Rome – after which she ended up under a train,' he added, for Fermi's benefit.

'So we can trace the receiving number,' Rosa said.

'Already done,' Mal grunted. 'My friend texted me that a little later.' He passed the number to Fermi, who excused himself and hurried out.

'What about calls to Roberts at Holy Spirit?' Rosa asked.

'Yeah. According to my friend, Dalton got there before us.'

'What can we do? We're flying without warrants here, and your source can hardly take the stand.'

'One dragon at a time, partner,' Mal said lightly.

Fermi was back. 'I have someone tracing the number for me. He will call me back as soon as possible.'

'What do we do now?' Rosa asked.

'We wait,' Fermi answered.

His mobile phone rang. He listened for a moment and pocketed it.

'That was quick,' Mal said.

'Not my friend; someone else. We go to the Colosseum now.'

The Colosseum

Michael watched Detective Fermi walk along the passage and freeze between the stumps of a ruined wall. 'Detective,' he called, but Fermi didn't acknowledge him, as if he hadn't heard. He's found Sebastiano, Michael thought.

Rising painfully to his feet, he came up behind the detective and stood in silence. Fermi cleared his throat and spoke with effort. 'Who is this?'

'Monsignor Sebastiano Spenza,' Michael said, and knew by the flinch of Fermi's shoulders that he recognised the name. 'I came in late on the action; he was already dead.'

'And his killer?'

'It was pretty dark, but he was dressed like a Benedictine. He used a crossbow.'

'But why did he do this?'

'Because the monsignor knew too much and talked.'

Fermi sighed and turned. 'Are you hurt?'

'No.'

Fermi looked at him critically. 'Why, every time I see you, there is a little less to see of you? ... Ah, the others have arrived.'

Michael turned and found himself face to face with Mal. A young woman with a very large handgun stood slightly behind him, her eyes roving among the ruins. Good cop, Michael noted absently, but his eyes were locked on Mal.

'Hi, Michael,' Mal grunted.

'Hi, Mal.'

So this is Michael Flaherty, Rosa thought, finally convinced that the ruins were free of snipers. She stashed away her gun and gave her full attention to the two men.

'Meet Detective Rosa Torres,' Mal said flatly.

'There's a crossbow, somewhere over there,' Michael told Fermi. 'Might be good for prints; he didn't wear gloves.'

Now that the spell was broken, Mal and Rosa caught their first sight of Sebastiano. Mal rocked on his heels and then walked steadily around the corpse. Rosa looked as if she was about to throw up.

'Rosa, you okay?' Mal asked.

'I'm okay. I don't think I'll ever get used to seeing things like this.'

'You won't,' he said. 'At least, I hope you never will.'

They were distracted by Fermi's phone.

'*Si...si...*' He started to pace back and forth. '*Grazie,*' he murmured, and turned to the others.

'Where were those calls to?' Mal asked.

'Castel Sant'Angelo.'

As they left the Colosseum and the others crowded into Fermi's car, Michael went to Emilia Spenza. He saw the bunched police cars and the paramedics unloading their equipment from an ambulance. She was standing with a policeman, and she stiffened when she caught sight of Michael.

'Sebastiano is dead,' she said calmly.

'Yes, Emilia, he's dead.'

He put his arms around her, and she rested her head on his shoulder.

'And the one who did this?'

'I'll find him.'

'Be careful,' she said, and kissed him.

He got into the front of the car, and the tyres screamed as Fermi gunned the engine.

28

The Irish College, Rome

As Hugh moved the razor around his face, a twinge in his right elbow reminded him of the Pantheon. He checked his chin and found the swelling. He knew Michael Flaherty had hit him to protect him. Afterwards, in the police station, the doctor had treated him efficiently, but she had made no eye contact with him; neither had the detective, Fermi. All the time, in the station, Hugh hadn't been able to tear his eyes from Michael's battered face. He resumed shaving, careful to run the razor around the perimeter of his bruise; careful not to look himself in the eye.

Habit had always been his friend: the conscious repetition of actions until they became unconscious, reflexive. Habit, the spiritual masters preached, is what brings you to perform when you don't want to.

'That's a two-edged sword for a surgeon, Hugh,' Tom had argued. 'If you'll pardon the awful pun. Sure, it takes you right in there to the ulcerated duodenum, even when you've been on a bender the night before and the nurse had to help you into the gown this morning – but it kills creativity. It stops you thinking sideways, man, gives you such a narrow focus that all you can see is all you can see. Hello? Earth calling Hugh O'Neill?'

'I have to go, Tom.'

'What? Why? Jesus, I'm running you theologically ragged here, Hughie boy, and you "have to go"… where?'

'To pray. I always pray at this time.'

Tom had looked at him incredulously. 'If He's there at all, lad, then He's as much here as anywhere else, if you follow me. Ah, go on, then – up to the top of the mountain, young Hughie, or the sky will fall and flatten the little chickens. Try not to mention me in your prayers; I don't want Him to notice me just yet.'

Hugh tried to smile at the memory, but he couldn't.

The sacristy was comfortably normal. Vestments lay pooled along the polished bench, waiting for priests to duck their heads and come up fully garbed for mass. A student peeled away from his companions in the corner and preceded Hugh to a side altar.

Habit, Hugh reminded himself: you start the action, and it's like dropping in a catalyst – the reaction creates something else. Not this morning. Every utterance was an effort; every word of the ritual phrases fought for its own solid space in his mouth, refusing to coalesce with the word before or after it. '*Vox et praeterea nihil*' was what the wise ones had warned them against – 'Voice and nothing else.'

He turned to impart his blessing, relieved that the mass was ended.

In the sacristy, he shrugged out of the vestments, folding them carefully in preparation for the next celebrant. There was an agitated whispering coming from the corner, and he glanced at the huddle of servers.

'Dr O'Neill.' The sacristan appeared at his elbow and leaned in for privacy. 'It's the rector, Monsignor Brennan, Doctor; he's having some problem.'

Hugh followed the sacristan through the chapel to one of the side altars. The server looked up, with a mixture of unease and relief, as they approached. 'He just stopped,' he whispered helplessly.

'I'll take care of him,' Hugh replied, and they hurried away.

Monsignor Brennan stood immobile, his arms outstretched. 'Monsignor,' Hugh whispered, coming up beside him, 'it's Hugh O'Neill.'

Brennan turned his head slowly, and Hugh was staggered at the change in him. The flesh seemed to have melted from his cheekbones, so that his skin was taut and shiny. His mouth was open, and a tendril of saliva tethered his chin to the vestments that hung huge on his bowed shoulders. Only his eyes gave any evidence of animation, and they were bright with fear.

'Hugh? I... can't say it.' Brennan's finger trembled towards the words of consecration in the missal – the words that would transform the bread and wine into the body and blood of Christ.

'I'll say it for you,' Hugh said gently. He took his handkerchief and dabbed at the old man's mouth; then he stretched his arm across Brennan's shoulders and began to read.

When they came to the sign of peace, he turned Brennan to face him. 'Peace be with you, Monsignor,' he said.

Brennan made an attempt to reply; then he dropped his head on Hugh's chest and began to sob. Hugh felt his own muscles tighten and urged himself to relax.

'Hugh,' the muffled voice said brokenly.

'It's okay,' he whispered, patting the monsignor awkwardly on the back.

Brennan raised his head, and Hugh was relieved to see a spark of the old intelligence in his eyes. 'Listen to me,' he whispered fiercely. 'I was ambitious, Hugh – ambitious for my own advancement, not for the sake of the Church. Every rector before me became a bishop. I wanted that, Hugh. The convenor promised me it was in his gift if I

became part of the Remnant. It was all a lie. A letter…
I got a letter today. I am to retire on the grounds of ill
health.' His tears dripped from his chin, freckling the
blood-red chasuble. '"It profits a man nothing to gain
the whole world and lose his soul," and I lost mine –
for what? The promise of a bishopric back home in
Ireland. I believed the lie because I needed it to be
true, so badly.' He was panting, his breath coming in
short gasps. 'It's too late for me, but you… it's not too
late for you. Please, Hugh,' he begged through his
tears, 'forgive me.'

'Dr O'Neill.'

The sharp voice startled Brennan into silence.
The vice-rector stepped to his side.

'Thank you, Dr O'Neill. The rector is unwell; we
will take care of him now.'

Hugh glanced at the dean of students, hovering
behind the vice-rector, and something snapped
inside him. The memory released was of a day in the
schoolyard when he had been confronted by a
taunting boy. He remembered his fist shooting from
his shoulder, as if of its own volition, and the surprise
on the bully's face as he sagged to the ground.

'Don't touch him,' he said fiercely.

'I beg your pardon—'

'I said don't touch him.' Hugh tightened his grip
on Brennan's shoulders.

'You forget yourself, Dr O'Neill.'

'No, I do not forget myself, and if you or that
creeping Jesus put a hand on him—'

Brennan placed his hand on Hugh's chest. 'Hugh, it's all right. There's nothing you can do for me now.'

He raised his hand and laid it gently against Hugh's cheek for a moment.

'I'm ready now, John,' he said to the vice-rector. The two men led him away between them, and their footsteps faded from the chapel.

Hugh rested his hands on the altar and bowed his head, fighting for self-control. He walked out of the chapel, startling the chattering group of servers outside the door. Something in his face carved the group in two, and he stalked between them, striding down the corridor. What could he do? The door of the common room stood ajar and he registered the bass voice of a news anchorman. '...Leclerc...'

The name rooted him to the spot. With an effort, he forced himself to step inside the door and lock his eyes on the television. He was just in time to see a mosque sink from view as the camera zoomed to the human head impaled at the top. 'Jean-Baptiste Leclerc,' the reporter intoned, 'a Roman Catholic archbishop based in the Vatican...'

Hugh was running, running flat-out down the corridor, scattering students from his path. Cardinal Thomas, he thought wildly. Thomas is the only one who can save me now.

Castel Sant'Angelo

Luigi Parma examined the photograph against the face of the bearer, double-checked the signature and held the papers to the light to look for the watermark. Then he handed the document back to the irate art restorer.

'I've been working in the Hall of Apollo for the last six months,' she snarled, 'and you're still doing this ridiculous routine.'

Luigi was unfazed. 'Signora,' he said mildly, 'if you're as careful with your work as I am with mine, perhaps one day you'll restore the Sistine ceiling.'

She stormed off, her bag of brushes rattling with indignation. Luigi stood to attention at the entrance to Castel Sant'Angelo. And one day I may stand at the door of the Vatican, he thought. Parma knew the other staff thought him fussy. Some went so far as to call him Napoleon. Well, the little Corsican had come from humble beginnings... He swelled his small chest and stretched to his full five feet in his carefully polished, raised shoes.

Then he saw the man approaching from the bridge, and much of the elation left his body. That damned Benedictine, he thought, may God forgive me.

Some months before, Luigi had asked the Benedictine for ID; after all, it was his duty. The papers had been in perfect order – but he shuddered at the memory of what had followed. He remembered standing before the governor's desk, on tiptoe so that he would not be dwarfed by the furniture. The governor had been furious and explicit.

'Father Stefan is a professor of art, Signor Parma. He is a world-renowned expert on the restoration of frescoes. We are privileged to have him take time from his other important work to perform such a service to our institution – and you ask for his ID?'

'But, sir—'

'I haven't finished. As if this weren't bad enough, you asked questions of a member of the Benedictine Order who has taken a vow of silence for life.'

Oh, Jesus, Mary, Luigi had thought miserably, easing down from his toes and wishing he could claim sanctuary under the desk.

'Once more, Parma, and you can exercise your talent for officiousness by picking up horse shit from the street outside. Do I make myself clear?'

'Yes, sir.'

As Father Stefan approached, Luigi averted his eyes. The Benedictine swept past, his face hidden, as usual, by the cowl. He looks a bit tattier than usual, Luigi thought. And he's limping. Maybe he's had an accident. Nothing trivial, I hope – may God forgive me.

That thought restored his good humour, but his eyes narrowed as a car came speeding over the bridge, the revolving light sweeping other motorists

to the left and right. It screeched to a halt on the
cobbled forecourt, one wheel perched provocatively
on the pavement. Luigi was already bristling when a
tall man in a lived-in raincoat flashed a police ID in
his face. 'Your name?' he hissed.

More accustomed to asking questions than to
answering them, Luigi was thrown. He spluttered his
name, trying to lean away from the towering figure.
Behind the tall man were two men and a woman.
They wore identical expressions of such intensity
that Luigi dropped his eyes – but not before noticing
the swollen face and blood-encrusted ear of the
younger man.

'Who's come into the castle today?' the
policeman snapped.

'Er… the Signora Agnelli. She's always the first.
She's a restorer – very capable, I—'

'And after her?' the policeman prompted,
leaning so far forward that Parma's spine creaked.

'Father Stefan.'

'Who?'

'The professor who's restoring the Hall of
Justice.'

The policeman practically dragged Luigi to the
kiosk. 'A map of the castle, and fast. Show me
where he is.'

Parma waved a trembling finger at the Hall of
Justice. 'There,' he whispered.

The policeman flipped to the centre-page
spread, a detailed cross-section of the castle.

*

Fermi barrelled along the Staircase of Alexander VI with Michael dogging his heels. Mal and Rosa brought up the rear. A wide stairway opened to their right and Fermi shook open the map, his finger moving across the page.

'The Hall of Apollo is up there,' he whispered. 'The target is in the Hall of Justice, beside it. Mal and Rosa, you take the next staircase and come up the other side. Michael and I will take him or flush him out to you.'

Mal hesitated and then nodded.

'Give us three minutes,' Fermi said, and Rosa and Mal moved on.

At the top of the stairs, Fermi held Michael's arm. 'Do you have a weapon?'

'No.'

The detective fished in an ankle holster and handed Michael a small pistol. 'It will stop, not kill,' he whispered. Could he kill another priest? he wondered but didn't ask. 'The Hall of Apollo,' he said. 'We need to cross it.' On a count of three, he turned the handle noiselessly and pushed the door open just wide enough for Michael to slip inside, his gun held straight-armed, panning the room.

Michael heard a gasp, above him and to his right, and swung his weapon in a tight arc. Signora Agnelli perched on a stepladder before a fresco, her eyes round as saucers, her cleaning brush dripping from a trembling hand. Quickly, Michael lowered the gun and put his finger to his lips. Her enormous eyes slid sideways as Fermi appeared, similarly armed. He whispered to her in rapid Italian and she nodded woodenly, without blinking; her voice sounded choked as she replied.

'She says there is a door to the Hall of Justice, but it's locked,' Fermi translated.

Michael took up a position in the centre of the room while Fermi stood beside the door, his gun aimed two inches above the lock. He nodded. Michael charged; Fermi held his fire until he was two paces from the door, then squeezed the trigger.

Michael's momentum carried him tumbling into the room. He rolled to his feet in one smooth movement, his gun already swinging. Fermi was behind him, to his left, frantically searching for a target.

'The bird has flown,' Fermi gasped.

Wearily, he went to the other door and opened it for Mal and Rosa. He shook his head. 'Gone,' he said, 'we don't know where or how long ago.' He looked at the fresco of an angel on the far wall. 'And that is the Angel of Justice,' he said bitterly.

He remained looking at the angel, as if he could extract some information from it, while the others explored the room. Mal found a music stand and glanced at the music sheets. 'Mahler's 'Resurrection Symphony',' he grunted to no one in particular. Fermi snorted. Rosa, moving around the walls, stopped short at a statue of the Virgin. She gazed at the bubbled paint and gouged eyes. 'This guy's *loco*,' she breathed shakily, and crossed herself furtively before continuing.

She, Mal and Michael converged at the desk and stared at the computer monitor. The screen-saver showed a picture of the Pope.

'Looks too high-tech for me,' Mal said.

'Yeah, that and the abacus,' Rosa said dryly. She sat on the swivel chair and swung her legs under the desk. 'Well, here goes nothing.' She wiggled the mouse. 'Okay, baby wanna password, boys. Any of you hotshots stepping up to the plate?'

'Try "Remnant",' Michael said, after a pause.

Rosa's fingers danced over the keys. 'Strike one,' she sighed.

'Try "wrath",' Fermi prompted, joining them.

Rosa typed and slumped. 'Strike two,' she said through gritted teeth. 'C'mon, fellas, rub some resin on the bat.'

Fermi was about to speak, but Mal stayed him. 'I figure we got one more chance and then we're out of the ball game – am I right, Rosa?'

'You said it, Coach.'

'This guy likes to play mind games. He murders people and hides them in plain sight – you know, like symbols. My bet is he's done the same thing with his password. What are we missing here?'

Rosa and Fermi exchanged shrugs. Michael had drifted away to the centre of the room, gazing at the angel on the wall. 'The screen-saver,' he said abruptly. 'What was it, Rosa?'

'It was the Pope… you know, at the window.'

'The Pope standing on the balcony in St Peter's Square,' Fermi said thoughtfully.

'What was he doing?'

'He was blessing,' Fermi said, looking quizzically at Michael. 'He does it every week.'

'Yes, but there's a big one, isn't there?' Mal chimed in. 'A kinda special blessing. What the hell is it called?'

'*Urbi et Orbi*,' Fermi breathed.

'For the city and for the world,' Michael translated.

'Need a little help here, guys,' Rosa said, spreading her fingers. She kept pace with Fermi as he called out the letters. 'Open Sesame,' she said, and pressed Enter.

There was a buzzing sound and the screen glowed. 'Home run, team,' Rosa said excitedly.

Abruptly, the screen went blank.

'Oh, shit,' Rosa breathed, and dropped her head in her hands.

Mal fished for his phone and punched in a long series of numbers. 'You calling God, partner?' Rosa asked, without looking up. 'It's a local call from here.'

'Terence,' Mal said, 'I need a favour. Yes, another one, goddammit. Uh-huh, yes, I know about taking the name of the Lord in vain and all that, but I tried prayer and He's busy. You're the next best thing. I'm passing you to my partner, Rosa Torres. She'll fill you in.'

Quickly, Rosa began to talk Terence through the sequence they had followed on the computer. Mal inclined his head, and the others moved away from Rosa's shoulder. 'Let her breathe,' he said diplomatically.

'Detective Fermi,' Michael said quietly, 'is it likely that our man's just doubled back to the main entrance?'

'No, he would have to come back through the Hall of Apollo.'

'And he's not going to stick around, holed up somewhere, until we leave.'

'No. We have, as you say, blown his cover; he is gone. But where?'

'I'm a little vague on the history of Sant'Angelo, so maybe you can help me here? I seem to recall reading somewhere that one of the popes took refuge here during the sack of Rome.'

'Yes, it was Clement the Eighth.'

'How did he get here?'

Fermi's eyes widened. 'Oh my God,' he whispered, 'the Vatican Corridor.'

'What corridor?' Mal asked.

'There is a corridor that goes from Sant'Angelo to the Vatican Palace. It has not been used since...' Fermi's voice trailed off.

'Can we find the entrance?' Michael asked urgently.

'Yes, yes, of course. I will show you.'

'Just a minute.' Michael turned to Mal. 'Mal, I

need a real gun.' He took Fermi's ankle-pistol from his pocket and passed it to the detective. 'I don't think stopping will be enough, this time.'

Mal looked at him thoughtfully. 'Are you sure about this, Michael?'

'Yeah, I'm sure. Look, if you have any problem with this, I could ask Rosa.'

'No.' Mal plucked the Walther from his waistband. 'Take mine. I'll stay here with Rosa. And, Michael...' He didn't seem to know how to continue.

'I know, Mal,' Michael said quietly. 'See you later, okay?' Fermi was already holding the door.

Rosa was becoming more agitated, and Mal placed a soothing hand on her shoulder. 'Take it easy, partner,' he said. 'Terence is the original pain in the butt, but he's the best.'

She turned anguished eyes in his direction. 'Mal, he's one part cyborg and two parts Bible-freak. Yes, Terence,' she said quickly, hunching over the keyboard. 'Could you just run that by me one more time? I'm flying a 747 here and I'm just cabin crew, you know?'

She listened intently and tapped. The computer sighed, and the glow of the monitor lit up her face.

'Terence, honey,' she asked sweetly, 'are you married?'

29

The Vatican

Hugh raced past the receptionist and took the stairs two at a time before the Swiss Guards could react. He heard them pounding along the corridor behind him; he slammed his shoulder into Cardinal Thomas' door and tumbled into the room. The two burly young men were hauling him to his feet when the cardinal appeared, in pyjamas and bathrobe.

'Enough,' he said sharply, and the struggle ceased. 'Thank you for your concern,' he told the guards. 'I'll deal with this.' They glared at Hugh and withdrew, muttering to each other as they stamped down the corridor.

'Please close the door, Dr O'Neill. If the hinges still work.' Cardinal Thomas sat down behind the desk and inclined his head towards a chair. 'Sit,' he commanded.

'I have betrayed you,' Hugh said simply.

The cardinal sighed and took off his spectacles, kneading his eye sockets with the heels of his hands. 'Why is it no one ever repents during office hours?' he asked tiredly. 'Okay, in your own time.'

Hugh told him all of it, without embellishment or excuse. When he had finished, Cardinal Thomas held him in a flat stare for some time.

'You are either a dangerous fantasist, an attention seeker, or… Tell me why, Hugh,' he said tiredly.

'I believed I was acting in the best interests of the Church, Eminence.'

'And do you still believe that?'

'I believe my motive was sound to begin with. As things… developed, I began to see things differently. Archbishop Leclerc's blood is on my hands, and I believe the people I supplied with information will no longer be content with the elimination of archbishops.'

'Oh? And how high do you think they'll go?'

'As high as you, Eminence.'

'You have proof of this?'

'No. I'm a lawyer by profession, albeit a canon lawyer, and I know what I've said can be dismissed as circumstantial.'

The silence stretched as the cardinal sat in thought.

'Would you be willing to tell what you know to the Pope? It would mean admitting your involvement.'

Hugh took a deep breath. 'Yes, I would.'

The cardinal sprang to his feet. 'Go to the Pope's quarters now. Tell them I'll be along presently. Go.'

Hugh hurried from the room and mounted the stairway to the papal apartments. He expected Swiss Guards at the top of the stairs, but there were none. With mounting concern, he walked briskly towards the door leading to the apartments themselves. There was no guard; an empty chair stood outside the door, and he felt a cold premonition clutch his heart.

He knocked. After a few moments, a voice called cautiously through the locked door. 'Who is it?'

'I'm Dr Hugh O'Neill, attached to the office of Cardinal Thomas,' he said clearly, his heart hammering. 'His Eminence asked me to come here. He will follow presently.'

After a beat, the lock clicked and the door opened. Hugh stepped inside; he was caught in an armlock and slammed against the door.

'Let's have a look at you, Dr Hugh O'Neill,' the big man said. He was dressed casually; a stethoscope dangled from his neck. 'Pass your ID – very slowly, please. Any sudden movement and I'll break your arm.'

He applied a little pressure to underline the threat, and Hugh winced. Carefully, he took his driving licence from his top pocket and thumbed it open. The man compared the picture to the face but didn't relax his grip.

'You don't look like an assassin,' he said. 'How did you get here?'

'There are no guards on the landing or outside the door,' Hugh answered.

The man's eyes widened a little, and he released his grip. 'I'm Dr Eli Weissman, the Pope's physician. He's sleeping.'

Hugh glanced over Weissman's shoulder at the figure wrapped in rugs, sleeping in a wheelchair.

'He has a respiratory problem,' Weissman said, by way of explanation. 'He can't lie down.'

'Dr Weissman,' Hugh said urgently, 'could you call the security desk and ask why there are no guards on the papal apartments?'

Weissman hurried to a telephone, listened briefly, and dropped it back in the cradle. 'Dead,' he said shortly. 'I take it that both of us are unarmed?'

Hugh nodded.

'Then what are we to do, Dr O'Neill?'

Hugh told him.

'That plan has no hope of succeeding,' Weissman said.

'Do you have a better one?'

'No.'

★

Michael burst from the Vatican Corridor and skidded to a halt, his eyes roving, trying to orient himself in the Vatican Palace. Think, he commanded himself. Where are the papal apartments? On impulse, he took the corridor to his left and sprinted up a flight of steps, his breath ragged in his chest.

A doorway loomed ahead, flanked by two Swiss Guards. Before the door, a hawk-faced cleric brooded behind a desk. Michael recognised the gaunt face: he was on the right track for Cardinal Thomas' apartments. The papal apartments would be overhead.

Raising an imperious hand, the cleric at the desk strode forward to block his passage. Michael hit him on the run. The man slid across the marble floor on his back, and Michael was running down the long corridor before the Swiss Guards could react.

★

Cardinal Thomas stopped outside the door to the papal apartments and waited. The pistol touched the back of his head.

'Knock, your Eminence,' the voice commanded.

He knocked. 'Who is it?' a voice demanded from behind the door.

'Cardinal Thomas. My assistant, Dr O'Neill, is already with you.'

Eli opened the door and was pushed back into the room. Cardinal Thomas was shoved inside by a man who held a pistol to his head. 'I'm sorry,' the cardinal said dully, 'he was waiting for me at the top—'

'Enough,' the man hissed, grinding the gun into his neck. Hugh moved to block his view of the wheelchair. With his gun butt, the man clubbed the cardinal, and his unconscious body fell to the floor.

Stefan swung the gun and pointed it at Hugh. 'Stand aside, Dr O'Neill,' he commanded. 'It is too late for you to become a hero.'

Hugh looked into the enormous muzzle of the gun.

'No,' he said calmly.

The sound of the gunshot was deafening in the small room. Hugh was punched back and fell away from the wheelchair.

'Now is it consummated!' Stefan shouted. 'You have betrayed the Church by bartering with the unbeliever.' He fired twice into the figure in the wheelchair.

The gun swept sideways and locked on Eli. He stared back unflinchingly.

'You are to live.' The gunman smiled and backed through the door.

For a heartbeat, Eli stood frozen. He had been ready to die; his brain couldn't accept that he was still alive. Then he rushed to Hugh and felt for a pulse in his neck. It was faint as a butterfly's wings beating in a boy's cupped hands. Frantically, he tore at Hugh's jacket and shirt, and groaned when he saw the enormity of the wound. Tenderly, he raised Hugh's head and shoulders from the floor, cradling him in his arms.

Hugh's eyelids fluttered and opened. 'Tom?' he whispered, the name bubbling through the blood in his mouth. His hand clutched convulsively at Eli's jacket, and then his body went slack.

★

There must be a stairway, Michael thought. Where the hell is the stairway? Damn – it's behind me. He turned and found himself looking at two Swiss Guards. The one on the left jerked his gun upward, gesturing for Michael to put his hands on his head. The other tried unsuccessfully to still the trembling in the hand holding his gun.

'Listen,' Michael said desperately. 'Do you speak English?'

'I do,' the one on the right said coldly. 'Now put your hands on your head.'

'I am Father Michael Flaherty. There is an assassin in the building, and the Pope may be in danger. We must go to his apartments, now.'

'If you do not put your hands on your head, we will shoot,' the guard said angrily.

Michael whipped the gun from the back of his waistband and pointed it at him.

'So will I,' he said.

★

Stefan raced down the stairs to the first landing. He heard the sound of raised voices and risked a glance over the balustrade: two armed Swiss Guards were holding a man at bay. Silently, Stefan swung over the balustrade on their blind side and dropped, rolling and running in one fluid movement.

He heard shouts behind him and a shot whined over his head, gouging chips from the corridor wall. Without breaking his stride, he swung his gun behind him and fired. The pursuers checked, and he sprinted for a lighted doorway.

He hurtled into St Peter's Square, slipping the gun into his pocket, slowing his pace. He weaved through the throng of pilgrims making their way to the massive doors of the Basilica.

Hide in plain sight, Magda murmured approvingly. He sensed her walking before him through the throng. Remember what I told you?

'To be invisible,' he answered.

Yes. And to be invisible, you must remember that straight lines are rarely found in nature. If you would cross a valley, let the valley take you across at its own pace and in its own way.

He allowed the eddying crowds to carry him back and forth, so that a watcher would not see someone breaking the flow. He sensed there were watchers above the colonnade on either side, shielded by the statues of the apostles and saints. He knew they would have small field glasses and high-powered rifles. Flight was their friend; a sudden movement would flicker in their vision and spur them to track and fire.

He set his sights on one of the bollards surrounding the base of the obelisk. The stream of pilgrims flowing into the square was thinning; across the mouth of the Via della Conciliazione stretched a blockade of police cars, bumper to bumper, diverting people to the right and left. Stefan sat on the bollard and sheathed his arms in his long sleeves.

The Papal Apartments

Eli closed Hugh's eyes with his thumb and placed him on the bed. He crossed the room to Cardinal Thomas and settled him in the recovery position.

Footsteps pounded on the landing outside, and the door burst open. Armed Swiss Guards crowded into the apartment, followed by Cardinal Richter. Richter saw Cardinal Thomas on the floor and stopped.

'Cardinal Thomas will recover, Eminence,' Eli said quickly. 'Please come.'

He drew Richter to the still figure on the bed.

'Who is this?' Richter asked hoarsely.

'His name is Hugh O'Neill.'

'And the Pope?'

Eli went to the double doors leading to the balcony and opened them. The Pope was propped on a chair in the corner. He stirred when he saw them. Carefully, the two men led him back inside and supported him as he whispered a blessing and made the sign of the cross over the body of Hugh O'Neill.

When they had settled him in the wheelchair,

Cardinal Richter turned to Eli and whispered, 'You have saved the Pope's life, Doctor. We are in your debt.'

Eli inclined his head toward the figure in the bed. 'It was him,' he said. 'It was his idea. He insisted we take the Pope to the balcony and switch off all the lights except the small light behind the wheelchair. He said we should arrange pillows and rugs in the chair, cover the head and put the oxygen mask where the face would be.' Eli realised he was babbling. I am not dead, he thought. I am alive and I shouldn't be.

The Pope coughed, and Eli went to kneel before him. He felt the furnace of the Pope's forehead and listened to the faint heartbeat.

'Cardinal Richter,' he said gravely. 'Please summon an ambulance, immediately.'

The Pope's eyes opened and he looked at Eli.

'Is it time?' he mouthed silently.

Eli took his hand and held it firmly. 'It is time, Pope,' he said softly. 'It is time to stop watching.'

The Pope lifted Eli's hand to his lips and kissed it. His lips moved once more.

'Thank you, Eli,' he said.

St Peter's Square

Do you remember that first time in the forest, Stefan? Magda asked.

'That fool boy let me walk right into the camp. I

remember when we stood against the others. They said, "There are six of us and only two of you." And you said, "We don't care." Nothing can hurt you if you don't care. I should have died in my church and with my people, Magda. I missed my chance at martyrdom, and I wasn't sure how to survive my survival.'

So you made a pact with the Devil.

The square had become eerily empty. A discarded red-and-white flag flapped like a wounded pigeon, unable to rise. Before the police line, a tiny cyclone of papers and debris twirled in a sudden gust of wind and settled.

And what did the Devil offer, Stefan?

'The possibility of putting some form on the… emptiness. And the promise of an end to it.'

Is this the end?

'Yes. I have kept my side of the bargain.'

Do you care?

He didn't answer.

You remember what I said in the forest about not caring?

Her voice was becoming fainter and he lifted his head, straining to hear her.

I didn't care then, Stefan. But later, when we were together in the forest, I think I did begin to… a little.

He heard her laugh and craned his head to follow the sound as it faded.

'Magda?' he whispered. 'Magda?'

The Papal Apartments

Cardinal Richter held the door as the ambulance crew wheeled the Pope through. Cardinal Thomas had regained consciousness and had been taken, under protest, to the infirmary. Somebody had pulled a sheet over Hugh O'Neill's face. Eli sat in a chair against the wall, his head in his hands.

'Dr Weissman?'

Eli straightened and looked at Richter.

'Dr Weissman, I have instructed them to take the Pope to the Gemelli Hospital. It is nearer than your own and, under the circumstances… I trust you are not offended?'

'We've said our goodbyes,' Eli said.

'I believe the assassin is in the square,' Richter continued. 'There are policemen everywhere; he will not escape.'

Slowly, Eli stood up. 'I'm not sure he wants to, Eminence,' he said.

'Can I get someone to take you home?'

'No, thank you, Eminence. I may be needed by the police.'

St Peter's Square

Stefan sat on the bollard in the empty square. Magda was gone. He felt nothing. Slowly, he eased himself to his feet and walked towards the blockade. He stopped about twenty paces from the line.

'Place your weapon on the ground,' a voice called, the echoes skipping around the columns of the colonnade. Stefan traced the speaker, a tall, thin man in civilian clothes. Detective, he thought, and so are the man and woman behind him. There was a subtle difference in their body language and clothing that marked them as foreigners. She has a gun in that shoulder bag she keeps close to her right hand, he concluded. He does not, and this makes his hands fret. Magda would have been pleased with her pupil. Slowly, he raised his hands and pushed the cowl back from his face.

'Put down your weapon and come to me, please.'

The tall, thin detective had moved a little in front of the others. Almost casually, Stefan reached into his pocket and raised the gun, centring the muzzle on the detective.

'The police will open fire if you shoot,' the detective said calmly.

'I don't care,' Stefan replied. He swept the weapon along the line before him until the muzzle found and steadied on the woman.

'I am standing in the Vatican State, Detective,' he shouted, for the benefit of all the uniforms in the line. 'I am a priest of the Roman Catholic Church and under its jurisdiction and protection. You are on the wrong side of the line. You can't shoot me.'

'I can,' said a voice behind him.

Oh, Magda, he thought, am I such a bad pupil, or is he very good? I didn't hear or sense him.

Slowly, he turned and bent his elbow, bringing the gun upright beside his face, the muzzle pointing at the sky.

Michael had used the obelisk as cover to make his way across the square. He had positioned himself so that, when Stefan turned towards him, the light was in his eyes. In Michael's right hand, a handgun hung beside his thigh.

'You are the gladiator,' Stefan said. 'I should have killed you in the Colosseum.'

'You prefer your opponents tied, as I recall,' Michael said coolly.

Stefan flinched and then laughed.

'Rosa,' Mal whispered, 'give me your gun.'

'Sebastiano Spenza was a nothing,' Stefan said. 'He was a pebble in my path. I kicked him aside on the way to fulfilling my mission.'

'Not yours, Father,' Michael said, raising his voice. 'Not your mission. You were just the weapon. Someone else pointed you and pulled the trigger. Who was that, Father? Who was the master who let you off the leash to—'

The three shots sounded to Fermi like a string of exploding firecrackers shattering the silence of the square. Belatedly, he raised his own weapon, even as he saw the Benedictine punched sideways and then back. Fermi was over the line and running. In his peripheral vision, he saw Mal following at speed.

His brain was racing through the permutations. The first shot had caught the Benedictine in the shoulder, so he had begun to spin; the second shot, a chest shot, had knocked him back. That had been the killing shot, Fermi knew, as he knelt beside the sprawled body and searched for a pulse. Slowly, he pulled the cowl over the dead man's head.

The third shot, he thought suddenly. Where did...?

He looked up and saw Mal on his knees, cradling Michael in his arms, calling his name over and over. He heard ambulance sirens butting at the confinement of the Via Della Conciliazione before they burst into the square.

30

St Peter's Square

Eli had just emerged from the Vatican Palace when the shots rang out. He started to run, his long legs carrying him to the huddle of people around the man on the ground.

'Let me through, please.'

In the back of the blaring ambulance, he worked feverishly, stringing the drip and placing the oxygen mask over the ashen face. He sensed someone behind him and turned.

'Is he…?' the older man whispered, in English.

'No. We'll be at the hospital very soon,' Eli said reassuringly. He saw the anguish in the man's face and concluded he must be the patient's father.

Santa Sabina Hospital, Rome

Rosa disliked waiting rooms. She had had a particular and passionate dislike for hospital waiting rooms, ever since Pepito... Don't go there, she admonished herself; this isn't about you. She worked at distracting herself. Why are the chairs so uncomfortable? Why are all the damn magazines out of date? Because frightened people get so focused on what might be happening in the theatre, they don't even see this place.

Mal wasn't going blind; he was just going, pacing the small room, driving her crazy.

'Get you a coffee, Mal?'

'No – no, thanks, Rosa,' he muttered, without checking his stride. She moved to the large window. A man walked by wearing a huge bandage on his head. She was about to turn away when she saw the surgeon.

'Mal!' She inclined her head and saw him swivel to the window. Oh, God, she thought, he looks so scared.

The surgeon was a tall young man with steady brown eyes. 'I'm Dr Eli Weissman,' he said. 'You are family?'

'You could say that,' Mal said.

'Ah, yes... very well. Please sit. Father Flaherty was shot in the chest. The bullet passed through his ribs and lodged in his left lung.'

Mal's face lost its colour, and Rosa put her hand on his arm.

'I have removed the bullet and stopped the bleeding. He is a young man, very strong, so we will hope.'

'Hope?' Rosa whispered.

'Yes, Signorina. There is no certainty. He is a very sick man; if he is to get better, he must fight. Is he a fighter?'

'Yes,' Mal said vehemently, 'he's one hell of a fighter.'

'Can we see him?' Rosa asked.

'Yes, of course. Please come.'

They halted inside the door of the recovery room, shocked by the tangle of pumps, tubes, drips and monitors. The upper half of Michael's body was swathed in bandages and his face was waxen. Ay, *Dios*, Rosa thought, he looks so small, so like Pepito… Her vision blurred and she planed her palms across her eyes, hoping that Mal wouldn't notice. But Mal only had eyes for the man in the bed. He moved to stand beside him.

'You may speak to him,' Dr Weissman said gently.

Mal bent until his mouth was close to Michael's ear. His body trembled and his face contorted.

'Hang in there, son,' he said brokenly.

Weissman took his arm and led him to a chair. 'It is good that you see he is alive,' he said.

Rosa slipped her hand into Mal's and tried not to wince when he squeezed it fiercely. The pressure eased as he drew in a long breath.

'Hell of a fighter,' he said.

Michael was in a world of water, huge slabs of maddened, green water that towered and fell, blinding his eyes and roaring in his ears. He was reaching across the upturned boat, his fingers locked in his brother's. He spat the bitter salt from his mouth. 'Liam,' he shouted.

The Monastery of the Resurrection, New York State

Hanny turned a corner on the path and stopped. The deer gave her a sidelong look, twitched its velvet ears and ambled back to the trees.

She stood still a moment longer, savouring the experience, and then checked her watch. She smiled as she recalled one of Raphael's mini-sermons on watch-checking: 'Do you wear the watch, Hanny, or does the watch wear you?' She had to admit, she had grown fond of the old coot. Funny old world, she thought: I'm almost filleted by a priest, and Cardinal Wall thinks I should recuperate in a monastery. She shivered and put up the collar of her coat. Takes time, old girl, she reassured herself. Takes time.

Cardinal Wall had pulled in all sorts of favours to get her released from the hospital into his care. Then he had insisted on driving her to the monastery himself, all the way upstate. She had called Mal en route, to tell him all about it, but he had been distant on the phone, not himself at all. 'Get back to you, Hanny,' he had said, and then, as an afterthought, 'You okay?' Yeah, well, okay will do for now, she thought.

She remembered her first meeting with Raphael and smiled. She had taken one look at his ensemble and asked, 'Who's your tailor?' Later, when Cardinal Wall had left, they had sat on either side of the fire like the unlikeliest Darby and Joan, she talking as usual and he nodding his head, until she found herself talking of Mal and Michael; the whole kit and caboodle. And the tears, rivers of tears from some dam breached deep inside... Remarkably, for a man, Raphael hadn't scooted or suddenly discovered a slew of platitudes. He'd just sat there, sipping his tea, holding the mug between those god-awful mitts.

Hanny looked up and saw the roof of the monastery begin to appear above the rise. A bird was giving it holy heck in a tree that seemed made of fire. There had to be birds in the Bronx, she thought, but who ever heard them? A cloud dimmed the sunlight, and she felt suddenly cold and anxious for no good reason.

'Hi, Hanny. How was it?' Raphael was already filling the kettle for tea. The Irish and the Chinese, she thought: can't live without the leaf.

'It's really nice out there, Raphael,' she said, hanging her coat on a hook, 'but, boy, my feet are killing me.'

'Tell me about it,' he said, and they both laughed. 'Sit down, Hanny,' he said, bringing the teapot to the table.

She sat slowly, watching him grip the teapot between his gloved hands to pour. 'Okay, Raphael,' she said, 'there's something wrong, isn't there? Back home, my mother always poured tea before she dropped the bomb. Spit it out.'

'I got news while you were out, Hanny,' Raphael said slowly, his eyes fixed on hers. 'Not very good, not very bad.'

'Is it Mal?' she asked, setting the cup to rattle in the saucer.

'No, it was Mal who called. Said he'd call back in an hour.'

'Michael, then,' she breathed. She didn't know why she wasn't surprised. A hard knot began to tighten in her stomach.

'Mal said Michael was shot,' he said. 'Shot pretty bad, Hanny, but he's in good hands.'

Hanny's brain fastened on the phrase 'in good hands'. Christ, she thought, it's right up there on the scale of dumb-ass things to say with 'as well as can be expected'. She bit down hard on her anger. Don't shoot the messenger, she chided herself.

'Michael is strong, Hanny,' Raphael said softly.

She wanted to take that word and bounce it off the walls. He's like all damn Irishmen from way back, she wanted to yell: muscle outside and mush inside. Always being so damn heroic that they never get sorted and the wheel goes round and round. And one day they realise that 'hero' isn't all it's cracked up to be, but it's too late, because they're too old to get off the pedestal and the plaster's set too hard.

'Hanny, I can hear you thinking, right over here. You want to talk?'

She picked up her tea and tasted it. 'Maybe we could have something stronger?'

'Top cupboard on the right, with the sauce bottles.'

'Where else?'

She poured two full tumblers and sat.

'*Sláinte*,' Raphael said, and they clinked glasses. 'Michael taught me that,' he added innocently.

'I think...' Hanny began, and fortified herself with a sip before continuing. 'I think if his mother had lived, Michael would never have been a priest.'

'That's a new take on the traditional Irish story,' Raphael said, smiling.

'Yeah, I know, I know. But when you lose a parent so young, there must be such a gap in your life. Back home, boys can grow to men awful fast, at a time like that; too fast. It's kinda expected. Everybody says it's brave and manly and all the rest of that bullsh...' She stopped.

Raphael smiled. 'Bullshit is a very popular ingredient in Chinese medicine.'

'Anyway, when you're brave, and tough, and all that other... Chinese medicine, it's mighty hard to be… real. You gotta keep running faster and faster to stand still, if you get my meaning.'

'Oh, I get your meaning. Heroism can be a big pain in the fingers, believe me. When people tell you all the time how heroic you are, you think maybe you should be, for their sakes. Heroes can be terminally polite.'

'Yeah, it's like everyone wants a piece of the action. I know I did. I wanted the son I never had – me and Mal both. So I kept house and cooked dinner and got on Michael's case about clean shirts and wearing the damn dog collar. Anything except sitting him down and saying what I'm saying to you now, 'cause I was afraid to lose him. If… when he gets over this thing, I wish he'd just go home, back to the Island, do whatever the hell Island folks do and maybe figure out a good reason for being himself.'

'I'll drink to that,' Raphael said.

'You needed a reason?'

Santa Sabina Hospital, Rome

Michael's eyes were open as he floated up to the light. When he broke through the surface of the water, he saw a young woman. She was sleeping with her arms resting on the side of the bed, her head cradled in the angle of her elbow. Her black hair was close-cropped – like moss on a stone, he thought. The face slanted towards him was creamy brown, with high cheekbones buttressing slightly slanted eyes.

Slowly, her eyes opened and they gazed at each other. Michael saw a spark of recognition ignite in her brown-black pupils and blaze through her face. 'Mal,' she said.

Another face bent to join hers. It was stretched from sleep and stubbled with a few days' growth, but the eyes were as blue as ever. 'Mal,' Michael whispered.

Rosa flung herself from the room and hared to the nurses' station at the end of the corridor, skidding as she negotiated the doorway. Dr Weissman held an x-ray negative against the light, his head tilted.

'Good morning, Rosa,' he said calmly.

'He's back,' she panted, and Weissman smiled as he put down the x-ray and followed her.

'Welcome back to the living, Michael Flaherty,' he said warmly, easing Mal aside. 'I am Dr Eli Weissman. I think you know these people. You are in hospital, in Rome. Do you know why?'

'Shot,' Michael whispered. 'Pope?'

'The Pope is dead, Michael.'

Weissman saw the bleak look in his eyes. 'No,' he said quickly, 'he was not shot by the assassin. Dr Hugh O'Neill – you know him?'

Michael nodded.

'Dr O'Neill had an idea. We took the Pope to the balcony outside the apartment, and made a figure with pillows and rugs on the wheelchair. When the assassin came, with Cardinal Thomas as a hostage, Dr O'Neill stood before the chair to block his view. He refused to move, and the assassin shot him.'

'Dead?'

'Yes. I'm sorry.'

'Cardinal Thomas?'

'The assassin knocked him unconscious before he shot Dr O'Neill and what he thought was the Pope. The cardinal has recovered.'

Michael's lips moved, but no sound came.

'You?' Weissman read the silent question from his patient's lips. 'You're asking why I'm alive. I don't know. Perhaps some providence spared me to save you. You must rest now. Your body and your mind need sleep.'

But his patient had already anticipated the command.

31

The Women's Refuge, 42nd Street, Manhattan

Sister Martha sat at the long, gleaming kitchen table and sighed.

'I'm tired,' she whispered, 'so tired.'

Tired? From doing what? When I was your age...

She let Momma's voice run in her head until it faded. 'You can let her rant, Sister,' the counsellor had said. 'It's just old tapes stored in your head, put there by a cranky old lady a long time ago. You can just let it in one ear and out the other.'

Shows how much you got between your ears, girl.

'Can I ask her to stop?'

'No, but you can tell her to stop.'

The counsellor was a Sister of Martha's own order, a friendly, open-faced young woman. One of the bright new… Martha squeezed her eyes shut, but Kathleen O'Reilly rose up accusingly in her mind.

'Oh, Sister Kathleen,' she whispered, 'I am so sorry.'

She wished she could tell the counsellor about it; this terrible guilt she dragged around with her every day. She couldn't pray. She couldn't bear to join the other Sisters for any length of time. She thought they were sure to see something in her face that would betray her.

There was a knock on the door, and she dried her eyes hastily on her grubby apron. 'Come in.'

Teresa, the younger of her two assistants, opened the door. 'Sister Martha, you got a visitor.'

'A visitor? Oh, Lord…'

She just had time to remove the apron and roll it into a ball before Cardinal Wall walked into the kitchen. 'Thank you very much, Teresa,' he said.

'You're welcome, honey.' Teresa smiled and backed out, closing the door behind her.

'Nice lady,' Cardinal Wall said to Martha.

'Oh, yes, your Eminence, she's very nice. She's some kind of a Baptist, your Eminence, and wouldn't know how to address you. I'm sorry.'

'No need to be, Sister Martha. Can we sit down for a few minutes? I'd like to talk to you.'

'Oh, yes, of course, Eminence. Won't you sit here?'

She resisted the urge to polish the seat of the chair with the balled apron and waited for the cardinal to sit before she sat herself.

'Sister Martha,' he began quietly, 'I've had some information from Rome that I'd like to share with you – in confidence, of course.'

Martha nodded, not trusting herself to speak.

'It concerns Sister Kathleen O'Reilly.' The cardinal saw the colour drain from her face and her eyes fill. 'I'm sorry to tell you, but Sister Kathleen was murdered.'

Martha's mouth opened, and a tear dropped on the table. Automatically, she wiped it away with her apron.

'You should also know that the person who did this terrible thing is also dead.' He looked away from the distressed woman. 'I liked Sister Kathleen, liked her a lot. She could be feisty and opinionated, she had all those new ideas that scare people my age – but she had great courage. Every time I bawled her out, she just bounced back for more, because she wasn't in it for herself. I feel guilty about that sometimes. I thought you'd like to hear this because I heard you two were friends. Kathleen was blessed with many friends, but it takes one to make one.'

He let the silence gather in the big kitchen. Martha dabbed her eyes with the apron one more time and decided.

Least said, soonest mended, girl.

'You go to hell, Momma,' she said defiantly.

'Pardon?'

'No, sorry, it's just…' Martha composed herself, sitting upright in the chair and holding her hands in her lap as she had been instructed to do, all those years ago, for her interview with Cardinal Wall before she took her final vows. Lord, she had been so nervous then. How should she address him? Should she kiss his ring?

'You're smiling,' the cardinal said.

'I was remembering the last time we met.'

He looked at her blankly.

'Oh, it was years ago; you won't recall it. I was very young and very nervous.'

'I'm sure we both were.'

'I don't remember any of the interview, but when I was leaving, I was dithering about whether I should kiss your ring or not; and you took my hand and… you called me by my name, my own name. I got Martha with my vows. You said, "Jane, try to be happy. Otherwise, what's it all for?" I never forgot that.'

'And are you happy, Jane?'

Martha's face crumpled and she covered it with her hands. Huge sobs racked up from her stomach until the tears leaked through her fingers. When the crying had eased, Cardinal Wall took a handkerchief from his pocket and passed it to her.

'Give it a good blow,' he said. 'You'll feel a hell of a lot better.'

At last she tucked the handkerchief into her sleeve and began to speak. 'Sister Kathleen... she was kind to me. I never felt stupid, or lumpy, or anything like that, when I was with her. She was so smart – all those books and lectures and everything – and I...I was kind of jealous.'

The cardinal nodded. 'Kathleen was a hard act to follow for any of us,' he said.

'Thing is, I'm not very bright, and when she talked to me about the Church and women priests and stuff, I got so frightened. The Church is the only home I've ever had. I used to feel safe, accepted. But then everything changed, and Sister Kathleen was saying those things...'

'Was there no one you could talk to, about your fears?'

'Oh, I tried to tell my confessor, but he... well, maybe he thought it wasn't very important. And then I found Monsignor Dalton.'

The cardinal felt himself tense.

'He was very comforting,' Martha continued. 'He seemed to understand how I felt really well. I thought, well, someone else feels the way I do, so I mustn't be such a fool. He asked me if I could get some of Sister Kathleen's papers, so he could study the stuff she was working on. He said he'd be able to help me if he could read it. I photocopied them here and brought them back later. She never knew. But it bothered me more and more. Sister Kathleen was so generous; anything you ever said was nice...

When I tried to tell the monsignor how badly I felt, he said it was God's work and for the good of the Church. But it wasn't, was it?'

'No, Sister,' Cardinal Wall said, 'it wasn't.'

'What can I do?'

'About the past – nothing. And God knows I think you've suffered enough for that. Do you have someone you can talk to now, about these things?'

'Yes, I see a counsellor – well, I've only seen her twice, but she's very kind. I've been trying to work up the courage to tell her about this.'

'It took a hell of a lot of courage to go see her, Sister, and even more to tell me what you just did. You don't lack courage, Sister Martha. You've lived through some of the greatest changes in the history of the Church, and you're still here. And maybe your counsellor can help you get back some of the joy.'

After the cardinal left, Martha put the kettle on to boil. As it started to sing, Teresa put her head around the door.

'Batman gone?'

'Yes,' Martha said, smiling, 'Batman's gone. Like a coffee? I'm going to use the special stuff we keep for visitors.'

'Lay it on me,' Teresa said, and slumped in a chair.

Momma's outraged voice came from the coffee jar. Wilful waste is woeful want, girl.

'And let's have real cream,' Sister Martha said.

St Patrick's Cathedral, New York

Cardinal Wall peeled off his heavy overcoat and slumped at his desk. The meeting with Sister Martha had left a bitter taste in his mouth. A vulnerable member of his flock had been mauled by a wolf, on his watch. He glanced at his open diary and sighed. Time for the bibulous bomber, Larry Breen.

Father Breen sat in the chair, a resigned expression on his florid face. The purple network of veins in his nose radiated to his cheekbones; his eyes, filmed and flecked, stared defiantly at a spot above the cardinal's head.

'How are you, Larry?'

The use of his first name and the genuine tone seemed to shake Father Breen out of his protective stupor. 'I am as you find me, Eminence,' he said uncertainly.

'I see. I was thinking, before you came in, about Sister Kathleen O'Reilly.'

'Ah, yes, Kathleen – grand girl. Always nice to me; gave me a bit of a lift, you know, whenever that bas— whenever the monsignor tried to get a few kicks in.'

'You don't like Dalton much, do you, Larry?'

Father Breen sucked in a wet breath and considered the question. He leaned a little forward in the chair and cast a wary eye at the door before replying. 'It's like this, Eminence. Sometimes – most of the time – I'm a drunken bastard. You know that and I know that. But Dalton is a sober bastard, and believe me, Eminence, they're the worst kind. I seen him in action – you know, out there – week in, week out. He never gets much satisfaction from me; with my complaint, you get a kind of talent for rolling with the punches. That pisses Dalton off, big time. Now, Kathleen, she didn't give a flying f— damn. She knew he was just a little man trying to pump himself bigger by stepping on some other man or woman. She could see right through that fella and his little piggy eyes and his parading around like he had a broom handle stuck up his ass – saving your presence, Eminence. And, by God, could she punch above her weight; full of spit and vinegar. I was very sorry to hear of her accident.'

'I'm sorry to have to tell you, Larry, that she was murdered.'

'Wha…?' Father Breen reared back in the chair. The colour left his face, the webbing of veins turning it into the face of a very old porcelain doll. 'Ah, Holy Jesus,' he gasped.

'I'm sorry to have that kind of news for you,' Cardinal Wall said. 'I know it's a shock. You and Kathleen were close.'

Father Breen had regained his colour, and he rubbed his fists roughly in his eyes. 'I couldn't say we were close friends, Eminence, not with her being up there' – he lifted a hand – 'and me…' The hand dropped back to his knee. 'But she never talked down to me, you see. I get a lot of that. I suppose it's well meant – most people get kind of antsy around a drunk – but it makes you feel like shit.'

He lapsed into silence, nodding and rubbing his knee reflectively. The cardinal let it stretch while he gathered his thoughts.

'I think I've failed you, Larry, as your bishop,' he said quietly.

Father Breen scratched his head. 'Well, I don't know. I mean, I have been out of order – what with the IRA thing and the bottle. It's just... I dropped the ball, Eminence, if you follow me. Things just got away from me, and I couldn't get them back. I felt, what the hell? This is what I am.'

'Well, I can't agree with all that, Larry. A lot of people have told me you're another kind of man, when you're not...'

'Drunk? Say "drunk", Eminence.'

'Okay, drunk. But that doesn't take from what you feel for Kathleen. She had a gift for people, didn't she? And she sure as hell saw through me.'

'You?'

'Yeah. I couldn't faze her with all the huff and puff; she just sat me out, and then we talked like ordinary, normal people. I really miss that. I surely do.' Cardinal Wall sighed. 'I have a suggestion to make, Larry. How's about you take a break for a while, get yourself properly fed and rested, give yourself a chance to think things through? I have a friend, Abbot Raphael, who runs a monastery upstate.' He saw the look in Father Breen's eyes. 'No, we're not talking spiritual boot camp here, Larry. I give you my word.'

Father Breen bobbed his head a few times before replying. 'Can't hurt, I suppose.'

'I'll take that as an enthusiastic "yes", then.'

Cardinal Wall stood up and extended his hand. Father Breen looked at it for a long moment before taking it.

'I'll make the arrangements, Larry, and you'll get a call.'

★

When Father Breen had left, Cardinal Wall scribbled a note in his diary. Monsignor Dalton opened the door from the waiting room.

'There are no more interviews for today, Eminence.'

'Actually, there is one more, Monsignor.'

'Oh, really? Who?'

'You. Sit down, Monsignor.'

The cardinal waited until Dalton sat primly in the chair.

'I think we can cut to the chase, Monsignor,' he said. 'You're fired.'

Dalton flinched as if slapped and struggled to his feet. 'Your Eminence—' he began.

'Sit down,' the cardinal snapped. 'Now hear me and hear me good, Dalton.' He leaned forward, his fierce gaze boring into the other man. 'I know about you.'

The monsignor struggled for composure, and when he spoke, his voice trembled with rage.

'You know about me? You don't know me; you never have. I am invisible to you, Eminence. It was always "Dalton, do this; Dalton, do that". I served you well, and for what thanks? Did you think of me when you appointed your assistant bishops? Did you consider for one moment that my years of service, my proven abilities—'

'Yes, as a matter of fact, I did consider you, Monsignor. And I thank our Lord Jesus Christ that I had the wit to look beyond you. As for your proven abilities… I know about your powers of persuasion when it came to poor gullible Sister Martha. I know about your proven ability to eavesdrop on telephone calls, and to pass on information that led to the death of Sister Kathleen O'Reilly.'

Dalton's mouth opened and closed. 'Kathleen O'Reilly fell under a train,' he gasped.

'She was pushed,' the cardinal roared. 'Murdered, Monsignor.'

'I had nothing to—'

'You provided information to those who had.'

Dalton lurched back in his chair, and the cardinal saw a flicker of cunning in his eyes. 'You can't prove that,' he said tonelessly.

The cardinal said nothing.

'You can't prove it, can you?' Dalton said, and

began to smile. 'You thought I was such a fool that I'd be taken in by the ranting from your office whenever she came for her interview. You thought you could conspire with the enemies of the Church and I would stand idly by. What does it feel like to know that all your silly games were for nothing? You think I didn't know about the congressman, or that policeman O'Donnell? You think I would simply let you betray your sacred trust by opening confidential files from the archives to outsiders?'

'What sacred trust was that, Monsignor?' the cardinal said levelly.

'To defend the Church and cleanse it of perversions. Under all your bluff and bluster, you were weak. You protected Kathleen O'Reilly, who criticised the Church and would have spread scandal about its ministers. You passed over faithful priests for promotion and you sent your pet policeman to hound one of them—'

'So you warned Father Roberts?'

'Yes, I warned him, and he escaped. Just as I sent your precious Sister Kathleen's filthy writings to…'

'To whom, Monsignor?'

'To someone you will never know or find, Eminence. To someone called by God to bring low the mighty and raise up His loyal servants.'

'If you mean Father Stefan, the convenor of the Remnant, then the man you speak of is dead, Monsignor,' the cardinal said flatly.

'Liar!' Dalton shouted.

'Really?' Wall pushed the telephone across his desk and read a Rome number from his diary. 'Call it,' he hissed. 'Push the damn buttons, Dalton. There's no one home. You can say "*sursum corda*" until you're blue in the face, but no one will answer.'

The monsignor stretched a shaking hand to the telephone and then drew it back. His face was stricken.

'There are others,' he whispered desperately.

'The Church authorities know about them, every last lousy one of them. Most of them are dead, murdered by your Wrath of Righteousness. The rest, like you, will face the law of the Church and state.'

'I claim sanctuary,' Dalton whined through bloodless lips.

'The sheep-fold is no place for a wolf, Dalton,' the cardinal said grimly, and pushed a button on his desk.

The door opened and a young black man stepped inside. Dalton's head swung wildly from one man to the other.

'You have what you need, Detective?' the cardinal asked.

'More than enough, your Eminence,' Detective Staines replied.

32

Santa Sabina Hospital, Rome

Michael was feeling stronger. He knew they had cut back on the sedatives, because his chest hurt like crazy and his vision had lost the halo effect.

'Mal?'

'Yeah?'

'How long have I been here?' The sound of his own voice was still strange to him.

'Oh, a while,' Mal said vaguely, his eyes roaming to the monitor over the bed.

'Mal.'

'Okay, okay. Two weeks, maybe.'

Michael digested this in silence for a while. 'How long have you been here?' he asked.

'I've been in and out, you know. Fermi needed a little help with the paperwork and stuff.'

'You look like death warmed over.'

'You should talk,' Mal shot back, and then turned his face away.

'Where's Rosa?'

'She's lying down on the campbed.'

'There'd better be two, Mal, or Hanny's going to put you in traction.'

'Hanny's with Raphael. She had a bit of a scare, and Cardinal Wall thought she'd be better off at the monastery. I was talking to her last night. Lots of lip, now she knows you're... out of the woods. Raphael says you're to get better quick; the leaves are piling up again, whatever that means. Oh, hey, you got mail.' He dug into his jacket pocket for the envelope and held it uncertainly in his hands. 'It's got an Irish stamp.'

'Will you read it for me? Please, Mal,' Michael added as he saw the hesitation in Mal's face.

Mal slit the envelope and flattened the letter on the side of the bed. He patted all his pockets before he found his spectacles, and the familiarity of the ritual warmed Michael.

'It's from your sister, Fiona.' He cleared his throat. '"Dear Michael, I was very shocked to hear of your accident."' Mal looked up guiltily. 'Sorry about that,' he mumbled. 'Didn't seem right to tell her you'd been shot, and her so far away. Anyway...' He resumed reading. '"Mal tells me you're making a full and speedy recovery—"'

'Hyperbole, Dr O'Donnell?' Michael teased.

'"We are well. Daddy's condition hasn't changed much since you last saw him. Some days he's like his old self, reading and arguing. He's teaching Liam, Kate's boy, to play chess, and he still hates to lose. Speaking of Liam, I have him in my class in school, and a strange thing happened recently. Being the totally dedicated teacher I am, I set the class a few maths problems so I could have a rest. At the end of the class, they put them on my desk before they charged off home. Liam had done a drawing of a man lying on the ground, framed in a huge square."' Mal's voice faltered.

'Read on, Mal,' Michael said quietly.

'"Later that evening, I was up with Kate, getting Daddy's medication, and I asked Liam about it. He waited until Kate had gone out of the room, and then he said, 'He's hurt.' I asked him who was hurt, but then Kate came in and Liam went back to his book. I was puzzling over it all the way home. The minute I got in, the phone rang, and it was Mal, telling me about your accident. Isn't that the strangest thing? I'm putting the drawing in the envelope to cheer you up. I know Mal and his friend Rosa have been with you..."'

Mal coughed and looked up. 'That's about it,' he said. 'She's put lots of kisses and those circles at the bottom.'

'They're called hugs, Mal.'

'Yeah, yeah. You want to see the picture?'

It looked fragile in Mal's blunt fingers. Michael

saw the figure of a man, drawn with a black crayon. His eyes traced the lines of the square that framed the fallen figure.

'Mal, what happened after I left you in Castel Sant'Angelo?'

'Look, all in good time, okay? You've been—'

'I need to know now.' He had spoken more sharply than he had intended, and his chest blazed. 'Sorry,' he gasped.

'You want me to get the nurse?'

'No, damn it. I want you to tell me.'

'I'll give you the headlines,' Mal said grudgingly. 'Rosa and Terence cracked the computer between them. Hell of a thing. All the info we needed was there, in a kind of... I dunno, maybe like a conversation, like this Stefan guy was talking to someone else. Rosa found the file under "Magda"; she thinks that's who he was talking to. Anyways, it had everything – names, dates, locations, the whole nine yards. This guy had a lot of blood on his hands, Michael, and he had help from a bunch of other people. "The Remnant", he called them; means nothing to us.'

'The Scriptures say that, in the final days, a small, select remnant of true believers will be saved from Armageddon,' Michael whispered, ignoring the hammering of his heart and the knife-pain twisting in his ribs. 'Go on.'

'Then Fermi got news of an explosion in some catacombs, lots of dead bodies. Some guy he knew was on site and phoned him. He said the bodies he saw coming up out of the hole were priests. Then someone took the guy's phone and gave Giuseppe an earful. I asked him about it, and he just did that Italian thing with his shoulders. "None of it ever happened," he said. There's nothing much in the papers,' Mal said thoughtfully. 'Nothing at all on the guy in the Colosseum, the guy in the water or the bunch in the catacombs.'

'And me?'

'The big story was how this deranged Father Stefan Koff busted into the papal apartments, knocked out Cardinal Thomas and shot a young priest. Koff was shot in St Peter's Square while resisting arrest. You got half a line, Michael. Quote, a second priest was accidentally wounded, unquote. If you ask me, the Vatican locked everything down tight. Now, it's yesterday's news and the papers are filling up with rumours about who's gonna be the next pope.' Mal stooped and plucked a newspaper from the floor. '"Conclave Called to Elect New Pontiff,"' he quoted.

'When?' Michael asked absently.

'Tomorrow.' Mal turned a page and grunted. 'This Thomas guy has been all over the news. He says this Koff was an assassin hired by conservatives inside the Church to whack the Pope. Says no one can put the clock back, the Church needs to move on, that kind of thing.'

Michael closed his eyes and ran the reel in his

head, going over everything Eli and Mal had told him about Hugh's death. Behind his closed lids, he watched Eli and Hugh create the illusion of a body in the wheelchair, and he smiled at the crazy plan. What if Stefan had come with a bomb or a knife? What if he had stepped just a little closer to the figure? What if…?

Eli's face swam into focus, and Michael remembered the pucker of incomprehension that had formed between the doctor's eyes when he had asked him why he had survived. The images in his head wheeled faster and faster, until he thought the tornado would suck him up – and then they were gone, leaving just one face. He opened his eyes.

'Too many survivors,' he said aloud.

'What?' Mal asked anxiously.

'Too many witnesses, Mal,' Michael said hoarsely. 'Father Stefan would never have left witnesses, unless…'

'You want me to call Eli?' Mal asked, rising from the chair.

'No. I want you to get me out of here, tonight.'

'Where the hell are you going?'

'To the Vatican.'

'Are you crazy?'

'Mal, we don't have time for this. Listen to what I have to say, and call Fermi.'

★

Rosa struck a pose in her nurse's uniform. 'The lady with the torch,' she said, smiling.

'Lamp,' Mal grunted, 'unless you're standing in New York Harbour. C'mon, give me a hand here.'

Mal wore a long white coat, which he had liberated from the changing room beside the theatre, and a stethoscope he had found in the pocket. They manoeuvred Michael into a sitting position.

Rosa felt his forehead; it was cold and clammy. 'You sure you want to go through with this?' she asked anxiously.

'Just give me a minute,' Michael said in a tight voice. He looked at Mal. 'Fermi ready to roll?'

'He's in the ambulance, right outside the main entrance. Okay, let's do it.'

As gently as possible, they lifted Michael into the wheelchair and bundled him in blankets.

Angela was doing the nightshift, again. She caught a flicker of movement through the glass wall of the reception area; straining her eyes, she saw a doctor and a nurse pushing a patient in a wheel-chair. Small nurse, big doctor, she fumed, and she does the pushing. Testily, she opened her door and began to advance on them.

Mal saw her coming and tensed. 'Better step on it, Rosa,' he whispered. 'We got company.'

As he turned to confront the receptionist, Eli Weissman came through the main door and inter-posed himself neatly between Angela and Mal.

'Ah, Angela,' he said quickly, 'I'm so sorry. Everything's been so hectic, I forgot to tell you.'

'Forgot to tell me what?' she snapped, peering over his shoulder at the trio.

Weissman stepped closer, obstructing her view. Taking her gently by the elbow, he began to lead her back to the desk, speaking in a confidential whisper. 'More orders from the Vatican. Father Flaherty is to be transferred to the Vatican infirmary, immediately.'

'I didn't get any notification of any transfer.'

'Did you get one when they took the Pope?'

'No, but…'

'You know how they operate. *Omertà*,' Weissman whispered dramatically.

Angela's eyes widened. She knew only too well about the *cosa nostra* vow of silence. Anyone who broke the code… 'Are these people trained?' she asked, tilting her head towards the door.

'You could say that,' Weissman replied sagely. I'm starting to like that phrase, he thought. If I use it often enough, I might learn to lie like Detective O'Donnell. Reluctantly, she allowed him to usher her to her desk.

'Good night, Angela,' he said.

He rejoined the trio at the door. 'Quickly,' he whispered, 'and don't look back.'

Fermi held the ambulance's rear door open as they raised the wheelchair and climbed in after it. The ambulance slid silently away from the hospital forecourt.

Weissman checked Michael's pulse. 'Near enough to normal, considering the circumstances,' he said darkly.

He rounded on Mal. 'So, Detective, I see an ambulance and question the driver. He is miraculously struck dumb. Then I see you two in the reception area, kidnapping my patient.'

'It was my idea,' Michael said wearily. 'I needed to get to the Vatican.'

'I suppose I should not ask why you want to go there?'

'No.'

'I see. Then it is my duty, as your doctor, to accompany you.'

The Vatican

The cover story was concocted by Fermi. Anyone who asked would be told that Michael was the priest who had been wounded in St Peter's Square; he was being returned to the Vatican on the orders of Cardinal Richter, as a security measure because of the media presence at the Santa Sabina Hospital.

Mal was unimpressed. 'That story has more holes in it than...'

'Than I do,' Michael offered, and the men laughed until Rosa glowered at them. The ambulance drew to a halt in a courtyard behind the Basilica.

'Where to now, Father?' Fermi asked calmly.

'Dr Weissman will take me to the Sistine Chapel. The rest of you need to leave.'

'No way I'm leaving you here,' Mal protested.

'Mal,' Michael said firmly, 'this is something I have to do alone. Dr Weissman's been here before; he knows the game. If we run into obstacles, he can bluff his way through. You three can't really operate inside the line, can you, Detective Fermi?'

'No,' Fermi said bitterly.

Mal still looked unhappy. 'You take good care of him,' he said gruffly to Weissman.

'Yes, Doctor.'

A pearly light hung like a halo above the great dome.

'It's a false dawn,' Weissman muttered, and began to push Michael's wheelchair.

The Sistine Chapel

Getting inside the perimeter proved to be the most difficult task. After that, Vatican security seemed to accept that, if you were inside the line, you were meant to be there. Only once did a Swiss Guard bar their way. He scrutinised their passes and peered suspiciously at Michael.

'Do I know you?' he asked. 'Have we met?'

'I'm sure I would remember meeting you,' Michael said, and coughed. The cough seemed to come all the way up from his toes, and Weissman took his cue.

'The patient needs to get to the infirmary, immediately,' he protested.

'The infirmary is the other way,' the guard said obstinately, his eyes still ferreting at Michael's face.

'Cardinal Richter is this way,' Weissman said. 'He wants to see Father Flaherty before morning.'

At the mention of the cardinal's name, the guard stepped back smartly. 'His Eminence is in the Sistine Chapel, overseeing the final arrangements for the conclave. Please proceed.'

They wheeled down a long, sombre corridor.

'What's a conclave?' Weissman whispered.

'It means "with a key". The custom was to lock the cardinals in the Sistine Chapel until they elected a pope. It tends to concentrate their minds on getting the job done as quickly as possible.'

'That guard seemed to know you.'

'He threatened to shoot me some time back.'

'Oh, of course,' Weissman said, so casually that Michael laughed. He regretted it instantly, arching back in the chair with pain.

A sound of hammering grew in volume as they neared the Sistine Chapel, and when they stopped at the open door, they saw workmen swarming over the interior, putting the finishing touches to the tiered seating for the cardinals. The unmistakable figure of Cardinal Richter stood inside the door. He seemed to sense their scrutiny and turned slowly.

'Isn't this an unusual hour to bring a patient to view Michelangelo's masterpiece, Dr Weissman?' he asked dryly.

It was Michael who answered. 'I didn't come to

see Michelangelo's work, Eminence. I came to see you.'

'And you are?'

'This is Father Michael Flaherty,' Weissman explained, 'who was shot by—'

Richter held up a hand. 'I recognise the name. Father Flaherty, the Church owes you a great debt for your—'

'Eminence,' Michael interrupted, 'the Church owes me nothing. I need to speak with you alone.'

Richter looked quizzically at Weissman.

'I'll be outside,' Weissman said quickly, and left.

'If you would push me to an alcove, Eminence, we can talk privately.'

With a bemused expression, Richter took the handles of the wheelchair and did as he had been instructed. The alcoves were makeshift bedrooms constructed around the perimeter of the chapel; they would house the cardinals for as long as it took to elect a new pope.

Richter sat on a simple wooden chair. 'I have made some enquiries,' he began. 'You are a very remarkable man, Michael Flaherty. I must apologise for not visiting you in the hospital. We have been working very hard to... contain the happenings of recent times. If I had visited you, it might have been construed to mean that you had played a more prominent part in the affair. The ladies and gentlemen of the press would have pursued you. I hope you understand.'

'Yes, I understand.'

'I knew you would. Now that these matters are safely in the past, we must go on.'

'Eminence, these matters, as you call them, may not all be in the past. Please,' Michael said firmly, as Richter made to interrupt, 'hear me out, without interruption.'

Cardinal Richter struggled with this for a moment, and then nodded.

When Michael had finished speaking, the cardinal sat in silence for a long time, his hand to his forehead.

'Have you any proof of this?'

'No. But, with your help, I may be able to get it.'

33

Cardinal Thomas' Apartments, The Vatican

Cardinal Thomas stood before the full-length mirror in his apartment and adjusted his robes. He had plenty of time left before joining the procession of cardinals into the Sistine Chapel. Arriving at the last moment always excited interest, he thought, and smiled.

The knock at the door swung him from his reflection. 'Come.'

The knock was repeated.

'Come in. Oh, to heck with it…' He hurried to the door and swung it open. For a moment, he stood gazing down at the man in the wheelchair.

'Why, Michael Flaherty,' he said, 'home is the hero. Come in, come in. Here, let me do that,' he added, as Michael struggled with the wheelchair. Cardinal Thomas manoeuvred the chair to the centre of the room and went to sit behind his desk, a bemused smile on his face.

'Well, well. What brings you to see me on this fine morning?'

'You didn't come to see me.'

'Hey, Michael,' Thomas protested, 'that whole business was shut up tight. You know how Richter is – all that need-to-know, within-these-walls malarkey. Can't say I blame him; just imagine what our friends in the Fourth Estate would have done with a story like that.'

'I hear you got some coverage.'

'Yeah,' Thomas said, with a deprecating wave of his hand. 'Someone had to go public, spin our story. You can't leave an information vacuum; someone's bound to start sniffing around. It isn't every day a priest gets shot in St Peter's Square.'

'Tell me about it.'

'Sorry – I should have said two priests. That was some piece of work. You're an amazing guy, Michael. That mad bastard nearly took you out.'

'But he didn't kill you, Eminence,' Michael said.

The cardinal's eyes narrowed. 'I figure he had bigger fish to fry. Gave me one hell of a thump on the head.'

'He shot Hugh O'Neill while you were unconscious.'

'I was sorry to hear that,' the cardinal said sombrely. 'You know, Hugh came to me and confessed his part in… well, doesn't matter now. Seems like the poor guy was suckered into all that stuff. I suppose we could say he redeemed himself in the end.'

He sat back in his chair, and they regarded each other in silence.

'Eminence,' Michael said, 'you and I were both in the Marine Corps, right?'

'Yeah. God, that's a lifetime ago. But, as I recall, you were Special Forces. I didn't have that kind of… talent.'

'Do you remember the saying, "no ranks in the locker room"?'

'Sure. As a matter of fact, I had that kind of no-holds-barred conversation with O'Neill – much good it did.'

'Want to go to the locker room now?'

'Why not?' Thomas said slowly, and squared his shoulders.

'Okay,' Michael said evenly, 'I'll start. Cardinal Thomas, you are full of it.'

Thomas blinked in surprise and leaned forward on the desk. 'You forget yourself, Father,' he growled. 'I'll take your condition into account and excuse—'

'No, I don't forget myself, Eminence. I remember only too well how you spun me a yarn about enemies within the Church. You were very convincing, and now I know why.'

'You know nothing,' the cardinal said dismissively. 'You're a sick man with some bug up his ass. You brought that baggage with you, Flaherty. I know all about your little fracas on the Island. You were an untouchable, and I took you in.'

'Oh, you took me in, all right. I've had a lot of time to think, Eminence, and I've got a lot of questions I can't answer.'

Michael raised a finger. 'One: Archbishop Leclerc. I took it for granted that Hugh passed on some information on his mission to the Remnant. But where did he get it?'

'I told you. He—'

'Yeah, I remember: you told me he must have read the memo on your desk while you were out of the room. So I'm wondering why you left it there. You knew he was coming; he had an appointment. And yet you left a top-secret memo in plain view and then left him alone with it. Best-case scenario, you were careless; but someone doesn't get to be a prince of the Church, with responsibility for a high-level mission that could alter East–West relations, by being careless.'

The cardinal bristled, but Michael ploughed on.

'Two.' A second finger rose to join the first. 'Father Stefan puts a gun to your head outside the Pope's door. What did you do? You're a persuasive guy, I know that. Did you try to talk him out of it? No; you talked Eli into opening the door so this guy, with a gun, could walk right into the Pope's presence. Now, correct me if I'm wrong, but, as I understand it, every rookie Swiss Guard swears an oath to guard the Pope with his life. But a hot-shot cardinal and ex-Marine passes up that particular option.

'Three: Father Stefan shoots Hugh O'Neill and what he thought was the Pope. But you, he knocks unconscious. Let's look at that scenario, Eminence. Okay, Hugh O'Neill got in his way – but why shoot the Pope? Why would the leader of the ultra-right-wing Remnant shoot a right-wing pope and leave the liberal Cardinal Thomas with a little lump on his head?'

'That's enough,' Thomas grated.

'I'm not finished,' Michael snapped. 'I can finish here or in a more public forum.' Pain lanced through his chest, and he closed his eyes until the spasm passed.

'Four: Eli Weissman is spared. Why? Because someone has to tell the tale of the murder of a young priest and an elderly pope and explain how the cardinal survived. And afterwards, because the Church needs to spin a story and cover up the sickness within itself, that cardinal comes large as life, via media satellite, into every home in the world.'

'You done?' the cardinal asked.

'Almost done,' Michael replied. 'Five: this cardinal's message is a simple one. Stefan and the Remnant are the conservative Church. Now we need to reach out, move forward, yabba yabba. The thing about television is, people don't take in much of what's said; it's mostly tone, not content. But they see who's saying it. They got to see you,

Eminence. Even though Stefan didn't kill the Pope, the plan still played out. The Pope was dying anyway; a conclave is called to elect a cardinal to the Throne of Peter, and one candidate had wall-to-wall coverage all over the world. You.' He leaned back in the chair and wiped a trembling hand across his forehead. 'I'm running out of fingers here, Eminence. Maybe you can help me out.'

Cardinal Thomas stared hard and then clapped his hands together in mock applause. 'You can throw it all and more, Michael, but none of it sticks.'

'The police have Stefan's computer. They have names, dates—'

'Not my name,' Thomas said confidently. 'Stefan is dead, thanks to you, and it all dies with him.'

He leaned back and looked at Michael with bemused eyes. 'Is that your best shot, soldier?'

Michael sighed, and his shoulders slumped with exhaustion. 'I just wanted to know why,' he said softly.

'Why?' The cardinal surged up from his desk. 'Why? What sort of dumb-ass question is that?'

He strode from behind the desk and looked down on Michael, addressing him as if explaining to a particularly slow student.

'I told you why already, but you were too stupid to listen. The Church needs to haul its ass out of the fifteenth century and engage with the modern world. We've stayed inside these walls so long, we think this square mile of the Vatican State is the world. Richter and his ilk think that, if they just sit in here long enough, the world will come to its senses and beat a path to our door, begging for salvation.'

He bent closer and whispered into Michael's ear, 'There's no one coming. There never will be.'

'So you decided...'

The cardinal swung upright and towered over him. 'Yes, I decided. I thought it through and I acted. *Veni, vidi, vici*: I came, I saw, I conquered. Julius Caesar, Michael. He needed a foreign war so that he could own Rome. If he could frighten the Romans with the Gauls and then slaughter their fear, they'd give him the keys of Rome on a silver salver.'

'So the Remnant were the Gauls?'

Cardinal Thomas clapped a heavy hand on Michael's shoulder. 'Son, you got it in one. The Remnant were nothing – a bunch of disaffected, disappointed whiners – and Stefan played them like a harp.'

'But they killed the very people who wanted to modernise the Church.'

'Oh, boy, did they ever. And you know what? The cardinals in the conclave know that. They already know about the mad assassin and his band of merry murderers, and it scares the shit out of them. Now, anyone who holds to the old-time religion gets tainted with the blood the Remnant spilled. Now, everyone wants to be on the side of the martyrs who gave their lives for a vision of the Church as it might be in the modern world.'

'You mean martyrs like Leclerc?'

'Leclerc had clout with the Muslim moderates. I sent him to Mali and set up the memo for O'Neill, and the sucker ran straight to Stefan.' Thomas spread his arms wide. 'It was on television, worldwide, Michael. Imagine the impact. Muslim extremists cut off an archbishop's head and stick it on a mosque. Moderates on all sides were shocked into a common condemnation of such extreme action. It put Catholic conservatives on the back foot and pushed my moderate colleagues a little closer to a liberal agenda.'

'Your agenda.'

'Yes.'

'And Sebastiano Spenza?'

'Sebastiano thought he was one step away from ruling the airwaves. He was salivating at the prospect of preaching the same old, same old to the huddled masses. Sure, he got the money to put the station on a war footing, but he was always a liability, never knew when to turn off the damn microphone. Still, thanks to Sebastiano, we now have a world-class media outlet for our message. You could say that nothing in his life became him like the leaving of it.'

'And Hugh O'Neill?'

The cardinal beamed. 'Hugh was absolutely perfect. God, they don't make them like him any more. He was young, naïve and passionately conservative, in a way that only a young, naïve guy can be. And he was lonely. Just the kind of guy to be sucked in by a mob like the Remnant. I needed someone who would do exactly what Hugh did: leak information to the Remnant. When the leaks came to light, I needed to point the finger at someone and say, "That's where they came from; that's the guy."'

'And why me, Eminence?'

Cardinal Thomas waved an dismissive hand. 'You asked me that before.'

'Humour me.'

Cardinal Thomas sat down behind his desk and took a long breath before replying. 'Stefan was doing his job effectively – but his job was nearly done. And, once it was, I knew he'd turn into a serious liability. Stefan was crazy, but he wasn't stupid. As soon as he saw the way things were going, he'd realise what my real agenda was – realise I'd used him against everything he believed in. Can you imagine what kind of havoc he'd have caused? He could have wrecked the whole thing. I didn't want any blowback. I could convince Stefan to get rid of the Remnant for me – he was big on cleansing, was Stefan – but I needed someone who would get him out of the way. I talked to some people in the US State Department – people who appreciate what an American pope, a black American pope, could achieve for his Church and his country. I needed someone special, someone capable of looking after himself and idealistic enough to be...'

'Manipulated?'

The cardinal shrugged. 'They sent you. I guess they figured, if there was a hitch with Stefan, you could fix it.'

'And I did.'

'Yes, you did. And for that, you'll have the eternal gratitude of the Church – not that anyone will ever acknowledge that publicly. But the labourer is worthy of his hire, Michael, so you just name your price.'

'There's nothing you have that I want, Eminence,' Michael said tiredly. 'I think I'll be going now.'

Laboriously, he turned the wheelchair toward the door. Cardinal Thomas made no effort to help him. He strode to the door and stood with his back to it.

'There's one last thing, Father Flaherty,' he said softly. 'If you consider reporting this conversation to anyone, ever... Well, you're a clever guy; you know I won't come after you. That might give your insane accusations some credibility, even posthumously.'

He bent forward until his hands rested on the arms of the wheelchair.

'There's an island off the western seaboard of Ireland, and there's a woman there who has a son. Your immunity doesn't extend to them. Do I make myself clear?'

Slowly, Michael lifted his head and stared at him. Something in his eyes caused the cardinal to step back and swing the door open.

★

Eli Weissman was waiting, in the colonnade of St Peter's Square, a concerned expression on his face. 'Where have you been, Michael?'

'In the dragon's lair.' Michael pulled up the front of his shirt. 'Could you get this thing off me?'

Eli withdrew the black box from Michael's belt and followed the cable to the tiny microphone in his collar.

'What now?'

'Call Fermi. Tell him to wait outside the line.'

The Sistine Chapel

Cardinal Richter lifted the headphones from his ears and tossed them aside, his ascetic face bone-white with fury. On Michael's instructions, he had invited the directors of the most powerful Vatican departments to the little alcove; one by one, they removed their headphones and looked to Richter for guidance.

'It is time to call the conclave,' he said.

★

A ripple of interest passed through the queue of cardinals standing outside the great doors as Cardinal Thomas arrived. He smiled a greeting and made his way to the rear; an African cardinal gestured to him, offering his own place in the line, but Thomas shook his head modestly and continued. A man wearing the distinctive headdress of the Eastern Church broke ranks and kissed him warmly on both cheeks. 'Peace, brother,' he whispered.

'And to you, Patriarch, and to the world,' Thomas replied solemnly.

Finally, he took his place behind his confrères.

'*Procedamus in pace*,' the leader intoned. 'Let us go forward in peace.'

Cardinal Ranieri – the Cardinal Chamberlain, who had responsibility for convening the conclave – stood inside the doors, flanked by Cardinal Richter and other senior prelates. They nodded greetings to the other cardinals as they passed.

As Cardinal Thomas approached the door, he slowed his steps, to ensure that most of the others would be already seated and he could walk under their gaze. Cardinal Ranieri stepped into the doorway before him, his assistants coming to either side.

'Cardinal Thomas,' he said, in a strong, carrying voice, 'you have betrayed our holy Mother Church. There is no place for you here.'

Cardinal Thomas' eyes glazed with shock. 'I... you have no power to refuse me entry,' he gasped.

'According to the law of the Church,' Ranieri said tonelessly, 'in the interregnum between the death of one pope and the election of another, the guidance and governance of the Church is in the hands of the Cardinal Chamberlain. My confreres have invested that power in me, and, in their name, I cast you out.'

He nodded, and the doors closed.

Thomas staggered back as if he had been struck, his face a mask of disbelief. His lips moved feverishly, but no sound came.

From inside the Sistine Chapel, he heard a clear voice intone, '*Veni Creator Spiritus*' – 'Come, Holy Spirit' – and the massed voices of the cardinals joining to pray for guidance in their choice of pope. With an animal cry, Thomas flung himself against the locked doors, his fingers raking the surface. 'I am worthy!' he screamed. 'I am willing! Let me in, in God's name!'

The singing voices soared louder, and he dropped to his knees, whimpering. 'In God's name...'

'Cardinal Thomas.'

Dazed, his face contorted, he turned slowly to face a captain of the Swiss Guard, four guards standing two abreast behind him.

'You will come with us,' the captain said curtly.

Led by the captain, the four guards marched, with Thomas between them, to St Peter's Square. A straggle of pilgrims watched the strange procession, unsure how they should react. Some raised their cameras furtively, as if they were recording an accident. As they passed the obelisk, Cardinal Thomas raised his eyes and saw Detective Fermi standing just outside the line, the light of a police van pulsing behind him. The captain came to attention before Fermi.

'By order of the Cardinal Chamberlain of the Vatican State, I am to transfer this man to the custody of the Police Department of the City of Rome. Who will accept him?'

'I will,' Fermi said.

The captain stood aside, and Cardinal Thomas stepped over the line.

'Welcome to Italy, Eminence,' Detective Fermi said grimly.

34

Leonardo Da Vinci Airport, Rome

Three days later, Detective Fermi divided the mayhem of the departures area with all the drama of Moses dividing the Red Sea, steering Mal and Rosa to the Promised Land of the VIP lounge. Rosa was almost swallowed by the luxurious couch; her knees rose to her chin.

'We could get to like this kind of living,' she said, accepting a glass of champagne.

'Maybe you could,' Mal said, raising his own glass in salute. 'Some of us were born to it.'

Rosa watched him sip and wondered. They had detoured to the hospital and been disappointed: even Angela couldn't account for Michael's whereabouts.

'He was here, and then Dr Weissman comes, and he is gone.'

'Maybe you'd give him a message from me,' Mal had said awkwardly. 'Tell him I said he was to... take care.'

'That's all?'

'Yeah, that's it.'

Rosa glanced at the monitor. 'Time to boogie,' she said reluctantly. She stood up, and was lifted from her feet in Fermi's hug.

'Did you throw three coins in the Trevi Fountain?' he asked.

'How could I?' she answered, laughing. 'I was too busy hunting dragons.'

'I will do it for you,' Fermi promised, 'and you will return to Rome.'

He turned to Mal.

'You try that trick on me, Giuseppe, and you'll end up in a truss,' Mal said, smiling.

Fermi embraced him anyway, kissing him loudly on both cheeks for good measure. 'Thank you, Mal, my friend,' he said huskily. 'Now it is time for the carriages to roll, no?'

'Wagons,' Rosa corrected automatically, and they laughed.

As they turned at Passport Control to give Fermi a final wave, they saw Eli pushing Michael's wheelchair in their direction.

'Hey, Rosa,' Michael said, 'what ever happened to goodbye?'

She leaned over the chair and hugged him, but not too tightly. 'I'll see you on the plane, Mal,' she said, and went through without looking back.

Fermi and Eli moved away in animated conversation.

'We called to the hospital,' Mal said, 'but you'd flown the coop.'

'We went to see Emilia and Vittorio Spenza and got held up in traffic,' Michael said. 'I was afraid I'd miss you.'

'Look,' Mal began, 'we didn't get a chance to talk about…about all that stuff before. And I…'

'Hunker down here and listen to me, Mal,' Michael said, and the big man crouched beside the wheelchair. 'Whatever you did, I know you did for the best. I know that now. Sorry it took me so long to figure things out. Tell Hanny I love her, okay?'

Mal nodded dumbly.

'Bring her to the Island, Mal.'

'I think she'd like that.' Mal rose to his feet.

'Hey, Mal,' Michael said, and opened his arms. 'When in Rome…'

*

When Mal slumped into his seat, Rosa was sipping from a plastic cup.

'They serving drinks already?'

She shook her head and took a long swallow.

'Okay, I give in. What've you got there?'

'A very large bottle of entrapment, Mal. I liberated it from the VIP lounge.'

'You know what you are?'

'What am I?'

'You're one hell of a detective.'

'I know that.'

'And modest, too.'

'It's my only failing.' Rosa dipped in her bag and produced a second plastic glass. 'Care to join me?'

'No peanuts?' Mal said as she poured. 'Ah, well. Listen, Rosa… I was talking to Hanny last night. She says you might like to come over some evening – you know, if it suits you. She says we got a spare room now, so any time you want to stay over…'

'I'd like that, Mal. Say thanks to Hanny for me. That way, I can take the stand as a witness for the defence when she finally pops you one.'

Some hours later, she surfaced briefly from sleep to find Mal tucking her fallen blanket around her shoulders. She smiled and slept.

Santa Sabina Hospital, Rome

Tentatively, Michael raised his arms and grabbed the bar suspended above the bed. Taking a deep breath, he raised himself. Sweat popped on his forehead and every muscle in his body seemed to vibrate. There was some soreness, but nothing he couldn't handle. It was the boredom he couldn't cope with, the tedium of the hospital routine, the daily sessions with the physiotherapist and the word 'soon', Eli's stock answer when he asked 'when?'

Like a genie summoned from a lamp, Weissman eased through the door. His eye caught the swinging bar. 'Good,' he said. 'Tarzan is almost ready for the jungle.'

'When, Eli?'

'Soon.'

There was a knock on the door. When Eli glanced up, he was looking at Pope John XXIV.

'*Shalom*, Dr Weissman,' Richter said, smiling.

'*Shalom*, Pope,' Eli replied, and the Pope's smile grew broader.

He handed Eli a small parcel. 'A small token of gratitude for all you did for my predecessor,' he said. 'You are a gifted physician, Eli, with a generous heart. It is the best combination. Again, thank you. Now, if you will be good enough to allow me a little time with your patient...'

'He's all yours,' Eli said.

'Oh, I doubt that,' the Pope said wryly.

When the door had closed behind Eli, the Pope sat in the chair beside the bed. 'How are you, Michael?' he asked.

'Getting better.'

'Good. I want to thank you also. You saved the Church from Cardinal Thomas. Some would say that, by doing so, you condemned the Church to me.'

'I think you'll do okay.'

'And why do you think that?'

Michael paused to gather his thoughts. 'Because you didn't want it, did you?'

'No,' the Pope said, 'I did not. I am an academic. All my adult life, I have found it easier to lose myself in theological questions than to deal with the ordinary challenges of human life.'

'Still, you trusted me when I asked you to. That wasn't a theological issue.'

'Yes.' The Pope smiled ruefully. 'I put the future of the Church in the hands of a man who could barely sit upright in a wheelchair, because I trusted his courage. And now, the Pope needs the courage to trust the people of God. And what of you, Michael?'

'I'm going home, Holiness.'

'Ah, yes, to the Island. I hope you don't mind, but I read your file. The Church needs – I mean, I need – men like you, to keep the Church honest and to challenge the Pope to trust.'

'I have people on the Island, your Holiness, people I care for... deeply. I must go back.'

'Well, the Scriptures tell us that Peter returned to fishing until he was needed again. Perhaps he needed to earth himself in the normal things. You are fortunate to have people you care for, and I think the Pope will sleep easier knowing you are somewhere in the world. Is there anything I can do for you?'

Michael considered this for a moment.

'Yes, Holiness,' he said. 'There is.'

The Weissman Apartment, Trastevere, Rome

'Dinner in ten minutes,' Sarah called from the kitchen as Eli closed the apartment door. He placed the parcel in the centre of the table and came up behind her, lifting her from the stool and carrying her to the couch.

'Oh, Eli, I have to—'

'Uncle Ari,' he called, 'can you come in here, please?'

He heard a shuffling, and his uncle opened the door.

'Dinner is ready?' Ari asked.

'No. Sit with Mama.'

Mystified, Ari did as he was bid. Eli went to the table and put his hands on the parcel.

'This is a gift from the Pope,' he said.

'Which one?' Ari asked.

'How many they got?' Eli shot back. Carefully, he peeled away the paper and lifted the lid of the box inside. He slit the long white envelope and withdrew the letter. The writing was barely legible, and he knew immediately who had laboured over it.

'"Dear Sarah Weissmann,"' he read, '"there are centuries of hurt standing like walls between your people and mine. There is much that needs to be forgiven but never forgotten. If we do not remember, how will we know the evil if it should come again?"'

Ari nodded his head and took his sister's hand.

'"And to you, Ari Cohen, I say that I have tried to keep watch, as you have. And yet, all the walls and watchmen could not save either Jerusalem or Rome. We must trust the next generation to create a world where even watchmen may sleep. Thank you for the gift of your son and nephew, Eli."'

With trembling fingers, Eli lifted out the contents of the parcel.

'What is it, Eli?' his mother asked.

'It's the last pope's own copy of the Old Testament, Mama,' he said. 'Look how worn it is.'

They passed the book reverently between them. Ari held it in one hand, rubbing the cover gently with the other.

'Today, nephew,' he said, 'we will talk about a pope.'

'Which one?'

'This one,' Ari said, placing the book on the table between them. 'I am listening.'

The Monastery of the Resurrection, New York State

'Tea, Hanny?' Raphael asked.

'Where do you put all that tea? You got a hollow leg or something?'

Hanny had her outdoor coat buttoned up and her suitcase stashed by the door. Mal had said he'd be there sometime after three, depending on traffic.

The kitchen clock showed two-thirty and she was pacing already.

Raphael smiled and poured two cups. He would miss Hanny. He would miss the rough edge of her tongue, her salty vocabulary and her pragmatic kindness. He would miss the companionship he had calibrated in endless cups of tea.

He saw her stop her pacing and tilt her head to the window, and knew Mal had arrived.

'Would you look at him?' she said softly. 'Wearing a bum-freezer jacket on a day like this.'

Raphael thought that, as a declaration of love, it ranked right up there with 'How do I love thee? Let me count the ways'. 'Hanny,' he said.

'What?'

He inclined his head to the door.

When they came inside, Raphael rose to greet the thickset man with the innocent blue eyes. Mal's handshake was remarkably gentle for such a big man, and he sat easily at the kitchen table.

'We'll have fresh tea,' Hanny said, and ran the tap.

'Where do you put all that tea, Hanny?' Raphael said slyly.

'Michael's going home, Hanny,' Mal said, when she sat down.

'About time, too,' she said hoarsely.

'He wants us to come over for a holiday, and I said we would.'

'Did you, now?'

'I did. We might even go to Ballina to visit your crowd. They deserve a second chance.'

She was laughing and weeping all at the same time.

★

'Maybe you'll come up and see me sometime?' Raphael said.

'You've seen too many old movies, Raphael,' Mal said roguishly, 'but yeah, we'll do that. Ready for the road, girl?'

Mal took the suitcase to the car.

'Neighbour of mine knits gloves,' Hanny said brusquely. 'I'll get her to do you some proper ones.'

Raphael opened his arms.

He watched until the car had disappeared over the rise, holding the moment against the cold of the empty kitchen behind him. The black limousine eased into the forecourt and stopped. He recognised the registration plates and the man who stepped out of the back.

The Papal Nuncio placed a box on the kitchen table. 'Abbot Raphael, it is a pleasure,' he said in heavily accented English. 'I have a letter from the Holy Father.'

Raphael slit the envelope with the bread knife and read the contents.

*Fraternal greetings to our beloved brother, Abbot
Raphael. At the request of Father Michael
Flaherty, we entrust the enclosed to your care.
May it be a source of joy and consolation to you.
John XXIV*

The box was made of rough, unvarnished wood.
Raphael's eyes were drawn immediately to the
Chinese characters stamped on the lid.

'Prisoner 1742,' he whispered, 'enemy of the
People's Republic of China.'

Tears leaked from his eyes and dropped to the
plain timber.

'You are sad?' the nuncio asked solicitously.

'I am happy,' Raphael replied through his tears.

Archbishop Modena nodded uncertainly and
gave silent thanks to God that he had not been
appointed to the Diplomatic Mission in Beijing.
Who could understand such a people? he
wondered.

When the limousine had departed with the
nuncio, Raphael carried the box to a small bench
sheltered by a stand of flaming trees. Carefully, he
opened and tilted the box so that the wind caught
and lifted the ashes. An updraft swept them above
his head, and in the last of the slanting sunlight they
seemed to dance like tiny stars.

'*De profundis clamavi ad te, Domine,*' he whispered.
Out of the depths I have cried to thee, O Lord. And
my prayer has been answered,' he added.

Tomorrow, he resolved, he would call his Chinese friends to the monastery to celebrate the release from captivity of Bishop Yuang.

The Island, Ireland

Kate shifted her nurse's bag to her other hand and opened the school gate. Fiona was framed in the open door of the schoolhouse, her red hair flaming about her head in the wind that gusted from the Atlantic. Her pupils passed Kate on the path, greeting her formally before their feet quickened to catch the last few hours of daylight after school. Liam was always last; there was always a picture to finish or a story to resolve. He smiled at Fiona as he came through the door, and she tugged his raven hair into an exclamation mark before releasing him.

'Tomorrow's Saturday, Liam,' she reminded him. 'My father's expecting you for chess. He's out for revenge.'

Liam led Kate through the gate and along the path to the headland. The sky above them was speckled with hovering larks, and he swung full circle, head uplifted, mimicking their repetitive song. Kate stood quietly and marvelled at her son's gift.

She saw him stiffen and turn to the sea. Drawn by the intensity of his gaze, her eyes swept out along the encircling arms of the harbour walls to the beaten-silver expanse that stretched to the mainland in the hazy distance. A boat carved twin furrows in the dazzling water as it angled for the quay.

Liam turned and hurried back to his mother. He took her hands and placed her palms against his cheeks, as he had always done when something fired his heart beyond the ability of his speech. A tremor ran through her at the joy that seemed to light his sallow face from inside.

'It's Tess,' she whispered uncertainly, 'bringing in the ferryboat from the mainland.'

'He's coming,' Liam said.

Acknowledgements

I owe a debt of gratitude to all at Hodder Headline Ireland and to my editor, Claire Rourke. My thanks also to Jonathan Williams, my literary agent, for his guidance and support.